The Captor's
Shadow

Books by M. C. Topham

Shadows of Light series:
The Captor's Shadow
The Power of Silence *(Fall-Winter 2025)*

FBI Suspense Series
Ice in the Heart
Ashes in the Soul *(Summer 2026)*

The Captor's Shadow

Book 1 of Shadows of Light

M. C. Topham

This book is dedicated to my brother, Justice
You inspired me with your writing
to start creating my own stories.

Acknowledgements

First off, I have to thank my mom and dad, of course. They have been there for me every step of the way, teaching me to follow my dreams. I am forever grateful for their teachings, their patience, and most importantly, their love.

My family and friends have always supported me along my path. Thanks for always being willing to listen to my ravings about my books, no matter the time. And thanks for the input that has helped my books become what they are today.

I am thankful for all my teachers and church leaders that have helped me in my writing projects, of which are many. Mrs. Mauer especially encouraged my writing in the many classes I took with her, helping me with many steps of the process. Mr. Simmons because he'd always encouraged me to share my thoughts and writings in his class as well. Jamie Blanchard, for the kindness and support. Thanks to all of you (written and not) for helping me and my confidence grow.

Thanks to the people in my previously used publishing company, Idea Creations Press, that helped me get this book out the first time around. You were both a great help making my dream come true at 16.

And now, a thanks to those who have helped me get it published the second time around; especially Jenna Topham who worked hard with school and work and still jumped in to help with my book editing.

Thanks to everyone else who has been a part of this project!

I am Shadow.

No, not darkness – not night.

Shadow.

I am those dark thoughts that you have, that thing lurking

behind you in the dark that you can sense but you can't see. I

am the sensation you feel when you drink or cut, those minor

things.

When someone beats you down, I am the bully, the one that

hits on you, as well as the one that follows you home,

whispering that the bullies are right.

No, I am not the dark that you get at night.

I am dark filled with dread.

I am the Shadow.

Prologue

DARRIN COULD HEAR humor in Michael's voice and could see the half smile that was forming. "Come on, it'll be fine." He insisted, leaning back on Darrin's couch.

"I don't think that will work." Darrin insisted, feeling himself getting flustered. The idea of Jessica going out with him was an absurd thought. He wasn't sure he could ever have the courage to ask her out. He hadn't gone out with anyone after his wife divorced him nearly ten years ago. His daughter was fifteen, but he never got to see her.

"You like her." Michael insisted.

Darrin shook his head. "Not happening." Darrin pulled away, eyes flickering around his bare house. Ever since his wife and daughter left, he hadn't tried to do much decorating, but the space itself was nice at least. "Did you come over to push about that, or to play some video games?"

Michael didn't answer the question. "Darrin, you're a good guy. One of these days you've got to let go of the fear. You've got to do something for you."

Darrin folded his arms. He most definitely was not a good guy. He wasn't a bad guy, he was just… nothing. He didn't have any special skills. No reason to be here. He couldn't keep a job, didn't do anything with his life. What girl—what person—would be crazy enough to stick with him? His wife sure hadn't.

Darrin studied Michael, his thoughts turning dark. Why did Michael even stick with him?

"I am." He gestured behind him. He had started to take some classes. He'd always enjoyed learning science. Always loved learning about the body.

"You know what I mean." Michael insisted. "You have so much potential in you."

Darrin darkened further, looking away.

Michael seemed to sense the change in mood, as he started to approach. Before he could move, however, the room around them flooded with darkness. They both froze, feeling a new heavy weight in the air, brooding. Overpowering. Chilling. It hovered over their heads. Darrin sensed Michael's panic, saw him take a few stumbling steps back. Darrin himself just felt frozen to the spot.

The darkness formed in front of him, vaguely forming the shape of a man, like a billowing shadow. Darrin found himself looking into the eyes of the shadow, and then everything turned cold. He was stuck.

Cold tendrils wrapped slowly around his body. He gasped, then felt the coldness rush into his body, trembling with the cold and fear. His mind felt empty... or heavy? He wasn't quite sure. But suddenly he felt an intense darkness in his mind. He fought it, trying to hang onto good. But he couldn't. An intense feeling of apathy seemed to tear him down.

His heart turned cold.

He found himself crouching on his knees, struggling for breath. He felt a new sense of energy in him, fingers itching, even as the darkness in the room dissipated, seeping under his skin. He was surprised when he felt a hand on his shoulder and realized it was Michael. He was still there.

"Darrin? You okay? What was that? Are you hurt?" He asked quickly, fear vivid in his voice. Darrin felt a small piece of him recognize his own fear before this new power forced it down.

Darrin stood again, barely noticing Michael beside him.

"Darrin?" When he still didn't respond, Michael tried a different tactic. "I'll call an ambulance."

"No." Darrin grabbed Michael's wrist before he could move away. "I'm fine." His mind felt distant, he just felt the strong force in him, telling him he had to get out of there.

"Darrin, we need to figure out what that was." Michael looked at him, confused and still scared.

Darrin pushed Michael back against the wall, hand on his neck. A deep sense of unease rose in him. Michael struggled to get free, hitting Darrin's arm.

"Darrin." Michael gasped a moment before Darrin's hand tightened further, the darkness swirling in him as anger. A strength Darrin had never felt overcame him, and he pushed Michael up the wall with his hold on the neck so his feet were dangling a few inches over the ground.

Michael tried kicking, tried to grab Darrin's hold to lighten the grip. His eyes wide and unbelieving.

The eyes tore deep in Darrin, a deep fear. The real Darrin. Underneath the new power that had overcome him.

Michael gaped, still trying for breath, face turning red.

That little bit of concern in Darrin made him unable to kill his lifelong friend. He let Michael fall to the floor, and he collapsed, coughing, and gasping breaths, trying to scramble away.

Darrin crouched next to his friend and Michael shook his head, trying to scramble away as he still wheezed.

Fury overtook him. The power in him rose to his fingertips. He pushed Michael back again against the wall, this time from the floor.

"Please." Michael barely managed the word.

Darrin put a hand to the side of his friend's head. He knew what he was doing, but he couldn't stop it. It wasn't really him doing it anymore.

Michael gasped in pain. Darrin could feel a sort of weakness wash over his friend as he struggled against the dark invasion in his mind, immediately causing a headache. The power in Darrin sought for control. The darkness knew Darrin's boundaries, knew that Darrin would never kill his friend. So it used that, using the connection he had to his friend to seek control over another. But unlike Darrin, the darkness wasn't able to get his hooks in Michael. Darrin's friend fought for freedom. He fought even as his consciousness faded.

He took a moment to debate. He couldn't leave Michael in his house, the man would go to the police. The power hadn't anticipated bringing another, but it figured having him there might help in the long run. And eventually Michael had to give in to the power.

He grabbed hold of Michael, lifting him with inexplicable strength, and went to his garage for his car.

The power inside him had control now, and they had places to go. Things to do.

₪   ₪   ₪

"We shouldn't have them do it. They are too young!" Glenda said. Henri glanced over at his wife, irritated that she kept insisting that their grandson was not capable of doing this.

"Well, who do you propose we ask to do it?" Henri asked in reply, deciding to use a different tactic rather than trying to reason with her. She didn't answer and he was relieved to have a quiet despite the tension in the large living room.

Glenda's foot tapped the floor at a fast rhythm as she glanced around the room, her gaze passing by all their décor, without focusing on it. Henri heard the phone ring and got off the couch after a moment when he realized that Glenda was not going to get it. He picked up the phone and held it close to his ear.

"Yes?"

"Henri?" a familiar voice asked him quietly.

"Yes. Who is this?" Henri couldn't place the voice even though he was sure he knew it. He'd always been terrible on the phone.

"Oh good. This is Frank. Have you done it yet?" Frank. His good friend, who was also the only other person that knew why they had to have their grandson and his friends do this… well uh, mission.

"No, I was about to call and ask if I can come over soon." It's not like Henri wanted the younger kids to do it, but Henri himself couldn't and no one else could know. It was a dangerous thing to do even for the most experienced people… Yeah people.

Henri felt doubt flicker into his mind; how could these kids do it if no one else had been able to? They weren't trained, barely even at an age where they might be marrying.

"Better get it done soon. It's getting harder." The phone line cut off, but Henri continued to hold the phone, almost unconsciously against his ear for another few seconds, as he tried to control his wandering thoughts.

He finally pulled the phone away from his ear and took a deep breath before dialing another number into the phone. Glenda walked in at that moment, giving him a small smile. He returned it apologetically and stared at the phone before pressing the call button and pulling it up to his ear.

"Hello?" A male's voice asked, it sounded slightly irritated.

"Hey, is Riley there? Or, uh, who is this?"

4

"It's John. Hi, Henri" Riley's husband was not a man that Henri approved of necessarily, but he tried to keep his tone kind because he knew that John made Riley happy.

Knowing that the man had probably identified him by caller ID, he continued. "Is Riley there? Or can I just come over a little later in the week?" He heard a deep exhale from the other end. Henri couldn't help but feel frustrated with his son-in-law.

"Fine, just come over some time." The connection ended and Henri's frustration vanished with it as worry swamped up again.

He sighed and placed the phone down. "Here we go, Glenda…"

Chapter One

HE GRUMBLED UNDER his breath, unable to get back to sleep no matter how hard he tried. Sitting up, he leaned his head into his hands. The sun had awakened him as it rose from behind the mountain and reflected off the snow to blaze into his room. *I need new blinds!* They had broken a little bit ago and he still hadn't gotten around to getting new ones.

He looked at the clock. Usually, he would be at school by 8:30 but they had teacher conference today so no students would have to be there. He was relieved; he had been a little behind in his schoolwork but now he could catch up.

The house was quiet. His whole family would still be sleeping. Which was not surprising since all his siblings were out of school too. He had three siblings; one older brother who was… well, he was out there at twenty, an older sister who was eighteen, and a little brother who was eight. Jacque himself was sixteen currently, though he knew he looked older than he was, like he belonged in the grade above. Or so he'd been told.

Most people his age would jump at the opportunity to sleep in, and he wished he could, but his internal clock refused to let him. Nonetheless, he still pulled the blanket over his head, dreading the cold air lurking outside his covers. *Well, you could just not get up,* he thought.

Jace—the name his friends called him—did not like to stay in bed when he was awake though, so he sighed and pulled the covers off in one fast motion, standing up.

Just as he suspected, the air was icy, his parents were going to fix the heater problem but hadn't gotten around to it yet. He put on a jacket, and, having already been wearing the jeans he'd slept in last night, he pulled on some shoes.

I wonder if anyone is up yet... His friends would probably still be sleeping. Well except maybe Hazel. He grabbed his phone off the table and unplugged it from the charger. His shivering made it harder to grasp.

Man, it was cold! He glanced up from the notification on his phone and looked out the window. There was a layer of snow covering the bush outside his window. It had snowed fairly heavily last night. That surprised him. Last night there had been a storm, but it had been warming up the last few days so the near foot or so of snow was surprising. It was snowing lightly, though it would probably melt by the end of the day.

A young girl was playing in the falling snow, a large smile on her face as she practically twirled and ran. The father, obviously done with standing in the morning cold, even if he was smiling fondly, scooped up his daughter and turned to go back inside.

They are up early. Still, it wasn't as big a surprise as it would have been if Jace's family had been up early. The kids' mom across the street had work early, so the family typically got up with her.

He glanced down at the phone in his hand and saw that the text was from Hazel. *That* didn't surprise him. Like him, she had a hard time sleeping past eight.

Are you up? the text read.

Hazel was one of those people who was positive about everything and liked to help other people. She loved writing and reading. She sent faces with each of her texts that matched her mood or the situation. Though she had a smile on her face all the time and was a bubbly kind of person, she felt a lot of internal pain. Jace personally thought she only acted happy to cope with the sad a little better.

Only Jace and their other friends actually knew that much about Hazel. She had trusted them enough to tell, and he sure as anything wasn't going to ruin his chances of keeping close to her. He opened the messages to text her back.

Yeah, I'm up. Wanna hang? Jace already knew the answer to that. Usually when she texted him it meant she was free. He grabbed his backpack, figuring he could find time while at her house to catch up on some of his homework. He opened the door to his room quietly, or at least as quietly as the hinges would allow. His door always made a loud scraping, screeching noise when he opened it, reminding him every time that he needed to tighten the screws.

Jace was surprised to hear talking as he started down the stairs, and was even more surprised to find his dad standing in the kitchen, facing the window.

"Who was that?" Jace asked as he caught sight of the phone that his dad had put down. Surprise lit up his dad's features as he turned toward Jace.

"What are you doing up? Where are you going?" His dad moved toward Jace, his hand rubbing his hair and neck and yawning.

"Woke up to the sun. I was going to go to Hazel's," Jace answered bluntly. "Who was on the phone?" Dad looked back at the counter where the phone was now lying.

"It was your grandpa. He's going to come over soon."

Jace cocked an eyebrow in surprise. He had been expecting something else, based off the look in his dad's eyes, but that wasn't bad news. In fact, it was more… odd than anything. He had barely seen his grandpa in the last year. He did know that his father didn't seem to get along the best with his grandpa – not like hard feelings or anything, just sort of indifferent to each other. Jace wondered if their relationship had always been like that.

"Grandpa? Why? When?"

His father shook his head. "I don't know when. Whenever he decides to. I am going to go back to bed, because even if you are not tired, I am." He gave Jace a half hug and a smile before turning away. His eyes became guarded and cold again, something Jace was positive had something to do with him. What had he done to make his parents so wary around him?

Before Jace could comment, his dad left the kitchen, and went into his bedroom. Jace sighed, slightly frustrated with his dad for closing up on him right when he seemed to be opening up.

A buzz in his pocket pulled him out of his reverie and he fumbled to grab it. As expected, Hazel did want him to come over. Choosing to ignore his parents' coldness to him, he put on a smile— much like Hazel did every day—and walked through the front door.

Though he could fake it on the outside he was unable to fake it inside; sadness seemed to unfold through his chest making him slower than he should have been, even if he was walking in the cold. It was early enough that the morning freeze made it hard to move.

He pulled out the phone as it vibrated again. *You doing okay? I'm sorry, shouldn't have had you walk in the snow.* It was just like Hazel to worry about other people… Also, just like her forget about the snow. He was almost to her house and there wasn't any point in turning around now.

The light snowfall when he first woke up was transitioning though, getting heavy pretty quickly now. He was able to text Hazel back before the wind started up and frigid breeze rushed through his jacket and made him stumble slightly in the snow.

Within a few steps, the snowfall turned more like a blizzard, maybe worse than the one last night; and he was walking in it!

He swore when his beanie was suddenly ripped from his head. Frantically he tugged at the hood of his coat, holding it tightly over his ears to keep the cold out, while wishing he'd brought gloves. Not the smartest move on his end; for saying he'd been freezing just getting out of bed, he should have expected it would be even colder getting outside.

He was surprised to see a slight dark movement of a silhouette almost directly in front of him. Curious, he walked faster to see what or who was out there.

It was a boy, probably around the age of eight, wearing a light jacket that was sure not to be warm – though, luckily, he was wearing thick boots. Jace ran to catch up with him. When he was about five feet away the boy stopped and looked around, confusion and worry bright on his pale face. He spotted Jace instantly.

"I can't get-t back home. I don't know w-what way." The boy shook and he had to speak between the chattering of his teeth. Jace looked around but couldn't see anyone and did not know who the boy belonged to.

Jace exhaled softly then took a deep breath as he shrugged out of the coat he was wearing. "Do you want to come with me? We can get you warmed up, then figure out where you live." The boy nodded sharply but tried to protest when Jace put the coat around him.

"I-I don't want-t-t to take that; you-you'll be cold." He put it over the boy anyway and the boy had no more complaints. Luckily Jace had worn a jacket underneath the coat, so he wasn't completely bare. He started to walk again, the boy holding his hand tightly.

Jace was sure that he was going to get sick later, but he didn't care. He just hoped that the kid wouldn't get sick too.

The boy tripped and Jace didn't hesitate to pick him up and

hold him. The warmth on his chest that came with holding the kid made him glad that he had.

"So, what's your name?" Jace asked him after a second. The boy looked up at him.

"T-tony. What-t is yours?" He put his head on Jace's chest after he'd finished talking. Jace didn't answer for a minute. He tried to ignore the cold air that went right through his jacket, which was thinner than what the boy had been wearing.

"Jace." They turned down the road that led to Hazel's house. Her house was the third one on the left but because it was cold it seemed to take ages to get to her yard.

He knocked on the door and a second later it opened. Hazel stood there and Jace was pretty sure that she had been standing on the other side to open it as soon as they arrived. She gasped when she saw the boy and frantically ushered them into the house.

"Why aren't you wearing a coat?" She asked Jace. He heard the worry in her voice, but she glanced at the heavy coat on the boy and sighed. She walked them to the fireplace.

"Mother!" Hazel left the room and a second later her mom came back with her. Hazel's mom was a lady in her early forties. Unlike her daughter's natural, almost black hair with only a few lighter strands woven through it, Maurice had blonde hair with a few streaks of brown; she had recently gotten it dyed again. Her blue eyes were wide as she took in the situation.

"Why were you out in that storm?" Jace identified anger in her voice. She took off the coat Tony wore, and the soaked jacket underneath before wrapping a large blanket around the boy.

"It-t-t wasn't that bad when I-I left," Jace told her as he tried unsuccessfully to control the chattering of his teeth. He did not want to get any of the furniture wet, so he instead stood near the fireplace.

"Take off your jacket," Hazel commanded as she grabbed another blanket off the nearby couch. He complied and placed the sodden jacket on the hook to hang near the mantel.

"Do you want some hot chocolate?" Maurice asked the boy. After a nod from him Hazel's mom turned toward Jace, and he nodded too. His fingers were numb. He couldn't even grasp the blanket that Hazel was putting around him. Hot chocolate would be the perfect thing to warm them up.

He was only slightly surprised when Hazel's arms slid around

10

him in a tight hug.

"You are too sweet for your own good," she declared with a small smile. Her nose was inches from his face, and he almost thought she was going to kiss him.

"Here you go, sweetie." Maurice returned with two cups and handed one to Tony. She flashed a smile towards Hazel and Jace. He wasn't sure if it was because she was amused that they were getting close or because she'd interrupted them, but it still caused Hazel to divert to give him a quick kiss on the cheek instead, before pulling away.

He was slightly disappointed because he really did like Hazel, but he was also relieved. His lips were too cold for kissing.

This time of the year was always a little chilled, but getting progressively warmer.

Maurice handed him a cup. It was warm, and within seconds it caused his hands to tingle. With a slight gasp he placed the cup on the mantel. He rubbed his fingers; they felt like someone had stuck a thousand needles into them.

"Oh. Sorry," Maurice apologized shortly, and Hazel glanced at him with something close to amusement in her eyes. She walked towards him and took his hands in hers. Tony held his cup with the blanket acting as a barrier, so he didn't burn his hands, smiling slightly at Jace.

"Thank you," he told Maurice, then looked at Jace with gratitude and something close to an apology.

"Where do you live? And why were you out in the snow?" Tony pulled the cup away from his face and licked his lips at Maurice's question. "I was over at a friend's house last night and started walking home this morning. I think I was lost within the first few minutes, but I continued, then the snowstorm hit. I didn't even know which way I was supposed to go." His voice was stronger now, not shaking nearly as badly.

"What's your last name?" Hazel interrupted before Maurice could say anything else.

"Vercet." A small smirk showed on Tony's face as he saw their reactions. "Yes. Like Mayor Vercet. I am his boy. Now that we got that figured out, can we find my home?" His eyebrows rose questioningly and Jace realized that this boy was not as soft spoken as he had originally thought.

"Phone number?" Maurice turned and grabbed the phone just

in time to type in the numbers that Tony threw her way.

It was silent for a moment until someone must have answered. "Hello. Is this the Vercet home?" She paused a moment. "Okay we–" Her voice cut off when she left the room and the door shut behind her.

"Thank you, Jace, for helping me." Tony said, with a hint of sheepishness, if that could be possible coming from this boy. Jace nodded shortly at Tony's praise, not wanting to make a big deal out of it.

"Why were you out in that thin jacket?" Hazel asked him a moment later. Jace understood what she meant. Since Tony was the mayor's kid, he should have nice stuff, including a good coat.

"I told my mom I did not want a coat. She did not force me to wear one." His voice had an edge to it, and he briefly glared at her.

Jace snorted a laugh. Hazel's glare towards him only made it harder not to laugh. Tony definitely acted like rich boys do in movies: a little bit spoiled.

"Alright." Hazel did not say anything else as her mom came back into the room.

"I'm going to drive you home as soon as the storm passes or calms," she said, looking directly at Tony. "Your mom is relieved that you're okay." She gave Jace a large smile "And she said to bring the young man who helped him through the storm so she could thank him properly."

Jace's eyes widened, and he took a step back. "I–I can't... I don't..." Jace couldn't get the words out. He did not want to meet the Vercets. It's not like Jace was anything special. Besides, he only did what anyone else would've done.

"You'll be fine," Hazel told him. It was her time to smile and hold back a laugh.

"You're coming too, young lady," Maurice stated. "We are going to have dinner with them."

"What?!" Hazel's startled voice mixed with Jace's.

"You heard me. Jace, you may want to tell your parents that you're not going to be home for dinner." Maurice knew how much both Jace and Hazel hated to mingle with other adults, preferring to stick with people their own ages; it was always awkward to try and make conversation with those older. Philips and Lisa were the two that liked being around adults.

"Aw. Mom, why? I didn't do anything." The way Hazel said

it made it sound like she'd done something bad rather than good. She looked like she was about to cry.

"You'll be fine," she repeated what Hazel had told Jace. "Now, I'd like to dry off the jackets so they will be warm for you guys." She stepped back out of the room with the coats, leaving a dumbfounded Jace beside the fireplace. He was sure that fear was showing in his eyes, although he did not necessarily know why he was afraid.

Tony looked back and forth between them, and then softly sighed. "My parents are really nice. You may not believe it, but they are great people." Hazel nodded, looking at Tony as if to reassure both herself and him that she was fine. Jace, however, did not reply. He looked outside to see that the storm was already starting to calm slightly. *Can I get out of it?* Probably not; they were the Vercets, after all.

ᴎ ᴎ ᴎ

Kory sat on the benches at the side of the indoor soccer field, wishing that his coach would let him get in the game. He watched the other team score another goal and couldn't help but feel irritated. His team kept making mistakes that they shouldn't be making due to Lance getting cocky and thinking he could keep the ball each time he got it – which only made the other team score more points as Lance had never been their best player. Usually his school played better – or maybe that just felt like the case when he was actually a part of the game rather than benched and watching all the mistakes.

"Can I play now?" he asked once again, desperately hoping that he could for once. Mr. Vin shook his head abruptly.

"You'll just slow them down," he snapped at Kory without looking over. Kory swallowed heavily, closing his eyes for a moment to keep from crying or punching a wall. He hated it when people told him that.

His coach was usually a very kind man and had never said anything like that to Kory before, but today was a very intense game and Kory knew tensions were high.

Why do you even let me stay on the team if you're not going to use me? he asked the man silently, frustrated.

Kory had asthma, though he didn't have attacks often

anymore. They only happened about once a month now – unless he pushed it. He'd only had an asthma attack once during a soccer game. But ever since then, his coach had refused to let him play, too scared that it could happen again. Sure, it had been terrifying, but it was just a part of Kory's life. He hadn't wanted something like that to ever happen in front of others.

He had started wheezing about halfway through the game and knew that he should have stopped, but he'd had the ball! He couldn't just drop it like that. Let the other team have it? No way.

So instead, he'd continued playing until he saw an opening to pass it to a teammate, passed it over, and put a hand on his chest as he slowed to a stop. He saw the other teammates pass him, but his eyes were scanning the crowd frantically, looking for one or both of his parents, or maybe a friend, who he knew had – or could get – his inhaler. He gave it to them for safekeeping at the beginning of every game so he didn't lose it from his pockets.

He couldn't find them. He didn't understand why his vision started to blur, why it became so hard to pick out details of the crowd. It was getting harder to breathe, and he could feel the heat leaving his face.

He turned around and finally found his dad on the other side of the field. He was running toward him, obviously aware of what was happening.

"Kory?"

Another teammate of his, Ian, appeared at his side. "Man, are you okay?" Ian's eyes widened and Kory knew that his face was pale. He gasped for a breath, black spots filling his gaze.

Then he'd fallen, not fully out of it yet, but unable to stand as his legs went numb and his vision went wonky.

His teammate grabbed him, slowing his fall to the ground. He heard people yelling in panic; his dad reached him a second later, though he only knew this because he felt the inhaler at his lips. He took a deep breath and, after a few minutes, found that he could focus a bit more.

He blinked open his eyes, squinting until they adjusted to the light. He saw his teammates gathered around him, his dad holding him in his arms. He could tell that most of his teammates were shocked and slightly terrified about what had happened. He had made it a point not to let them know about his asthma because he knew that if he had they wouldn't have been as tough on him, and he couldn't have handled being treated with kids gloves.

And now they knew. He was right. They treated him like he couldn't handle the simple things. They forgot the fact that he'd been on the team for years and had been fine until that game.

Blinking out of the memory, Kory stood up to follow the coach, who started down the line to watch the game better.

"Please, Mr. Vin," Kory begged him. "I can play, I'm good— you know that, and—"

"Kory. No." Mr. Vin turned to him for a split second. "If you have another attack in the middle of the game, we might not be able to get to you fast enough."

"More like you think I'll lose the game for you," Kory muttered, just loud enough for him to hear. "Mr. Vin, if you're going to be too scared to use me during a game, then there's no point in me being on the team. Don't lead me on! If you don't think I'm worth it, then kick me off!" Before his coach could respond he'd slipped into the crowd, making his way quickly up the rafters as he made his way to his family and Lisa, his only friend who'd been able to make it to his game this time.

He avoided looking at anyone as he walked, just silently fuming and swallowing back tears. Most people here knew that he had asthma now, and he didn't want to see what anyone thought.

"Kory, shouldn't you be down there with them?" His mom cleared a spot for him, next to her and his little sister. They both tried to make it to every one of his games. Lisa—who was sitting on the other side of Zory—gave him a sad smile.

Kory and his sister had close names. It wasn't planned that way. His parents just happened to fall in love with two foster kids with similar names, one African-American little girl and one Australian boy, and both adopted at the same time, almost four years earlier.

Zory was seven now, smart, and very cute.

"No, Mom." Kory suddenly felt his sister's arms around him. He put an arm around her. "He's not going to use me. You know he won't."

"You don't know that..."

"Yeah, he practically told me. Said he didn't want me having an attack in the middle of one." Their side cheered and Kory realized that his team had scored. He didn't join in. He was happy that they'd made a goal, but he was kind of frustrated at his coach and distracted by his own thoughts.

Lisa squeezed his hand encouragingly and he cast her a small smile, trying not to show how much it hurt him to sit out when he could be playing, just because they didn't think he could handle it.

He took off his soccer shirt, revealing a hastily donned T-shirt when he was running late for the game. It was almost all black but had some words that had faded so much that he could no longer read what it said.

He watched the game, but his heart was no longer in it. His mom seemed to notice and as soon as the game ended, she stood and gathered their stuff, getting out of there before most of the other people. The snow had been pushed off the sidewalk, but it was slippery. He followed her, anxious to leave, and itching to find something that would help him feel needed again.

It had always been hard for him to keep his thoughts happy, but recent years with his adopted family and friends had helped a lot.

But as he walked, an even darker feeling came over him, a sort of an ominous sensation unlike anything he could explain. It was as if someone was watching him, following him, which was strange because he didn't think that would be something he could actually feel. He looked around, but he saw no one.

Taking a deep breath, he closed his eyes for a moment. However, when he opened them again, he thought he saw movement, just a mere flicker of a shadow before it and the dark feeling was gone

Unsure what to think and suddenly antsy with more nerves, he stepped closer to his mom.

As soon as his mom emptied her hands, she pulled him into a hug, which helped bring warmth back into him. He hadn't realized how cold the air was today while he'd been stressing about the game. Should have brought a jacket. It was probably something his mom had told him to do before they left the house.

"I love you, Kory," she said. Her hand was in his hair. "They might not think they need you, but I do."

"Thanks, mom." He didn't cry. He rarely cried in front of people. He probably wouldn't ever cry in front of people since he found that the only time he cried was alone in his room when he thought about his past life.

And that past life was something he didn't want to tell even his best friends or parents about. He just wanted to forget that it ever happened.

When his mom pulled away, he walked to the passenger side and opened the door.

"Kory!" He looked back to see his coach running up to him. The man stopped with a huff next to him. "Look kid, you're right, I'm sorry. I shouldn't keep you on the team if I'm not going to let you play." Kory paled when he realized that he was probably getting cut from the team now, but the man continued without a pause. "Next time, next time I promise I'll get you in the game. Next Saturday, okay?"

"Really?" He was relieved—relieved that he wasn't cut, glad that he'd get to play again—and he knew that Mr. Vin could tell. He nodded. "Thank you." He let out a deep breath, "Really, thanks."

"I'll see you, Kory," Mr. Vin said. He smiled. "Be ready."

Kory bit his lip, nodding, then watched him walk away.

ℕ ℕ ℕ

"No way, I am *not* going."

"Yes, you are! You can do this for me!" Hazel sighed in exasperation as her older brother argued with their mother once again.

Karthus scoffed. "This isn't for you! This is for *them*, and I don't need to go!" he insisted.

"What else would you do anyway? We are having dinner with them tonight." Hazel peeked out her doorway of her room to see them facing each other in the hall near the family room.

"Anything but that. I'll figure something else out." Karthus was trying desperately to back out of this one, but Hazel knew that he was not going to win this argument. She turned away from them and went into the bathroom.

"Here we go again," she muttered to herself. "Ugh!" She felt tears dampen her eyes but blinked them back. "Why do they always have to fight? Here we are going to try and have a good time, and they have to ruin it!" Not that she thought having dinner with the Vercets would be fun, necessarily, but did everything have to be an argument?

Hazel was convinced that they just enjoyed fighting or, at the very least, enjoyed being right. She pulled the necklace from around her neck and placed it on the counter next to her.

"And now I'm talking to myself again!" She continued to

mutter to herself for a few seconds, despite her anger, not paying attention to what was actually coming out of her mouth.

She opened the bathroom closet then pulled off her shirt, placing it into the laundry bin on the closet floor.

She could hear them arguing from in here, but it sounded distant. The noise was dimmed as she turned on the water, and as she got in, she let her shoulders finally relax.

Thank you for my family, thank you for water, thank you for... She didn't know if anyone from above was listening to her silent rambling, but it helped her calm down to remember all the good she had. She continued to name random things that came to her mind, constantly repeating a few.

I miss you, dad. Why'd you leave? Her mom had divorced her dad about five months ago, and she had only been to visit her dad three times since he had decided to move to California.

A knock interrupted her thoughts and she heard her mother's voice through the door.

"Hurry up. William still needs to shower!" She sounded irritated.

"I just got in mom!" She rolled her eyes, then she lowered her voice so she couldn't hear. "Jeez, give me a minute, would you? We have three hours."

Her mom didn't answer, so Hazel turned the water up a bit more.

She was able to push aside her worries as the water ran down her back. She sang softly to herself; her voice was beyond terrible, but at least she didn't go out singing as loud as she could to the world.

They had driven Jace home about twenty minutes ago because, according to her mom, she'd had to get ready.

Jace was her best friend by all definitions, but they often most of their time with their other friends. Honestly, she counted them all as best friends.

They were kind of oddballs at their school because they stuck together and didn't really join in with other people or their gossip. She winced as she heard the front door slam and figured that her mom had won the argument and Karthus didn't like it.

She heard another knock on the door again and sighed.

"Yes?" Her voice was curt.

"I have to pee," William told her through the door. Hazel

smirked as the little voice reached her ears.

"Okay?" She didn't hear a reply but heard the door hit the wall as it was opened. "Are you serious, William? You can't go in the other bathroom?" She was just glad that her shower had a thick curtain rather than a glass wall.

"Mom's in it."

"And I'm in this one!" Hazel wasn't really mad, just frustrated. Not with William though, and she was pretty positive that he knew that.

"Where are we going? What was Karthus angry about?" he asked her quietly. She knew that he hated her brother and mom's arguing just as much as she did.

She felt a sense of anxiety at the thought that they would have to go to the Vercets house. The Mayor!

"We are going to go have dinner with the Vercets." She didn't know if he actually knew who they were but there was silence for a few seconds.

"How do you think they are?" He was washing his hands now. She could hear it running in the background, though the water was pounding on her back.

"I wouldn't even want to guess." She imagined him nodding since he didn't answer verbally for some long seconds.

"Why do we have to go?" So her mom and brother had been too busy arguing to explain to William what they were doing.

"We helped their son out. They invited us to dinner." She closed her eyes and carefully slid to sit on her feet on the floor of the shower. William didn't answer and she heard the door shut a second later. She continued to sit in there as the warm water ran down. She watched it swirl down the drain as her mind wandered to her most recent poem.

Flurries... The people went around in flurries. No, that's not right... The people moved around, like smudges to me. I couldn't bear to see the pain that the world would bring. Instead, I close my eyes, drowning out the sound, and it all moved peacefully before it began to—

She grumbled as a knock sounded on the door again, interrupting her thoughts. "What?!" she snapped.

"Time to get out. You've been in there for a half an hour now," her mom said. *Oh boy,* she thought, *the whole world's going to fall, isn't it?*

"Mom, we still have more than two hours, stop stressing!" She turned the water off though and grabbed the towel, quickly drying off. She hoped that her mom would be relaxed enough tonight.

Bound... it all moved peacefully before I was bound. She smiled in her mind. Yes, bound. Bound by what though

Chapter Two

JACE TRIED TO KEEP his mouth closed but the beauty of the house made him look jealously around. He had never cared much about expensive things, but this place strayed into the overly opulent.

Maurice had dropped Tony off about noon, once most of the snow had melted, and now Hazel's family and Jace and now they stood at the door listening as footsteps rushed around inside.

Jace had chosen to wear nicer clothes than he usually did. He didn't have any clothes as nice as a tuxedo or anything so his white button-down shirt would have to work.

The door opened and the very recognizable Mayor's wife stood in the doorway. Mrs. Vercet was a tall, thin lady with blonde hair that fell just past her mid back. She looked around forty-five.

Her slightly wrinkled face curved into a large smile as she invited them in.

"I am so happy you guys came!" She started toward Jace, then paused, "You don't mind if I give you a hug, right?" Jace shook his head and accepted her embrace. "You're the young man who helped my son?"

Jace nodded.

"How can I ever repay you?"

"No, don't worry about repaying me, I–"

"Nonsense!" She looked shocked, and then winked. "You think about it for a bit and decide what you want."

Yeah. Right. I'll just hope you forget. Mrs. Vercet turned away and pulled Hazel into a hug as well.

"Um… Mrs. Vercet, why am I here?" Hazel's little brother William asked quietly, almost apologetically.

"Because you guys helped my boy out." She turned towards

him and swooped down to hug him as well. Karthus, Hazel's older brother, just rolled his eyes.

"I didn't do anything," the young boy told her bluntly. Hazel turned toward Jace with a smirk. *Me neither,* she mouthed to him. Jace smiled back at her, though it didn't feel quite authentic due to his nerves.

"You're in the family, dear." Karthus reluctantly accepted a hug from her as well. He, of course, had a headphone in one ear.

Just had to get myself wrapped up with the mayor's boy, didn't I? Jace shook his head slightly and looked out the window. Of course, he didn't regret helping, not like he'd have left him in the cold, but he sure hadn't been expecting nor wanting a reward.

Well, she's a talkative one. Mrs. Vercet was still talking and he forced himself to listen as she let them into the house and shut the door behind them, then taking their coats to hang up in the coat closet.

He smiled when he realized that she had somehow figured out a way to turn the conversation to her kids.

"This is Tony, whom you know, and he's almost nine. He's our little troublemaker, as I'm sure you've figured out. And Mia is about your guys' age," She gestured toward Jace, Hazel and Karthus. "She is in high school, and she's a smart cookie, that one. I am excited to see what she gets into."

As she spoke, a girl, who Jace assumed was Mia, came into the foyer. She smiled brightly as she saw the guests. Jace smirked when he saw Karthus straighten under the new girl's gaze and take his earpiece out.

"Now you're happy," Hazel told him, then flounced away from the hands that attempted to pull her back.

"Shut up." Karthus's face flushed slightly as he avoided the gaze of Mia and focused his attention on Hazel.

"Hi, I'm Mia." She looked directly at Maurice. "You must be Mrs. Holland."

"Yes, I am." Maurice responded as Mrs. Vercet motioned them to follow her. Jace decided as they entered that the dining room was even better than the main entrance. Of course, that could have been because of the food pile on the table.

"Thank you so much for helping my brother, he's a stubborn one and doesn't like to listen to what we tell him." Mia smiled. Her blonde hair reached her waist and looked similar in style to her mother's. But it was her blue-green eyes that were the most noticeable part about her. They were framed with makeup that made them seem brighter and bigger than most people's eyes.

"You really should be thanking Jace, he's the one who brought him out of the snow." Jace shuffled slightly at Maurice's words and inwardly scolded himself. He was working on his nervous tics with little luck.

Mia looked as if she was holding back a laugh at his reaction. "Well thank you, kind sir." She curtsied in a way that made him think she was teasing him, but not in a way that caused offense. "And who are the others that came with thee?" She turned towards Karthus and flashed him a large smile. Jace wasn't quite sure if she was talking like that for fun or if it was actually the way she acted all the time. It was weird.

"This is William." Maurice pulled her younger son close. "That is Hazel, and the young man who seems to be besotted with you is Karthus."

"Mom!" Karthus's face turned red again but so did Mia's. Karthus was almost two years older than Jace and looked closer to Mia's age.

Mrs. Vercet just chuckled.

"Um… I'll go get Tony." Mia turned away and went towards the door across from them.

"Honey, I think he went out back," Mrs. Vercet told her. "Can you go get dad, too?" Mia started to nod but another voice cut her off.

"I am here, don't bother." Jace turned as the mayor entered with his booming voice. Mason looked a lot less intimidating without his large suit that he usually wore, and yet being near him while he's wearing simple jeans and a polo shirt was strange. Also made Jace feel slightly over-dressed.

"Sorry, I just got home. I haven't had time to change into nicer clothes," he told them after a moment's silence.

"You are absolutely fine," Maurice said.

"Oh, I'm sorry, I need to get to know my guests. You must be Mrs. Holland then, correct?" He took a step forward and took Maurice's hand in his.

"Yes, but call me Maurice, please."

"Gotcha I–"

"Go ahead and sit anywhere," Mrs. Vercet told them eagerly and grabbed a chair. Maurice turned away from Mr. Vercet and took the chair next to Mrs. Vercet, diving immediately into a conversation by complementing her house.

Jace turned his attention back to the mayor and realized he was standing in front of him, waiting to shake his hand as well. Jace hesitantly extended his hand, trying to figure out how tight he should squeeze. He could've been too tight for all he knew, but the man didn't seem to care.

"And who are you?"

"I'm Jace."

"Ah… And I assume you've already been thanked by the women in the household, so I don't need to?" He laughed. "I'm kidding. You'll get a thanks from me, too."

"No, you don't need to thank me, sir—"

"Don't fancy me with those names, Mason will work wonderfully," he said, laughter still in his voice. Then he whispered: "And don't worry, I won't make such a big deal out of this. I'm not to like being the center of attention, ironic, I know. But just so you know, my wife is a bit of a gossip…"

Jace looked away from the larger man with a smile, amused and surprised that he felt so comfortable with a man he just met. He was also confused at why he'd become a mayor if he really didn't like the attention.

Then he got distracted and stepped towards a window that seemed to frame the view of their town and the mountains that lay behind, and it absolutely stunned him.

"It's why we liked the house," Mason said softly, coming to stand next to him.

"It's beautiful," Jace murmured before he realized that he should probably sit down like he'd been asked. He took the few steps to grab the chair closest to him, which happened to be three seats down from Hazel's mother. The table was large but had good space for movement in the room. He wondered if servants had to function behind the chairs.

While everyone else had grabbed a chair already, Hazel had waited for him to choose a seat and grabbed the chair next to him, while her little brother sat next to their mom. Mason was chuckling as he moved away from Jace and sat in the head chair, which was on the other side of Jace.

Karthus shuffled uncertainly before sitting across from his

mom.

"Hi Jace!" Tony ran across the room and snatched the chair right across from Jace. He was beaming, and Jace couldn't help but smile in return.

"Hi, uh… you good?" Jace asked slowly, fidgeting with his hands. He looked around and noticed that other than Hazel's mother and Mrs Vercet, everyone else seemed to be about as uncomfortable as himself.

The boy nodded enthusiastically and turned to his dad, talking quickly to explain a game he'd been playing outside with their dog. Mason just nodded along with an amused smile toward Jace.

Mia came in a second later and ended up in the seat right next to Karthus. While Karthus stared at her, she avoided his gaze, instead becoming fixated on the tablecloth on the table ahead of her.

He hid a smile. Hazel had told him that Karthus had not wanted to come, but now he sure seemed to enjoy himself, a small smile, bordering on a smirk, on his face as he kept trying to get Mia's attention.

"Bet you a hundred that by the end of the night he'll have her number," Hazel muttered in his ear. She glanced at Karthus and Jace followed her gaze.

"I'll double that offer," Jace said under his breath. There was no way he would leave the house without it. Jace and Hazel both knew that Karthus could easily flatter a girl.

She glanced at Jace. "You're supposed to bet against, not with me," she said disapprovingly.

Jace gave her a pointed look. "I am not going to bet against you when your bet's more probable and I know it." He forgot for a second that he was in the dining room with the Vercets and quickly lowered his voice slightly, even though he was sure no one had heard — they were all busy talking.

Hazel bit her lips, clearly trying not to burst out laughing. "Fine, then we get to share the M&Ms with a movie," she said it like a threat, even though neither of them would find that a bad thing.

They had too many M&Ms. Jace still had some from his last bet with her. They always used M&Ms as the reward since they didn't have a lot of money. M&Ms was both of their favorite candies and Jace was sure that he would run out of money before they stopped betting with them.

He turned his attention back to what was going on at the table and found that Karthus was already flirting with Mia while grabbing some food. After making sure everyone was starting to dish out food and eat, Jace cautiously reached to grab a roll out of the nearest bowl.

"Can you pass the rolls?" Mia asked him. It took Jace a second to register what she'd asked, and he set his own roll on his plate and handed the bowl to her. She passed him the mashed potatoes and Jace sighed inwardly. *Yeah, this is so freaking awkward.*

Jace's mom had been excited about him having the opportunity to meet the Vercets – she actually smiled and nudged him out the door despite his protestations – and had told him he could borrow his brother's shirt – despite the fact that Jason himself off somewhere with one of his friends and hadn't given his own permission. Jason was rarely ever home these days though, and Jace still couldn't figure out if it was because he wanted some form of independence from their parents, or if they'd had some kind of fight.

Jason was the reason he had chosen to call himself Jace rather than Jack – even though Jack was more appropriate coming from Jacque. He was closer to his older brother than anyone else in his family and was the one he felt like he could talk to without being judged. Well, Jason and Korren, but his younger brother was much too young to understand most things.

Jace passed the potatoes to Hazel. He wasn't sure if he was supposed to pass everything or only the things the others asked for, but he just kind of grabbed what others held out to him and passed it to whomever reached for it.

He mostly listened to the conversations, only joining in when questions were directed at him. And slowly the night passed without any problems. As they drove home, he rested his head on the window and sighed as Hazel leaned on him. He suspected that she fell asleep before they reached his house.

Chapter Three

HE DIDN'T REMEMBER falling asleep last night, and immediately found his phone laying on the bed next to him – he must have drifted off before he could get it on the charger. But his phone was buzzing now; Lisa was texting him, wanting to know how the night with the Vercets had gone.

It was fine, he texted back. A few seconds later he received another message.

Want to hang out with us? At our spot. We are all thinking about being there about 10:00 or 11:00. He knew she was talking about their treehouse, and he didn't have anything else he'd rather do today. It had probably warmed up today after that freak-storm yesterday, that he referred to as third winter.

"Sure? Is Hazel coming too?" Hazel had texted last night, telling Jace that they were right and Karthus had indeed got Mia's number before they left dinner last night.

Yep, she's coming. She said to get your butt down here, we can watch the movie together... What is she talking about?

He smirked. They had decided to bring M&M's to their next movie. He knew he would get back to sleep now, but it was early enough that he wasn't quite ready to get out of bed yet. He wasted some time messaging his friends, scrolling social media, and playing some games on his phone, and before he knew it, hours had passed and he had to get going.

What a great timewaster. Or a terrible one, if you're supposed to get moving.

He rolled off his bed and pulled his shoes on, pausing only when he received another text. Lisa in the group chat: *If you haven't left yet, bring blankets! It's still a little chilly! And some tissues, I think the cold is making me drip.*

I'll get some, Jace assured them.

He had a bunch of extra blankets, so he grabbed three of the larger ones and shoved them in a garbage bag, adding the box of tissues to his other hand. Would mom or dad drive him to the tree house? He really didn't walk there while dragging a black garbage bag.

Jace quietly shut the door behind him, but then paused as he heard voices in the basement. Only the two oldest brothers had a room downstairs, Jace, and his older brother Jason. Jason must be visiting, as he'd been pretty much couch-surfing at friends' houses for the past two years or so. Instead of heading upstairs, he went that direction, recognizing his grandpa Henri's voice as he did so.

Freezing for a moment out of sight from the room, he quietly set the bag of blankets down before creeping closer. He would have just gone directly into the room to say hi, but it sounded as though they were having an argument, the tones sharp but still fairly quiet, and he kind of figured that they didn't want anyone else to hear.

"Whatever, Henri. There's no way!" It was Jason talking "There's no way I can do that. I wouldn't be able to save peoples lives' if I tried!"

"It's a quest, Jason. All you have to do is find the power before Darrin does!" Henri's voice came in insistently. "You don't even have to go far. I've been told it's nearby, you can take some friends. Just warn them of the danger.

"But, Jason, Darrin *cannot* get this. If he does the whole world will be ruined, I need you to get it. I would do it myself but I am too old and nobody else can know about it."

All was silent for a moment before Jason's voice came back in. "How would I even know if I found it? You said that it was in one of the close towns, but how will I know? It wouldn't just be sitting waiting for me in the open because then the darkness or whatever would have already gotten it."

Grandpa Henri paused and sighed. "It's in a cave." His voice was quiet "You won't be able to get to it easily, there will be a lot of adversity trying to stop you, and it could take a while to find."

"Why me?" Jason asked. He sounded as if he still didn't believe. "You can choose anyone—maybe someone who actually cares about this, or believes in it. So why would you ask me?"

Jace leaned closer to the door. It was getting harder to hear them as Jason had lowered his voice as though trying to talk rationally.

"I would choose someone else but their reactions would be much like yours is now, and they aren't related to me—and they have to be related to find it. You are the oldest; you might be able to do it easier."

"Not saying I am going to agree to this, because it sounds ludicrous to me," Jason told Henri, "But if I do, where would I start? And what would happen if the Shadow gets it? And how would I know what I was looking for?"

"If Darrin gets it, anything can happen. The power is the only thing that's keeping the world as sane as it is even now. You'll have to start in Kinstown and work your way around. We think that it's most likely in Kinstown or Jurade. You'll know you've found it once you see it. Please, Jason, we really need this. If we don't get it first then all will be lost."

Jason hesitated and, in that time, Jace had stepped further away from the door. What were they talking about? Why did it have to be Jason? Why not *Jace*? Why didn't anyone think that *he* was capable of doing anything?

Jace chewed on his lip, thinking. He could go out and get it— whatever *it* was. A power of some sort. It sounded like *they* didn't even know what it was entirely, and Jace didn't understand what his grandpa meant by shadow either. But he could do this *quest* just as easily as Jason could.

Grandpa said something that Jace missed and then he heard footsteps coming out. Jace quickly slipped into the bathroom as Grandpa Henri passed.

"I'm not going to do it, Henri," Jason called after him. "I don't believe in all that crap." Jace waited until he could hear no other sounds before peeking out cautiously.

Jace couldn't really say that he believed what Grandpa Henri had said either, nor did he get all the information, and yet something in him was yearning to do it; maybe to prove himself, maybe to get away and escape his life. His life wasn't bad, per se, but boring for sure, and... well, he wondered what his parents would think. Would they even miss him? He knew they loved him, and yet they didn't really show any interest in him or how he was doing.

Besides, Jace and his friends had always wanted an adventure; and one had practically fallen into their laps. He wondered if his friends would even actually want to do a so called quest now that it came their way. It was one thing to long for it, another to actually take the risk when it came.

He started back to his brother's room. It had been long enough pause that Jason's door was probably shut by now.

He knocked on Jason's door quietly and a second later the door opened.

"Hey," he seemed a little surprised to see him.

"Hey, sorry, I thought I heard your voice. Jace went in for a hug that his brother opened for. "It's good to see you."

"You too, bro." Jason ruffled his hair as he stepped back. "So what are your plans for the day?"

"Oh, I was just going to hang out with my friends. I was wondering if you could drop me off if you have a minute? If not, I can just walk. Or ask our parents."

Jason nodded his head. "Of course, I'll give you a ride." Jason went back into his room and grabbed some shoes. "Did you see grandpa?" He asked as he pulled them on.

"No. He's here?" Jace feigned surprise.

"He was. He may have left by now." He stepped out, shutting the door behind himself as he did so.

"Oh, that wouldn't surprise me." *No one really cares to see me often anyway*, he thought. Jace grabbed the bag with the blankets on the floor but paused by his door. "Wait one second," he added, going back in his room and digging through his drawer until he found a bag of M&Ms and stuffed them in his pocket. He also grabbed a heater that sat by his door. Now he had full arms. He was so glad he wasn't walking.

"What are you doing?" Jason asked. He eyed all the stuff in his brother's hands.

"We're going to hang out at the tree house," he said. "I thought that maybe a heater would help."

Jason shook his head in amusement. "You guys are going to get sick hanging out at that tree."

Jace snorted. "Yeah, probably." Jace told him as they went upstairs. "It's pretty out there though, you know, with the snow, though most of it is melted now."

"Yeah… Pretty cold!" *It's not that cold*, Jace thought. *Not during the day at least.* But Jason had always been more sensitive to the cold than most of them.

Their dad was in the kitchen at the top of the stairs, almost startling Jace when he spoke.

"Where are you two going?" Dad asked as he brushed his hands on his pants, as though trying to brush the flour off his hands. Clearly, he was making some fresh bread for the week. His eyes looked almost sad as he watched them. A little weary.

"Jason's going to drop me with friends," Jace told him quietly. He always felt really uncomfortable with his parents, unsure what to say to them at times, and he wished he didn't. Never knowing how to interact with his parents had then extended to pretty much any other adult as well, making him awkward with anyone who wasn't his own age or younger.

"Did you see Grandpa?" Dad asked him.

"No. Did he leave already?"

His dad nodded, his eyes narrowing in confusion at the denial, but then he shook his head and turned back to knead the dough.

"Alright, I'll see you later. Will you be back here after dropping Jac off, Jason?"

"Yeah, I will." Jason confirmed. "I'll be here for a few days, if that's okay?"

"Always okay, son." He smiled warmly. "See you in a bit."

Jace frowned at the obvious tone change with talking with his brother, turning to leave the house and walk to Jason's car.

"Holy crap, it's cold out here," Jason said.

Jace didn't even feel the cold until he got into the car, though it was quite chilly.

"Yeah," Jace agreed.

"So, where is your treehouse?" Jason asked as he pulled onto the road.

Jace stuck a thumb behind them.

"It's faster the other way." Jace leaned his head on the window with a quiet sigh. As Jason flipped back around Jace started talking again.

"How was Grandpa?" He wondered if his grandpa had even *tried* to say hi to him.

Jason hesitated. "He was good... I think. Just wanted to talk for a bit, I guess." Jace wondered if the look Jason shot him was because he didn't like the new direction of the conversation, or if it he was worried about giving something away. If Jace didn't know what they had talked about then he probably wouldn't have even noticed the nervousness.

"Oh, fun." He scratched his neck, feeling strangely uncomfortable with his brother.

"So what are you and your friends planning to do today?" Jason asked.

"Who knows what they're planning." Jace shook his head. Usually they just got together to hang out, then figured out what they wanted to do after that.

"Turn right here," he told Jason a second later as they got close. Their treehouse wasn't visible from the street, rather a few trees into the forest.

"I can't believe you guys are really going to hang out in the cold." Jason shook his head. "That doesn't make sense to me."

"It's not that cold." Jace protested. "Besides, I brought blankets and the space heater, and we all got coats. To be honest, it might be overkill within the hour anyway."

Jason snorted. "Yeah, sure."

Jace moved to get out of the car as it slowed to a stop, but Jason stopped him. "You might want to give me a hug. I won't be back for another few weeks and I'm leaving today."

For a second or two, Jace felt alarmed. Was Jason going to do what Grandpa Henri had asked of him after all? "To another friend's house?" he asked his brother, closing the door so that it was resting against his foot.

"Yes. I've had plans to go to Austin's house for two weeks now."

Jace didn't think that Jason was lying. He'd never been one to lie to anyone, if anything he was too forward about his opinions. But would he lie about something like this?

"Okay. I'll see you soon?" He gave him a quick hug.

"Yes, of course, in just a few weeks."

Only if I get back by then, Jace thought, slightly surprised because, until that moment, he didn't realize he'd fully decided on going. He pulled the door open again and grabbed the heater, pausing to wrap the cord around his hand. Then he grabbed the bag of blankets.

"Thanks for the ride." He lifted his hand in farewell as he stepped out. After he stepped off the pavement, he was in a bit of snow that had been more stubborn in the shade of the trees.

32

Luckily, he only had to weave through a few trees before he was staring up at their treehouse.

Kory had come up with the idea of this treehouse because he was interested in architecture and thought that it would be fun practice. They had all helped – or tried their best to. It was well made, sturdy, and no water had gotten into it yet. But, just in case, they'd bring and take home the most important things – like the TV and sometimes heaters, then cover the rest of the stuff with plastic wrap.

"Finally!" A voice startled him out of his thoughts "What took you so long?!" He looked up to see Philips' face. A second later Lisa's face peeked over as well.

"Good, you brought the tissues. I already need those!" She glanced at him in amusement. Jace smirked at her and tossed the box up to her.

"Catch!" He didn't warn her as fast as he should have, but she stuck her hand out to catch it anyway. Kory appeared suddenly and snatched the box from her grip. Jace grinned as he started up the ladder with the heater, leaving the bag of blankets down on the ground until he went back down to get them. He only had enough arms to carry one thing up, and he didn't want to set the heater on the wet ground.

"Hey!" Lisa reached for the tissues, but Kory smoothly tossed the box to Philips, and she was stuck going back and forth between the two in an impromptu monkey in the middle.

"Would you give it back?" She whined. When they still didn't comply, she huffed with a smile. "Fine, I'll just use you guys." She rushed to hug Kory and used his jacket shoulder to wipe her nose.

"That's disgusting!" Kory scoffed, shoving her –gently– away.

She smiled and flounced away, back into the room.

As Jace passed Kory, attempting to wipe his shoulder with the tissue, he laughed. "Come on, dude. That's why you don't mess with girls. They have a way of either getting what they want or manipulating the system." Kory punched his shoulder and Jace pretended to stumble close to the edge which prompted Kory to quickly reach out to catch him.

"I'm fine, bro," he said with a laugh. He snatched the box out of his friend's hands with a "thank you," then tossed it to Hazel, who was reaching for it.

Kory made his way to the ladder. Obviously, heading for the bag of blankets.

"You sure made a dramatic entrance," she laughed. Her nose was already bright red, and he wondered for a second if she was sick or if she'd been out in the cold long enough already. "Decided to join us?"

"Yeah, figured I might as well." Jace shrugged nonchalantly and put the heater down as Philips followed him back in the treehouse.

"Smart," she said about the heater as she reached to plug it in the long extension cord that reached all the way to Lisa's house. "Hopefully, it'll warm it up fast." Jace saw the light come on as she turned it almost as high as it could go.

"What would you do if the roof broke in and trapped us all under the snow?" Kory asked climbed back into the treehouse, tossing it into the room dramatically before making his way to the big black bean bag. He always said that he had never seen snow before he was adopted at age twelve, and snow, well, now it was one of his favorite things.

"I don't think you'd really be able to do much under the snow," Lisa pointed out. She jumped onto Kory's lap with a laugh and Kory grunted but wrapped an arm around her to steady her. "But I would try to dig myself out. Oh, and then help dig you guys out, if you haven't made it out yet."

Kory looked thoughtful. "Well, what if one of you guys came over – like Jace did – but instead of finding people or a tree house you found a pile of snow?"

Not that there was quite enough snow to really bury anyone at the moment, and even if there was, Jace didn't think he'd really want to be hanging out at the treehouse.

"If I saw that," Jace interjected, "I would start to dig while I called my brother back to help. Why are you asking?" Although he didn't really need to ask, Kory was always the one to come up with unlikely scenarios and listen to the ways everyone would react.

He shrugged and Jace nervously cleared his throat before speaking. "Well, I've got a possible scenario for you." He wished that they didn't all look at him. He leaned back as if trying to make it seem like a question just for fun, not asking it because it had actually happened. "If you were to be asked to go on a quest to save the world, would you do it, even if it was dangerous and you had no idea if it would really work?" He watched their reactions closely. Lisa looked thoughtful as she scooted off Kory and sat at his side. Kory smiled at

Jace.

"What brought up that idea?" Jace ignored Philips' inquiry for a second, wanting to hear their replies first. He didn't want them to know the details unless they wanted to take on the adventure. If he told them, and they weren't completely convinced that they wanted to help, there would be a chance they might tell someone where he was going, or even stop him from leaving. Also, it sounded so absurd to even him.

"I think that would be an awesome opportunity," Hazel said as she stood up. "I would want to go, even if it was just to see the reactions of my family."

"I have to agree with Hazel on that one," Kory said as he closed his eyes. "It's sad how we always think about impressing our families, but I can't help it. And it honestly would be cool, like in the great stories, the ones that really matter," he smirked at being able to bring part of a quote from Lord of the Rings, and Jace couldn't help but smile as well as Kory continued, "being able to do something that might actually save the world." Lisa nodded as well, but Philips was still studying Jace with his piercing gaze.

"I don't know how I would react unless it actually happened," Philips said at last. That was his response to most of the questions like that. He always said he knew how he'd want to react but not how he would in actuality. "Now seriously, what brought that up?"

Now that it was time to ask his friends the question, Jace found that he really didn't want to. Maybe he would just go by himself or not at all. "Nothing," he lied, glancing down, though he realized that looking away was just adding to his terrible lying skills.

Jace stood up quickly, trying to ignore their questioning eyes on him. He grabbed the blankets out of the bag and tossed one to Lisa and Kory. "I only had three extras." He explained to them. He didn't look at them, knowing that he would see disbelief in their gazes, and it would convince him to talk. He didn't think it would be smart to tell them anymore. *It was just some baloney thing I overheard. Jason didn't believe a thing his grandpa said, and I definitely hadn't received nearly enough information.* It was a stupid idea.

He gave another one to Philips and Hazel. "Are we watching a movie or talking for a bit?" He finally looked at them, knowing that he had to eventually. They had all stopped to watch him and Hazel's arms were folded in front of her.

"Are you going to tell us what's on your mind?" Hazel asked him with narrowed eyes.

No, he told them silently. "Maybe." They wouldn't believe him if he said nothing. *Why do I have to be so bad at lying?*

Hazel frowned at him. "Does it have something to do with your scenario?"

Jace shook his head. "Never mind, just forget I said anything, okay?"

"Oh, come on!" Lisa whined. "Tell us."

Jace blinked. He really did want to tell them, but who was he to ask them to leave when he didn't even understand everything?

But there was a bright look in her eyes that he had to look away from – toward someone who was more cautious, not the bundle of joy that Lisa was. Philips.

"Um… it's just…" Philips still hadn't moved and was just watching them, halfway smirking at the way Jace was practically stumbling over his words now. "Well…" Even if they didn't go, he could still see their reactions. It wouldn't hurt.

Taking a breath, he dived in, "I overheard my brother and grandpa talking. He was trying to convince Jason to go somewhere, one of the towns around here, for something. But my brother probably isn't going to go," he said quickly, curling his fist and glancing away.

"And is that something the thing that can save the world?" Kory asked in disbelief, able to put the scant details Jace gave together.

"Maybe, or my grandpa is old enough that he could just be confused," Jace shrugged. "I just thought that it would be kinda fun especially if it is true." He wondered how evident his nerves were, he sure felt shaky.

"Where is it?" Philips asked. He usually was the most mature and cautious in the group, so it would be hardest to convince him.

"He said that it was in one of the surrounding towns, like Kinstown and Jurade in a cave most likely." He slowed down his speaking, trying to get his thoughts together so maybe some more useful details could come out of his mouth.

"What are we looking for?" Philips' eyebrows rose.

"I don't know. It doesn't even sound like Grandpa Henri knew. He said that he'd know it when he saw it, and I guess only people related to him could find it." The sentence came out more like a question. He lifted his arms in an 'I don't know' way. "He said something about going out to find this… power. I'm not sure I understand it, honestly. There's not really a lot of information to work on, but it's enough and it would be something new to our lives." That would be the thing to convince them. They all had that in common; how they wanted something different to happen in their lives.

"What would we tell our parents?" Lisa asked. She looked like she was really contemplating this.

Which was terrifying.

He bit his lip as his answer. They couldn't tell anyone because no one would let them go.

"Okay. So you're planning on just leaving." She nodded curtly as if she figured that would be his answer. "Now? What about coming back after? Won't they be mad?"

Jace looked down at his feet. He didn't know what he'd do about that.

"Never mind, just don't worry about it," he said again. "I don't want you guys to stress over it."

"You're still going though, aren't you?" Philips asked him after a second of silence.

"Nah," he lied. It sounded a lot like *yeah* though.

"I'll go," Hazel said. She bit her cheek. "Like I said, it would be fun to try."

Lisa nodded. "If you are going, I'd like to go with you." But despite the nonchalant tone, she was practically bouncing.

"Dude, you know I won't let you go without me." Kory dug into the M&M bag and popped some into his mouth as he spoke.

"It might be dangerous," Jace warned them "This other guy — Darrin, or something like that is also trying for it, and we could run into him. I have no idea what he wants it for or what he'd do to us if we came across him."

"When are we leaving?" Philips gave him a look that said, 'don't argue, I'm going'.

"Do you think tomorrow would be enough time to get a bit of money, food and clothes?" Jace asked. "Don't want to bring too many things or else our parents might figure us out. And, we'll have to walk, and I doubt we want to carry too much."

"Yeah, I've gotten ready faster than that before," Lisa smirked. Her family was always taking impromptu trips.

"Okay." Jace felt another wave of anxiety. "Are you sure you want to? We shouldn't go if you guys don't want to, or don't feel comfortable with it..."

Kory shook his head to interrupt. "Jace stop it, we've already said we're going, and I think we all know that you'll go whether or not we do. *I* am at least coming." Jace chewed on his lip for another few seconds before nodding slowly.

"Okay, well, I'll have to tell you about everything I heard. We'll leave tomorrow after breakfast. Meet here."

Chapter Four

HAZEL WATCHED JACE approach the tree house. He seemed awfully worried about the prospect of them leaving today, not really for himself, but for them and for her. He had told her that much.

Jace looked up at her and smiled softly. Hazel was honestly nervous about leaving as well, but she knew that Jace would go either way. She knew that he was determined enough to do so, no matter what any of them said. She'd had a pretty bad dream last night about leaving that left a bad taste in her mouth, but it still hadn't erased the feeling that they needed to go.

As he got up the ladder, Hazel immediately asked him a question that she had thought about before falling asleep last night. "Jace, what if we are put in the missing kids ads? People could recognize us wherever we go."

Jace stopped in the snow on the deck and looked thoughtful as he shifted his bag to his other shoulder. "True. We may have to stay where no one can see us… Or bribe someone to let us stay with them." Jace sighed. avoiding her eyes. "Maybe we shouldn't do this. There are too many complications."

The attempt to keep them from coming was to no avail. Kory shook his head, stood up from the beanbag, and swooped his backpack in one smooth motion.

They were still waiting on Lisa. Hazel wondered if she would show up after all. This wouldn't work if even one person told their parents. Granted Lisa had seemed the most outwardly excited by the prospect of a quest, so she'll probably be here—

In that moment, Lisa came into view below and caught sight of them. "Sorry, my mom wanted me to clean my room before I went to hang out with you guys." She rolled her eyes with a beaming smile as she looked up at them. "My mom knows I brought my bag – not what's in it, and she assumed that we were just going to hang out and needed some games."

"It's all good," Hazel told her, unable to keep herself from smiling at Lisa's joy. But catching Philips gaze, she was surprised to find that he looked anxious. *So I'm not the only one with reservations.* Besides Jace, of course. They could all see his nerves.

Philips shrugged his own backpack on and stepped up beside Jace, putting a hand on his shoulder "Don't stress so much," Philips told him. "It'll be a fun chance to get out." His words seemed to contradict his previous expression, but it was a good attempt.

I hope he's right, Hazel thought as she watched them, her dream coming back to her mind. She pushed the fear aside.

Still, going out would at least have some fun aspects, a change in routine, but she was mostly glad to go because she knew that Jace would go either way, and she wanted to be a part of it. Big case of FOMO, huh?

She took a deep breath. She didn't really believe what Jace's grandpa had said, it sounded all a little too mystical for her, but that wouldn't stop her from going. Especially not when all her friends were going.

It could be dangerous... Everything is dangerous though, she argued, trying to calm her heart. She forced herself to give Jace a smile. They'd already made up their minds that they were going, and they weren't going to back out now.

What if everything he said was true? The thought flashed through her suddenly. *What if there really was someone or something out there who was not only trying to destroy the world, but had the ability to do so? What if we really did manage to do this and save the world?*

"Are you coming?" Kory placed a hand on her shoulder, startling her out of her thoughts. She had not realized that the others had already left the treehouse.

She nodded and shifted her backpack so she could climb down the ladder. When she got to the ground, she stepped closer to Jace, feeling the sudden conviction to stay at his side. She couldn't remember her entire dream last night, but something really had unsettled her, and she wanted to make sure her friend stayed safe. All her friends, but Jace... well, she was pretty sure her dream had been about him, and she couldn't fight the foreboding.

Jace's leg bounced in agitation, and he looked around at them again as he bit his lip. "We shouldn't do this," he started again. She looked down and realized that his hands had curled into tight fists. She'd learned ages ago that he did that when he was uncomfortable or overly stressed. "We shouldn't make our parents stress over something that probably isn't even real, and – and…" It looked like he was trying hard to find more reasons for them not to go. He started to put his bag down, his hands shaking slightly. "And you'll miss your soccer game, Kory…"

Hazel put a hand over Jace's, to stop both his movement and shaking. "Jace. Don't worry so much. We all know that you want to go, and I want to go. We will be back within a week or so and if it is true, we could save the world." She shrugged, not fully believing it. She pulled his bag back over his shoulders and tightened the straps. She didn't know why she felt like they really needed to do this, but deep in her soul she had a feeling that they had to go through with this.

Which was… terrifying.

"I don't care about my game anyway," Kory chimed in.

"What if something goes wrong?"

"Then we'll wing it."

"Winging it is *not* an emergency plan, Kory." Jace gave him a small smirk, despite the obvious despair. Hazel remembered a billboard sign that had said that.

"We'll be fine, Jace," Hazel soothed.

Jace still looked worried, hesitating as he chewed on his lip.

"Jace, listen," she tried again, opting for more sincere. "I know you're worried, and I am too, but for some unknown reason I really feel like we need to do this. It might just be the hope that it will change things, or it could be that this will turn out to seriously be important—important enough to save the world, or maybe there's just something we need to learn." She looked down. "But let's go, alright?"

It took another few tense seconds before Jace nodded. "Okay." He took a deep breath. "Let's go then."

"Wait. One second." Lisa stopped them. "What about our phones? We can't have them calling us or tracking them to where we are." Hazel pulled out her phone and looked at it. It still had a full battery, and she didn't really want to leave it where it would get ruined, but Lisa was right. They couldn't bring them.

She let it drop to the ground with a shrug, still wet from mostly melted snow. "Do you want to leave them somewhere else?" she asked.

Lisa smiled. They all knew that she cared little for her small blue phone and a second later – rather than dropping it – she threw it as far from the tree house as she could.

Kory followed her movement with more hesitancy. He actually liked his phone better than the rest of them, so Hazel was kind of surprised when he did it before the others. She saw his smash into another tree and shatter. Kory squeezed his eyes shut with a wince of immediate regret. "It's bad, isn't it?"

"Just don't look at it," Lisa muttered, grabbing him and pulling him away before he could freak out and open his eyes. She flashed Hazel an amused grin and patted Kory's shoulder consolingly.

"You're mocking me." Kory opened his eyes and went defensive. "You would be upset about something that *you* actually had to save up, buy and pay for *yourself*." He frowned and looked at Philips who had just let his phone fall to the ground and was also trying hard to hide his smile.

Kory rolled his eyes. "You guys have no appreciation for phones. They help our parents be calm about where we go. And they're not cheap…" He trailed off as he looked at them. Kory knew as well as the rest of them that they all had to work for their phones either by behaving or doing chores. Kory just had to use his own money. He shut up and laughed at himself, as though realizing how his complaints sounded.

"We should probably get food before posters go up everywhere," Jace suggested as his own phone hit the ground.

"Yeah, we should get a lot of chips and crackers since they last longer and taste better," Hazel agreed.

"Watch–" Kory tried to warn Lisa as he reached out for her, but the warning came too late. Her foot got caught underneath the root of a tree and she let out a short half cry. Hazel tried to grab her as well, but Lisa had stumbled to the opposite side. Lisa reached out an arm as if to catch herself on the tree, though she ended up on the ground next to it.

"Are you okay?" Kory quickly reached her side and helped her up. Hazel was surprised to see blood on the ground where Lisa had fallen.

"Yeah." Lisa lifted her arm to look at it. She had scraped the side of her arm on the tree trying to catch herself. Her nose scrunched up and she lowered her arm. "Yeah, I'm okay."

"Do you want to go back to clean your wound?" Philips asked her.

She shook her head. "If we go back, we'll never leave." She started to take her backpack off but paused. "I brought a first aid kit, but we should get out of here first." She stepped away and turned in the direction they'd be heading. Laughing lightly, she looked at them. "That was quite fun."

Hazel snorted. *Only Lisa.*

Shifting her backpack again, she scrunched her nose. They hadn't really even started, and it was already uncomfortable. How was she going to last long enough for them to get all the way to wherever they had to go? They had decided to walk since none of them had a car of their own. They could drive, technically, but they would have to borrow one of their parents' cars.

The nearby towns weren't too far anyway. Just might feel long for first timers, like they all were.

She blinked slowly as they started moving again. "Do you have any idea which way we need to head?" she asked anyone who would listen.

Philips nodded. "Just need to head a bit off west and we'll run into Jurade, and southeast will take us to Kinstown." He shrugged. "Where do you want to go to first?" he asked Jace who just shrugged in reply.

"Well, how about Jurade then?" Philips suggested, not having a problem taking the lead of that part.

"That sounds fine," Jace replied softly and turned in that direction. Hazel knew that he was still stressing over leaving. She wished that she could also calm down about it.

She closed her eyes for a second, taking a deep breath. *Please help us...* she begged anything that could hear.

Along with the sense that they had to go she also felt a sense of dread, and she knew that something was waiting for them, and she wasn't quite convinced that it would be good.

൝ ൝ ൝

Jace paused next to Hazel. They had been gone pretty much

the whole day now and were just arriving in Jurade. It was now after 10:00 p.m. and they needed to go find someplace to stay. Jace was pretty much drop dead exhausted, he usually didn't get that much exercise and he was now thinking that when he got home he was going to work out more often.

His feet *hurt*.

He leaned over to stretch his sore back and saw that Kory had grabbed his inhaler and was using it. If Jace hadn't become friends with Kory he never would have guessed that he had asthma because he was so active and optimistic, and he rarely had to use it. Jace watched him another minute until he knew his friend had been able to fully catch his breath, grateful that now they were out of the forest they could see with the help of town lights. Luckily Philips had thought to pack a flashlight, so they hadn't been walking blind through the trees.

Philips looked around. "Now what?" He folded his arms tight, obviously trying to conserve warmth. It was definitely colder without the sun out. Good thing they came prepared for the weather.

Jace smiled softly, trying to reassure them even though he needed some reassurance himself. "I've only made it this far too, you know," he told them when their gazes came to him. "But we shouldn't tell anyone that we're here, or why we're here." He was positive that he didn't really have to tell them that, but he did anyway.

Lisa turned back the way they had come. "I wonder if my mom is freaking out yet." Her lips puckered in concentration as she turned back to them. Jace knew that they had to be freaking out, they'd been gone since lunch and never came home for dinner. At the obvious concern in her eyes, he knew that she was more worried about stressing out her parents than she was about coming out here with her friends.

"Anyway, let's figure out where we are going to stay." They concluded that they had over a thousand dollars saved up if they counted it all together. It was enough for a bit, but they knew that they'd run out pretty quickly – especially if they had to pay someone to agree to help them and not tell anyone.

Would they be able to stay in a hotel without being recognized? Maybe a small one, probably run down? Or maybe they'd have to go knock on a door or two, and see if they could find someone willing to help, if not they'd stay in an alley or forest – they had some camping gear.

Again, though, if they didn't gain a helper, he didn't know what they would do for even food. Send one of them in to get fast food and other groceries while everyone else kept watch?

Man, this was more complicated than he thought it would be.

"What are you kids doing?" At the new, sudden voice, Jace startled and spun to find a man behind them. He was probably about Henri's age, though he was mostly bald, white hairs on the side the only covering. He looked concerned and confused, eyes flickering to their backpacks. Yet he gave them a soft smile. "Lost? You look like you just got back from a trip." Jace felt a moment of anxiety and his fist curled slightly.

"Um…" Jace began. He didn't know what to say and he was relieved when Lisa jumped in a second later.

"We kind of did. Would you help us?"

"What are you doing here?" His eyes were curious. He took a few steps closer. "What happened there?" He nodded toward Lisa, his gaze on the scrape she'd received from the tree.

"I fell." She shrugged and looked down at it.

The man went back to his original question "What are you doing here?" When they didn't answer right away, he continued. "Look, if I'm going to help you, I would like to know what you guys are up to."

They hesitated and he rolled his eyes and tried a different track, watching them closely. "Okay. What is it you need?" Jace shifted, unsure about the man that was watching them so expectedly, almost as though wanting something from them.

Well, he did. He wanted to know what they were doing. And he was right. It was only fair to give the guy at least a portion of the truth, but he'd just think they were crazy being out here and would probably have a conniption when they told him not to call the cops or send them back home.

Jace looked at the others and realized that they were thinking the same thing he was. They would have to tell the man something and hope that would help them out.

"We need someone who can help us get groceries and stuff without telling anyone where we are," Jace finally said when no one else answered him. The man's eyebrows rose as his eyes widened.

"Excuse me?" He folded his arms.

Kory said something before anyone else could respond; "We really need help." He hesitated for another second. "You'd find us crazy if we told you."

The man's gaze sharpened, that expectant look coming back even stronger as he stood up taller. Jace couldn't help but think that the man knew more than he was letting on. "You think so?" He flashed them another smile "Everyone seems to think I'm crazy, too. So how 'bout you tell me, and then I'll tell you if I think you're really crazy."

Jace once again looked at the others and found that they were contemplating what he had said. He personally thought that it might be worth the risk, yet… was this man *actually* crazy?

Once again, when no one answered, he spoke again. "I thought you were supposed to be older." His face once again furrowed in confusion as he studied them, seeming as though he hadn't realized that he'd said the words out loud.

"What do you mean?" Jace asked sharply, taking a step back. He saw the others shift uncomfortably as well. "Who do you think we are? Why would you know about us?"

The man didn't answer right away, as though debating what to say. "Henri sent you, didn't he?" He once again took a step closer to them, studying them closer. "He told me that you were twenty. You definitely don't look twenty. Plus, he said you weren't coming, though I did have a dream to come out here, so I guess…"

Dream? "Uh… twenty? That would've been my brother," Jace murmured quietly as he looked to the ground. "My brother told Grandpa Henri he wasn't going, but I overheard them talking so I came."

"So you didn't talk to Henri? You don't know why you're here?" The man rubbed his head, incredulity strong in his tone and expression.

"No," Hazel told him. "We only know something about having to… find something. Some power." Once again, the words came out as a near question. "It's true then?"

The other man shook his head with a sound that could have been a huff or a laugh. "You don't even believe it?" As they hesitantly shook their heads the man continued; "Why in Power's name did you come then? And why didn't you talk to Henri first? You really need to know about this. How much did you overhear?" The man uttered a few things under his breath that Jace figured were probably expletives.

After a moment of tense silence, the old man finally shook his head and sighed. "Come with me, I'll tell you what you need to know."

Jace didn't move at first. He didn't know if he should trust this man. But... he did know Henri, and apparently, he was expecting – well not expecting, since Jason said *no* – someone to come. And his dream?? What had that been about?

"We should be fine," Philips said. Jace nodded and started moving, but he wasn't sure he agreed with his friend. Man, why hadn't he talked with Henri before coming out here? Oh yeah, because he hadn't wanted to run the risk of hearing Henri say that he couldn't do it.

Well, that may have been idiotic of him. Yes, this whole thing had been stupid, which he'd known from the beginning, but still couldn't fight the desire to go.

The man led them over to the closest house, a tiny one that was cute, but a little worn-down. It strangely didn't detract from the style of the house though; it might have even added to the vintage look. The old man opened the door and held it open until they all slipped in behind.

"My name is Isaac. I'm the only one who lives here, so you don't need to worry about anyone else. And yes, I know about your... quest." As he spoke he guided them all into the family room and had them all sit. They squished onto the couch and chair, while Isaac took the one that was well-worn and obviously his. The man then grabbed something before continuing. "You can stay with me for however long you need, and I'll help you with all that I can."

He didn't wait for them to agree, instead he continued speaking, eyes distant, almost as if he were talking to himself. "I can tell you about it, but I am sure that Henri told – or you overheard – most of what I'll say. There might be something new, though, that could help you out."

Isaac closed his eyes and leaned back in a chair recliner, setting it rocking. When his eyes opened again, he began. "Now, this will be very dangerous, but by now, you're already wrapped up in all of this. You cannot back out now because the Shadow will try to find you whether you stay out looking or go home and decide to give up.

"He probably already knows that you're here and looking for the power, he seems to always be aware of that. And for how hard he'd always tried to get Henri, I think someone related to him will be pretty tempting for him, we've always suspected it needed someone in Henri's line."

Jace felt himself pale. Why him? What had Henri done to

garner this *shadow's* attention? He hadn't heard Henri say anything about a shadow, but if it was real, *and* it was looking for them, *and* it wanted Jace, then they wouldn't be safe… would they? He glanced at the others and found them looking at him anxiously.

If it was true that it would want Jace, he didn't want to be caught with his friends. He would never want them harmed by doing this with him.

He felt panic rise in his gut as his worst fears seemed to be confirmed. He might just puke.

"Shadow?" It was Philips who voiced the first question. Jace felt himself shrinking. Hazel grabbed his hand, while Kory leaned slightly into his side. He looked at each of his friends, Lisa half on top of Philips while they shared the chair, and Kory and Hazel at his sides, and wondered if there was any way they could get out of this, or if Isaac was right about not being able to escape this shadow now.

Even though there was a part of him hoping that all of this was just old man insanity, there was something in his gut telling him to beware that it was, in fact, true.

Isaac's eyebrows twitched a little in confusion. "Okay, you must not have heard as much of the conversation as I thought you might have." He sighed. "The Shadow. It's a force in the world, essentially you can think of it like the force behind any of the evil in the world."

"What will this… shadow do to try and get… well, what exactly does the shadow even want?" Kory was fidgeting with his hands.

Isaac shook his head. "Honestly, I don't know for sure what it will do to try and get the Power, and I can't even be sure what it wants to do exactly, it's been foretold that it wants to ruin the world, but… well, let's think of it this way. If something inherently evil has the power of the universe, what do you think can happen?" He paused, giving them time for that thought to sink in. "But for it to get what it wants out of you, if it believes you have the knowledge or ability to get the power, it will get it from you…" He trailed off for a second and grimaced. "By any means necessary. Even torture."

Jace felt like he was going to puke. Kory gave a laugh that sounded slightly hysterical. Hazel was gripping his hand just a little too tight. He wondered if he was losing circulation to his fingers by now. Lisa had made a little sound in her throat, and Jace could see

Philips rubbing a hand on her back soothingly.

"If he does know that he needs you then he will beat the info out of you, if needed, to make you take him to it." He looked at them sternly. "You must not let him know. You cannot tell the Shadow, just remember that if you do get caught and if you end up telling him anything, *everyone* will be in danger."

"Torture?" Lisa asked quietly, obviously stuck on the word. Jace was pretty sure his face mirrored hers; jaw locked and face pale. The others looked equally sick at the possibility.

The man looked between them. "You at least heard that it would be dangerous, didn't you?"

"Yes," Jace said after another few seconds. He shook his head with an exhale, pressing his free hand into his leg in an attempt to ground himself. "What is this power that he is looking for?" he asked at last.

"The Power." When curiosity showed in their gazes, he continued: "It is the world's power. You have the Shadow – evil – of the world. Hate, pain, trial, fear. It's what influences bad decisions. Then there's the Power, it's the good, love, kindness, strength… all that." He looked at them firmly. "You can't have one without the other or there would be no point to the world. If there is no evil, then there wouldn't be any good either. We would all just… be.

"The Shadow has been searching for the Power since the beginning of time but hasn't been able to find it. In this time, there has been occasions that the Shadow has overtaken a man, to have a physical form. Currently the man that has been taken is named Darrin. He is who you'll want to avoid at all costs. Just–" He cut off suddenly eyes flicking between them all worriedly. "You know what, I think that's enough for tonight. You guys are probably hungry and tired. Let's discuss the rest of this tomorrow, alright?"

Jace wanted to protest, but the older man was right. As much as he wanted to hear what this man said, he could barely concentrate on the words, and their dinner had been a few hours ago. Besides, he was pretty sure his brain was about to explode, and he might have a full-blown panic attack if he had to know anything more at the moment.

Jace started to stand but the Isaac just shook his head. "I'll bring you all something to eat, my kitchen is far too small for all of us to sit comfortably. What do you want?"

There was still a portion in him that wasn't sure if he wanted to trust this man with making them food, but he honestly was too tired to object. Besides, even if he did drug or poison them, wouldn't it be better than being found by the shadow – whatever *that* was? And if he really wanted to kill them, he probably would have already tried.

"Anything will be fine as long as it has no onions or nuts," Hazel told him, and Isaac nodded and pushed into the kitchen.

"We're going to be okay." Philips even managed to get a slight air of confidence as he said the words, even though his face still hadn't lost the worry lines.

Jace knew none of them fully believed that in the moment, but he appreciated Philips' strength.

"What if we get caught?" Lisa asked worriedly. Jace hated that she was so stressed, since Lisa and Kory were usually optimists and always had belief that things would work out, but even they were looking rather anxious.

Jace felt his free hand curl into a fist, while Hazel tightened her group again momentarily. He slowly exhaled. "I don't know, Lisa. I really *really* don't want to think about what might happen. I really don't want to believe any of this, and yet... I don't see why Henri and Isaac both would make this all up. It doesn't make sense that they wouldn't just send us all back home if we were searching for a wild goose egg."

None of them spoke for some long moments, then Jace eventually muttered; "We really shouldn't have come, but like Isaac said; we can't back out now."

Lisa looked down at her hands before meeting all of their gazes. "We can do it. We have to promise right now that if this is true, and we get caught, that we won't tell Darrin or this shadow anything. We can't have our families harmed because we couldn't keep quiet."

Kory nodded. "Yes, we have to stay strong." Then he seemed to deflate, eyes taking on a haunted look, eyes distant. It was a look Jace would see on him when he didn't think anyone else was looking, and Jace just wished he knew what sent his friend into such a state. He put his hand on Kory's back, and his friend shot him a grateful look as his eyes cleared. "But we don't know how it will be. There were strong people in the wars that were caught and tortured and they broke eventually. I don't even want to imagine how it must have been for them, and I definitely don't want to go through anything similar. Not when we have so much on the line."

Jace was about to respond, but Isaac came back in right then, carrying a plate. He had made and cut sandwiches into little squares and piled them onto the plate.

"Take what you want," he said as he sat down in his chair again. He looked defeated, stressed, and exhausted. Jace wondered why. Was it just because he was worried about the shadow? Was he worried about them?

Jace hesitantly bit into a sandwich. It tasted fine – good actually. He quickly finished and reached for another one. "So, how are we going to find this… power?" he asked as he swallowed. Yeah, he knew they would talk about it later, but he couldn't halt the questions. They were spiraling.

As Jace grabbed another sandwich square Isaac answered: "We don't know exactly. It will reveal itself when you enter the correct cave. That's what we've been told." The man looked troubled by this.

"So we should be prepared for a lot of hiking," Philips stated tiredly. It didn't seem like something he was too excited about. Of course, they were all tired of walking just from half a day's worth to get here.

Isaac smirked. "Yes, unfortunately. Would you like me to come with you to help?" He didn't give any clue as to whether he wanted to go or not and Jace honestly didn't care.

It seemed the others didn't either. "Whatever you want to do," Lisa told him. She licked her lips before taking another bite.

The man nodded. "Anyway, I'll be going to bed. I have a guest room that has a bed, and the couch in here, then the two recliners, you guys go ahead and figure it out. Extra blankets in the closet by the guest bedroom." He smiled at them. "Sleep well tonight. We will talk more tomorrow."

Chapter Five

JACE WOKE UP SHORTLY after seven, unsure as to where he was at first. The place didn't look familiar at all, and he knew that he wasn't at a friend's house. He blinked and sat up, working on getting his eyes to stop being blurry. His muscles were sore, so he stretched them wearily which finally reminded him why he was hurting. The long walk to this place had worn him out.

All their parents would know they had gone and be worried by now. He imagined that they would have spent last night or this morning calling each other, hoping to confirm that their kids were just at friends' houses, and just not answering their phones for some reason; only to find out that they weren't at any of the known places.

He felt his gut clench at the worry they had probably caused and wondered if his parents were grouped in the worried ones. He'd always known his parents loved him, yet, they'd always seemed to keep their distance, never really showing much concern for him. Maybe that was just middle-kid syndrome. Even though his sister was technically a middle kid as well – but she was their parents only girl, so that might have something to do with it.

He looked over at Philips and Kory. Kory lay next to Jace on the hide-a-bed of the couch, and Philips had taken the recliner. They were still conked out, though that wasn't surprising. It was early for them after all, but for some reason Jace had always had an internal alarm clock that woke him early.

He stood up, grabbing the blanket, and making sure to keep quiet, as he stepped outside to sit on the porch to enjoy the sunrise. The sun was up coming up over the tree line, the clouds stretching the orange and red light in a sunbeam way. It was chilly, but he settled himself on the front porch swing with the blanket and listened to the chirping birds. Their morning song was always his favorite time of day., and he needed this moment of peace.

The door opened a few minutes later, and Jace watched out of the corner of his eyes as Isaac sat next to him. His stomach was a bit pudgy, so as he sat it kind of folded on top of itself, but Jace found himself thinking that the extra weight wouldn't slow him down much. Isaac seemed like one to work hard, even if his stamina was being affected.

"You're one of those early morning people, eh?" Isaac smiled in wry amusement and Jace flashed him a confused look.

"And you aren't?" he gestured, signaling the fact that clearly the man was also awake early.

Isaac shook his head. "Not usually, just sometimes I seem to have more reason to wake up."

"Oh." Jace looked back at the sky and leaned back.

"What do we have to do?" Jace asked Isaac as a bird flew over their heads. He watched it land a good ten feet away on the tree in a Isaac's yard, waiting for Isaac to gather his thoughts.

"I think before we get started, we should have you visit one of my other friends," Isaac told him. "He was with us when we got the information years ago. We've been trying to find this Power since, but we are all becoming old men now." He smirked at that, leaning back into the seat as though he didn't believe his own words.

"Why should we visit him? If you were all together, wouldn't it be just as well to talk to you?"

Isaac shrugged. "A different perspective is always good. I mean it doesn't matter too much either way, but it could be nice for you if you have more insight. Also," he added with a wink, "my friend is rich. He could give you some resources to use."

Jace snorted half a laugh, which seemed to be Isaac's goal, if the twinkle in Isaac's eye was anything to go by.

"I don't think you all need to go to his house," Isaac continued. "You could if you wanted, but even if just two of you go, I think that would be fine. Just because my friend would feel like he'd have to play host to all of you guys, and the more of you there are the longer it'll take to get the information." His eyes held a fondness for his friend, a combination of amusement and exasperation. Jace wondered if he'd be lifelong friends with everyone in his friend group, and one day be sitting on a porch talking about them with the same look. He hoped so.

"If you think it would be good, then we can go." He agreed, then after a long moment, he asked another question. "How long ago did you guys learn about this power?" Jace asked. He was still fighting disbelief about all of this. He wanted to shout in denial and go home, and yet, he was still here, and still planning on looking. He wasn't sure what was true anymore.

"Years ago." Isaac's eyes went distant. "We were probably all in our thirties or so. But it wasn't quite as… I don't know… desperate, I guess, to do it when we were younger. It was more of a strong suggestion to go find the Power. Now it's more like a need. A desperate need for someone to find it. So few are trying at this point."

"There are others trying to find it?" Jace asked, surprised. "Around here?"

Isaac shrugged. "I couldn't know for sure, honestly."

Jace narrowed his eyes, thinking. He couldn't help but feel nervousness wash back through him. He'd invited his friends out on a journey, honestly because of the chance at some adventure. But he should have visited with his grandpa first, to get an idea of what he would be doing, the real danger that they might be getting into, if any of this was true anyway.

And that was part of the problem. He honestly didn't know what to believe. His grandparents, Isaac, a rich friend of theirs, and apparently someone else named Darrin, who was supposedly taken over by the shadow and became evil, all believed it to be true and have been searching for this power. But just because it was believed by some, didn't mean it had to be true.

He wished he could go back, or at least, send his friends home, but he had a bad feeling that, as Isaac said, now that they'd started, they couldn't return.

Before he could think of anything to say or ask, he heard the front door open beside them. Jace wasn't surprised to see Hazel come out, blinking in the light of the rising sun.

"All okay?" She asked, leaning on the railing in front of them.

"Yeah." He smiled at her, wondering how she could look so cute after just waking up.

"Good." She sat on the railing and looked up at the sky. "It's so beautiful, isn't it?"

Jace nodded and looked up as well. He knew that she didn't see his response, and that she didn't have to in order to know. The three of them settled in to watch until the sun reached above the tree line, then Isaac shifted and stretched.

"I think that we should get going early today. We have a long day ahead of us, and I think it would be better to get started."

Jace nodded in agreement and moved to stand.

"I'll go wake up the others," Hazel said, going in again.

Isaac put a hand on Jace's shoulder to stop him from following, and as Jace turned toward him he was surprised to see Isaac's gaze intense with warning, wrinkled face set in a frown, and an undisguised concern for them written in every line.

"Jace, you'll have to be very careful. The Shadow will try anything to get what it wants, including using you as a tool." He didn't understand how a shadow could use him, but he nodded warily.

"I'll be careful."

₪ ₪ ₪

It was decided the Jace would go visit Isaac's friend and Kory said he wanted to come with him. It wasn't surprising, because even though they were all sore from the previous day's walking, Kory couldn't sit still for long to save his life.

Even by breakfast, Kory's leg had been bouncing like crazy, his hands moving nonstop, and all his friends knew that he was anxious to get out of the house that morning. Jace could swear that the other teen had some serious ADHD or something, because there never looked to be a sign of Kory wearing down, even though everyone else would rather sit the day away.

Jace figured that Kory was just as stressed about what they got themselves into; Isaac's words of warning last night ringing loud in their ears, casting a layer so thick around the group, that it took Kory's joking and positivity, and Lisa's inherent joy to pull them out of it even a little.

So, after Isaac had called Walter and received permission for Jace and Kory to come over this afternoon, they left. Isaac offered to drive them to the front gate, but had decided to help prepare for the next steps of their journey. So Isaac had drove them to the store, then told them how to get to Walter's mansion, which was only a couple minutes from the store so they could walk to it. Isaac would shop while Jace and Kory talked to Walter, then Isaac would wait until Walter called him to come back and get them.

As they approached the gate, Jace's nerves actually deepened into a sense of dread, and he was *this* close to turning around and fleeing from the cameras' view. The house truly was *massive*, looking castle like with two separate turrets, three garages, including on that was tall enough for an RV, and the yard was rather immaculate. He'd be surprised if he found out that the house didn't have a pool in the back. Kory kept walking though, so Jace made sure to keep pace beside him.

Kory's fingers kept tapping on his pants, fiddling with his shirt, or weaving through his hair in the nonstop habit that Jace had become used to over the years of knowing his friend. Somehow the small familiar movements helped to calm him down.

So Jace pushed the feeling away as a security guard came out of the guard shack to greet them.

"Do you have an appointment to see Mr. Indole?" The man asked. Jace noticed another guard still inside the building, and Jace found himself trying hard not to shift uncomfortably under their intense stares.

"Yes, Isaac called him. He said we could come over."

"Ah, yes, of course." The man smiled at them, then waved back into the other guard and raised his voice a little. "I'll take them in. You man the gate?"

"Sure thing." The guard lifted one hand in quick response, then clicked the button to open the gate. They waited as it swung wide enough, then made their way in after the guard.

Jace saw Kory slip slightly closer to him, and while no one was around to see, he pulled his inhaler out of his pocket, and used it quickly, looking ashamed even as he did so. Jace knew his friend hated his asthma, seeing it as a huge weakness—he thought that maybe Kory had been teased about it in the past—so he avoided doing it in front of people as much as possible. It had probably taken him months before he felt comfortable using it in front of their group of friends.

They entered the house, the guard holding the door open for them, but before Jace could do anything more than briefly gawk at the inside of the house, the door shut tight and Jace heard a click. It was the sudden flare of dread in his gut, a warning deep in his bones, that had him turn back to the guard. Even with that warning in his gut, he still startled to see the barrel of a gun pointed toward him.

Kory hadn't noticed yet. "This house is nice." he murmured to Jace, but when Jace's hand flew to his arm suddenly, grip unrelenting, he quickly caught on. In what was clearly an instinctive move, Kory was in front of Jace, the hand that Jace held onto now behind his back and gripping tightly back.

"What's going on?" Jace asked, coming to the side of Kory just enough to face the other man too. No way would he let his friend stand against the man alone or sacrifice himself in some idiotic attempt to protect him. Besides, Kory was smaller than him. The man would be able to hit Jace if his aim was any sort of decent whether Kory was there or not.

The man gave a smile and, surprisingly, it didn't look like an evil smile, despite the enormous gun, which was… weird… and terrifying. "We've been waiting for someone to approach Walter about this *quest* of yours. It has been a long time in waiting, but Walter was the only one of your grandfathers' group of friends that we knew how to locate. Darrin has been waiting a long time to be able to get his hands on someone who can help him find the Power. We've been impatient and worried you weren't coming, and yet here you are. At last." His smile shifted into a smirk.

Ah, there's the evil smile. Oh, and yeah, the villain monologuing. At another time, that realization might have amused him, but at the moment he just wanted to do anything to get his friend—and himself—out of any line of fire. "We've orders to keep you here until he arrives."

Jace felt his hands tremble and could feel the same in Kory's body. The man gestured with the gun for them to move further into the house, down the hallway.

"Wh-where is Walter?" Jace managed to stutter out as he moved, looking back at the man as he forced Kory to move with him.

"He was expecting your arrival." The guard shoved Jace forward, as though they weren't moving fast enough. In their defense, Jace felt numb to the bone in shock and fear, so he honestly was amazed he was moving at all. Kory's grip on Jace's arm and his wide eyes and pale face told him that it was probably the same for his friend. "But Darrin won't have to worry about him anymore."

"You killed him?" Kory's quiet words were half question, half statement, but completely filled with horror.

Jace felt his gut flood with trepidation as the man merely chuckled behind them. *We shouldn't have come here.* Panicked, Jace tightened his grip on Kory, barely noticing that Kory had done the same thing. They'd probably leave bruises on each other. Or fingernail imprints.

Isaac had been right about one thing, at least. Whatever they had signed themselves up for was far more dangerous than Jace ever could have imagined.

The man kept them walking and Jace was unable to even enjoy the massive house, which was a little infuriating. They kept moving until they made it to a door, then they were shoved inside what was evidently a theater room. There were no windows in the room, which would make it a great theater, but terrible for trying to escape.

The man shoved them into the room, Jace landing hard on his wrist, and Kory practically tumbling over Jace and into the back of one of the couches. Jace immediately sat back up, staring at the man shut the door in their face with a smirk. "Someone will be guarding this room." Were the last words they heard before they were locked in near darkness.

Jace felt like his whole body was trembling, and his breathing had gone shallow—harsh. And in those breaths, he was suddenly gagged by a putrid smell. It smelled like some sort of animal had gone and died in there, and Jace couldn't keep his thought from the idea that it could have been another human.

Knowing the fate of Walter, he realized that might be exactly what it was.

"Jace?" Kory's whisper tore Jace from the near panic attack.

"Yeah?" His voice cracked and he forced some deep breaths as he sat up and made his way carefully over to where he'd seen Kory fall. In just a few seconds he managed to find his friend and he clasped his arm again. "You okay?"

"I'm not hurt, I don't think. Maybe just a few bruises." Kory took a deep audible breath. "It smells."

"Yeah." Jace didn't share his thoughts on what he thought it might be, he figured that Kory could figure it out on his own.

Kory was silent for a moment, then, voice even tighter than before, he spoke again. "There's got to be a light somewhere in here, right?"

Surprised at his tone, Jace nodded. "Probably."

"We should find it. We've got to find some sort of… way out or something to defend ourselves with." At this point, Jace wasn't sure if the tremble was from himself, Kory, or both, but there was a very evident tremble in Kory's voice.

Jace took another few seconds of deep breathing to calm himself further, then moved to sit up, ignoring the twinge from his wrist. It didn't feel too bad, not broken, hopefully no sprain or anything bad, just tweaked.

Kory stood up with him and they worked on feeling their way to the wall by the door, guessing the light switch to be near it. After a couple long minutes of searching, while their eyes adjusted only enough for them to see shadows due to the light from the DVD player or something, Kory finally found the switch and turned it on.

Jace was surprised at the sight of his friend. Jace was terrified, rightly so at this point, but Kory's face was nearly as white as paper, and the sweat on his forehead and the fact that his arms were folded tightly against his torso instead of fidgeting in some way, told Jace that his friend was in near shut down.

Jace crossed quickly to Kory, putting his hands on his shoulders. "You sure you're okay?"

Kory wouldn't meet his eyes. "Y-yeah." He took a breath, half stuttered, but then managed a more convincing attempt. "Yeah, fine. I'd just *really* like to get out of here." At last, he met Jace's eyes, a combination of defensiveness, pain, and fear taking his breath away. Once again, Jace couldn't help but wonder what was in Kory's past.

Now wasn't the time to ask; the look in Kory's eyes told him that. Instead, he squeezed his friend's shoulder before pulling away. "Okay, we're okay Kory. We're going to get out of here." It felt weird to be the one encouraging his friend. Kory was one of the most upbeat and optimistic people Jace had ever known.

Even with the obvious fear, with Jace's words, it took Kory only a few seconds to pull himself together. "You're right. Of course, we are. Let's find a way out of here. Or something."

Kory nodded to himself and immediately moved away, heading for the front of the massive home theater room. Jace turned away reluctantly, eyes darting for anything he could use. Maybe the speaker stand? He might be able to use that. Whack someone over the head right as they enter. Before they can aim a gun?

Yet, his gut squirmed uncomfortably at that. He was terrified, and knew he should defend himself, but he couldn't fathom hitting someone hard enough to hinder them that much.

"I found the, uh… smell." Kory's voice cut in, an odd tone to it that had Jace spinning around quickly toward his friend and saw a glimpse of hair that Kory was staring at, nose scrunched up. Jace wasn't sure if it was out of disgust or horror.

Probably both.

Feeling nausea rise in his throat, Jace shook his head and took a step back, avoiding looking back at what he knew had to be the dead body of Walter. "Don't tell me. Please don't tell me." Kory looked up at him, an eyebrow arched at Jace's obvious revulsion and sadness.

"Alright." Kory agreed. "Just keep looking over there, okay?" His voice was gentle.

Jace used to get crap for how sensitive he was. He'd never been interested in harming bugs or picking on his friends' grumpy cats. When he was younger, burning bugs with a magnifying glass or such things was a common entertainment among his peers, and Jace had always made his way back home when they would do so. He had no desire to see any form of creature hurting, and just the thought of being in the same room as someone who was now dead…

He turned away quickly, shaking his head, and bringing a hand to his mouth to fight back bile or tears, he wasn't sure which was more urgent.

Thankfully Kory didn't ever tease him for anything like that. None of his current friends had called him sensitive or anything of the like, and most of them felt the same as him; even if it wasn't to the same extent.

Out of the corner of his eyes he saw Kory gently pulling a blanket up over the recliner and its occupant head before rounding the corner of the couch to get as far away as possible as he continued looking for anything that could help them escape.

"Hey Jace." Kory was practically whispering this time.

"Yeah?" Jace looked up.

Kory tilted his head, gesturing him over, and Jace quickly came, a little seed of hope filling him. Did he find something? He didn't look over to the blanket and what he knew was hiding beneath it.

Still in a whisper, Kory continued. "I don't know if that security guard has ever really been inside this room," he murmured, a smirk on his face. "Because he doesn't seem aware that the bathroom has another door."

Feeling his face light up in hope, Jace quickly followed Kory back in, waiting impatiently as Kory opened it slightly and peeked through.

"So?" Jace asked him, just as quiet.

"We might be safe." Kory shrugged. "We should go. Better than staying here."

"I agree." Jace nodded, massaging his still hurting wrist with one hand.

Kory took a deep grounding breath, then carefully pulled the door wider and stuck his head through. Jace saw a wide hallway with big frames of sports jerseys. The frame closest to him had a picture of a teenager in the frame, so he figured all the frames were full of his kids or grandkids' athletic accomplishments.

Tears pricked his eyes. This poor family just lost a dad and grandpa.

It was all clear though, so Jace followed Kory through and entered the hall. He stayed close to his friend, keeping an eye out behind them for anyone, while Kory paid more attention to what was in front of them. Jace grasped the back of Kory's shirt lightly so he'd notice if his friend stopped suddenly while he was looking behind them. Also, it was a comfort to physically feel his presence.

Kory gave him a glance, as though he knew what Jace was thinking, but didn't say a word as they made their way slowly through the house. They made their way through the massive kitchen before, seeing the front door from where they were.

Hesitating, Jace eyed the path to the front door, unsure what he should do. Was the guard at the gate bad too? Was that the only way for people to get in? It had to be, otherwise there was no point in a fence. Maybe they could climb the fence, but they would have to get to the fence without being seen.

He stared at the gate, indecisively. At feeling Jace's hand fall away, Kory looked back, then stopped to half face him.

"What's going on?"

"How do we get out? They might see us. The guy at the gate might be in on this too. Do you think we could climb that fence?" At least it didn't have spires on the top, being just a smooth stone wall. Maybe they could give each other a boost.

Kory's forehead creased as he looked between the gate out the front door window and the fence out the side window. "I think we should try climbing the fence first. We should be able to help each other over." His hands had gone back to their fidgety selves after escaping the theater room.

Jace nodded, nervous about the risk of both, and possibly choosing the wrong option. But he knew they didn't have many other options. In unspoken agreement, they headed carefully for the family room, heading straight for an open window.

Jace felt as though his whole body was tingling with stress, even to the ends of his hair.

They climbed out of the window, right onto that immaculate grass. The sun was bright and almost in their eyes, but he was grateful for it. Much better than being in the dark theater or the house that Darrin was coming to.

They both kept watch around them as they made their way down to the fence, feeling completely exposed at the barren front yard. There were only trees far and few in between, a few perfectly trimmed hedges, and flowers lining the driveway. But they were heading out from the side of the house.

It wasn't until they were almost to the fence that they heard shouts behind them.

They both started to run. Once they'd made it to the wall, Jace looked back a moment. He saw movement and a couple men came rounding the house. A spear of panic shot through Jace. They were so close to freedom! No way were they going to get recaptured now.

"I'll help you up first," Kory told him. When Jace was about to protest, Kory shook his head, speaking quickly. "You're stronger and I'm lighter, you could pull me up better."

Unable to argue with that, Jace stepped into Kory's hands and scrambled for the top of the wall with urgency. With a little struggle from both of them, he was finally able to reach the top. He quickly sat on his knees, ignoring the sharpness of the wall he now kneeled on. His hands and legs would both be a bit bruised and torn from the roughness, but it was a small price to pay.

Kory barely managed to reach Jace's hand, and Jace struggling to pull him up was harder for both of them than the boost had been, but Jace refused to leave his friend. The men were getting closer, one even pointing a gun in their general direction threateningly, but not actually shooting. *Hurry, hurry, hurry,* he chanted in his head.

Kory had one hand to the top of the wall now, grasping Jace and the wall desperately as he started lifting his legs to the side as though to roll himself onto the wall.

Bang!

The sudden explosion of sound made Jace to flinch. Startled, Kory let out a gasp and twitched rather violently, almost causing him to fall back down. His eyes were squeezed shut in panic, and he almost lost his foothold on the top of the wall, but Jace kept his grip. He pulled harder as he realized that the sound had been a gunshot, and practically sent them both tumbling off the wall onto the other side.

Jace landed on his side, then his back, tweaking his wrist once again and definitely bruising his whole left side of his back and arm. Winded and not entirely sure what had just happened, Jace just lay there for a slightly too long moment as he struggled to catch his breath. Kory groaned next to him, but then staggered to his feet, tugging Jace's good wrist. "Come on."

Jace looked at him, saw some blood on his cheek and arms—scrapes from the wall and possibly the ground, but Kory didn't even stop to let Jace ask if he was okay, which was smart.

As soon as Jace was up, Kory was pulling him to run again. As Jace ran slightly behind Kory, he noticed that his friend was limping and bleeding. He wanted to stop Kory and examine the severity of the wound, wondering if it was from the bullet, but it wasn't bleeding *too* bad, and they really had to get out of there. There would be time to take care of it later. Right now, they had to get back to Isaac's house and the rest of their friends. For now, adrenaline and determination were fueling them both and neither dared to stop.

Jace luckily wasn't worried about getting lost, since he'd paid attention to the drive with Isaac to the store and the directions from Isaac to the mansion had been simple to follow, but he didn't want to stay on a main road in case anyone was going to follow them, and Isaac wouldn't know when to come get them until Walter called.

They had to stay out of sight of anyone that may be following them. He led Kory into the thick forest a little away from the main road and town. Neither one of them calmed down as they walked. Jace's eyes flicked all around, and he caught Kory doing the same. They jumped at every breeze that ruffled the leaves, and Jace's shoulders were tense.

After about four minutes, Kory took a quick pause to wrap his leg to stop the bleeding with the scarf he'd been wearing, but once he was walking again, he picked the pace back up.

"Didn't think you'd be getting a workout today, didja?" Kory muttered, slightly bitter, but with a ring of humor still. Jace just gave a snort as a response, not sure how Kory had breath to talk at the moment. He didn't think he ever fully got his breath back after the fall.

The sun started sinking in the sky, telling him that it must be past noon by now.

As they neared the house, Jace could feel his strength flagging, the adrenaline and panic having worn him out, and he knew Kory was feeling the same, the limp more exaggerated now. Jace moved closer, putting a hand on his shoulder, but he wasn't sure if it was more of a support to himself or his friend.

At last, they made it to the house, Jace breathing a sigh of relief as they climbed up the stairs—Jace helping Kory up the few steps since it seemed those last few steps were about the last Kory could give—and they stumbled into the house.

Isaac caught sight of them first.

"What happened?" He jumped to his feet and moved faster than Jace would've thought possible for a man of Isaac's age. Jace shook his head, staggering into the room with Kory. Kory immediately moved to the couch. Lisa and Hazel jumped up in time to let him collapse into it, Lisa immediately finding the scarf around his leg and fixating on it. Jace was right behind him, sinking into the couch in relief as their three friends and Isaac fluttered around them.

"Jace? Kory? Are you okay?" Hazel asked, kneeling between them. Lisa was already at Kory's side, gently checking him over.

"What's going on?" Isaac asked, all the questions from everyone coming quicker than Kory and Jace were able to respond.

Jace felt his eyes water, realizing for the first time that Walter had been Isaac's friend, and that he was going to have to tell him what had happened.

"Isaac, uh…" Jace swallowed hard, not sure if he could find the words.

Kory took over for him. "The guards let us into the house, but then one of them pulled a gun on us."

Hazel gasped, a hand tightening on Jace's hand. Jace squeezed her hand, lifting one to his eyes, pressing fingers over his eyes to try to keep the tears at bay. Philips put a hand on Kory's shoulder, unable to quite reach Jace with Hazel and Isaac at his side.

"They, uh… the guards somehow knew we were coming, probably heard Walter talking to you or something. They killed him." Kory squeezed his eyes shut, and Jace wrapped an arm around his shoulder. "He was, I mean… they intended to keep us there until Darrin came for us. They killed Walter to get to us. He was just there, they put us in the same room as… and he—" Kory cut himself off, shaking his head as though suppressing the urge to give all the details.

But then Jace heard him sob, and Jace realized… his friend had seen a dead body; someone he'd had a name of. He'd had just been shot at, adrenaline fueled for the run home, terrified, not to mention practically kidnapped, even if it had been for such a short time.

Jace had purposely avoided looking at the body, but Kory had found him, then had taken the time to cover him with the blanket.

Jace tightened his hold on his friend, wrapping him in a side hug, and Kory turned toward him. Not sobbing any more but taking a few long minutes against Jace to calm himself. Jace felt Kory's deep breathing and felt himself trying to match it to calm his own racing heart. The others just sat and watched them have their moment, just staying to help ground and support them.

Isaac took a few steps back and started pacing, a pained look in his eyes, worry showing in every line of his face once more. Jace knew that they would have to explain everything to them all, but for right now, they just needed a moment.

Jace closed his eyes, grateful to feel all his friends around him, everyone touching him and Kory in support, and Jace realized that they all knew how dangerous it was now, that this quest that none of them even fully believed in, now had definite consequences.

₪   ₪   ₪

The police stood at the scene, the media not far behind. Frank, the senior officer, was annoyed with the reporters back there, and always ignored questions until he *had* to answer them. He was expecting to have a kidnapping on their hands, and the subsequent questions of who was taken, who took them, why all of the kids we nabbed—as though he would know the answer to any of those questions—or if the police were *sure* they were runaways? He wasn't ready to answer any of those questions. The media was always the worst part of the job, but he didn't love breaking the news to their parents either.

Of course, Frank already knew what had happened to the kids.

He'd already talked to Henri and Isaac, and knew that they had taken on the quest, much to Henri's concertation—he'd been hoping to get the older brother, not having a teenager out there with his friends.

Frank couldn't tell anyone that though, so he had to continue searching for them anyway. The group of officers that had gathered at these teenagers' treehouse—which was a rather impressive treehouse, he had to admit—fanned out around the tree, looking for any clues, and Frank noticed blood on a tree. The snow had melted too much for them to have luck with tracks, but the blood made Frank worried. If they had just gone to do the quest, there shouldn't be any sign of a struggle, but Isaac had said they'd arrived safely at his house.

He would have to tell everyone that they were kidnapped, the likely story being that Darrin had taken them, as he's been the common culprit, though they hadn't been able to find the man yet. Their parents would panic and be inconsolable; they almost always were.

He talked with a few of the other officers, and they came to the same conclusion that he had. If he didn't know the truth and was working from scratch—they'd been taken.

He moved back to the waiting families and media, preparing something to tell them. Frank prayed for those kids; he knew Henri hadn't planned for his younger grandson to go.

Well, you see, your kids here, yeah, they are supposed to find the Power before the Shadow does, and now they are off in more danger than they ever have been before…

Despite the fact that that was the truth, he knew he couldn't say it. He'd probably get thrown into a mental hospital.

Still, he would much rather talk to the parents than the media, so instead of walking to a lady with a microphone, he moved over to the group of parents. There were a few reporters around but as he and Officer Sicx waved them off, they reluctantly moved away. Most reporters at least had the decency to pretend to respect someone about to receive some hard news.

"Do you know where they are?" one of the moms asked. He was pretty sure she was Kory's mother. According to his papers, Kory had been adopted when he was twelve, along with his sister.

The other parents looked at him expectantly, worriedly, and he could tell that most of them expected grave news.

"No." He took a deep breath. "We don't know where they

went, though I'm sure you've heard of the recent kidnappings that have been perpetrated by a man named Darrin." A few nods filled the space, the faint hope they'd been hanging onto slowly being replaced with an obvious horror at what he hadn't said yet. "We're pretty sure that's what happened here, but we are already looking for this man and we will stop at nothing until he is found." If they were indeed taken by Darrin, then this was the biggest group that he had snatched. He usually grabbed two kids at the most.

One thing was for sure, Darrin was getting too sure of himself, thinking that he could get away with whatever he wanted, taking random kids just because they were out… The police would have to step up their game to try and find this man, whether or not these kids had been taken by him.

Frank knew that Darrin wasn't really a bad person. It was the Shadow that was the problem, but the kidnappings were still happening. Frank would kill the man if he had to, if only to help the kids.

The reactions of their parents were as expected. Most of the mothers started crying and the fathers tried to hold them, though they weren't very successful at staying calm themselves.

"If you need anything, just let us know," he said before turning away, letting them grieve.

Inside he prayed that the Power would keep them safe.

Chapter Six

HAZEL HAD NEVER LIKED the idea of them going to this mansion to visit Walter in the first place, therefore she was just immensely glad that her friends were still okay. She felt bad for Isaac, that he'd lost his friend. His grief and concern seemed to run deep, though there was still a part of Hazel that struggled to fully trust the man. What if Isaac had sent them there intending them to get captured?

She forced the thought away. Isaac—along with Lisa—had done some amazing work getting Jace and Kory patched up, and Isaac was just as relieved as the rest of them that they had both made it back more-or-less okay. He'd been frantic about their injuries, slight as they ended up being, and was horrified at what the two boys had endured.

And he'd been devastated by Walter's death.

They'd tried to keep the two boys to take it easy the rest of the day. Jace was more muted, as though the concern he'd had from the beginning was suddenly tenfold, dragging him into the worries in his brain. Yet as soon as Kory was patched up, he'd found a way to be up moving around, his anxious energy keeping him up on his feet despite the healing wound on his calf. He'd become more animated, which Hazel knew was Kory's way of handling situations.

Two days after visiting Walter, they were out looking through the caves that they had researched the day before. Hazel's legs were tired from all the hiking, but none of them had been willing to stay behind at the house.

Even Kory had come with them, even though his leg obviously hurt. He still limped, though he hadn't complained a lick. Probably didn't want the attention, nor to be sent home.

She looked at the cave in front of her, remembering from her studies—let's be honest, it was all Philips studies—that the inside was very slippery. Water dripped from above onto the moss-covered rocks, making it hazardous. She could just imagine herself biffing it quite easily, and probably taking a poor friend down with her—whoever tried to catch her. Yep, she could definitely see that happening.

She smirked, then stopped when she noticed Jace. Her friend had his hands in his pockets. He seemed gloomy and tired; obviously regretting telling them about this quest. Hazel understood why. Her feelings had been dread-filled the day they had left home, and now their lives were in danger, and she couldn't go home and pretend like nothing was happening. Henri, Isaac, Walter, and the people who had taken Jace and Kory, all seemed to believe that the Shadow was real; and this worried her to no end.

She didn't like knowing that the Shadow wanted her best friend to get what it wanted, nor did she like that they were all in danger.

Jace was ahead of them at that moment and had pretty much refused to talk. Hazel couldn't be mad at him, though. She was fairly quiet herself and she just listened to Kory and Lisa converse, since they seemed to handle stressful situations better if they talked it out. Hazel was sure that Lisa had talked more the last few hours than she usually did, and that was saying something.

"I think that if this Shadow has been hunting for the Power for this long and hasn't found it yet, it's not going to." Lisa was arguing.

"Except that it now has people who can help it find the Power." Kory's voice was light, as if this was a normal conversation to be having.

"True. But think about it." Hazel looked back at Lisa and Kory, noticing that Jace did too. "Henri and his friends have known about it for ages, right? They would have looked for the Power and yet they haven't found it yet, and I'm sure they're not the only ones to look for it either. Maybe the Power can't be found because it doesn't want to be. I mean, it is *power,* right? Maybe it has everything it needs to stay hidden."

Hazel's interest sparked and she slowed her pace slightly so she could hear more of the conversation. For some reason the idea of the Power hiding left a bitter taste in her mouth. It was hard to admit that the Power they were supposed to be looking for would be impossible to find when they were now stuck looking for it.

Isaac said that the Power was the good in the world. Was it avoiding all humanity? If so, is there still good in the world? There had to be, I know plenty of good people.

She licked her lips, suddenly even more worried. Would they ever find the Power if it *was* hiding? There would be no reason for them to be on this quest – or to risk their lives.

Isaac wasn't with them on the hike. He'd offered and said he'd be willing to join them, but that if they were okay by themselves they would be able to move a lot faster.

"Why would the Power be hiding from us, though?" Kory's voice was still calm, as if sure that couldn't be the reason.

"I don't know." Lisa shrugged. "But think about it. If the Power hasn't been found yet, it's got to be hiding, right?"

Kory acknowledged her suggestion with a short nod. "Maybe it just wants to see if someone can find it, rather than show itself right away."

"Or maybe it can only be found in one place." Philips stepped up next to them. He had been lingering around toward the back of the group. "So, even if it did want to show us, maybe it can't, but that doesn't mean it can't send hints."

"True…" Lisa bit her lip. "The Power could mean anything." Hazel noticed Jace's clenched hand pull out from his pocket to wipe the sweat on his head.

It was a surprisingly warm day. She was sweating under her backpack and coat even though she'd had it unzipped nearly the whole hike. She was tempted to take it off fully at this point. Maybe she would after they got to the cave.

"It would help if we even knew what we were looking for, like what it looked like," Kory grumbled, wincing as he took another step. Lisa gave him a worried look, but she was the one who had told Kory it was okay to come—granted telling him he couldn't come wouldn't have kept him behind anyway, Kory was stubborn.

The wound wasn't too bad, now that they cleaned it up... maybe he needed just a few more days for it to heal enough that he won't notice it at all.

She glanced around at the trees. She had mistaken how long the hike really was. Distance wasn't her forte.

She thought that it was strange to think of the 'Shadow' as actually real – and not just real, but a being that could harm them. It wasn't a cheery thought, especially since it would want to use them to get the Power—another thing they never had heard of before.

Why are they called the Power and Shadow? From the way Isaac said it, they must be names of some sort, but why would they be called what they are instead of just 'the good and bad' in the world?

She seriously hoped that they would get lucky and this cave would be the right one, if there *was* a right one. Would the Power show up for them?

"I kind of think the names are cliché," Kory murmured, giving a small laugh as he evidently followed Hazel's line of thought, but of course, finding humor in it. "Like, seriously? the Shadow and the Power? Not very creative."

"Well, you know they were probably one of the first things in the world," Hazel suggested. "I don't think they had to have awesome names back then, and it was probably pretty creative at that point."

"Besides, how do we know that's what they are really called?" Jace finally joined in their conversation. "It could just be what other people call them but not what they call themselves."

"Yeah, I guess, but…" Kory shook his head. "I don't know, it's just weird."

"I sure hope they can't hear us talking crap about them." Lisa rubbed her cheek where sweat had gathered and smiled.

Jace grimaced. "Yeah, that would suck."

Hazel looked up, relieved to see the cave in front of her finally. Jace stepped up next to her as she stopped and looked at it before taking a careful step in. Hazel followed him carefully.

"What am I supposed to be looking for?" Jace asked, his quiet voice echoing back to her. She turned on a flashlight to give them more light.

"I have no idea." She watched his shoulders fall as he looked around the cave, obviously not satisfied.

She looked back at the others, who had carefully come in behind them. Kory was walking closer to a wall.

"Be careful," she told him, worried about his leg. He just nodded but continued on anyway.

Philips slipped, but easily got his feet back under him as they all wandered the cave.

After another few minutes Jace just sighed in defeat. "Let's go."

ℼ   ℼ   ℼ

Isaac paused while making dinner to glance at the clock once again. He was worried about the kids that had come to him. He had thought it was going to be older kids—already adults, but still kids in his eyes—but then these sixteen to seventeen-year-old kids had appeared in his yard instead. He'd found it amusing that they had walked rather than driven, but though a few had drivers' licenses, they didn't have their own car.

Still, he found himself getting attached to them. They had been with him for three days now and he couldn't help but enjoy the company of their lively spirits, though he knew it wouldn't last. Whether leaving to search more caves or being caught by Darrin, they'd be gone soon. The former thought bummed him out and the second terrified him.

He couldn't help but glance at the clock every few minutes, hoping that the teens would make it back okay, figuring that Darrin probably knew they were nearby made it even worse.

Isaac began to get a bit more restless when they didn't come back for close to another half an hour. He was in the middle of trying to convince himself that they were okay when, finally, the door opened. A weary and defeated looking Jace stepped in first, the rest of his friends following.

"Is everything okay?" Isaac asked him, as the boy plopped into a chair. He put his head onto the table as the rest of his friends also sat, Lisa perching on the edge of her chair. She shuffled her feet, looking uncomfortable, and Isaac figured that she wasn't relaxed enough in his house to join in much.

Jace nodded. "Just tired," he mumbled into the table. After a few seconds of silence, he pushed himself up and moved into the family room, maybe to take a nap. He definitely needed it. Isaac had noticed that both Jace and Kory seemed more tired since visiting Walter's house, and one time he'd gotten up in the middle of the night to find them both awake in the kitchen, and doubted they'd been getting much sleep. Maybe they'd been getting nightmares.

Kory followed him after a moment, limping on his leg, though obviously trying to ignore it.

"Nothing, huh?" Isaac asked. Hazel shook her head and Isaac deflated a bit, though he wasn't surprised. They *needed* to find the Power. It was their last hope to try and save mankind. He didn't even

72

want to try and guess what would happen if the Shadow ruled.

"Isaac?" He turned to look at Philips, who had a curious, uncertain expression on his face. "How do you know about this?"

"About…?"

"About us needing to find the Power, to stop the Shadow?" He folded his arms, as though hugging himself.

Isaac leaned back on the counter, setting the spatula next to him. He paused for a split second when Kory and Jace stepped back in, before rubbing his hands together. "The Power told us that we needed to find it; Henri, Frank, Nancy, Marcus, James, and me."

"If the Power told you this, why would you have to come find it? It was already there after all."

"I had asked it that," Isaac answered smoothly. "It told me that it wanted to see our persistence." He shook his head. "How much we really wanted to get there, and how easily we'd fall away from what we've been given to do. And I don't think it was quite… fully there. For me, it was while I was sleeping. I was about ready to dismiss it, honestly, but then my other friends were talking about it too. They described it like I had seen it. It had floated down in front of me, some kind of orb of pure power of the elements. Colorful, with all types of nature swirling in it, leaves swirling in the orb as though by wind. Lightning flashing across the entire thing, water and fire… Anyway, the point is, after we all shared the same experience, we knew it had to be true. No way could we all imagine the same thing like that."

"But you haven't found it yet," Lisa muttered, casting a worried look to Jace.

"No, so we had to pass it down to someone else. You see, we got this when we were in our twenties and thirties, now we're too old."

"So why us?" Jace asked this time. "Why do they need me, or uh… someone from Henri's line specifically?"

"Because you're Henri's grandson." He tilted his head. "Henri is the only one of us who got married, had kids, and didn't die trying to find the Power." He looked over at Hazel and found her curious gaze on him.

Jace's face seemed to clear slightly, as if a long-pondered question had a decent answer. "But why do you need someone related to one of you guys? Why not pick some random kid on the street and say 'hey you want to do me a favor?'"

"What was your brother's reaction to this news when he heard?"

"He thought Henri was completely insane," Jace admitted quietly, his gaze falling to the floor, his question obviously answered.

"I'm sure that would be the same reaction for anyone else I went to. We thought it would be easier to convince family members." That was only part of the reason, but he wasn't quite ready to tell the whole reason. It didn't seem they were aware yet, and he didn't really want to be the one to tell them.

Kory looked thoughtful. "Did the Power tell you why it wanted you to find it?" Isaac studied him for a second before he remembered that he was making food and turned to stir it.

"It said that we needed to find it so we can change the course of the Shadow's plan and get to the Power without the Shadow getting there first."

"Are you sure that the Power will come out for us?" Jace barely waited for him to finish.

"No, not necessarily, but we believe that it will."

"What if it doesn't?"

"Then we're all dead." Isaac said it with a shrug as if it wasn't such a bad thing. In reality, it set his nerves on edge.

The Power can't be found by me. Isaac thought. *I've fallen too far to do any good.*

Luckily that seemed to satisfy the rest of their questions—for now—and they were all quiet.

Chapter Seven

JACE WAS SO TIRED, his legs had locked up ages ago, and now he was trying his hardest to breathe fully. On top of that he wished that he had exercised a lot more before going on a quest.

Stupid quest. Stupid hike. Stupid caves. Why was the Power in a cave anyway?

He reached the cave, finally, and sat on the floor heavily. His friends crowded along next to him, all equally exhausted.

"Jeez… You would think that the Power would come out now that we've put so much energy into finding it," Kory wheezed. Despite having had no time to rest, his bullet graze had healed itself very well; it had been only four days since he'd received it. He still limped sometimes but it was way better now.

Jace was feeling better too, despite being tired and sore from overwork. Seriously sore. The scrapes from the fence were practically gone now, the bruises weren't as painful, and his wrist was pretty much back to normal. Luckily.

After a few more seconds Kory grabbed his inhaler, and put it to his lips.

They'd had to search a few caves that weren't really on any trail. Luckily, the rangers were a bit more relaxed on the 'stay on trails' signs now than they had been years ago.

"That's so unfair," Philips teased Kory as he used his inhaler. "You have something to help you catch your breath."

"Aren't I lucky?" Kory smirked and put the thing back into his pocket and stood up.

Jace groaned and pushed himself to his feet again. This hike had been exceptionally hard—he was already sore, and they'd had to hike close to ten miles *off trail*.

Uphill.

Ugh.

"How 'bout we get some ice-cream after we're done?" Lisa said, getting back on her feet as well.

"Sounds good to me." Hazel swore as she stood up. "Lisa," she moaned, "is there anything you know of that will help with soreness?"

"Sure, plenty but I didn't really think to pack any of it with me."

The walk had been long and very unimpressive. Sure, it was pretty, but no Power had showed itself, so they probably weren't in the right cave.

They were all tired because they'd had to wake up earlier than normal to get to the caves before dark. Now that it was about three in the afternoon, everybody wanted to head back to the house.

It was a good thing Isaac was a part of the group. Jace enjoyed Isaac. He was funny, and was one of those types of people you just couldn't help but get along with. And Jace could tell that he really cared about them. It was nice to be able to stay at his house for a bit and having the man willing to cook for them.

Surprisingly, Jace heard more footsteps entering the cave. Jace turned to find a man entering the cave. He seemed surprised to find that they were in there, but he smiled wide and warm. The kind of smile that one couldn't help but return.

He was clearly Hispanic, hair and skin a bit darker. He had a jacket and a backpack on—one of those Camelpack kinds with water, which was super smart of him to bring. They really should go buy one of those since they would be doing so much hiking.

The man greeted them, but it was in a different language—Spanish Jace guessed since the first word that came out of his mouth sounded something like 'ola'—not that he knew anything about the language. He'd chosen French as his elective.

Luckily Philips did. Sort of. After a second, he started talking back to him, slowly and unsurely.

"He said there's more to this cave," Philips said after another minute of conversing. He scratched his head. "I think."

"Really?" Jace looked at the other man, studying the happy eyes and nice hiking clothes. Since he was barely out of breath Jace knew he was obviously a lot fitter for this than they were.

The man studied them closely, and Jace wondered if he may have seen them on a poster or something with the long look he was giving them.

"Look tired," the man said after a few more uncomfortable moments. Philips startled in surprise.

"You speak English?"

"Little." He held his fingers about an inch apart to show what he meant. "New here, not learn much yet."

"How new?"

The man rubbed his chin. "Days? Few I think?"

"How many?" Hazel held up her hands, as if counting off the days on her fingers.

He held up his fingers, showing a seven.

"Seven." Philips nodded in appreciation. "Good job on getting the language thus far." The man narrowed his eyes and Philips translated in the man's language.

"More cave?" The man asked after a second of contemplation.

Lisa nodded, though Jace had a feeling she wasn't quite sure what he was trying to say.

"Here." He walked past them, into a corner, then gestured to something hidden from Jace's view. Jace moved closer, cautiously, but the man just continued watching them with a smile.

Jace looked to where the man was pointing and realized that there was a gap in the wall, big enough for a person to walk through. He'd missed it before because it hadn't looked like there was a gap from where he had been standing.

"Go." He nodded "It's pretty, be careful."

Jace bit his lip, not really wanting to squeeze through the gap, but knowing he had to. He walked in slowly, gripping a flashlight in his hand and trying to calm his breath, which had started going shallow, and his heartbeat that felt like it was going hyper-speed. Sweat gathered on his forehead despite the chill in the cave.

Why—why do I have to be so claustrophobic? Having to explore caves with that sort of fear was the worst combination possible. At least he wasn't scared of the dark too.

After a few steps in he felt a gentle hand on his back. "You okay?" When Jace gave a look back at the man who had followed him in he saw a worried expression. Jace just gave a short nod.

"He's just claustrophobic," Philips told him.

"Klos-to-fobic?" His voice appeared confused at the use of the big word, and the pronunciation was awkward.

"He doesn't like small spaces," Hazel explained, and Jace gave a quick look back to see her making the gesture small with her hands.

"Oh."

Jace wiped a hand on his pants to dry the sweat from it, before stopping in surprise. In front of him it opened up into yet another cave. Out of all the caves he had been to thus far he could almost believe that the Power might be here, because it was rather beautiful.

"What's wrong, Jace?"

"Wow." His voice was breathless as he moved forward quickly, trying to get out of the way of the others following from behind. He studied the cave. The one wall was open to the outside, where water came in, making a pool about twenty feet wide.

Kory gave a low whistle as he stepped out. "Wow is right."

The man looked sharply at Kory. "How do you do that?" he tapped his lips.

"Whistle?" Kory looked surprised, slightly uncomfortable.

"Yeah…" the man hesitated, looking about as embarrassed as Kory did at the sudden question. "Whistle. How?"

"Uh…" he looked over at Jace for help, but Jace just shook his head with a silent laugh and turned away, leaving Kory to explain it to the man while he looked around. "Well, you round your lips… and uh…" Jace stopped listening to Kory when something caught his attention. He walked away from the others and moved to the wall.

Carved into the wall were some engravings, but he had no idea what they said at all, yet as he stood there touching the rock, he could hear—no, *feel*, a voice.

"Jace, you've done excellent work searching for me thus far." There was a momentary pause as Jace felt himself stiffen, nearly jumping in surprise, straining his ears as though it could help him hear better. He couldn't quite put a name *to* the feeling. It was strength and vulnerability at the same time. *"Keep looking. Don't stop trying. You are on the right track. Hard times will come soon. Very soon. I'm warning you—don't let them break you. You are the only one who can find me. Be wary of anyone who hasn't been with you since the beginning.*

Jace looked up at the Hispanic man that had finally figured out how to whistle and was now laughing. Was the voice warning Jace against him?

He wished that this was just some cruel joke, and that someone would step out and start laughing. He had a sick feeling about the 'Don't let them break you' part and wondered what it meant... *Break you*... His mind was swirling, wondering if he'd imagined the whole thing. Yet somehow, the feeling he got when it spoke... he wasn't sure he could have made that up. It was like it spoke straight to his soul.

Jace shook his head and walked slowly back over to the others. Suddenly the beautiful cave didn't seem half as magnificent.

The feeling of dread that washed over him was just as real as the feelings of awe that had accompanied the voice. He walked over to Hazel, intending to grab her and the others and leave.

But then something sounded in the darkness and Jace shone the flashlight back to the place they had entered. Stunned to suddenly find two more men in the cave with them! They were staring at Jace and the others, glaring against the light of Jace's flashlight, and blocking the only way out. Jace thought about directing the flashlights away from their eyes, but something about the way they were staring was freaking him out.

Who were they? His friends followed his gaze, obviously all noting a new tension riddling the air. The Hispanic man glanced between them worriedly, stepping closer to Jace and Hazel as though he too sensed something off.

"Hey, didn't know there'd be more people here," one of the newcomers said, almost casually. That dark feeling continued to grow stronger, like a shroud surrounding him and sinking into his skin. It made his body feel like it was itching, like they needed to *run*, ad yet the men were in the way of their exit. Jace shuffled his feet, hands clenching, and stepped closer to Hazel.

"Hazel, we need to leave," Jace murmured in her ear. He took a step back as the strangers came closer, bringing Hazel with him.

A snap rung through the air and without knowing how, Jace found himself on the ground, dazed and pain exploding behind his eyes. He heard his friends scream out for him, but his vision wasn't working well, and he was pretty sure he was about to pass out...

As his gaze cleared, he saw what had hit him. What looked like half of a stick—walking stick or tree branch—lay near him, split. Even with his dazed mind he figured that the other half must still be in his assaulter's hands. The Hispanic man was also on the ground, a man standing behind him, having hit him with another piece of wood.

Four men? Where had the other two come from? The two at the entrance to the cave were still standing there, but these other two seemed to have come out of nowhere.

As Jace fought to keep conscious, trying to get his fairly uncooperating hands underneath him to push himself off the floor, one of the mysterious men had tossed the Hispanic man in the water. Kory instinctively jumped in after him. Jace watched, his eyes bleary with tears, head pounding in pain. Everything felt… completely warped. His head weighed a million pounds, his arms felt like limp noodles. His mind might not be working fully, but he still worried when he didn't see Kory pop back out of the water yet.

It took a few long seconds before his friend's head appeared above the water, gasping and holding onto the other man.

One of the men, scowling, grabbed Kory and jerked him out, Kory's vice-like grip helping to get them both onto land.

Kory was wheezing.

Wait… Jace thought distantly, unable to get his mouth to form the words. *His inhaler*…

One of the men pulled Jace harshly to his feet. His head fell forward despite his greatest effort to keep it up, his knees sagging.

He saw Hazel near him, breathing hard and glaring, hands in fists. Jace knew that she could've taken out a few of the men despite her smallness due to years of martial arts training, but she seemed to be holding back, probably to avoid provoking the men holding her friends.

Even with his head mostly down he could see the last man stepping toward them all, his eyes on Jace as he approached.

"Hello, Jace," he said as he stopped in front of him. Jace barely managed to lift his eyes enough to meet his.

The darkness seemed to be radiating off this man like a stench, and Jace felt himself shrinking.

The man touched his cheek. His hand was cold. Jace flinched, turning his head to the side – or trying to. The man grabbed his chin.

"You know who told me where you are?" He smiled, one of those smiles that twisted Jace's insides. This was a cruel man. "Your friend. Isaac." Jace felt his insides shatter and tears well in his eyes, not just from the pain this time, but from the betrayal. "I will say that he needed a good deal of persuasion before he would talk, though."

The man rubbed his hands, and Jace wondered what he had done, how he'd 'persuaded' the older man.

Jace didn't respond – he didn't know how to. Isaac had warned them that they couldn't "break" if they were caught, yet that same man had broken and told these creeps where they were headed.

On one hand Jace couldn't blame him, though. Who knew what the man had done in his attempts to break him or get him to talk?

"Darrin, we really need to get going," someone from the shadows barked, making Jace jump. *Darrin?*

In a split moment, getting hit with a sudden clarity amongst the ache in his head, he realized the crony had to be addressing the radiating-dark man in front of him.

The man they'd been warned about was standing in front of them all now.

Darrin was in front of them.

Before he could panic further, a quick movement and sudden spike in pain told him that Darrin had whacked his ear, the same spot where the branch had hit him moments before. Jace's vision blurred and he fell.

His last thought? *Please don't hurt my friends.*

ॱ ॱ ॱ

Kory watched Jace fall, though he didn't hit the ground. The man holding him kept him up, wrapping one arm around his chest, the other hand gripping his arm, and Jace was out. Completely out.

The man gave a look at the rest of them, and Kory felt his fear rise up to challenge him. He fought to not show it. Nevertheless, he wasn't able to meet the man's dark gaze, so he looked back at Jace. He watched the blood traveling down his face and neck. The wound on his head looked deep and wide, hair knotted with it.

He inhaled sharply, feeling his breath catch. He needed his inhaler, but he forced himself to wait. If he took it out now then the men would most likely confiscate it. He needed a moment when they weren't looking, if that was possible before he passed out.

"Cover them."

Kory was confused at the command, but a moment later he figured it out. The last thing he saw was Jace's limp head being covered just before a bag was pushed over his own eyes.

What would they do if someone saw them? Others would wonder why these big men were holding kids with bags over their heads. Yeah, no one in their right mind would walk past that without at least calling the police.

He heard a splash and stiffened. Did they put the Hispanic man back in the water? After Kory *nearly killed* himself to get him back out? Another splash. No, they weren't putting the man back in there. They were putting *his friends* in there! Were they just going to kill them all and take Jace?

Kory tried to twist out of the man's arms. But the man covered his mouth when he tried to scream, and Kory felt the man's mouth next to his ear. "I can break your neck right now, Kory. Kill you off now if you'd rather." It wasn't the threat that sent a chill down Kory's spine. It was the fact that he knew his name.

Before he could react, he was pushed forward. He hit the water quickly, face first, and found that he was sinking. He couldn't even move. His legs were too sore, and he hadn't been able to catch his breath before being shoved in there. He couldn't figure out if he was going up or down, and the pressure of the water on his chest felt like heavy weights.

He inhaled water and started coughing, which made him inhale more. He tried to kick up, but failed, his backpack and clothes dragging him down. He'd already done this once, with a limp body, doing it again seemed impossible.

A hand pulled his arm, and he was dragged up through the water. He barely noticed when his face emerged since he was still struggling to breathe through the bag over his head.

He coughed until all the water had left his lungs, but by then he was starting to lose feeling in his extremities. He knew that the lack of oxygen from his asthma was starting to wear him down, but he couldn't grab his inhaler with the guy gripping his arm and being herded like blind, drowning cattle. The man was nearly dragging him along, feet barely keeping up.

He heard his other friends coughing. So the men weren't trying to kill them. Yet.

Minutes later they pulled him into a vehicle—he thought it might be a truck when the door slammed shut. He wasn't sure how they got a truck all the way out here, but that wasn't a worry at the moment.

The man let him go and he dropped to his hands and knees like a puppet. His chest ached and his mind wouldn't think. He needed… what did he need?

His inhaler. He needed it, but he couldn't feel it's bulkiness in his pocket. *Oh, right, it's in my backpack, not my pants.* He felt like laughing at the irony that it was so close, literally in the bag that was resting heavy on his back, and yet he couldn't get himself to move to get it.

Help me, someone, please. He couldn't even figure out where he was, let alone his inhaler.

He wheezed, trying his hardest to get air in.

"What's going on?" one of the men asked. His voice sounded confused. He probably thought Kory was playing a trick.

"Please," Lisa begged, though Kory couldn't see her. "Please, let me help him. He needs help—fast. He has asthma. I just got to give him his inhaler." He was surprised to feel Lisa's gentle hands on him a second later, proving that they had let her go. The bag over his head came off and he caught sight of a blurry Lisa's knees.

"Hang on, Kory." Her hand was searching his pants pockets and he shook his head.

"Where is it?" she asked him.

"Bag," he coughed out. He grabbed her arm, hoping that doing so would provide something, if not air, then at least comfort. He was pleased to be able to have at least a little relief at the touch—as much as he could get while trying not to die from lack of air and from being kidnapped. Though holding onto Lisa made it harder for her to look for the inhaler, he just couldn't let go.

She frantically went through a few pockets of his backpack, until, finally finding it, she thrust it to his lips. Despite the speed, she was still as gentle as always.

He took a breath and then just sort of keeled over onto Lisa's lap, taking another breath greedily when she didn't pull it away. Lisa's hand found his hair and he watched with half closed eyes as the men left the back of the truck, grabbing all of his and his friends' belongings, though luckily they left the inhaler with Lisa.

"Are you okay, Kory?" Hazel asked as the door shut behind them.

He didn't answer, but Lisa did for him. "He's fine." *Yeah, I can breathe now, but that doesn't really matter. We're probably all going to die anyway.*

Hazel bit her tongue, then whispered: "We're so dead."

Kory took one more deep breath, then pushed himself up carefully and looked over to where they had let Jace fall to the ground. His friend still had the bag on his face, but everyone else had pulled theirs off.

Lisa was moving faster than him, already helping Hazel gently take the bag of Jace's head.

He watched Lisa work on Jace's head, having taken off her jacket to get to her flannel underneath. She kept the T-shirt beneath the flannel on and used the other to stop staunch the bleeding by tying it around his head. Hazel had already scooted away, turning toward the wall and covering her nose. She'd had always had a weak stomach when it came to blood.

"Well, think of it this way," Kory murmured, giving them a fake smile and noticing Hazel's attention flick to him. "At least we don't have to walk back."

Chapter Eight

JACE EYED DARRIN CLOSELY as he grabbed a few things from some cupboards, though he could not see what. Jace knew he was not going to get out of this; this was something larger than anything he'd previously had to face. This man wanted something and he would go to extremes to get it.

His head pounded from the beating he'd received but thanks to Lisa the wound had stopped bleeding.

Jace looked around the room the best he could, trying to see if there was anything in there that could help him. It looked like he was in a run down and rather barren kitchen; he was sitting strapped to a chair where the table would be.

"You know if it was just a shot I needed you didn't need to bring me here," Jace told the man when he saw the injection needle in his hand, swallowing nervously. Man, Kory must be rubbing off on him, he was starting to handle stressful situations with humor.

Darrin didn't respond and silence filled the room again.

"Where are my friends?" Jace tried again. "Hello? Guy with the freaky needle and mysterious expression!" Jace sighed, regretting even speaking. His nerves were showing, and the man didn't even look toward him as he spoke, let alone respond.

He fumbled with his fingers, which were tied behind his back, trying to regain feeling in them. His feet, too, were tightly tied to the chair legs and they were pounding. No matter how much squirming or picking at the ropes he did, he could not free himself from the chair.

He had awoken in the chair and had sat there trying to figure out what had happened for who knows how long. He had woken earlier in the truck but had quickly passed out again from the pain, and now he almost wished that he was out again.

"They are fine for now," Darrin told him, coming closer. "Probably better than you." Jace met his dark gaze, frustrated with the man in front of him. "Now, sit still." He smirked, knowing that Jace had no place to go.

"Please, just let my friends go." Jace looked up, just in time to see Darrin's hand flash, a sudden pain in his cheek whipping him to the side, nearly knocking the chair over with him in it.

Slowly, Jace righted himself. "What do you want?" Jace tried looking past his tear-filled eyes, but all he saw was a blurry blob. He tried to say it in defiance, but his voice cracked.

"Where is it?" Darrin asked in response, crouching down next to him. "Maybe if you tell me, I'll let your friends go."

"Where is *what*?" He blinked in faux confusion, ignoring the last part. As much as he wanted his friends released, he knew the man would never actually do so.

He wants the Power. But I don't know where that is, or even what it is.

Darrin must have seen something in his gaze. He shifted, grabbing Jace's foot, held just a couple inches above the ground where it was tied against the chair, as he spoke again: "Ah. You *do* know what I am talking about. Good. Where is it?" He slid the needle into the heel of Jace's right foot, though he did not plunge whatever was inside yet. The pain was sharp, and quick. The metal cold.

"I um, I don't–" Jace couldn't keep his eyes from nervously flicking down at his own foot, shoulders tensing at fear at what might be inside the syringe, and soon inside himself. What kind of drug was the guy going to give him? Did he know what he was doing, or was Jace going to be killed by an overdose?

"We can do this the easy way or the painful way. Although it will end the same either way, *I* would love to make you hurt first." Darrin shrugged his shoulders and his dark hair fell into his green eyes, casting them into shadows. "So where is it?"

"I don't—I don't know…" Jace was unable to keep his thoughts in order, though Darrin must have taken his hesitation as a signal as he pushed down on the needle.

Immediately, agony tore into Jace's body, and he curled over his side, falling to the floor, chair and all, and gasping for breath. Confusion fought with the desire to tell Darrin what he wanted to know. *Why keep it from him? It doesn't matter.*

The pain slowly decreased, leaving him uncertain. His thoughts tried to convince him to tell Darrin while something inside told him to keep quiet.

"It's…" Jace hesitated as the alarm inside his head grew more desperate, trying to warn him of danger. He pushed away the growing pain, forcing himself to remain collected even in his despair of not knowing why.

He took a deep breath. "No." Pain flared as spoke the word.

"What?!"

"I said, no."

Darrin was obviously not expecting *that* as an answer. "Where is it?" He took a step closer to Jace, looming threateningly above him. Jace tried to scramble away from the man but he was still tied to the chair, and he suddenly realized by the throbbing in his arm that the chair and the floor were trying to press it into a pancake. Darrin grabbed the shirt that hung loosely from Jace's chest, lifting him and the chair back up to so it was sitting, but shoved him backward. Jace's head slammed into the wall behind him.

"Tell me where it is," the man repeated.

Jace didn't answer, he couldn't, pressed as tightly as he was against the chair and wall. He couldn't even breathe. And the pain was nearly blinding.

"Dang it, boy!" Darrin pushed him further into the wall before releasing him, letting the chair fall back to all fours again. He grunted and watched warily as Darrin turned around and went back to the kitchen counters.

"I do not think that is wise, sir." Jace startled as he heard another voice to the right of him. He turned to see a man walk out of the shadows. He had obviously been there awhile, but Jace had not noticed him.

"And why not?" Darrin asked, irritated with this man. He did not stop what he was doing at the counter, though, and he did not seem surprised by this man being here.

"More than one injection this soon could kill the boy before he talks." The man looked at Jace with sadness in his eyes—no not sadness, defeat maybe? Or respect? Whichever it was it almost made Jace like him.

Darrin shrugged his shoulders. "Do you think I care? He's not going to talk if I don't anyway."

"Might I suggest something?" The man asked, flashing a look

at Jace that he couldn't quite understand.

"Whatever, Michael, say what you want." Darrin finally turned away from the counter and folded his arms. But whatever good thoughts Jace had about Michael were disappearing quickly.

"Why don't you kill his friends?" Michael took a step closer to Darrin and lowered his voice. "Not yet of course. You must first wear him down, make him weaker." Darrin was glaring at him and Jace was sure that the man saw the horror that washed over him in that moment.

Michael was speaking again, but Jace was having a difficult time hearing him; the fear was so strong.

No! Don't kill them! I'll just tell you! But he couldn't. As much as he wanted to avert his friends' deaths, Jace couldn't tell him. But could he handle his friends' deaths? He'd rather die first. He'd rather just tell them what they want to hear—if there was any guarantee that they would let them go if he did so.

They wouldn't let us go. They'll just kill us if I say anything.

He closed his eyes and took a deep breath then forced himself to look stronger than he actually felt.

Darrin nodded at Michael's suggestion, then turned to continue mixing ingredients together. Michael looked surprised. "You're still going to do it." It was a statement more than a question.

"Well, if the first time didn't even get him to talk..." He looked over at Jace. "I don't think the second time will kill him." Jace couldn't agree with him, the first time had felt bad enough and he thought he was going to explode or something.

"You never know with this sort of thing," Michael protested, though he backed away, probably considering it useless to argue his point further. Jace didn't know what to think of the strange concoction that seemed to swirl deep within him; he felt so vulnerable.

He thought of Hazel's soft brown eyes layered with love and hope, her dark hair that seemed to frame her face perfectly. He sensed that she would be as freaked out as he was, if not more so. He needed to stay strong for his friends.

Grandpa, what did you get us into? Granted, it wasn't his grandpa's fault. He hadn't even intended for Jace to know.

He remembered how his parents had been distant to him all those years. The main reason he had decided to leave the house to do this was because he felt his parents wouldn't have cared. His friends had come with him because they hadn't wanted to leave him alone. But maybe they should have.

We are going to die. The thought entered his brain for the hundredth time since they had been kidnapped.

And it probably wouldn't be the last.

He glared at Darrin as he approached, angry that this man had taken them. That he was trying so hard to get information from Jace that Jace didn't even have the answer to.

"Are you just going to tell me, or are you really going to make it difficult?" Darrin asked him sourly. When Jace did not answer, Darrin slipped the needle in his foot, pressing down again. Jace prepared himself for the worst that would happen.

It didn't come. He blinked in confusion. Even the pain was only a slight disturbance. He felt… why couldn't he feel anything? His breath—he was still breathing, right? Yes, there it was. He could feel it, sort of. It felt like he wasn't even a part of his body, unless he focused on something specific.

Darrin said something with a smirk, but Jace was unable to concentrate and so he didn't hear it.

Nothing… It was all gone. His thoughts, though there, seemed more like he was hearing them while he was sitting in water.

"How's that one?" Darrin's voice finally caught up with his mouth, though it still took Jace a minute to process what he said.

"We could do this all day." Jace hated the smile that spread across Darrin's face. "Yes, I have a bunch of other concoctions that I have been unable to test on anyone else yet. You would be a fun experiment." Jace hated the way Darrin's words came so delayed, it made him think of when he'd watched movies and the words were out of sync with the mouth, although the experience was a thousand times worse in reality.

"Michael," Darrin turned to the other man, his voice suddenly lapsing back into the correct time, startling him as everything else snapped back to full awareness as well. "I think he'll need to be moved into my office."

Then, turning back to Jace, he watched him with a curious look in his eyes. "There's something different about you…"

Jace didn't think that Darrin knew he was hearing things at the appropriate time since he paused for a second after that statement. Jace had no intention of telling him either.

"Okay, let's go." Someone, possibly Michael, came back out

of the shadows, cutting him out of his ropes expertly before grabbing his arm to pull him to his feet. Though Jace did not really want to be carried he couldn't really hold himself up either. Even though the time lapse had corrected itself, Jace was still unable to feel anything strongly. He didn't care to see what was around him. He couldn't with the darkness that filled the room, so he didn't try.

All the other pain from before flooded back the moment he got his feet under him, and if it hadn't been for the man holding him up, he would have fallen back to the floor.

"Ah, it's subsided already, huh?" Michael asked, in a way that seemed rather loud in his ear.

"I'll be in there in a second, Michael. You take him and watch him." Michael nodded and pushed Jace out. He stared at the ground as he left the room. He saw the shoelace from Michael's shoe hitting the floor.

"You should probably tie your shoes." Jace bit his tongue and closed his eyes tightly at the remark that came out of his mouth. *Really? Shoelaces? Idiot.*

The man's laugh startled him. "You know, of all the people that guy has brought in, you are by far my favorite." The tight grip on his arm relaxed. "Can you walk by yourself?"

"Maybe." He already knew he couldn't, though, and it was confirmed when he took a step and fell immediately. Michael caught him before he hit the floor.

"Guess not." Michael shook his head "I am sorry this is happening to you; Darrin just doesn't get that pain is not always the way to get things he wants. He doesn't… well, he isn't the same man I once knew." His tone grew wistful.

"Where are my friends?" Jace asked stiffly, not sure if this man was for real. He seemed sympathetic, but then he was a part of this whole thing too, so Jace wasn't going to trust him.

"They're actually in that room there." He pointed down the hall towards a door. "They're okay. Scared, but okay. They keep asking about you, and I can't tell them anything."

"Why is he keeping us here?" The information loosened some of the stress in his shoulders. He might not trust the man, but if he was answering he'd take advantage of that.

They turned left down the hall, away from his friends.

"He just wants information that you have." He lowered his

voice. "He's going to kill you, you and your friends, whether or not you tell him."

"Why are you telling me this?" Jace looked at the other man.

He shrugged. "You asked."

"Yes… but why are you answering?"

"Because…" Michael looked down at him. "I've been here for years and known Darrin for even longer. He's a good guy—well, he was, before all this Before the Shadow… I can't leave him. I'm not able to. I'm trapped here, captive in a way that even you aren't." He grimaced, a haunted look in his eyes. "And with me here, I can reach the little bit of humanity Darrin has left. I feel I would lose him completely if I left, even if I was able to." He paused, sadness in his eyes. "And being stuck here… it requires me to do some things I don't like." He stopped talking, probably lost in his own thoughts, but it gave Jace time to think.

He seems genuine, but is he? Jace didn't know him well enough to decide.

"What is this stuff he used on me?" Some kind of drug? But what kind of drug would be able to cause that extreme agony? Or the sense of nothingness? Jace looked down at his foot, annoyed at the pain that flashed up with every step.

He felt Michael stiffen and looked back up at him. "What?"

"I don't know exactly what's in it…" Michael's voice was barely above a whisper, "…but it's rather deadly if used too much, and it's never pleasant, it basically takes away your free will. Somehow, you were able to resist it though…" He pushed open a door—it was dark inside, like everywhere else in this building so far, lights barely illuminating the shadows. Jace was surprised to find a plant on the desk—alive or dead he couldn't tell. Besides the desk, a chair was the only other piece of furniture in the room.

Michael let him slide to the floor slowly.

"Hold on, boy." He retreated back into the darkness leaving Jace confused. *Hold on to what? Or perhaps he was getting something?* Jace didn't know what to think.

The door was pushed open again, interrupting his thoughts, and Darrin came in with one swift motion.

"Found some new ones!" He smiled wickedly at Jace. "I've never used them, so I don't know what they'll do. It's late tonight, though, you may want to get comfortable now." The small smirk on his face told Jace that he understood how Jace was never going to actually be comfortable there.

Jace frowned, unsure of how to reply. Darrin sounded excited about the prospect of testing more liquids on him and Jace fought a shudder.

"Michael, get some rope and tie his hands to the pole. I'll be going to bed now." Darrin took on a new tone, one that was almost carefree, and Jace felt like he was getting whiplash at the change in his demeanor.

"Of course, go to bed," Michael said, stepping out of the shadows again.

"Good. We will start again tomorrow." Darrin turned to the door, and once he was gone, Michael turned to face Jace.

"Michael… I can't do this. What does he put in those things?"

"The liquid in the syringe you mean? I don't even know the answer to that." He turned towards the lonely desk and opened a lower drawer.

"What if I have to pee?" Jace, who had been struggling to sit up into a more comfortable position, forced himself to give the other man a small smile.

"Do you want a bucket? I am sure that would be the most you'd get." He grimaced in sympathy.

Jace shrugged and held out his hands for Michael as he came back with rope. No point in fighting it, he was too weak to do so anyway.

"Better than nothing, I suppose." Then he eyed his wrists. "Although I don't really know how I'd even go with no hands so… whatever."

Michael chuckled lightly and pulled the rope tight, causing Jace to wince.

"Sorry."

Jace didn't respond, just closed his eyes and took a deep breath. He could feel himself already slipping to sleep, completely drained.

"It always was the hardest to..."

As hard as Jace tried, he was unable to open his eyes and concentrate on Michael's words. Instead, he found himself in darkness with no sound to disturb him.

₪ ₪ ₪

"What do you know?" Hazel winced as the man once again hit Philips in the gut, causing him to gasp and curl himself slightly. Philips was pretending to know more than he actually did so that the others would not get beaten.

"I won't tell!" Philips glared at the man. His hands were tied above his head like everyone else's—Hazel's, Kory's and Lisa's. All of them were suspended so that their feet barely touched the ground, probably to make it harder on their wrists and easier to deal with them.

The man pulled back to punch Philips in the face again. He already had some blood on his chin from previous hits to the face. Tears streamed down Hazel's face, and she could see Lisa's face was wet as well.

Hazel couldn't take it anymore. "Please. Please stop!" she begged. The man paused and turned towards her, eyes gleaming eagerly, reflecting the light in the room.

"Hazel." She heard Kory warn her from other side.

"Talk." The man took a step closer to her.

She took a deep breath "He doesn't know."

"Hazel, don't," Kory tried again. The man glanced at him suspiciously and elbowed him sharply before turning back. Kory glared at him but didn't react. "Well, who does know? You?"

Hazel had finally been able to get control of her thoughts— she'd convinced herself not to tell him. It may be true, she might know a little more than anyone else in this room, since she and Jace would chat a lot in the morning before the others woke.

Although Kory and him would also talk at night when neither of them could sleep. Hazel had awoken from strange dreams to find them sitting in the kitchen talking. Jace probably knew the most, but he was not in the room with them.

"Where is my friend?" she asked him, unblinking.

The man smirked. "Like I would tell you. Darrin has something else planned for him." Hazel didn't think it would be good—whatever it was. If anything, Hazel knew it was probably worse than the treatment they were getting. The man moved over to Kory, curling his shirt in his fist and before Hazel could blink, he kneed Kory between his legs.

Kory grunted in pain and his eyes widened slightly as he instinctively pulled his legs closer to his body. Hazel swallowed heavily, wishing that she could help. But the man wasn't finished.

With one quick movement, he stuck his hand in Kory's pocket and pulled out his inhaler. With a smile he drew away, slipping the inhaler into his own pocket, before turning back to Hazel.

"Now… I know one of you guys, if not all of you, knows something, and I intend to get it out of you." He turned back to Hazel. "Personally, I think you are the one who knows the most."

"No," Lisa piped in from the other side of Kory. "He gave bits and pieces to each of us." She closed her eyes.

"Lisa!" Kory hissed.

The man chuckled. "I think you were not supposed to say that." He paused. "Well… might as well get started if I want to get you all to talk."

As the man shifted his stance, preparing a punch—which Hazel only saw the signs of the punch coming because of her years of Martial Arts training to help—Hazel twisted her hands in the rope above her head to get a grip, and prepared herself for the hit that came a second later.

She didn't know what possessed her to do what she did next, but as the man turned to punch her again, she kicked forward, aiming for the same spot where he had just kneed Kory. She hung from the rope as the man stumbled forward, and Hazel swung her legs up and wrapped her legs around his neck.

Off to the side she saw some guards coming toward her so she let go of the man, the pain in her wrists doubling as she felt a slight bounce on the rope. She glanced up at the ceiling momentarily, noticing that the rope was not tied to the ceiling, but instead there were small holes in the ceiling.

Huh.

Kory was grinning.

Gasping for air, the man gestured for the guards to step back and turned his attention back to Hazel.

"Someone taught you how to fight, huh?" He rubbed his neck, a weird sort of smirk on his face. "Why didn't you finish me? You could have killed me long before the guards got over here, of course then they'd kill you without hesitation, and we wouldn't have the information that you still have to tell us." Hazel felt a little blood from her wrists trickle down her bare arms and shivered at the warmth of it.

"We could be doing much worse to you guys, you know. We have many torture techniques and machines. You should be happy that you're not receiving worse than a beating." He paused.

"Let her down." He barked toward the guard closest to them.

"Thomas?" The guard coughed in surprise. "Sir?" He looked at the other man incredulously.

Thomas glared at him. "If she wants a fight, she can have one, but we are going to make it fair for both sides. Let her down."

"No!" Philips looked at her. "No, Hazel." She flexed her fingers. They tingled sharply as they brought her down. She had once taken up boxing classes, at least before they'd changed it so girls couldn't join in. After that she'd taken up karate, then moved into other styles, having enjoyed learning it all. Many of the girls had said that she should try out for something that girls are *supposed to do*—like dance or cheer—but that hadn't stopped her, and now she was glad that she hadn't listened.

She didn't even have time to get in stance before the first blow came and forced her to the ground. Instantly, her training came back to her—she did not fight back, not yet at least. Instead, she waited until Thomas was done with the first few punches, absorbing them the best she could, ignoring the pain that threatened to take over. She would let him think that he had won.

She wiped blood from a gash on her forehead as it dripped into her eyes. She shifted into a better stance as he circled her with increasing confidence, as if judging whether or not it was really going to be this easy.

Then Thomas attacked.

Striking upward, she pushed Thomas's fist away, and jabbed him in the gut, then curled her other fist and hit the side of his face.

Thomas's eyes were filled with nothing less than astonishment, as were the eyes of her friends. They knew that she trained but had never really seen her in action. Jace was the only one that usually came to her practices, and unlike most sports, they didn't really have performances. She knew they probably would have loved to go, but she was always self-conscious at having people watch her. Her family and Jace being the only exceptions, and barely at that.

Her mentor's favorite words flowed through her mind, *"If they expect you to be weak, use it to your advantage; you will throw them off."* She suddenly realized that Thomas was on the ground.

She let go of him for the second time that day and backed off as the other guards approached. One of them grabbed tightly onto her.

Hazel turned and kicked the one who held her, knocking him

to the ground, and in the same movement she brought down the other guard who was right behind his friend.

The other guards had reached her now, managing to hold her back. But that was okay with her. She had finished what she wanted to do.

"Sir, if I may?" The guard who had untied her, and protested Thomas' decision, spoke up, humor palpable in his voice. "I don't think you made it more even. I think it would have been more even if you had left her strung and fought her." She heard someone – who she assumed was Kory – snicker behind her.

"Yes…" Thomas stood up. To her surprise she found no anger in his gaze. "I think you are right, Bryan. It's been a while since I've had a decent fight. I think, with that one, we'll have to tie both her arms and legs." He took a step closer to her, then another until he was directly in front of her. She attempted to turn her head away from the face that was barely a few inches from hers, but Bryan grabbed her hair tightly.

"I like you…" He trailed his finger down her face.

"Leave her alone!" Philips pulled against his restraints. Thomas's gaze snapped toward him.

"Or what? You have nothing to threaten me with. I can do what I want." Thomas turned back to Hazel. She bit her cheek and tried to pull away from the hands that held her.

Her jaw tightened as he leaned in and she realized, with disgust, that he was about to kiss her.

She didn't want her first kiss to be with someone she didn't know, let alone someone trying to hurt them. She wanted her first kiss to be with a kindhearted guy. Someone who made her smile and laugh. Some who made her feel safe. Someone she could share everything with.

She wanted to kiss Jace.

That realization shocked her. She liked Jace, always had, but had never thought she wanted to be more than friends—until she felt the lips of another man against her own.

She kept her lips pressed tightly together, and a second later Thomas pulled away, looking... well, she wasn't quite sure about the expression on his face.

"Tie her back up. It's time to go eat." Thomas turned away. She let the others pull her back, sighing softly as she felt the rough rope wrap around her sore wrists.

"Are you okay, Hazel?" Lisa asked quietly, attempting to look around Kory. Hazel nodded numbly in reply. Her mouth was still closed, and she started to feel pain from clenching her jaw.

"Are you going to feed them?" Bryan looked between Thomas, who was leaving, and them.

Thomas waved the comment away dismissively. "Maybe tomorrow." She heard Philips' stomach growl as if in protest. Bryan laughed then turned to follow Thomas out the door.

Hazel was not sure if they were alone or not, since she couldn't see the whole room.

"Whoa! You kicked his butt!" Kory's voice broke the tension. "I can't stop replaying that in my head. I would be laughing if this wasn't such a depressing moment." He paused, then chuckled, "No. I'll laugh anyway. You never said you were that good!" Lisa's laugh came in softly a second later, but Philips' gaze remained hard.

"Hazel... I didn't—I was going—" His eyes pleaded silently with her as he stumbled over his words. "I don't want you guys to get hurt."

She smiled softly at him. "I don't either, but we got ourselves mixed up with this, so we're going to get hurt. I'm not just going to sit quietly while you take it all." He looked as if he was going to argue, then relented with a soft sigh. He studied her with narrowed eyes, his eyes scanning down her body, as if gauging how much pain she was in. She looked down as well and found that she was already bruised in a few places and bleeding in others, although she was in about the same shape as Philips, and probably ten times better than Jace.

Oh Jace... where are you? She wanted to get out of here, and she wondered if she could if she were by herself, but she wouldn't leave her friends. She had to look after them. Kory was still rambling on about how 'awesome' she was.

"Then you took down the other two?!" He grinned at her, and she laughed at how carefree he was able to be, even in the worst times.

"How are you so happy?" she asked him quietly.

He attempted a shrug. "We haven't been beaten yet. Also, I am lucky to have lived as long as I've lived; might as well make every day a party." He exhaled slowly. "Why did you tell them that we all know bits and pieces, Lisa?" He turned away from Hazel, speaking quietly so that she barely heard. "You know that's not true."

"Because..." Lisa smiled happily. "Then they can't kill any

of us in case they kill the one who knows the important pieces." Hazel drew her eyebrows up, surprised at her logical thinking. "Besides, it's kind of true…"

Hazel decided to try something she'd thought of during the fight. Looking above herself at the hole in the ceiling, she grasped the ropes between her hands again and pulled on them. Instantly she felt the bounce again, or the catch of the rope. She saw Philips give her a confused glance.

"What are you doing?"

She didn't look at him "Trying something. They will most likely be gone for the night. I am going to get comfortable."

Kory raised his eyebrows skeptically. "How do you intend to do that?" he asked.

She ignored the question, continuing to pull on the ropes, once again ignoring the sharp pain that came consequently. If she could just get the winch to release her…

"Are you trying to break it?" She sighed in exasperation at Lisa's question.

"Something like that." She finally felt the give, the winch rapidly unraveling and dropping her to the floor like a rock. She winced when her butt hit the ground, but she stood up as soon as the rope stopped coming down, pleased with her success.

"Now…" She turned to Kory. "I can sleep more comfortably."

"What about when they come back?" Lisa looked worried, but Hazel just shrugged.

"Then, oh well," Kory interjected, and started tugging on his as well. "They're just going to try to kill us anyway."

"How did you know it would do that?" Philips looked at her, confusion creasing his brow.

"When I attacked Thomas, I felt it catch. I think they are using a winch to wrap it up." She sat back on the ground, putting her hands in her lap and trying to ignore the ache in her shoulders.

She saw Philips shake his head, laughing softly.

She watched as Philips and Lisa started tugging silently on their ropes, then laughed as Kory finally managed to loosen his and land on his back.

"Well, this is way more comfy!" He continued to lie where he'd dropped. Hazel stood when she saw Lisa struggling with her rope and went to go help her.

What do you think about that, Thomas?

Chapter Nine

JACE AWOKE TO THE SOUND of a door shutting, but he didn't open his eyes. He knew exactly where he was. Instead, he let himself drift back to sleep, not wanting to deal with what he knew awaited him.

"I believe it's time to wake up." He opened his eyes irritably as he was pulled from his semi-dream.

Darrin held a plate in his hands with a few sandwiches cut into four pieces, and Jace felt his stomach clench at the thought of food, both with need and disgust.

"Want one?" He held out the plate. Jace eyed him distrustfully.

"I am not going to kill you; we need to keep your strength up if I'm going to continue testing these on you." He waved the syringe in front of his face and placed the plate on the floor before untying the ropes binding his hands. Jace didn't actually want to keep his strength up, because he didn't want there to be a chance of him revealing what was better kept secret.

"Take one while you can, you may not get another chance." Darrin's eyes darkened when Jace still didn't grab one, although Jace wasn't sure why it would matter to him. Yet, upon seeing the anger in the man's eyes he hurriedly grabbed a sandwich. He was already not going to enjoy this, he didn't want to make Darrin angrier and risk any other consequences.

"Good." Darrin stood back up and turned around. "Now we can continue." With the sandwich in his hand, Jace couldn't resist a taste. Then, realizing how hungry he really was, he ate the rest in another bite few bites. Darrin took the plate before he could grab another one.

"You do have an appetite." There was a challenge in his eyes when he looked at him.

Jace felt the drowsiness of sleep threaten to take him back, as if he hadn't slept at all last night. That wasn't like him. He'd always been an early riser. He might be a little tired when he woke up, but he'd usually have energy to get the day started.

"What time is it?" Jace yawned, trying to act as if he wasn't in a place that was worse than his nightmares. His eye caught sight of the syringe lying on the floor next to it.

"Around nine." As soon as Darrin turned away from Jace, his attention diverting to the desk, Jace was reaching for the syringe. "Don't you dare." The man snapped, and Jace inwardly cursed himself as he spun back toward him.

Darrin grabbed the plastic syringe with a short huff.

"Can't leave anything in your reach, can I?" Jace barely caught the mumbled words from him.

"I guess not." Jace shrugged. "But you can't blame me for trying, right?" He felt himself shiver.

"I suppose not." He turned toward Jace. "Are you going to tell me what I want to know?"

Jace looked down at his hands, something deep inside him trembling. To avoid further torture, he felt tempted to reveal information that he didn't really have.

He had already tried telling Darrin that he didn't know where the Power was nor how to find it, but Darrin hadn't believed him. The little information he had wasn't even enough to help *Jace* find the Power, let alone this other man.

His right foot was still sore from yesterday's pricks, and he was not looking forward to the multiple sensations from the liquids that he'd go through today. He dug his fingernails into the flesh of his arms to stop himself from shouting the words.

"Alright, works for me." Darrin grabbed a vial that held a bluish liquid inside and pushed the needle through the hole to fill the syringe.

It was in that moment that Jace noticed the reaction on his foot that expanded from the bottom of his foot. Bright red lines seemed to trace his veins' pathways starting from his heel where he'd been punctured. It looked like some kind of extreme spider veins, but in a bright red tone that was almost unnatural. His stomach flipped unnervingly at the sight and he looked away, deciding to worry about that more if he ever got away from here.

He winced as Darrin grabbed his foot aggressively and pulled it closer to him.

"That looks tender." He traced the veins with his finger, causing Jace to shiver uncontrollably. He let out a short yelp when Darrin pushed his thumb into the arch of his foot.

Darrin's smile grew when he heard the sound, and he slid his finger up and down the foot painfully. He leaned in closer to Jace.

"Are you sure you don't want to tell me?" he asked quietly, as he traced the veins again this time with harder pressure. Jace guessed that the liquid that was running through his veins was giving him a major reaction or infection in his right foot, and could also see that his foot was bruising along this same path.

He closed his eyes, forgetting what Darrin had asked. He bit back a yelp when he felt the needle slide into his bruised foot. He felt utterly unprepared for whatever new torment this new liquid mingling with his blood would bring.

The liquid was pushed into his foot. He felt the coldness moving through his bloodstream, tapering off about halfway up the leg as it obviously warmed up. He sat the re for some long moment, trying to figure out what it did. Nothing seemed to happen really.

He opened his mouth to comment on it but paused as he realized that speaking was the new desire he felt. It was almost as though his brain was circulating too many thoughts, and they all wanted to spill over past his lips. Was this some sort of truth serum?

He remembered hearing once that truth serums didn't necessarily make you tell the truth, but rather made you more prone to talking and lowering inhibitions in order to answer the questions asked.

"I would like to know what that one does if you'd tell me," Darrin said.

He breathed out deeply at the words, biting his lips hard. *Nope. Nope. Nope. Nope. Nope. No.* He felt ridiculous being so determined not to speak even a little, but if he answered one question, he wasn't sure if he'd be able shut up after that.

He desperately dug his nails further into his skin, and, finally, the feeling faded as he continued to resist the taunting going on in his mind.

He relaxed the grip on his arm, relieved that the desire passed so quickly.

"That one went by fast." Darrin said as Jace opened his eyes. "What did it do?"

He ignored the question and concentrated his attention on the liquid that Darrin had already started on.

"Should I start on the other foot, and give this one a break?" Darrin didn't wait for an answer though instead he grabbed the same foot and ran his finger up and down it again. "This has never happened before. It's quite strange that it's happening to you. Of course, no one else has denied me this many times, nor lived this long through it." He pushed on Jace's skin again, making Jace hiss in pain.

"That obviously doesn't hurt as bad as some of the things I've done yet, since you can still react." He scraped his nail across Jace's foot again, and his breath caught as he felt the pain flash through his stomach. "But I do love seeing how bad the pain is." His last words echoed in Jace's mind like it was bouncing off the walls, over and over again. "Even if you don't tell me now, I'll get it out of you."

Jace thought that Darrin may have had some of that blue liquid that made him want to talk, because right now he was on a roll. He would have laughed at that thought if Darrin wasn't so close to him, holding his foot threateningly.

"Did you know that I got a bachelor's degree in anatomy when I went to college?" Darrin asked nonchalantly. "I know the points on the foot, where the liquid goes, where it can help." He paused and placed his thumb to the side of Jace's foot. "And where it hurts the most." Jace felt dread, knowing that Darrin actually liked causing pain – he did it for fun, not just as a pressure tactic

Darrin's hand whipped to grab the syringe, pausing right before meeting Jace's foot. He then extracted the green liquid from its bottle, and injected it forcefully into the large bruise on Jace's sole. He bit his tongue to suppress the cry that wanted to escape.

"The poison is causing these marks to spread up your leg faster every time I inject a new one." Darrin paused thoughtfully, not quite injecting the liquid yet. "I wonder what will happen when it wraps around your whole body. If you last that long anyway."

Jace didn't like the thought of the poison in his veins making its way around his entire body; Darrin would use that to cause more pain.

Darrin finally pressed down on the plastic syringe plunger, and, unlike the other injections, the shock was instant.

A piercing scream filled the room as his pain doubled, causing Darrin to jump in surprise. The crumbs on the ground from the sandwich felt like thorns against Jace's hands and legs. He could feel each individual vein, each thing that touched him. He felt like a pin cushion. He vividly heard Michael shuffling his feet behind him, and the beating of his heart was unnaturally loud. Scraping reached his ears from who knows where—probably from some hidden mice or something.

He could see the marks on the floor, little dents in the wood. The light from the window was so bright that it felt like he was outside, not inside a dark building, and he had to squeeze his eyes shut. He could smell food, some kind of meat cooking not too far off and nearly gagged.

But as fast as it came, it was gone. The pain seemed to disappear, everything sounded muffled, and he felt… numb.

"What did it do?" Darrin asked quietly, almost repressed.

Jace looked down at his hands that he had pulled off the floor because of the pain. He was confused. What had just happened? Why had the pain been so intense?

He pulled his arms close to his chest in a protective manner, tucking his hands to stop himself from trembling. Nonetheless, he was unable to control his panic, and he shrunk closer to the wall. He didn't know why he was freaking out about this particular injection when he hadn't even reacted with some of the other ones. He didn't know how to explain it, but for whatever reason, he couldn't control his trembling.

"What happened?" Darrin tried again. He reached toward Jace with his other hand.

"I don't know! I don't know!" He scooted away from the hand painfully, and tears fell from his eyes. He lowered his voice. "I don't know… Please don't."

"I was told that that one of these would have serious effects. I believe you are experiencing those. It's supposed to enhance senses; your reaction suggests that it did." Darrin looked away "Of course, they all are supposed to have strong effects in the moment, but it's not common to have side-effects after it runs out. It's very interesting to see how it's affecting you. No one else has lasted this long. Not like you'll last much longer though, You're definitely too weak for much more."

He's right. I am weak, and I always will be. Jace knew it was true. He always knew that he was weak; he was always just a boy in the background. No wonder Grandpa Henri had asked Jason to do this quest, not Jace. Jace just *had* to go out and prove he was worthy. What a joke. He'd never be worthy.

He felt idiotic, having come out here, and he just wanted to curl in a ball and die now, but he couldn't. He was here now. He had to try his best. He couldn't give up with the first sign of the storm, he had to walk bravely through the tempest... and quite possibly die trying.

He took a breath, raising his eyes up to glare at the man, fighting to keep his defiance. It felt like the only thing he had now. He didn't know if his friends were okay, and he was stuck in a dark, bland room with a man that wanted nothing more than to tear him down.

"If you're trying to get any information out of me by making me feel small, then it's not going to work." He looked up at the man. "I may be weak. I may be the worst person for this job. But I will not give up. You'll have to do much worse than this."

"I can do worse." Darrin grinned, his eyes flashing with an intense thrill. Hatred. "I can do much, *much* worse if you'd prefer to do it that way." He ran his finger up Jace's foot again. "But I think I'll take it slow, more fun that way."

Jace turned away from Darrin, and searched for Michael in the darkness, before turning back to Darrin.

"Can I get some water?" He hadn't wanted to ask this man for anything, but his mouth felt like sandpaper, and he was starting to get rather desperate.

"Ah. I suppose that would be necessary to have if I want you to live much longer." He stood up and turned around. "I am about ready for a snack anyway." He left the room, whistling cheerfully, and once again, Jace felt like he was getting whiplash at the change in the man's demeanor.

Jace ran his hands through his hair and pulled his legs closer to his body, dimly noticing the pain that flashed from his leg, and took a trembling breath. He ran his hand down his injured leg slowly, trying to figure out how high the infection had penetrated. His whole leg throbbed, so he wasn't sure where it ended. He pulled up the end of his pants, and saw that it ended just about mid-calf.

"Are... Are you okay?" Michael's voice nervously arose from the shadows, and he appeared a second later.

"Yeah. Well no. Not really." Jace leaned against the wall stiffly. "I feel dead."

"Can you hold on?" Michael asked anxiously. Jace blinked as he remembered the conversation they'd had the day before. *Hold on...*

"Hold on?"

Michael took a frantic step closer to him.

"You need to hold on you can't–" The door opened, and Darrin came back in carrying a few things.

"Now I have to do some paperwork." Darrin nodded toward his desk. "Here's your water." He handed him the glass.

"Thanks," Jace said sarcastically, yet he was honestly grateful for the break he'd been given. He wondered what kind of paperwork the man would have. Did he actually have a job or something?

He could tell that Darrin did not like the paperwork and was having a hard time concentrating, frustration evident. Jace couldn't blame the man, it was terrible thing for nearly everyone.

Probably about a half hour later, Jace finally spoke up. "Can I use a restroom?"

Darrin's head thumped against the desk with a loud sound, and Jace held in a laugh at the timing of his interruption, not sure if he'd want any ire directed at him. He wished he didn't have to go so he didn't have to attract the man's attention.

"Why don't you just go?" he said to Jace, turning his head to look at him.

"But... You wouldn't want to work in a puddle of my piss, would you?"

Darrin's gaze darkened as he met Jace's gaze, then he turned to Michael. "Show him where it is. You may need to help him as well."

Chapter Ten

THOMAS HADN'T BEEN OVERLY upset about the teens pulling loose to be on the ground. Instead, he had chuckled and sent one of the guards away with a quiet word.

Instead, he had mostly seemed amused. "You sure know how to think things through." And it wasn't even a moment later before Kory was suddenly jerked by the arms. They'd winched the rope back up, and Kory had let out a short yelp from pain and surprise. Such a rude awakening.

That was yesterday. Today, it had pretty much been like the day before except yesterday they'd been given food and water. Not a lot though, she still felt her stomach clench every few seconds—she wanted food so badly. Water even more.

She didn't know why Thomas kept going straight for her, more than anyone else in here, unless it was the fact that she'd kicked his butt, but she was relieved. Because of her training she knew she could probably handle the pain and empty stomach better than the others could. Maybe.

Thomas cut her ropes with a knife; one she hadn't seen before. "Let's go on a little walk, shall we?" he whispered into her ear, though she could tell the others still heard it—and she was pretty sure that had been Thomas' intention.

"Where to?" She tried to control her beating heart; positive he could hear it.

"Eh, I don't know." He shrugged and glanced maliciously at the others, which made Hazel feel like he was trying to get more of a rise out of her friends than her.

She looked down at her wrists as Thomas pushed her forward. Her friends, who had long since learned that protesting was useless, just stared at her in panic as she left the room. She stumbled as Thomas pushed her forward again. She was slightly surprised to see that they were alone. She didn't think that he'd be alone with her after she'd beat him the last time.

She could actually see the bruise she had left on his chin and left eye, and she felt a weird calm when she looked at it, as if it was a reminder that she would be okay. They walked past a handful of doors in silence. She was confused. Why walk with her if he wasn't going to say anything or try something? Still, she was relieved that she could stretch her muscles.

"Why are you doing this?" she finally asked.

Thomas just shrugged. "Which part?" He asked the same thing that she had just wondered in her head.

"I guess all of it, any of it." She didn't think she'd get much out of him, but it couldn't hurt to ask.

"You just need to tell us what you know." He didn't elaborate, which was to be expected. She stiffened as he turned toward her. "You could just tell us. Tell us and all of this will stop." His voice seemed to vibrate through the wall that she had unconsciously backed up against. It almost seemed soothing. As if he was promising security.

No! Knock it off, Hazel! You've got to stay strong! She shook her head forcefully and tried to shake the weird feeling that she was being manipulated.

"How can you promise that everything will stop?"

"I have you here in this position. I can stop it whenever I want." She shrank down the wall as Thomas stepped closer.

"You wouldn't stop though. If I told you then you would just kill us." Hazel forced herself to look at him, to hold his gaze that darkened.

Thomas opened his mouth to respond but was cut short as a scream filled the air. Hazel jerked up in surprise and fear.

It was Jace. She knew him; knew his voice, even if that scream was something she'd never heard before and never wanted to hear again.

She pushed past Thomas—who was not expecting the movement—and stumbled to the door that the sound had come from. But a second later Thomas was grabbing her, pulling her roughly away from the door.

"Let go of me!" She kicked him in the shin, and he

108

immediately let go, but a barely a moment later, as she tried to take another step she was jerked back by the hair, and tightened against his chest.

"You can't go in there, sweetheart." His mouth was right against her ear. Tears came unwillingly out of her eyes from the tug.

"What is he doing to Jace?" she gasped out.

"Magic." He said it sarcastically, yet there was a serious tone to the word, and she wasn't sure if she should believe him. "It seems he doesn't like that one very much."

"Which one? What is he doing?" Hazel knew that Jace was going to be worse off than her or the others, but she didn't want to think about how bad it could get.

Thomas pushed her back down the way they'd come, and she forced herself to pay attention. She needed to keep track of which way they were going. She would have to ignore the frustration and terror that plaited inside her. She remembered watching movies and reading books in which the characters were tortured, and she didn't like the thought of any of that happening to Jace. What Hazel and the others were going through was bad enough.

The door to her room opened but she didn't allow Thomas to push her in. Instead, she rammed her shoulder into him, and he hit the wall outside of the room. Hard. She was going to get answers. Now.

"Why are you doing this to us?! To Jace?!" She barely noticed the guards heading in her direction or her friends calling out in warning. "Why are you so heartless!?" She pulled him back and slammed him back into the wall. Tears slipped down her face, but she didn't care.

Thomas shoved her back until she'd hit the opposite wall, beside the doorway, fast enough that black spots blurred her vision.

"Heartless? Hardly." His voice was quiet, for her ears only. Blood appeared in his hair. "What do you think the walk was for?" He let her fall to the floor, her knees hitting hard, as he took a step back. His hand found the back of his head and lightly touched the blood. He looked at the blood for a second before lowering his hand to the side, his eyes slightly wide with shock.

As the guards stepped next to her, Thomas took a few stumbling steps down the hallway, into the shadows. This whole building seemed full of shadows, light barely trickling from the ceiling and most windows boarded.

Bryan went around her and followed him with a quick pace,

giving her a glare as he passed. Something like blood began to dampen her own hair.

The other guards didn't move. For a second, Hazel just sat there on her knees, trying to stop crying. She felt slightly sorry for hurting Thomas so much. She hadn't wanted to do it, not even to someone who deserved it. Though she didn't necessarily regret doing it. She needed to know what to do next, without the voice of any other person's opinions. For once she needed to decide for herself what she was going to do.

And she did, right then and there. She was going to get out of here, and she was going to have all her friends out with her.

What do you think the walk was for? What *was* the walk for Thomas? She asked herself silently as she was finally pulled up to her feet. She had thought that Thomas had just been trying to provoke them, but she wasn't so sure now. He'd been harsh, that's for sure, but altogether, their beating hadn't actually been too torturous, not compared to what he could be doing. What was happening to Jace— now that sounded *brutal*.

And when Hazel actually looked at the man, meeting his eyes, and a few of his actions… well, it just wasn't lining up. It occasionally seemed as though there was something in him that was pleading for her to understand. To…something. To help, maybe?

If that was so then why wouldn't he just help us get out of there?

But if Darrin was as bad as he sounded, then he would kill them—anyone who helped them escape—without hesitation. Maybe Thomas was trying to keep himself safe in his attempts, and if so, maybe, just maybe they had a chance.

It was a hope she clung to, even if she didn't believe it fully. A hope that maybe not everyone in this dark dump wanted them dead. That they might be able to make it out.

She was surprised when the men just tied her hands and left. No punishment, no pain?

"What happened?" Kory asked first, breaking the silence. She let her head fall to the side, onto her arm, and closed her eyes. The tears continued to fall.

"I know what room Jace is in." She shuddered as his scream echoed in her mind.

"You saw him?" Diminutive relief was heard in his voice.

"No. I didn't see. I just heard." She rubbed her cheek on her arm to get rid of the tears. "Kory, they aren't going easy on him, they're hurting him worse than they are us." She opened her eyes and looked at him just as his own eyes closed and he took a shuddery breath.

"Are you okay, Hazel?" Philips asked after a second. Pain laced his words.

"Not really. I am tired of all this." She wanted to tell them that they were going to try and escape, but she wasn't sure if there were hidden guards or cameras, and she didn't want to get caught.

She felt helpless. The chances were about one to a hundred that they'd be able to survive long enough to escape, and the escaping part was even more unlikely than the surviving.

"We need to get out of here," Hazel murmured softly, so softly she didn't know if anyone heard, and she didn't look to see if anyone did either. She ignored her aching stomach and other pain, and closed her eyes again.

ↁ ↁ ↁ

Jace had a fitful night's rest. Most of the night had been spent trying to go to sleep, and the other fighting the urge to scream as he awoke from nightmares—nightmares which he was confused by, dreams filled with darkness. No, not dreams of Darrin or his new trauma from torture. Fears of something new. Like he was searching for something without knowing what, stuck in a darkness that wouldn't lift, lost and alone.

He was awake when Darrin came in, and unlike yesterday, he did not pretend to still be sleeping. Instead, he stared at him as he came into the room.

His stomach was aching with the desire for food. Darrin did not give him much, just enough to keep him alive; but he felt his will to live fade a little more every time Darrin entered the room.

Darrin, for once, did not say anything as he sat down in his chair, breaking the routine. He usually enjoyed investigating the spread of infection first, then pumping Jace with more drugs.

Another man came into the room after a second. He looked edgy; but who wouldn't be with Darrin as their boss? Jace didn't hear most of what he said until the man mentioned his friends. Then he strained to hear the rest of the conversation. He caught only a little bit, but the words he heard were easily put together. "...So far... all still giving us trouble."

Darrin looked at him with a smile and he returned it, as smugly as the one he'd been given. He felt relief that his friends had been able to hold on. It was the *so far* part that he didn't like.

The other man left soon after, and Darrin continued to struggle with whatever he kept on his desk.

Jace's eyes closed for what seemed like a second, at least until he felt that unknown feeling of dread and darkness standing over him. Darrin. Darrin was standing over him. He raised his eyes to him questioningly. He didn't know what the man was doing anymore. It was always something new.

"What do you want? What can I do to get you to tell me?!"

He only half heard what Darrin said next, but the fact that he was saying anything for once, rather than tormenting him the whole time, almost made him even more scared than the pain had.

Jace's face flushed as Darrin continued to talk, his voice quiet and nearly gentle for once, which was strange and a little alarming. "I've not been very nice to you, it's just the stress…"

He didn't mean to miss the words that Darrin spoke, but he was pretty sure he missed most of them. He couldn't concentrate on anything.

"I had just wanted you to tell me, but it doesn't seem like you will."

Jace turned away from the man, trying to get his thoughts in order. Did he think that talking like this would make Jace more likely to speak?

"What can I do?" Darrin tried again.

Jace's jaw clenched. He didn't really want to say anything. Darrin was almost out the door before the voice came out of him. "You could let my friends go." He didn't know why he was saying it. He didn't know that it was even his voice that was speaking it. His throat was so hoarse that it made him feel like someone else was speaking in his place, as if that person had swallowed a bucketful of sand. "But I know that's not going to happen, you will just kill us all, even if you say that you'll let them go." Darrin didn't respond, he just watched Jace for another few seconds before leaving the room completely.

Jace looked into the shadows again. He was sure Michael had

been there the majority of the time, but he hadn't spoken much since he'd told Jace to hold on.

Again his thoughts lingered on those two words. *Hold on...*

Does that mean they were going to be okay? Maybe it meant that they'd get help at some point, or maybe it had been said to keep him from saying anything. Jace shook his head trying to ignore the thoughts. He didn't want to give himself false hope.

He closed his eyes, leaning his head on the pole. His wrists were still tied tightly, and he tried to twist them into a different position. The rope just dug into the sores on his wrists and began to bleed even more.

He must have dozed off because when his eyes opened again Darrin was back in the room, and he was only a few feet away. Darrin's interest in his foot seemed higher than the desire to try out the new liquids. Not by much, though.

He blinked as Darrin grabbed his foot again. He didn't really care anymore; it was all painful and he was growing accustomed to the pain. Part of him just wanted Darrin to finish it off and kill him. He didn't want to be this weak anymore.

Tears fell from his eyes as Darrin pressed down on his foot again. He slid Jace's jeans up to check if the red lines had grown anymore but wasn't even able to push the pants up enough.

Jace panicked for a second as Darrin pulled up his dirty shirt but was relieved when he saw the veins just above the hip. But his relief that they weren't any higher was overlaid with the fear that the further those lines went, the closer he came to—his best guess—dying.

Darrin turned and Jace realized he was starting to get the items for another liquid. He recognized the few items he got out, and that one of them was a green color. His jaw quivered as he realized what liquid the green was. A chill traveled through him.

"Are you going to tell me?" That question—the one that, if he answered, could end this pain right away—filled Jace with fear. One way or another, whether Darrin killed him or let him go, he would still be free.

The green one made everything stronger; it enhanced his senses. He didn't like hearing what could be happening around him and feeling the multiple pricks of pain from every little crumb, and the dim light seeming to burn his eyes.

He tried to prepare himself better this time, now that he knew what was coming. He tried hard not to react to it, but just like last time it surprised him by being far too painful to ignore, especially with Darrin pushing on different spots on the bruise-like lines.

He screamed again, it may have been a little less high-pitched this time, maybe not. Darrin seemed to push harder on his side when he realized how much it truly hurt Jace.

It took him a long moment to even calm down slightly, breathing heavily. The light was intense, and he squeezed his eyes shut. He heard movement from Michael's corner, and then he heard a shuffle and sharp inhalation from outside the door. Surprised, his breath froze in his chest. He heard Hazel outside the door. He knew her sounds, knew that little gasp she gave, any time she was stressed or something startled her during a movie.

She was so close yet so far away.

The extra senses were gone too fast for him to be sure what was going on. He could no longer hear much of anything. That was one good thing about this one. He'd be in excruciating pain for ten seconds or so, but for up to an hour afterwards he barely felt anything.

He rubbed his arms, feeling goosebumps up them. He didn't think he was cold, but it could be some more of those side-effects that Darrin had talked about.

Darrin stood, as if realizing that pain doesn't faze Jace as much right after that particular liquid is used, but Jace's thoughts still stayed on the fact that Hazel had been right outside the door. How did she get there? Why was she there? He shook his head. He couldn't focus on that right then; his head was already pounding, and he was sure any thinking would make it worse.

He lay back on the pole again as he tried to ignore his bladder that was telling him he needed to pee. But then he decided that he didn't really want to pretend, he liked the break it gave him from the room.

"Can I use the bathroom?" he asked heavily, blinking for a minute as he tried to keep his eyes open. Darrin didn't say anything but waved his hand dismissively, and a second later Michael came out of the shadows and untied his wrists before pulling him to his feet.

The bathroom was right outside the door, so he didn't have to walk far, which he was glad about, because at the moment he really couldn't move well. Michael locked the door behind them and turned away, he obviously didn't care to help Jace, and Jace didn't want help for this.

Michael leaned back on the door and tilted his head to the ceiling as Jace tried his hardest not to fall over. He shifted his weight to his left side and gripped the wall.

"I wish that he'd stop with this fixation," Michael mumbled, seemingly disheartened. "He had much better ideas when we were teens, but now he just lets the power take over." Jace didn't reply. He didn't really know how to, not knowing what he meant by power when that idea was seemingly what they were looking for, so he let the silence stretch on for a while longer as he washed his hands. He let the cold water run over his hands, letting it numb his wrists. He looked up at his reflection in the mirror, seeing the blood that was still on his face from when they had knocked him out to get him here. He tried washing his face, but he couldn't get the dry blood off without pain, so he gave up.

Michael finally pulled the door open, forcing Jace to be done. Jace glanced down the hallway for a second—freezing when he saw movement. Kory was being pushed to the bathroom that they had just left. He glanced up at Jace at the last second and gave him a small smile, but didn't try to talk; his eyes just scanning Jace worriedly in the dim hallway.

Jace didn't say anything either. From what he could see, Kory had been beaten pretty badly, and he had lost a lot of his spirit.

Shame filled him. He looked to the ground, choking back tears. In his mind, he couldn't help reprimanding himself. He shouldn't have brought his friends with him, shouldn't have left without talking to his grandpa about it. He shouldn't have even left in the first place! What had he been thinking? The few reasons he'd had—they'd had— seemed dim in comparison to the trouble they now found themselves in. He wished more than anything to just be home already. For his friends to be safe.

As soon as they were back in the room, Jace held out his hands for Michael to tie his beat-up wrists again, idly wondering if he'd even live long enough for his wrist or head wounds to get infected, as he sat on the floor again. He barely felt Michael's tightening of the ropes, and instead, leaned his head on the pole. He didn't want to be here anymore, to do this any longer.

Darrin stood up and turned to Jace again, and Jace mentally prepared himself for what he knew was coming, even without moving his body.

Just let me be done now... he pleaded to anything that could hear him. Receiving no answer, of course, he sighed softly as Darrin knelt next to him again.

"Are you going to tell me?" the man asked again. Jace shook his head slowly, hoping that by doing so he would be able to keep any form of strength.

Darrin stood and went back over to his desk, taking his sweet time on making another liquid. Jace dug his nails into his arms and was surprised when he felt blood.

Instead of letting it go he pushed harder, allowing his head to hit the wall. *How much longer?*

Chapter Eleven

BACK AT HOME IN HIS BEDROOM, Jace's older brother, Jason, paced, but his thoughts were directed at the larger problem, not the ground under him. He hadn't been able to sleep since he had gotten home two days ago. It was then that he'd learned that his brother had left the house and hadn't been seen in a week—just the day after Jason had seen him. *If only I had been here. I should have been here.*

He had heard the missing child report on the news at a friend's house. The friend hadn't known that Jace was his brother, so he'd just come down to the theater room talking about some kids being kidnapped a few days ago that still weren't found, then he'd mentioned Jacques's name. Jason had run up the stairs to listen to the last of the report before hurrying home.

Jason could only guess that his brother had gone out on the quest that Grandpa Henri had been talking about and was angry that his grandpa had gone on blabbering to his younger brother because Jason had said no. Jace wasn't even an adult yet! What was the man thinking?

The cops had tracked their phones to his brother's tree house. It looked like they had been kidnapped or something because there was blood on the tree nearby. The recent hot weather had made it impossible to follow any footprints, since most of the snow melted.

As Jason continued to pace, his bedroom door opened and his grandpa, parents, and sister Laura came in.

Jason turned on his grandpa immediately. "This is all your fault!" He stepped closer to his grandpa, wanting answers. "Why'd you have to go telling everyone about this—this thing!?" *And how come I heard the news that Jace was missing from a television set?* Not a single person from his family had thought or cared to give him a call to tell him about Jace missing.

"I only told *you* about it," the old man said calmly. "He must have overheard somehow."

"What are you talking about?" Laura slipped past their parents and grandpa irritably, eyes flicking between all of them with an angry glint.

His parents exchanged a quick look that Jason didn't think he was supposed to catch. They didn't look overly worried about Jace being out there alone. He turned to them next, looking for someone to take his anger out on, even though he knew it was his own fault for not going himself.

"You knew this was going to happen?!" Jason shouted.

Grandpa Henri looked toward Jason's parents in surprise.

Jason lowered his voice. "Why didn't you tell me?"

"What's going on?" Laura's voice came in forcefully again. "Where is Jace? And where are his friends?"

"His friends?" Jason drew his eyebrows together in surprise. "They went, too?"

"Excuse me, but I'd like to know if my brother is okay!" Laura snapped before anyone could respond.

"I guess we should tell you—it's out in the family anyway," Jason's mom said, sighing heavily.

"Tell us what? What's going on!" Laura nearly shouted.

"Your brother went to go find something, a… Power," Henri told her slowly, as though he knew how it would sound. "He took his friends too."

As Laura looked at him quizzically, Jason's mom searched Grandpa Henri's eyes.

"Do you know where he is?" A desperation for her middle son, that Jason had rarely seen in her eyes, showed clearly, despite her attempts to hide her concern.

"Yes and no." Henri shrugged heavily.

"How does that work?"

"I know that, um…" Grandpa hesitated. "That Darrin has him."

"Darrin!?" Jason hit the wall in desperation, making his hand sting. "How… how do you know?"

"A friend of mine talked to a witness who was with them when they were taken. We kind of figured out that it was them," said Henri.

"Who's Darrin?" Laura looked fearfully at them.

"Okay, you won't believe this. Jason didn't either," Henri said. Jason looked away from him in disbelief as he continued. "Darrin is an evil man, likes to bring pain. And he has… magic."

"That's impossible, Henri." Jason interjected, watching in surprise as his mom and dad grabbed each other's hands, eyes suddenly filling with that worry that Jason felt like they should have had from the beginning. They must have thought Jace was safe, but there was nothing safe about any of this, especially not now that Darrin has him.

"Pain? Jace is with a man who wants to hurt him?" Laura said, exasperated. She stood up and began pacing the room. "Where does this man live? I am going there right now!" Honestly, Jason was surprised to hear the anger in her voice, the protectiveness. She had sort of separated herself from her brothers in recent years as her desire to be around her friends got stronger, but she obviously still cared for them. She made Jason think of a mother bear, ready to tear someone apart for taking away her family.

"We don't know. All we can do is hope that Jace figures out a way out by himself." Henri sighed, taking a step to the door and opening it. "We are still searching for them, and I do hope we can find him, but Darrin has been avoiding the police for years now."

"This guy has magic, and you think that Jace will get out alone?" Laura stepped in front of him, stopping the door. Jason felt a flash of annoyance at her acceptance to believe that magic was real.

"He's not alone. He has his friends, and yes I do. Or, I hope he can." Henri slipped out the door, flashing a grim smile back. "I will do my best to find out where he is."

His mom and Laura followed Grandpa Henri out the door, Laura arguing some more, and their mom looking like she wanted more answers now that she knew how much danger Jace was truly in.

Jason fell back onto the bed, listening to the silence. "This is my fault. I should have gone. I shouldn't have fought him on everything," he said out loud. He ignored his pounding head and closed his eyes. As soon as he did so he regretted it because his lids didn't want to open back up.

"You look terrible, Jason, you should get some rest." He felt the bed sink down as his dad sat next to him.

"I don't want to." He forced himself to sit back up, fighting back the dizzy spell. He did need rest. And probably food. He didn't do well when he went too long without, but his stomach was twisted in knots of worry for his brother. "I'm fine." He stood, brushing past his dad and slipping through the door that Henri had left open.

He heard Laura's voice as he walked slowly down the hall, but didn't focus on what she was saying.

He's with Darrin. And it's your fault. He exhaled heavily. He had to do something—now. How could he leave it up to Jace to figure a way out? If, in fact, he was still alive. He had to at least try.

Slamming the front door behind him, and hating the sound of it, as it increased the pounding in his head, he went in search of his brother.

But first, he'd wanted to talk to his friend, Devin.

He looked up and stopped in surprise. There Devin was, standing on the bottom step, paused from coming up as Jason came out.

"Dude, you look..." Devin caught his glare and paused, sighing. "Is there any word about Jace?"

"Not anything helpful." He didn't stop to talk, and Devin turned to match Jason's fast pace.

"But there has been something?" Jason looked over. Hope and worry fought in Devin's blue eyes. Jason sighed, slowing to stop and face him.

"I'll tell you something, but you can't tell anyone. Okay?" Jason curled his fists as the words came out.

Devin gave him a blank look. "Jason. Come on." He spread his arms wide. "Who would I tell?" Upon seeing Jason's unrelenting gaze, he shook his head and let his arms fall. "Okay, I promise not to tell anyone." Jason nodded and continued walking.

"Hey, wait! Aren't you going to tell me? You can't just say that and walk away!" Devin hurried to catch up with him.

"I'm going to tell you; I'm just going to the forest first." They walked in silence for a handful of minutes, until Devin finally broke the tension.

"This is ridiculous," he said with a soft sigh. "Why would he just leave? Why aren't your parents doing more to find him? And why do you seem more mad than worried? Do you think they're actually kidnapped?"

Jason stiffened at Devin's questions, forgetting that his friend was one of the most introspective people he had ever known.

120

He quickened his pace anxiously, trying to force the tiredness from his body before he collapsed to the ground. A hand grabbed his arm tightly, and he tried to pull away, but Devin made him turn and look into his eyes.

"Jason, are you okay?" He tried to turn away again, but Devin just tightened his grip. "Jason! Focus here! Knock it off. You need to get some rest. You need to stop it. It's not going to help Jace if you do this to yourself. You need to be strong so that you are able to do whatever it takes to help."

Jason looked around. People nearby were staring curiously at them.

Devin's voice softened. "I know you're worried, I am too, but you need to calm down and focus or you will only make it harder to do anything."

"You don't get it! I can't concentrate! It's… It's—" People were now slowing down to watch, or hurrying faster while casting furtive glances at them, but he didn't care.

"Of course, I don't get it, I haven't lost a brother, or anyone for that matter." Jason turned his angry gaze back to Devin as his friend continued. "But I know that if the roles were reversed you would not allow me to act the way you are right now, so you had better shape up, and help me figure out a way to find your brother!"

Jason sighed heavily and his shoulders slumped. "I don't know how we're going to do that."

"I don't either, but we *are* going to find a way." Devin turned and led Jason towards the forest again.

"Devin!" Jason snapped at his friend. "Devin! I already know who has him!"

Devin's eyes were bright with surprise as he turned around.

Jason continued. "I know who has him, but I don't know where he is."

"Why didn't you tell me?" Devin asked, a rejected look on his face.

"I only found out right before you came to my house." Jason shook his head. "But we need to go somewhere else to talk, people seem to find us entertaining." He glared at the closest man until he walked away.

"Jason, be nice," Devin said as he started walking again. "Let's go, and you can tell me, and then you are going to get some sleep. I don't care if it's at my house or yours, or even in the forest, but you will." He cast a disapproving gaze. "And, of course, there are going to be people watching, we are talking about this in front of them, and it's in people's nature to be curious."

Jason imagined strangling his friend, but in reality, he appreciated his friend and couldn't help but smile.

"You're right of course. I am being an—" He broke off as he saw a little girl close to his side and changed his wording. "A really big grump, I'm just worried about him."

"I know you are. Who wouldn't be?" Devin nodded to the side, and Jason watched as the little girl walked up to them.

"Are you okay?" she asked Jason as she got closer. Jason smiled a little. Her small smile reminded him of his little brother, Korren, who had been at school today.

"I'm…" He found that he couldn't—or didn't want to lie to her. "I honestly feel sad."

She nodded slowly, her nose scrunched up. "That is not fun to feel like. But I think that's what I feel like too." She sighed. "I don't know where my brother went either, you know? I miss him. He used to play with me, but he left a week ago."

"What's his name?" He exchanged a look with Devin, figuring that it had to be one of Jace's friends.

"Kory." He looked deeply into the eyes of the young girl, and saw that he found a sadness that went deeper than his own. Tears filled his eyes.

"One of my brothers' friends." Jason smiled sadly at her. I'm going to do my best to find both of our brothers, okay?" He barely made the promise before her mom was calling her back.

"Zory, you can't just go and talk to people," her mom scolded gently, her eyes bright red like she had been crying for a while. Even though she sounded stern with Zory, she cast a grateful and hopeful look towards them.

"See there." Devin grabbed Jason's arm. "Now, that's nice." He smiled at him. "I'm happy you told her that. They both need hope."

Jason nodded, but he was too busy trying to hold back his own tears to reply.

He ignored the drafts coming from the cars to his left, his jacket blew out in front of him. The snow that had come weeks ago was now practically gone and it was fairly warm.

Well, except for the chill that continued to linger in his soul.

He looked up at the trees that towered over him and felt a small smile appear on his lips. Nature always calmed him.

"So, what is it?" Devin asked as soon as they left the buildings behind.

Jason took a deep breath, trying to calm his fears. "You'll find me insane," he told his friend truthfully.

"More than I already do?" Devin looked at him reproachfully. "Don't forget that it's me you're talking to. I'm open to a lot of things. I don't brush off everything just because the majority doesn't believe it."

"Yeah… I guess." He sat down. "My grandpa Henri, came to me a few weeks ago, when I came home. He seems to think that I needed— that I am…" He put his head onto his hands and massaged his temples. Ugh! It's much harder to say it when you don't believe it!" He could see that curiosity was bright in Devin's eyes, as well as confusion and wariness. Yet, despite all that, he stayed silent as Jason got his thoughts in order.

"He said that I was supposed to go find something, something that could save the world. I didn't believe him and brushed it off as an old man's fantasy. My brother overheard and apparently did believe, and so he went out to search for it, I guess, with his friends."

"So, he's okay? You seem too stressed for that to be all." His eyebrows rose accusingly.

"That's because Grandpa Henri said that a witness saw some kids getting captured by this guy named Darrin, who is working to get the thing that will save the world, and he…" He hesitated. "Likes to cause pain… And, according to my grandpa, has magic."

Devin blinked and took a step back.

"Magic?" his thumb moved to his lip, and he rubbed it thoughtfully. "Well, I guess it's a possibility, though not a very likely one. Where does this man live?"

"We don't know, I guess they've been trying to figure that out for a while."

"Well, Darrin has to live around here. They wouldn't go far to take some kids, right?"

"Well, we don't know that for sure, but we have no idea where Jace was when he got caught even if he wouldn't."

"Simple," Devin smirked. "Where does this witness live or where was he when they got taken?"

Jason looked at his friend, once again surprised at his insight.

"You're a genius, man." He stood up too fast and felt a wave of dizziness that almost took him to the ground.

"You need to sleep," Devin said firmly, but Jason ignored him and waited for the darkness to pass before taking a step.

"I'll sleep later. Right now, Jace needs me."

"Well, you can't really help when you're this tired," his friend reasoned.

He was right, but he chose to ignore the advice anyway. He needed to do something, and if he went to sleep... "If I sleep, I might be too late," he said, starting to walk. "Come on. We've got to go talk to Henri before he leaves."

"Jason…" Devin was close to whining. He stood up slowly. "You need to rest. I won't let you go without sleep. You've probably already gone nonstop for days."

"Yeah, since I found out," he admitted softly. "I can't sleep when I know my brother is out there, especially since it's my fault."

"It's not your fault, and you are going to sleep even if I have to hold you down till you start snoring!"

"But for now we are going to get my brother." Jason continued to walk but quickly realized that his friend was not following him. He glanced back to see Devin run his hand through his hair. He was staring up into the sky for a moment, then he ran to catch up.

Jason felt a pang of guilt. He was making his friend and family worry about his stability because he was unable to think straight without the sleep and probably looked like the walking dead. The thought made him laugh, quite hysterically, causing Devin to look at him with even deeper concern.

"I must look really insane, huh?" Jason shook his head. "Like I belong in a mental hospital? Sorry, man. You're right, I do need sleep. I just don't get how I'm going to sleep easily while he's out there going through whatever the he–" He caught the cuss word then continued, "crap that he's going through."

"Yes. You look like a zombie though, I think." Devin smiled. "You'll sleep then?"

"Soon, I'm going to ask my grandpa first."

Devin sighed. "Fine, I can live with that." He pulled Jason in the opposite direction from the one in which he was heading.

"Where are we going?"

"To my house, a car will be faster."

124

Jason nodded and allowed himself to be pulled in the direction of his friend's house. His house was luckily only two minutes away from the forest and it didn't take them long to open the front door.

"Devin! Is that you?" Jason smirked as his friend's mom entered the room, as if she couldn't wait for a response from Devin to know if it was him.

"Oh good, I need you to get—" She paused at the sight of him. "Oh. Jason. Good grief, boy, you need some sleep! I didn't recognize you! I thought that Devin must have gotten another friend!" She smiled pleasantly at him, although there was some sadness there as well. "Are you guys doing something?"

"Yeah, we are kind of in a hurry to get back to his house." Devin took a step towards the garage.

She nodded. "Okay, get going." She waved them away and turned back to the other room.

Devin blinked in surprise before opening the door. "Well, that was easier than I thought it would be." Jason hopped into the passenger seat and leaned his head on the window while Devin got in the other side.

He fought to keep his eyes open and finally relented and let them close. They'd be there in a minute anyway.

Was my brother even still alive? Would I be able to help at all?

"Jason!" He felt someone shake his shoulder and jerk him out of his thoughts, or maybe a dream. He wasn't quite sure, but he forced his eyes open and looked up to see Devin's triumphant gaze.

"So, you don't just look tired, you actually are!" He pulled away and waited for Jason to get out. "I was calling you for like a minute. I was starting to think I should let you stay sleeping while I go talk to your grandpa."

"No way." He saw Henri step out of the front door, and head for his car. "Grandpa!"

Henri's gaze whipped around until he found the source of the voice.

"Yes, Jason?" he asked as he and Devin stepped closer.

"Where was that witness when he saw Jace and his friends?"

He blinked. "Why?"

"Please? I have an idea."

"I don't know, I'll have to ask." He narrowed his eyes at them. "Do you have your cellphone, or do you need our landline?"

"It has to be now?" he asked wearily. Jason just nodded.

"Okay, let's go inside then." He turned and opened the door back up.

Jason's family wasn't downstairs, but he could hear them talking upstairs. He wondered if they had even moved since he had been here.

He sat on the couch and watched anxiously as Henri dialed the number, but within a minute he found that he could no longer hear anything. His eyes had drifted shut, his family room fading from view, the sounds of his grandpa talking becoming background before disappearing entirely.

He was in darkness but as his eyes adjusted, he started to see the outline of buildings, worn-down houses and small shops, and he was standing on broken pavement.

Where was he? How did he get here? Had he fallen asleep? He walked anxiously through the town trying to wake himself back up. He wasn't sure how long he walked, but it felt like he was trapped in this town, and he had no way to get back out.

Had he been here before? It looked familiar, but he was struggling to pinpoint where it was. He furrowed his eyebrows, surprised that it felt as though he could feel the wind on his skin.

It was too dark. But he knew these buildings. He *knew* them!

Suddenly, a light burst from one of the smaller buildings. He walked toward it slowly. Peeking in, he saw a desk and a chair. The room was empty. He sighed and started to turn away, but a small movement drew his attention back to the room.

Jason leaned closer, a palm flat on the cold surface, a cold that seemed to seep every warmth from his body, drawing him closer.

And in that moment, he saw the small form huddled on the ground.

It was—

Jerking awake, Jason sat up too quickly. He found Devin asleep on the couch next to him. It was dark out. He had slept through the rest of the day!

"Devin!" he hissed quietly, trying to wake him up, the sight of the huddled form ingrained in his mind, a form that he knew instinctively was that of his brother. "Devin!" he said a bit louder and reached over to nudge him. Devin finally sat up and rubbed his eyes.

"Dude, you were out." He slurred, mumbling and barely able

to keep his eyes open. "We tried to wake you up, but you wouldn't budge. Henri found out that his friend was in the next town over—"

"I know where he is!"

WHEN HE HIT THE GROUND, Kory jerked awake; already aching back throbbing from the fall. He looked up to see Thomas standing above him, with the usual smirk on his face. He'd obviously recovered from Hazel's attack.

He still couldn't believe that Hazel had attacked him—well, he could, but… she just seemed so gentle. He had to admit that it was freaking amazing to watch.

Before he could move—with his brain too foggy from waking up to understand what was happening—Thomas kicked his torso, causing him to automatically curl up on his side as he groaned. He squeezed his eyes shut at the onslaught of pain in his head as he was clearly kicked there as well.

And then his arms were jerked away from his torso, and the tightness from his tied wrists told him that he was suddenly getting dragged along the ground by the ropes.

His shoulders screamed at the change of movement, first from the fall, and now this.

His friends were calling for him.

As his vision cleared, he caught sight of his friends, each of them frantic, trying to get to him, though their movements were futile as they swung on the ropes.

Then Kory was dragged out of the room they'd pretty much lived in the last couple days. Days? How long had it been? Now he was in the neighboring room, that looked sort of like a dining room. He could see a table and chairs, but not much else from the floor. He wondered what else was in the room with him.

The *who else* was more concerning.

He looked up at Thomas, then over to the other two people in the room, trying not to cower at their feet, though he was sure he looked pathetic. One was Bryan, the other was a girl that looked like she might have still been in high school, maybe just a bit older than Kory. She had red-ish brown hair, and she shot him a glance that Kory could only describe as thoughtful. Not mean, not necessarily sympathetic, just thoughtful.

The two men backed away slightly and the girl came closer. She had a syringe in her hand. A second later, she pushed it into his arm despite his squirming, and he felt a cold liquid entering his veins, slowly spreading up his arm.

She leaned in closer to his ear as she pulled the needle back out of his skin. He shivered at the chill of the liquid, wondering what he'd just been given, but his eyes caught hers, and he was surprised when she stared at him with her intense gaze, seeming as though she wanted to tell him something.

He couldn't speak, and as he laid there, he felt his strength draining from his body. He couldn't do anything but watch her.

His chest tightened, breath turning shallow, and his gaze blurred before darkening. A sudden pressure in his pocket grabbed his attention as the voices became muffled, and he saw the girl moving her hand away after having slipped something in his jeans.

He couldn't…couldn't breathe. Couldn't move. His mind was screaming in alarm, but he was fading, and he couldn't do *anything*.

The darkness quickly found him.

₪ ₪ ₪

Hazel fruitlessly tugged on her ropes, but this time the ropes and the winch above both refused to give her any leeway. She wasn't strong enough, even with determination. Not anymore, and she figured the tiny bit of food and water they were given had weakened her already.

Biting back a sob, she did her best to turn where she hung to see the door behind her that they'd taken Kory through. Their friend hadn't awoken when Thomas had come in, and she hadn't tried to wake him. That had been a mistake. He had been so tired, plus he usually was the deepest sleeper out of all of them, so it didn't surprise her to find that he hadn't woken up right away, and she would have felt terrible about waking him up just because the men were back. But because she hadn't, Kory hadn't been able to prepare himself for any form of attack.

Philips was also staring toward the door they exited before turning to Hazel and Lisa, his expression worried.

"What did we get ourselves into?" he asked them quietly. Before either of them could respond the door opened again, and Thomas and Bryan entered, surprising her at how short of a time they were gone. Bryan was holding Kory like a sack of potatoes, and he let him drop to the ground in front of them. Hazel swallowed heavily, trying to assess what was wrong.

Kory had fallen to his side, his face pale, his arm falling across his chest limply. He hadn't reacted when Bryan dropped him or to Thomas's kick. He just rolled over from the push.

Hazel's lip trembled as she realized what was wrong. He had to be dead. What else could it be?

"Kory…" Philips murmured his name quietly, tears forming in his eyes.

"Are you ready to talk?" When none of them answered, Thomas just rolled his eyes. "Not yet then? Well, when you're ready I'll be here." He tied Kory's hands to something sticking out of the ground before leaving again.

"He's dead…" Hazel closed her eyes tightly, turning her head away from them. Intense sorrow washed over her, and she forced herself to take a deep breath.

"Hazel?" Lisa's voice was soft, but Hazel didn't answer. "Hazel?" Hearing a slight surprise in her friend's voice, Hazel opened her eyes.

"What?"

"Do you want to tell me why they'd tie his hands up if he was dead?" Lisa was studying Kory closely, as if trying to see something and Hazel realized that she was right. Why would he do that?

She also turned her attention to Kory, looking for a sign that he was okay. She watched him and grew increasingly worried when he didn't breathe for another ten seconds. When he finally did inhale, his breath was so shallow that she could barely hear anything, but it was enough to reassure her that he was okay. Alive. For now.

She gave a soft sigh, watching as, seconds later, his arm muscles gave a small twitch. As relieved as she was that he was alive, there was a part of her that realized that it would be a lot easier if these men would just get it over with and kill them. The end result was going to be the same anyway, and this way there would be a lot less suffering first.

No. I am escaping, with all my friends. She took a firm determined breath.

Kory was bleeding from the curve of the elbow, as if they had stuck him with a needle.

Lisa jerked on her rope, struggling to get down, and Hazel followed her movement, noticing that Philips also tried.

After another few minutes Lisa finally got her winch unraveling again. She landed on her knees then scrambled back to her feet and moved over to Kory, just barely able to reach him.

"Kory, please wake up." She put her ear to his chest, her arms twisted across her body by the rope.

Hazel finally broke her restraints, but she couldn't get close to Kory. Instead, she stayed about five feet away. Philips was next to her.

Lisa rested her head on his chest, letting out a sigh. "I think he was drugged."

"Do you have any idea with what?"

She shook her head, "There are only a few drugs that I know of, so I can't be sure."

They continued to watch Kory through the day, scared that each preceding breath would be his last. It was probably about five hours from when he'd first come in when his leg finally jerked up, his knee bending slightly closer.

"Kory?" Lisa followed her gaze back toward him. She seemed a bit more hopeful. Kory didn't respond, but Hazel saw his eyelids flicker as if he was trying to wake back up.

Philips turned toward him as well, his eyes studying him as if to find out how he could help.

His breathing became a bit deeper and his eyelids flickered again. After another few minutes his eyes opened. They were dark and distant, as if he wasn't sure where he was.

Philips swore. "Kory, are you okay?"

His mouth opened as if to respond but nothing came out at first. He tried pulling his hands up, but the rope just caught it. He stared at it and his confusion slowly melted away into recognition and sorrow.

"Kory?" His gaze came back to them, and he opened his mouth, taking a long few moments before words actually came out.

"Lisa?" His eyes closed tightly, laying his head back on the ground. "I thought I was dead."

"So did I." Lisa's voice caught in her throat. Hazel's jaw was shaking. She was sure that if she could feel her hands they'd be shaking as well.

Lisa sat up a bit more, trying to get closer and Kory opened his eyes again.

"What happened?" Hazel asked.

Kory's gaze was still shadowed and confused as he shook his head. Could he not remember?

"How are you feeling?" Hazel asked again.

"Tired."

She tried the first question again. "What happened?"

"They put something in my arm." His breath hitched. "I wish I had my inhaler."

"Do you know what he put in you?"

He just shook his head again with a sigh. His breathing sounded painful, and Hazel couldn't help but wish that he had his inhaler too. His gaze, though dark, searched the room almost frantically, then, looking worried, he sat up and tried reaching into his pockets. He could barely get his hand in with his wrists tied.

"Kory?" Hazel narrowed her eyes.

He looked up at them with wide eyes. Before he could say anything, a young lady stepped in, looked at Kory, then at the others.

"Are you ready?"

Kory's pulled his hands out of his pockets and scooted away from the girl, a flash of panic going through his still wide eyes. But before anyone could speak, an object came clattering out of his pocket from him removing his hand.

They all looked down at it before looking back at her in disbelief.

Chapter Thirteen

JACE'S JAW WAS ACHING from how hard he was clenching, teeth grinding as he fought back tears that wanted to rip out of his aching body. He was missing time. He wasn't sure when Darrin had come back in the room, and to see the man just standing at the countertop, mixing a new batch of something for Jace, so casually, so…

This man didn't care. He didn't care that he was hurting people. Didn't care that even the people working for him felt trapped. He only wanted the information that he believed Jace had.

And Jace didn't have it. That was the real kicker. The knowledge he had came from what Isaac had told him and what he'd overheard from Henri, and that wasn't much. He couldn't tell Darrin where the Power was when he had no information.

His foot was throbbing again, unfurling from there and spreading up his leg and into the rest of his body, and it made him want to sob, to curl in a ball, and to have his mom or dad there to run their fingers through his hair. He remembered them doing that when he was sick as a kid.

The distance he felt from them now hadn't really started until he was in his teens, and he was never sure what had changed. Had he done something wrong? He wasn't rebellious. He didn't think he would have said or done something to make them suddenly hate him.

But he didn't care at this point that his parents had been withdrawn for years. He wanted them more than anything else at the moment. He wanted them and his friends.

If only he could know that his friends were okay.

He blinked, and somehow Darrin was in front of him again, crouching, looking as though he'd been talking. The darkness and curiosity in his eyes, the interest and nonchalance of this whole ordeal, and the pain, fear, and weakness washed through him; it all rose to a boiling point in his mind.

He didn't want to cry in front of this man, so words came out instead.

"What do you expect to get out of me anyway?" Jace snapped, glaring at his captor. "Obviously you hate that I won't say anything, but really what do you think the Power is going to do if you try to find it anyway? Maybe the Power doesn't even want to be found by you, have you thought of that?

"And how is torturing a whole bunch of High School students going to help you find the thing? You could have spent all this time looking for it instead of trying to get something from us! You're psychotic!" He could see that Darrin was going to interrupt. He had anger boiling brightly in his eyes. He looked like an eagle eyeing its prey.

Frantic, Jace's words rushed out before the man could speak, a tremor having taken deep root inside him.

"It's not like I even have anything useful for you anyway! I'm just a freaking kid. I wasn't even the one chosen for this quest in the first place, you know? My uncle didn't come to me with it, I just overheard the man. I was an idiot to believe that I could accomplish what nobody else has been able to do yet." He looked down at his lap to hide the tears in his eyes.

It was hard to fight back sobs, feeling broken but still determined enough not to cry in front of his captor. The lump was large in his throat, and he swallowed it back with much effort.

It wasn't until he managed to blink back the blur in his eyes and finally look up that he caught sight of the anger in Darrin's gaze.

In fact, it wasn't anger anymore. It was rage; and it was ready to overflow. Jace was honestly relieved; he had been anxious to know to what lengths Darrin would go to retrieve information, and now that he knew Jace had no answers, then maybe they could get this over with. Unless the man didn't believe that he knew nothing.

Jace frowned as he caught sight of the empty syringe for the first time that lay beside his foot. It hadn't even been his own bravado or annoyance that made him so bold to speak his mind. It was the liquid. He hadn't even noticed Darrin emptying the syringe into his foot, his mind having been much too blank for most of this morning.

134

The torture was getting to him. There wasn't a part of him that didn't ache, not a part inside that didn't want to end this quickly.

But now Jace recognized the fading feeling of the liquid that Darrin had used was the one that made him want to talk. And it had worked. Everything Jace had been worried about had spilled out, and he wondered if the man would just kill them all now because Jace had broken and admitted that none of them knew anything significant.

If he'd just signed his friends' deaths by his words, he would never forgive himself.

Jace felt something probing at his mind. It reminded him of an oncoming headache, although about a thousand times more intense. He looked over at Darrin and found him glaring back at him. The pain intensified, as though fingers were twisting his brain, and he shifted to his knees in a desperate attempt to shield from more pain.

You want to know what I can do? Jace thought he heard it in his head, but he wasn't so sure; Darrin might have said it out loud. He vaguely recognized that there was water dripping down his face: tears and probably sweat, as the pain built up in his head. It continued to envelop him until he was sure that he was going to die; it swelled down his neck, then deep into his chest and back, until it seemed to envelop his entire body.

Darrin is doing this to me! He felt a brief flash of anger at the realization, but it quickly settled into a weak resignation. He didn't know how long he sat there, but sometime while he was still crouching, the door had shut, signaling that Darrin had left. The pain did not.

When had the man given him another liquid? Had he spaced out again? Why was this one so bad?

Minutes—or maybe it was only a few seconds—later, he was finally able to breathe through the pain and nearly whined as he looked up. The room was dark except for the sunlight filtering through the blinds of the single window in the room; the angle of which told him the day was almost over.

He grimaced as he sat up; a sharp tingling traveled down his spine, like when his arm would fall asleep and it would take a while to wake back up. He groaned, pressing his hand to his head as he tried to blink away the dizziness that surrounded him like dark fog.

What did he do to me? For the first time since he had been here, he felt a real, absolutely paralyzing fear slide into place where it should have been a long time ago; he was unable to detect what was wrong with him. His muscles were weak, barely able to hold himself up; his head blazed, and as hard as he tried, he could not blink back the tears that were welling in his eyes.

Idiot, you just had to talk. He braced himself against the wall to keep himself sitting up. He gasped in another breath, pulling his hand to his chest as if urging it to hold onto the breath that had been robbed of him. It was as if a giant fist was squeezing his chest, not allowing him to breathe in deeply or move freely.

He squinted as he lifted his head, finding himself alone. Not even Michael was hiding in the corner of the room at the moment.

His attention caught on some movement out the window, but if there had been, it was gone by the time he looked over. He focused his attention on trying to find the unknown source of pain, hoping Darrin would not go to his friends and harm them. As far as he knew, they were left alone by Darrin's hands, but now that Jace had said all that, he wasn't sure if that would still be the case.

"Help me… please help me..." He could not stop the pleading coming from his mouth, even though he knew no one was going to come. His head was pounding too much to concentrate on anything but the pain. His eyes closed against his own will, and he wanted to curl back up into a ball. Instead he brought his good leg up to his chest the best he could, grimacing at the shifted weight onto his infected leg.

And in one brief moment, he felt a moment of serenity, of peace.

He was going to die, he knew it; he could feel it. He wondered if it had been Darrin's intention to kill him.

Whenever he'd read books where the character died, they explained that right before death they had peace, much like he was having. *It's definitely not one of those fast or easy deaths* he thought wearily as, once again, he tried to push away the pain. He did not want to die without finishing the quest, or without being able to go home once more, but it hurt so bad!

Jace pushed past the anguish and opened his eyes. He was surprised to see that it was darker now, much darker than before. *I must have passed out...* He did not remember the rest of the day and now the moon was clearly up.

Even with his nap he did not feel any stronger. If anything, he felt, in some ways, worse off: more physically and mentally exhausted, even if the pounding in his head had lessened slightly. He was a little surprised to feel vivid sadness emerging beyond the pain. He was upset that he wouldn't be able to help his friends and see his family again. What would happen to everyone else?

He heard a loud noise and turned his head toward the door where it had sounded from, persuading himself to at least try to get up as panic speared through him. He hadn't cared to move much before, but he couldn't imagine letting Darrin come near him again, even if he couldn't do anything to stop it. If only he could run.

He grasped the pole, using it as he pulled himself up. He was shaking from the effort when he heard someone fumbling for the door handle. He sighed heavily. He couldn't face Darrin right now, sure that if he did, he would say something more that he'd regret later. He was too weak. He just couldn't do it anymore.

He leaned heavily against the pole, resting his head on his supporting arm. Light flooded the room, surprising him. It had seemed dark for so long, and it was only in that moment that he realized that Darrin had never really used any lights when he came in, just whatever dim hue that came through the blinds during the day.

He blinked down at the ground, eyes squinting.

"Jace!" Surprised to hear a voice that was not Darrin's, he racked his tired brain for whomever it belonged to.

Hazel? What is she doing here? He tried to lift his head to look at her but had to grab the pole to keep from falling over. He heard footsteps and realized it wasn't just Hazel who had arrived. All his friends had come. A second later, many hands grasped his arms, and the connection to them was grounding in a way that surprised him.

"What did he do?"

The quiet voice held astonishment and deep worry. This time it was Philips; it was also Philips who had grabbed his right arm. Jace forced himself to look up at his friend's face. Philips was worried and Jace noticed the bruising around his left eye. There were probably other bruised places that he could not see. It was painful to keep his eyes open.

"How did you get out?" Jace forced the words out of his mouth.

"We'll talk later. We need to get out of here *right now,*" Kory's voice broke in before Philips could respond. Kory had started untying the rope around Jace's wrists.

The last of his strength drained slowly from his body.

"You guys go. I can't," Jace said as he leaned his back against the pole and continued to struggle. His breath that had still not received its normal rhythm.

"We won't leave you!" Hazel said indignantly, grabbing his arm. "We have to go, and you have to come with us!"

Jace shook his head tiredly and gripped the pole tighter as another wave of dizziness swept through him. He saw Philips exchange a look with Kory before his eyes closed.

A second later the hands that were gripping his arms shifted, sliding under his shoulders on each side.

"Okay, let's go then," Hazel said. He opened his eyes. Hazel was smiling at him, though she quickly turned away, ignoring his weak protest about staying behind. Hazel signaled for him to be quiet as she turned toward the open door.

There was a loud, clattering noise down the hall and Jace winced as the sound echoed in his ears.

"That would be our distraction," Kory whispered in his ear, humor palpable in his voice. Being out in the hallway, Jace found his energy returning slightly. He pushed away from Kory and Philips determined not to have them carry him. As he did so, the pain in his leg flared up again.

"Dude, you're—" Jace shook his head sharply, interrupting whatever Lisa was going to say.

"I'm okay." It did not ring true to even his own ears and he could tell that he had not convinced Lisa—or any of his friends—either, but she didn't object as Hazel led the way down the hall. She glanced warily down the next split before making her decision to turn left. He tried his hardest not to limp, because he didn't want Lisa to question him quite yet about the red veins that went up and down his leg, or his side.

"Someone took pity on us and helped us out," Lisa explained quietly as she fell into step beside him, Hazel kept a slow pace probably because of him and the fact they needed to stay quiet. "She was the one who caused the distraction. She said she would try to make it look like an accident, and hopefully she succeeded."

He nodded in reply, grasping the wall as Hazel stopped at another fork. He took a deep breath. Though they were not moving fast, Jace still found it impossible to breathe.

Lisa gave him a worried glance before turning her attention back to following Hazel quietly. They took a right.

He was surprised at how easily Hazel was able to navigate through the halls, confident enough with choosing the turns, even though she was cautious before she rounded the corners.

Jace let his eyes flick around his friends, noticing the bruises and blood encircling every one of his friends' wrists, the visible abuse that each of them had taken. By the way they each moved—limping or holding ribs—he knew there was a lot more hidden under clothes.

Lisa looked back at him, and suddenly the hall went dark, the footsteps stopped, and the distant noises were gone.

Jace stood in the hallway not daring to move in case he ran into someone or something. They stood in a silence that seemed to encroach deep into his soul, and he vaguely heard his friends shuffle closer so he was definitely touching a few of them.

So when the sudden whispers, almost like a rush of wind, and completely undistinguishable to his ears, started, he jumped, shoulders tensing even further. Kory's hand pulled away sharply from his shoulder before gently laying back on his arm. When had he gotten there?

"Are you okay, Jace?" Kory's voice was louder than the whispering, even as his friend clearly tried to keep it down.

Jace didn't bother answering. A cold presence slithered down his spine, and Kory's hand tightened on his arm as he pushed closer, clearly feeling it too. He jerked forward, pulling away from the darkness behind him and running into a solid body as he did so.

A sharp yelp from Lisa echoed in the hall. He rushed to grab her before she hit the floor.

"Sorry," the words came, though he was not paying attention to her anymore. His thoughts were once again on the all-encompassing whispers that seemed to surround him.

"Did you hear that?" he asked, frightened of the sounds that crashed through his head. He honestly couldn't tell if he was hearing the whispers, or if they were coming from somewhere deep inside him.

"Hear what?" Kory snapped. At the confirmation that he was the only one hearing them, he swallowed hard and strained his ears to listen to the whispering voices.

They seemed to be warning him, the tones panicked more than threatening, as though trying to keep him from the edge of a dark chasm. He felt as though he was looking into the chasm, a vertigo washing through his head, his legs jelly.

And then a louder whisper spoke over the top of the others, in

Darrin's voice:

Run, run, run as fast as you can… I will find you my dear man. Far, far, far you could go, I'll still see you, you'll still show, his voice taunted in a singsong tone; a deep growl fading into the deepness of the dark.

Jace couldn't help taking a few steps backward as violent tremors chilled down his spine or the steps that he took backwards until his back was against the wall.

I am here… You will not make it far… The darkness takes your freedom away… Please help us… Run away… the voices spoke over each other, Darrin's having faded, but bringing others to the forefront.

The onslaught had him cowering; he pressed his hands over his ears and bent forward to let himself slip to the ground. Anything… he had to—he was frantic for the voices and Darrin's laughter to *stop*.

Then all the voices stopped, but one. Darrin's. *Go, and I will find you and your pitiful friends.*

"Jace!" Philips pulled on his arm before he could make it to the ground, breaking him out of his trance. Philips had found a phone, who knows from where, and was using it as a light, though it only lit up a small area. He wondered if they had called for help, or if there was no service in the building.

A sharp sound like a switch went off to the right of him and a second later Philips' phone light went out as well.

"Crap!" Once the light was off, the voices started again, and the dark presence returned. He felt it inside him, but this time he swore he could see a silhouette, an area in the dark corridor that was even more shadowed than the rest…

He watched as darkness coalesced behind Philips, growing large as though about to pounce on him, and Jace jumped toward his friend, shoving him out of the way of its blow a second later. A sharp slice on his cheek startled him as they both fell to the floor. He hadn't been fully expecting the shadow to actually be tangible, but of course, why shouldn't this whole thing become even crazier than it already was?

He breathed shallow and quick.

"Jace, are you out of your mind?!" Philips pushed Jace off angrily, and Jace could hear the thread of panic in his voice.

"Maybe so." His reply was soft, barely there, and he was once again scanning the darkness for any movement, eyes flicking quickly, breathing still unsteady.

"Are you okay?" Hazel's voice cut through the tension. Jace was unsure if she was talking to him or Philips, so he didn't answer. Honestly, he doubted he could answer.

What was happening?

Philips obviously didn't care who the question was for. "No. I am not. He tackled me to the ground. I did not really care to hit the floor today. If I did, I would have kept walking—"

"Shh!" Jace snapped as he heard another sound.

"No! You have–"

"Shut up!" Jace's demand came out sounding like a plea, but it finally shut Philips up.

He sensed the dark company behind him—a slight movement of the air, or maybe a sound, or maybe it was just the sweat dripping down his back. He started to turn, but and arm wrapped around his waist and pulled him against something solid. One hand clamped on his mouth as he tried to scream in pain and fear, his infection growing up his side aching at the touch.

The arm tightened as he began to squirm.

He heard the others call out in a panic, scrambling to figure out what was happening.

Then the light flipped on.

Jace couldn't see who was holding him, but Darrin's voice was a dead giveaway. "That was quite fun. The most fun I've had in ages, actually. I especially love how you used the girl to do your dirty work." As he spoke, he gestured to the side. Two guards came forward, dragging a girl barely older than Jace in between them. Her red hair was in a messy ponytail and her eyes held fear.

"I'm sorry, please forgive me," she begged, trying to get free as she pleaded with the same man that held Jace's life in his hands, literally.

"Kill her," Darrin told the guards severely. Though she tried harder to get away, it was useless, just as it had been for Jace.

"No!" Kory tried to jump forward but Hazel and Philips held him back.

Darrin continued to ignore the girl's pleadings, and Jace felt the horror rise in his gut, threatening to make him puke, as he watched the knife poke through the front of her gut. The man behind her was impassive as he dropped her, knife sliding back out of her body as she fell to the ground; struggling for breath, blood seeping through her shirt, and eyes darting between Jace and his friends frantically.

Jace swallowed hard as her struggles slowed and finally faded. The man dropped the dagger, letting it fall back to her now lifeless body, his expression indifferent… a strange darkness in his eyes, as though he'd lost all care.

Jeez… he was going to puke. Seeing a dead body in Isaac's friend's house had been hard enough, but seeing someone killed in front of you was something else entirely. He couldn't help the tremors that ran through him, making his legs quake.

"You know, Jace you're just like your grandfather. Defiant to the end—except you broke." Darrin started next to his ear. "Of course I missed it in my anger, if I'd just been patient I could have forced the rest of the truth out of you. Because even if I believe that you don't know exactly where the Power is, I know you would have the information from Henri and Isaac. I just needed to keep you talking, because you finally were getting to information that I could have used."

Jace couldn't look at his friends, knowing that they knew how weak he'd been.

"Unfortunately, I was so used to you opposing me that I was not expecting to get results. So," he paused, pulling Jace tighter and moving his head up so he had to look at his friends. "Are you going to tell me what your grandpa told you about where the Power is? Or will you watch your friends die in front of you?"

"Don't do it, Jace!" Philips took a step closer, only to be pulled back by Michael who had gotten behind him. Philips was struggling against the grip, while another man approached his friend wielding a knife. Michael opened his mouth, pulling Philips back further as though to protest, and Jace tried to pull out to get to his friend as well, but could only watch as the other man grabbed his friend by the shirt, pulling him from Michael, and pushed him into the wall, the knife slicing into his arm.

"Philips!" Hazel's scream was almost washed out by Philips's own. His eyes squeezed shut and he took a breath that shuddered, as though he was trying hard not to cry.

"Let's see how talkative you are when your friends die." Darrin pulled his hand away from Jace, pointing it toward his friend, and Jace felt that darkness once again as Darrin merely flicked his finger and Kory was suddenly thrown against the wall. A sharp gasp

142

of pain escaped his mouth.

And Jace *froze* as he finally understood what he'd been missing this whole time. Magic. *But that's impossible, there's no such thing as magic.* The logical side of his brain lost the argument because *this* was obviously magic. And it made sense now. The attack against his mind and body in the room earlier hadn't been from another liquid, it had been this magic, the darkness that seemed to radiate from the man in his most terrifying moments.

Michael and one other man grabbed Lisa and Hazel, pulling them away from their friends. When he redoubled his efforts to get out of Darrin's tight grip, it seemed the man had enough, as he shoved Jace toward the guards. Jace landed a short distance away from the guards and struggled to his feet. Before they could reach him, he started running towards Kory— who looked as though he was choking on air.

Out of the corner of his eye, Jace saw Darrin make a slashing motion with his hand and he himself was jerked back by nothing, towards the waiting guards. The pain from the invisible force surprised him, but he ignored the blood that trickled from his nose as he was once again held tightly.

His mind went numb, his fingertips tingling, and he felt coldness flood through his veins. He'd failed the mission, but more than that, he was about to lose his friends. They had been so close to getting free. They should have just *left him.* They might have been able to get away if he hadn't slowed them down.

In the numbness, he was startled at the wetness against his cheeks. Tears flowed slowly down as he watched his friends struggle, but his body was too numb to pull away from the guards. He clenched his hands as desperation flooded his mind. He was angry—at himself, for getting his friends into this mess. At Darrin and these other men.

This quest was going to get them killed!

Kory struggled more frantically, completely uncoordinated, his nails scratching at his neck, lips starting to turn blue, his face losing color, and his eyes panicked as they flicked around the room.

Jace was horrified to watch as his hands slowly lost strength and fell to his sides, eyes starting to droop.

No! This can't happen!

Suddenly a loud bang reverberated through the room. Heat flashed through his body, causing him to flinch.

Kory fell to the floor, finally loosed from whatever unseen

force held him to the wall.
All was dark.

Chapter Fourteen

HAZEL STOOD THERE IN shock for what was probably too long, staring in at Jace who had fallen to the floor along with everyone on the side of the room. Magic. Darrin had clearly been using magic against her friends.

But it wasn't just Darrin who had magic. Jace did as well. Before everyone fell to the floor, including her friends, he'd flashed a bright white light, momentarily blinding them all. When she'd been able to blink back the afterimage, she'd found the whole other side of the room unconscious.

When? How long? Has he always had it? Did he know?
Did that really happen?

Finally snapping out of her shock as she watched Jace's chest rise as he breathed, she pulled away from Thomas who was staring at Jace in surprise as well.

She wanted to go to Jace first, to make sure he was okay, but she forced herself to check on Kory who had fallen to the ground on his side. Her friend had been close to suffocating to death, and she had to make sure that Darrin's magic hadn't succeed in killing him.

Hazel had been panicking since they started their escape, but her anxiety rolled in her gut as Kory didn't budge.

But right as she crouched next to him, Kory shifted weakly, stumbling to his hands and knees as he started coughing and gasping for breath, face still far too pale and blue for her liking. She sighed in relief and put a grounding hand on his shoulder as he kept struggling, willing strength to her friend.

As soon as Lisa saw Hazel make her way to Kory, she had rushed over to Philips to attempt to stop the blood flow seeping from the wound in his arm. Relieved to know that two of her friends were being cared for, she turned her attention to Kory, recognizing his scrambling movements for what they were, an attempt to find his inhaler from his pockets while trying not to fall over.

But Kory didn't have it on him anymore. Thomas had taken it.

Hazel looked toward Thomas with a determined expression "Please…" Hazel begged him, swallowing heavily, not knowing how to plead with her captors to help save her friends life. She felt like she would have better luck fighting it off the man.

But she was surprised when he merely pulled it out of his pocket and passed it to her. She caught it and held it up to Kory's mouth feeling him take a deep breath in before grabbing it from Hazel's hand, his eyes closing in obvious relief, and body relaxing from the crouched position, into something more like a fetal position on the ground now that he didn't feel like he was dying.

The man that had been holding Philips walked slowly over to Jace and Hazel quickly rose to her feet, Kory's hand slipping from her arm as she did so.

"Leave him alone!"

The man was crouching over Jace by the time she'd taken even two steps, having ignored her yell.

"He's alive," the man informed them, glancing at Hazel softly. She was bewildered to see some sort of kindness in his eyes. "You guys have to leave now, before everyone wakes up."

"What are you doing, Michael?!" Thomas stepped towards him. "If we let them go, he'll kill us!"

"What else do you suggest, Thomas?" Michael said back.

Hazel watched them warily, unsure if she should trust this man named Michael.

Michael looked back at her and said: "You need to help him now or he won't survive." He paused and closed his eyes, as though still in debate about whether he should say something or not.

"You need to take him to Henri," Thomas interjected forcefully. Hazel blinked a few times at how willing they seemingly were to help, but unsure of how these two seemed to know Jace's uncle.

Hazel wasn't the only one surprised. Michael had a look of astonishment as he looked at him. She stepped closer to Jace slowly, then stopped as she noticed something for the first time. His arm showed lines of bright red, traveling up it like vines. They reached about halfway to his elbow.

"What happened?" She crouched and instantly traced a line with her finger.

"It's not what happened. It's what's happening." Michael shook his head and pulled Jace up. She scrambled to her feet as well, keeping hold of her friend to slip under his arm. "You need to get him to Henri, or those things will kill him." Kory's hacking had calmed down while they were talking, and now he was rubbing his neck like it was still painful as he made his way to his feet and over to them, slipping under Jace's other side and forcing Michael away.

"Why are you helping us?" Kory asked. His voice was rough.

"Because I do not like what Darrin has been doing." Michael didn't elaborate, instead he turned away and walked quickly back down the hallway, Thomas following after a quick, nervous look at them.

"Well, that was strange," Lisa said, eyeing Jace's leg. Hazel looked down and realized that the red veins also spread to his right foot. In fact, it looked worse there, and she wondered if that's where they originated from.

"Let's go," Philips said, looking over Darrin and the other people who lay on the ground. "Before they wake up."

Hazel nodded and adjusted her grip on Jace, trying to ignore the dread she felt as she saw the marks crawling slowly up his arm. She vaguely realized where she was going, her mind wandered like her feet; she hoped they were leading her somewhere good.

Minutes later, she'd pushed open a door and was breathing a sigh of relief. The moon was above them in the sky. She didn't think she could miss something so simple so much.

And it was as they all got out the door that she felt Jace move. She looked into his eyes as they opened.

"Jace, are you okay?" He managed to place a foot underneath him and took his arms off both of their shoulders, though his eyes widened as he caught sight of the markings that went almost to his elbow.

"How long have I been out?" he asked in confusion, then anxiously looked around until he met Kory's gaze, sighing in relief. "You're okay." He then scanned his eyes over the rest of them, as though making sure they were all there and accounting for injuries.

"You've been out about ten minutes." Hazel caught him as his foot gave out, none of them having moved far from him.

"The marks grew that fast?" He sounded worried, and she understood why. It would be more than a little nerve-racking to have marks all down your arms—even worse, marks that could grow and kill.

"What happened to you?" Lisa asked from behind them.

Jace hesitated. "I don't know." He averted his gaze from theirs, seeming uncomfortable with this topic. Obviously, he knew more than he was letting on.

He changed topics: "How did we get out?" He pushed away from Hazel, wincing as he took a step onto his right foot.

"You... You don't know?" Hazel shook her head. "Of course you don't, you passed out." She stepped in front of him. "Jace. You used magic."

"Excuse me?" He coughed lightly. "I don't have magic. I couldn't have done anything."

"And you would know? You passed out, remember? I was watching. You flashed white and everyone behind you and to the side of you collapsed along with you. I don't know what you did, but it was definitely you." She turned with him so they could continue to walk, interrupting him as he opened his mouth to protest. "Don't argue. Right now, we need to be going."

"Wait." Jace limped even after Kory slipped under his other side again. "You said to the side and behind. What happened with the ones that were holding you?"

"Oh, they helped us get out. They also said we need to get you to Henri fast, or those markings will kill you," she said bluntly, with far less emotion than she was feeling.

"Well... we will never get there in time," he said as he glanced down at his arm. She followed his gaze, and he continued. "Not with how fast it's spreading and how slow we are moving."

"Where are we?" Philips asked quietly.

"At the abandoned city, it's about a half hour drive to here." Jace looked at them. "And there are never many people on the road." Hazel felt her hope disappear but she refused to relinquish full hold on it.

"Then we'd better hurry, and hope."

₪   ₪   ₪

148

As soon as Devin stopped, Jason got out of the truck, feeling a chill that had nothing to do with the evening breeze. He'd only come here twice, once with friends, and once with his brother. This town had been abandoned for years due to unexplained weather phenomena that had damaged the buildings significantly. In recent years it had been a little better, but nobody had the courage to move back yet. Other than this kidnapper, apparently.

He had to admit, it was probably a wonderful place to disappear. Everyone was terrified of being here, and only daredevils or idiot teenagers—like Jason himself had been—even visited anymore.

"Ready?" Devin asked as his friend got out of the driver's door, also eyeing the building around them cautiously, but he could see the determined set to his shoulders that matched Jason's.

Jason was about to answer, but instead his eyes narrowed at a flash of movement from behind his friend, near the bed of the truck. He took a step closer to the back, peering into the darkness.

"Hi." A face appeared right behind Devin. Devin gasped and, startled, spun to face the man, pushing him back a few feet instinctively.

"What the crap?!" Devin put his hand to his chest. Jason burst out laughing at the response, even as he kept an eye on the random man. "You scared the crap out of me. Who the freak are you?"

"Oh, sorry, name's Robert – though *you* get to call me Rob." He pointed over his shoulder to the truck. "I was sleeping in the back, I hope you don't mind." Rob looked like he'd just come out of a dumpster. His clothes were dull and tattered in various places, his hair long and shaggy.

Despite his forlorn appearance he wore a grin. "Who are you?"

Devin – who was still breathing heavily – did not answer so Jason stepped in for him, feeling a little cautious, but mostly amused that it seemed that they had attracted a homeless man.

"I'm Jason. The one you just about scared to death is Devin."

"Sorry 'bout your heart man." Rob grabbed Devin's hand and shook it a little too vigorously. Then he turned towards Jason with the same smile and took his hand as well. "What are you doing here?" He looked around the dark buildings with curiosity.

"Getting my brother," Jason answered softly. "You can stay

here, or you can keep up with us." At that, Jason turned around to sprint down the alley, not looking back to see if they were following him, though in moments he heard footsteps to show that at least one of them was.

His legs cramped up as he slowed to a stop. Which direction had he traveled in his dream?

Looking over his shoulder he was relieved that both Devin and Rob had followed him. Even though he and Devin were breathing heavily the new man wasn't even winded. He didn't know this Rob, but he felt safer with another set of hands, just in case. They hadn't wanted to contact the police because Jason wasn't entirely sure if his dream was a fluke, or a memory, or a miracle, and if it would even be accurate.

"So, where's your brother?" Rob asked, hopping from one foot to the other.

"I don't know…" Jason looked around anxiously.

"Then how are you supposed to find him?"

He heard a noise and spun around—he couldn't see anything in the darkness, but still, someone was there...

"Jason?"

Jason startled at his name, but the voice had come from the same direction he was peering into, and he saw one of Jace's friends step out of the shadows of the alley—Kory, if he was remembering correctly. Relief shot through him to know that the little girl's brother was okay.

"Kory! How are you?" Jason took a step closer to him.

"Fine, but…" Kory hesitated. Jason didn't like the hesitation. Kory looked back behind him, where Jason couldn't see. "It's fine. It's Jason, guys." He lowered his voice—his obviously hoarse voice—now turning back to talk to Jason. "How did you find us?"

"We'll talk later," Jason told him, not really wanting to explain that he'd had a dream. It sounded a bit insane now that it had turned out to be true and not just a desperate hope.

"Okay." Kory rubbed his neck and Jason could see the bright red swelling that was slowly bruising his neck. His other hand was holding a small object—an inhaler. He held it tightly as if worried that it would be torn from him.

"Jason?" Jace stepped—limped—out from behind Kory, and Jason stared at him for a second, hardly believing that his brother was

150

really there. He ran up to him and pulled him into a tight hug.

"Are you okay?" He pulled away slightly, studying Jace's eyes desperately, searching for answers. He frowned when he realized that the whites of his brother's eyes were practically scarlet red. Dried blood stained his brother's face, some from his nose, some from a cut on his cheek; a lot had dripped down from a gash in his head, traveling down his neck. His skin was practically stained red.

"I'm fine," Jace said quietly, looking away from his eyes and drawing his arm behind his back. Jason had a better look at the gash on the side of his brother's head. It looked deep.

"No, he's not. Don't listen to him." Jason turned to see Philips emerge from the shadows. Lisa and Hazel came out to the side. Jason nearly cried at how beat up they all were, an anger at the people that caused their pain rushing through him. They all had marks around their wrists and bruises lacing their bodies; Philips had dried blood down his left arm coming from a ripped part of his shirt that was wrapped around like a bandage.

None of them were 'fine.'

"Jace needs to get to Henri, or he will die," Philips said, nodding to Jace, eyes firm. "Show him." Jace's gaze hardened, and he turned away, taking a step back into the darkness.

"Jace?" Jason tried to see what was bothering him, but in the shadows he couldn't see much. "What is it?"

"Jace! He's going to find out either way!" Hazel's voice came in forcefully, "We need to be going!"

Jason's dread grew as his brother continued to stare at the ground. Then he finally sighed heavily, and stepped closer to Jason, pulling his arm back out from behind his back. Jason gasped at the sight of the pattern that laced his arm.

"What happened?" Rob asked from behind.

"Can we go right now, explain on the way?" Lisa turned toward him.

"Who are you?" Jace glared at the new man.

"Oh. That's Rob." Jason grabbed hold of Jace and was quickly pushed away.

"I can walk on my own!" Jace said sharply.

"I know you can, but we're kind of in a hurry," Jason consoled, confused as to why he was so snappy.

"Jace, come on." Hazel put a hand on Jace's arm, looking at him. "We need to get you to Henri and get out of here before someone comes after us. Just let Jason help you." She ended her words with a gentle kiss on his cheek, which clearly startled Jace.

Before Jace could say anything, she moved away, turning her attention onto Devin. "Where'd you guys park?"

"Somewhere his direction." Devin said, unfazed by the sudden tension. Jason himself was surprised, since Jace and Hazel had been friends for years.

Although, maybe he should have expected it sooner; since the two of them were crazy close.

Jason snickered at how Jace's face still hadn't cleared from his confusion, nor had he moved, "Come on little brother, and you can tell me what happened to you – before the kiss."

His brother smiled, but only slightly. "What part?" he asked quietly, moving forward, but his footsteps were uneven. Jace was barefoot and with how tentative he was walking, Jason wondered if he was bleeding from the bottoms. But when he looked down, he clocked the marks that seemingly followed the path of his veins layered on the right foot as well.

Jace stopped suddenly. "I don't want mom and dad to know."

"We are going to Grandpa Henri's before anything else," Jason began, not promising him anything. He knew the rough relationship he had with them, but he hadn't seen the very real worry their parents portrayed when they found he'd been kidnapped. He altered the topic. "Why did you leave in the first place?"

Jace blinked away tears and looked down. "I didn't think anyone would miss me," he choked out eventually. Jason's heart ached as he realized he hadn't been all that good of a brother.

"Do you remember where we parked?" Devin asked, looking back, completely trusting that Jason knew where they'd come from. Jason picked up with Jace so that he was leading.

"We're about halfway there. We should probably pick up the pace. It is just to the end of this alley." Jason lowered his voice. "Jace, I didn't sleep at all as soon as I heard you were gone."

"Did mom and dad miss me?" he asked, a near desperate tone to his voice, though Jason figured he tried to hide it.

"Yes." Jason tilted his head. "I think there's something they need to tell you. You guys should all talk."

Jace winced at the thought but nodded slowly. "I'm sorry." He exhaled shakily. "I shouldn't have left. I didn't mean to make you worry. I was just trying to—"

Jason shook his head sharply. "No. I'm sorry. I should have been there to help you."

Jace frowned at him but didn't say anything.

"Now, what is this about you dying if we don't get you to Henri?"

He felt Jace stiffen. "I don't know."

Jason felt slightly frustrated because he was sure Jace did know. "Jace…" he began, trying not to whine, "I need to know what you're dealing with."

"I don't want to talk about it."

"Please? You can tell me anything, I just…" He trailed off, wondering if maybe he should leave the conversation for when they were safe and alone. Before he could apologize though, Jace was suddenly speaking, an underlying panic ringing through his tone.

"He was using these uh… It was some kind of liquid that he put into a syringe, then into my foot. Different ones made me feel different things. They made it so I didn't—couldn't think straight."

He hesitated a long moment, some sort of indecision fluttering quickly on and off his face, before saying forcefully: "It was magic. He used magic inside me and it's killing me now." He held out his arm. "These marks go up my right side, and I think that if it gets all the way around it'll kill me. It's moving too fast." A half-sob came out of Jace's mouth.

"What do the liquids do?" Jason asked, aware that all the others ahead of them were listening to their every word.

"Michael explained them as basically taking away the control of my body. They all made me feel different emotions or had effects that hurt or made me feel weird. One made me want to talk, another one was really painful, one made me feel… well… nothing, and another I think enhanced my senses. That one was the worst, and I believe there were a few more, but I don't remember. The liquid is what I think is causing the marks." Jace went to touch them, but hesitated and dropped his hand instead.

"I broke though. He used the talking one on me and I said what was on my mind. I'm just happy that it wasn't what he wanted to know." He closed his eyes. "But it only caused him to use magic to manipulate my mind. I thought for certain I was going to die."

They'd reached the car, and no more was spoken, but Jason worried over the words his brother had already shared. How could one manipulate another's mind?

He used magic inside me…

It is real. Magic.

"Devin, you drive. I'll call Grandpa Henri and tell him we need to come over." He hesitated as he realized they only had two seats inside the truck, and that Jason would have to be in there with Devin to show him where to go.

"It's okay, Jason." Jace smiled weakly at him. "Let's just get there."

"You guys will have to sit in the back and hold onto something," Jason said as he looked up. The sky had brightened. It was near dawn.

He helped Jace into the back after Rob had climbed in, the other man giving him a hand.

Jason looked into the truck and was surprised to see a few blankets inside the truck's bed.

"I had them with me," Rob told him lightly. "It gets cold outside."

Rob was right. It was rather cold. Jason realized he hadn't even offered his coat to Jace or any of his friends who were wearing thin shirts. But he did his best to help the others in the back, then Rob handed out the blankets to share since there weren't quite enough for them to each have their own. Jason got into the passenger seat, shutting the door behind him while Devin slid in on the driver's side.

"See, this is why I keep an open mind," Devin began as his door shut. "Never would have guessed that your dream was right, but I didn't shut it down, and magic—as it turns out—is real. Who woulda thought?" he laughed lightly, then frowned. "Get your grandpa on the phone. Which way do I start heading?"

"Take a left and get on the freeway." He grabbed his phone, and was surprised that he had a lot of missed calls and texts from some of his friends, checking on how he was, probably a little worried as to why he hadn't answered for three days. He ignored the messages and found 'Grandpa Henri' on his phone.

"Please answer…" He tapped his fingers; almost certain no one was going to pick up with how long it took.

"Hello?" It was a female's voice on the other end, and she sounded tired.

"Grandma! Thank goodness you answered!"

154

"Jason? What's wrong?" The tiredness he'd heard immediately left.

"I found Jace, we need to come over fast, and we need Grandpa's help." There was silence on the other side of the line and then Henri's voice came in.

"Jason, what's wrong with him?"

"I don't know—" Jason started, but Henri interrupted quickly.

"I need to know what to grab. You gotta give me something."

Jason ran his hand through his hair. "He had marks on his arm that travel up like veins. He said Darrin inserted different liquids in through a syringe."

"Whoa. Jason, how far have these veins spread?"

"He said that it was up his right side, almost reaching his wrist." They drove onto the freeway. "I'm about twenty minutes away, will you be ready?"

"I hope so." Grandpa paused. "Jason, this doesn't work on some people, I can't guarantee that it will work for him."

Jason hesitated before shifting the phone to the other ear. "We have to try."

ПJ   ПJ   ПJ

Jace winced as they hit a bump. He scooted his butt back against the bed of the truck and looked back down at his arm, really getting worried as it approached his wrist.

"So… why were you there?" Rob asked, trying to strike up a conversation. Jace didn't feel comfortable talking to him since he had never met him before tonight, which might have been one of the worst nights to meet someone new. He vaguely listened as Kory caught the man up on what was going on, focusing most of his attention on trying to hide his pain.

He lifted his eyes to the sky and tried to use Hazel's trick of counting his blessings instead of fixing on the dark memories, and his thoughts turned back to the kiss that Hazel had given him. What was it for? It may have only been his cheek, but something in Hazel's eyes told him there might've been something more.

I guess I can put that on my list of things I'm grateful for.

He turned his gaze back to Hazel. She shook her head at Rob, a small smile stretched across her lips.

"No, I had only just met your—his brother," he nodded toward Jace, "and his friend Devin, like ten minutes before we found you."

"Wow." Kory raised his eyebrows, and Jace could bet that only he could see his friend's discomfort. Kory had always been good at hiding it. "Get along fast, don't you? Just met someone and then you're off saving people with them." Rob flushed slightly, and his quick tongue was stalled for a minute.

Jace chuckled at the look that Rob flashed at them.

"What will my mom think?" Hazel looked at them nervously.

Jace saw the others' smiles disappear quickly.

"My mom will probably be crying her eyes out at the police station twenty-four seven," Lisa said softly.

"I don't want to see my parents, don't want to see the pain that I caused." Kory shook his head. "But we'll have to alert the police and we'll most likely be in the news as soon as they know we get back. We won't be able to hide out at your grandpa's house forever."

Jace's head jerked up. "I don't want to be in the news." He slid his arm closer to him, as if hiding what he'd been through.

Jace felt the car swerve slightly to pull off the freeway, catching a glimpse of Jason looking through the back window at them. Within minutes they were on the street that led to his grandpa's. He watched as the moon slowly sunk behind the mountain, being lit up from the sun that was rising on the opposite side. *You are not hidden… I'll always see you.* He turned sharply as he heard Darrin's voice in his head again. He could not see the source of the sound, no man and nothing else, so he eventually turned back to Kory; to see him looking at him worriedly. *Must just be my imagination…*

He hoped.

"Are you okay, dude?" Philips asked tiredly, his hand gripping his wounded arm as the truck went over another bump, eyes clearly in pain as well. They went over another bump and Jace's face scrunched up for a second before smoothing out, then saw that both Philips and Kory had winced as well. He wasn't the only one in pain, yet they were worried about him.

"I'm fine. Why?" Jace answered stiffly.

"You seem a little…" Philips struggled with finding a word.

"On edge?" Lisa suggested.

"Tense?" Rob jumped in before Philips could say anything.

"Determined," Hazel stated calmly.

"Determined?" Kory looked at Hazel skeptically, rubbing his inhaler with his thumb in his grasp; an unfamiliar nervous move as Jace had never seen the inhaler in sight for so long. Kory hated that particular 'weakness'—as he always viewed it—and would always use it quickly and hide it even faster, hoping no one would be able to see it.

"Yes, pretty determined that he's not going to show us what's wrong, but it's coming through anyway." She held his gaze. "What's wrong, Jace?"

Don't tell them. You can't tell them anything. His thoughts were stubborn. As much as he wanted to tell them that he was hearing Darrin's voice, he couldn't. He had been with the man for at least four days, constantly having to keep quiet in fear of saying something that could get them killed, and that made it so much harder to be open now.

He shrugged. "I don't know." He blinked away the tears that wanted to form. He couldn't do this.

Hazel scooted closer to him. "Why are you lying to us, Jace?" She rested her hand on his arm. "If you can't trust your friends, who can you trust?" He closed his eyes. There were too many voices in his head, too much noise. He wasn't sure how he would be able to push past the walls he'd built up in a mere four days, but these *were* his friends.

He took a deep breath, trying to gather courage, but when he opened his eyes he realized that they were pulling to a stop in Grandpa Henri's driveway.

Hazel squeezed his arm reassuringly, and when she slipped out the blanket they shared to get out he saw Kory gave him an arched eyebrow that made him wonder if he was blushing as hard as he felt.

Don't get too attached... They'll be dead soon anyway. He shuddered as the voice took over his thoughts.

Why won't you leave me alone? Jace crawled over to the side to jump out of the back before anyone could help him, then opened the blanket back up for Hazel as she came closer, shivering. She sidled back up next to him, seeking refuge from the wind.

Jace ignored the pain as he walked up to the door. He shielded his arm with the blanket to keep it out of view of the neighbors who had been out. One person grabbed a phone with wide eyes, and Jace sighed. The police would probably be there within a half hour, the news reporters not long after.

Grandpa Henri opened the door as they approached and let

them in, guiding them quickly through the hall, and into the first door, clearly the sitting room. He didn't even pause to examine Jace's arm.

"Can you keep the people away from me? The police and everyone?" Jace asked his grandpa anxiously. "At least until you are done? And I can get a jacket?"

"You won't be able to hide it from everyone," Grandpa replied calmly, turning his gaze to the others. "Glenda will get you guys settled in and fixed up," he told them, eyes flicking through them all worriedly.

"What will I tell them then? Can't very well say it was magic, now, can I?"

"They might believe it to be spider or varicose veins. Besides, if this works right, you hopefully won't have them anymore."

"And if it doesn't work?" Jace's anxiety grew as his friends left him, heading in the direction Grandpa Henri had pointed them in, through what Jace knew to be the door to the kitchen. But Jason stayed.

He'd be okay with Jason there.

Grandpa Henri didn't answer for a long moment. He carefully grabbed Jace's arm, studying the veins, and Jace had to fight back the urge to jerk away. "If it doesn't work then you could quite possibly die." He met Jace's eyes as he spoke, looking nervous.

Jace nodded. He had already guessed that would be one of the options. He looked over and was surprised to see Devin and Rob still waiting. His Grandpa had also noticed.

"You guys should probably wait out there." Grandpa Henri nodded towards the door. "When the police come, please tell them to give us a minute, okay?"

Devin nodded and stepped out, Rob following him slowly, but Jason didn't move.

"You can stay *if* Jace is okay with it," Grandpa Henri told his brother without looking up.

Jace was relieved. He did not want to be alone again with someone, even if that someone was his grandpa. "Please stay," he said quietly, almost begging. Jason nodded, possibly looking more relieved than Jace felt.

"You're going to hate me, I think." Grandpa sighed. "How many times did he use the liquids on you, Jace?"

Jace shrugged uncomfortably. "I don't know, around ten

times before I flipped out."

Grandpa looked up quickly at that. "You flipped out?" He ran a hand through his short hair. "What did he do when you flipped out, and what did you say?"

"I didn't tell him anything that you would want to keep hidden," Jace answered shortly, choosing to ignore the first question.

"And what did he do?"

"I don't know," Jace repeated. He hadn't wanted Jason to know what Darrin had done to him, and he especially didn't want everyone else to know. He'd already said a lot since he'd been out. *Don't tell him!* The voice repeated anxiously, *they already know enough.*

"He said Darrin... manipulated his mind," Jason told their grandfather bluntly, but his eyes betrayed his concern.

Jace glared at his brother, avoiding his grandpa's gaze. He halfway wished that he hadn't allowed Jason to stay in here.

Grandpa ran a hand down his face, the concern deeper now.

"Jace... You're in... This really isn't good." Grandpa Henri shook his head, meeting Jace's eyes head on again. "You can hear him, can't you?"

Don't tell him! This time it was Darrin's voice that he heard. He felt the color drain from his face and shook his head forcefully. There was no doubt that Jace had not convinced Jason or Henri of not hearing anything.

"No." Jace pulled his arms close to his chest.

Jason looked at him in alarm. "You can hear him?"

I'll kill them, the voice insisted.

"No!" he said desperately. He wasn't sure if he was talking to the voice in his head or Jason, but his voice sounded too panicky, even to his own ears.

"Can you help him?" Jason asked their grandpa, his eyes pleading the other man.

"I can try, but we have to help him not die first." Grandpa looked deeply into Jace's eyes, and Jace couldn't help but notice the kindness in them. It was maybe the first time he'd felt so much pure love from his grandpa. They never visited them too often, even with their proximity. "You... I need to do something that will be painful, and you will probably resist it, but if I don't do it you are *going* to die."

"What are you going to do?" Jace's voice was barely audible. He heard the quake in his voice.

"To get it out I have to get more liquid in."

He felt his face pale, opening his mouth to protest, but grandpa rushed on. "If you panic, the stress will cause the liquid to have a reverse reaction, and instead of healing, it will kill you. You have to stay sane, and conscious." Jace closed his eyes tightly, rubbing his hand with his thumb and feeling his heart pounding hard in his chest, echoing into his ears. A hand rested on his shoulder and he knew it was Jason. He leaned into his brother's grip.

"Can you do that?" Henri asked him. *It's just like all the other times.* He thought to himself. *I have to stay calm. I need to be strong.*

Jace nodded slowly, biting his lip.

"Good. Jason, help keep him calm too, okay?" Grandpa Henri guided them over to the sitting room couch, letting the two of them sit next to each other while grabbed a syringe, and Jace's heartbeat doubled. He didn't think his heart could go any faster than it was already going.

Jason grasped Jace's hand tightly, pressing his entire body down the side of Jace's. Jason's hand was slightly sweaty, and he was shaking even more than Jace himself. Seeing that his brother was nervous for him made it surprisingly easier to calm his breathing. He smiled shakily at Jason for being there.

He winced as the syringe slipped into his foot, the tenderness unsurprising, but the fear nearly crippling.

And then the sudden pain made him freeze, eyes wide. He felt the liquid move slowly through his body, as though it were trying to burn him from the inside out!

It was too painful. He tried to jerk his hand away from Jason's, scrabbling at his leg with his free hand since Jason wouldn't let go; his lower leg at first, until it became obvious he couldn't move it, then anything he could get a grip on. Anything that would stop the course of the fire.

Tears streamed down his face as his breath hitched. He heard himself give a scream, muffled to his ears, and weak due to the seeming breathless nature of his lungs.

His friends burst back into the sitting room.

"Stop it! Stop it! It hurts!" He vaguely recognized that he sounded like a child throwing a tantrum, but he didn't care. He just wanted the pain to go away. He vaguely saw the sorrowful looks that his friends and Jason's friends cast at him.

Hazel tried to get to him, but Grandma herded them out of the room.

Jason pulled him firmly back into his side, wrapping an arm around his shoulder, and practically hugging him, and it was only then that Jace realized he had been trying to writhe away from his older brother, as though getting away could somehow stop the agony.

"Help me…" Jace begged. He could barely get the words out.

"Shh… It's okay, Jace. Calm down, it's okay…"

It's not okay! Jace wanted to yell. His brother had no idea what it felt like! Jason rocked him back and forth as the liquid burned his insides. He couldn't think straight.

Through his tears, he saw the marks crawling up his hand, wrapping around like small snakes. He felt terror at actively seeing the marks move under his skin slide in with his pain and the next scream of pain was stopped in its tracks at the reminder of why this pain was necessary.

Get a hold of yourself! They're trying to help! You have to be strong! He remembered what Grandpa had said. He didn't want to die. He had to make it through, and to do that, he *needed* to *calm down!* He gritted his teeth, trying to control the urge to scream. He collapsed into Jason's arms, finally stopping his frantic attempts to escape, and breathed a deep, shaky breath as he gripped Jason's T–shirt with his hand. His exhale was more of a sob, but he followed with another inhale.

"It's okay… Shh…"

Jace listened to Jason's soft murmurs, allowing himself to slowly relax his tight muscles. His heartbeat slowed, but the tears continued to flow down his cheeks because of the pain. A few sobs continued to escape as he sat there for probably long minutes until the pain dulled, the excessive pain fading into a lingering fatigue.

He wasn't sure how long it was, but eventually he opened his eyes to see Grandpa Henri's overwhelmed gaze watching him, but his eyes felt so heavy, and he couldn't keep them open. He still kept a tight grip on Jason's shirt and tears were still rolling, but he felt like they were more from relief at this point. Relief and gratitude. He was glad to be back with people who loved him.

Jason's cheek rested on Jace's head, and he didn't stop rocking him even though he had relaxed. Jace settled further into his brother's arms, letting his hand slowly let go of the tight grip—the last part of him that was holding tension—as his mind started to blur into a state of oblivion.

There was a distant sounding knock on the front door that jerked him out of the half-sleep that he'd slipped into. His eyes flew open, and he jerked, startling Jason. But when Jace looked down at his arms, he sighed in disappointment as he realized the vein-like marks still reached all the way to his hand.

"It's still there."

Grandpa looked as confused—and worried—as he felt. "I don't know why it didn't fade all the way. It was supposed to work."

"It doesn't seem to be growing anymore. Is that a good thing?" Jason asked Henri.

"I think if it's not growing it will be fine," Henri sounded unsure.

"I need a jacket and some socks," Jace said. If the marks would not go away, then he would have to hide them. He couldn't handle the questions that would come if anyone saw them.

"Got it," Henri said, nodding to the desk. He grabbed a white jacket and handed it to him, his other hand landing gently on Jace's shoulder—the one free of marks – and rubbed it gently, shifting to cup Jace's cheek. "I'm really sorry, Jace. I hate that I hurt you."

Jace carefully grabbed the jacket from Henri's hands, hearing the new voices in the hallway by the front door. His grandpa let him go as Jace went to put the jacket on.

"It's okay, it's not your fault, Grandpa," he said, and then glanced up at Jason. "Thank you, Jason." Tears stained his brother's face, probably mirroring his own. Jason smiled at him and wiped Jace's cheeks.

Jace shifted off his brother—and when had he ended up practically in his lap?— and looked down at his hand. Yeah, those marks were still visible. "I need some gloves too, if you have any?"

"Jason, they are in that drawer. I need to get the others to agree on a fake story." Grandpa gently touched Jace's head, slightly turning his face so that he could see the large gash. The look in his eyes betrayed the sorrow his grandpa felt at the sight, tight around the eyes and mouth. After a long moment, Grandpa Henri let go, once more rubbing Jace's cheek before leaving the room to do as he said.

Jace had forgotten about the hit on his head and suddenly became hyper-aware of the throbbing and dried blood that surrounded it.

Jace pulled the rest of the way from his brother, embarrassed to have broken down like that, and busied himself with putting on his socks. "I'm sorry, Jason. I didn't mean to—"

"I'm just happy that you're okay," his brother cut him off. As soon as he finished with the socks, having to move carefully with his right foot, Jason gently pulled Jace up so they were both standing. Jace ignored the flash of dizziness and pain.

"I won't be able to just hide in here, will I?"

"Probably not, but I'll be with you and help you the best I can." Jason grabbed the pair of gloves and gave them to Jace to don.

He flashed him a grateful glance as he pulled the gloves on. "I'll be right back." Jason told him gently, looking at him for a long second. "Are you okay?"

Jace paused and met his brother's eyes. Was he okay? He felt drained, fatigue settling deep in his bones, and the pain was still intense. He wanted to hide from everyone, sleep for a week, and maybe never come out again. But he was home.

He was home.

"Yeah… I think I am. At least… better," he said finally.

Jason nodded and shut the door behind himself. Jace continued to stand, staring around at the sitting room as he heard the muted sounds of talking through the door. He hadn't been here much, but the room was inviting, warm colors, soft carpet. He wanted to sleep on that carpet.

He felt slightly disappointed that he had not finished what they had set out to do. He dreaded the idea of going back out, and yet he felt incomplete now that he knew magic was real. If magic was real, did that mean the rest of it was as well? What if there really was a Power?

But he didn't think he could go at it alone, and he couldn't bear to take his friends with him again. It was far too dangerous for them.

I'll have to reevaluate later, when I get strong enough to try again.

For now, he had to use the bathroom. He'd only been to his grandpa's house one other time in recent years, but he knew where it was. It would just require him to walk past the cops. He summoned his courage and walked to the door. He lowered his hood over his face so that it hid a little more of his face and opened the door slowly.

At once the conversation was cut short and they turned

towards him. Jason and his friends were in the hall keeping the cops company.

"It's Jace, right?" one of the cops asked him, slightly eager. His eyes scanned him and Jace knew he was taking in his appearance. Not a good look at the moment.

Jace nodded stiffly. "Yeah," he croaked out quietly.

Jason looked at him pointedly and touched his neck as if trying to tell him something.

Jace put his hand on the spot to which he was gesturing. He couldn't feel anything, but he knew Jason wouldn't worry over nothing. He turned away quickly and closed the distance to the bathroom, locking the door behind him before leaning back on it with a breath that was more like a gust of release. He stood there a long moment before looking into the mirror and moving his hand.

The veins had moved up his neck slightly. They were mostly hidden by the jacket, and blended slightly with all the blood, but the problem was still visible if he turned his head. He sighed in annoyance. It would be a lot harder to hide the ones on his neck.

He had forgotten about the bloody nose that Darrin's magic had given him, and the cut on his cheek that he had received from pushing Philips out of the way. Now the blood from those two wounds had dried along with the head wound from days ago, mixing as though into one and causing a rather gruesome sight. Even with a lot of it having been brushed off, it still tinted his skin red.

How many days had it been since the initial hit? Was his wound infected? He knew that Michael had given him something for it, but he hadn't really taken the time to fully clean it off.

Jace didn't really want to take the time to wash it off even now, rather wanting to just fall face-first in bed, but he turned the water on anyway and took off his gloves. He waited for the water to fill his hands before gently scrubbing his face. He got most of the blood off, but doing so started up the bleeding from the gash on his head, so he decided to stop trying to clean the rest. He bet that it needed stitches. He gently dabbed at the wound with a paper towel until it slowed down again, his gut flipping as he did so.

He turned to use the toilet, glad that he didn't have to stress over someone standing behind him as he went anymore.

He wasn't in any hurry to get back out there, so after he washed his hands, he rested his head on the mirror for a moment. He really didn't want to go over everything with the cops, especially not before he could take a nap. He didn't know what to do about the reporters either. He knew that the news had presumed them kidnapped from the very beginning, which probably helped their case, but he didn't think they would give him a pass if he just pled too traumatized to talk about it and asked them to leave him alone.

They were going to make a big deal out of everything, and now he was going to be fussed over.

When he finally made his way back out of the restroom, he was met by one of the cops leaning on the wall across from the bathroom. He looked over to see the other one casually blocking off the way to the family room, where he figured his friends were.

He wondered if they had purposely done that.

"Can we talk?" the cop across from him asked gruffly. Jace looked for Jason desperately, seeing him just down the hall behind the man. His brother shrugged heavily, looking helpless. He was the only other one still in the hall.

Unconsciously, he folded his arms, holding them tight to his chest. "I guess. Won't really let me leave without talking anyway, will you?"

The cop sighed. "No, sorry."

"Okay, uh… my brother can be there too, right?" He asked, watching in relief as Jason pushed his way past the cop to wrap a comforting arm around Jace. Jace leaned into him in relief.

"Of course." He smiled at Jace in what was supposed to be a reassuring way, but it didn't help calm his nerves.

"Okay." He turned away from them and was relieved when they didn't follow right away. He hoped to talk to his friends for a second before they followed him in.

When he entered, everyone looked at him, and he was glad that his brother was still beside him. This might have been the first time in ages that he was uncomfortable with all his friends. Even though he'd not seen his grandparents too often, he'd always felt pretty comfortable with them as well, but not today. Would he ever feel comfortable again?

"What's our story?" Jace asked tiredly.

"We were thinking he took us to get us to work," Philips told him quietly.

"So, kind of like slavery," Jace started. "Sounds like as good an answer as any. The officers are right behind me. Let's get this over with." Jason pulled his arm away to get the cops and Jace found his way to the couch and sat in between Hazel and Kory.

The cops entered with Jason right as he sat down.

His grandparents' visiting room typically had plenty of seating, but even with all the couches and chairs, Jason and Devin had to pull a chair from the kitchen, letting Rob sit on the couch.

Grandpa Henri and Grandma Glenda greeted them, but grandma left the room saying that they'd give them some time, leaving only their grandpa in the room with them, his sharp eye focused on the officers.

"Do you want any tea or cookies or anything?" Glenda asked before she left. Even though Jace was starving he didn't answer because he didn't know if she was talking to him or the officers. He heard someone's stomach growl but was unsure whose it was.

Glenda winked at him, catching his eye, and Jace realized he must have made a yearning face or something.

"I think I'm okay, but it sounds like *he* would like some," the cop, who had first asked his name, said with a compassionate pointed glance at Philips. Philips wrapped his good arm around his stomach, his other one supported in a sling and clearly bandaged underneath a new, clean shirt. He blushed a little as he settled back in the chair, not looking at any of them as his hand gripped tight to his shirt.

"I'm sure they all would," Glenda said. "I'll bring a plateful."

The officers didn't waste a second, immediately breaking the silent tension before it could fully form. None of his friends were making eye-contact with the cops except Hazel.

"I'm Officer Kilauea, and this is Officer Jenkins," the gruffer one said firmly. "We're going to need you to answer the questions that we ask. Can you do that?" The question was more of a statement, and no one objected.

Jace turned his attention to his friends. Hazel was sitting tall on the couch next to him, a tendency she had when she got uncomfortable, clearly a trained thing from her martial art training.

Jason was trying to look encouraging across the way from him in his own chair, but Jace could tell that his brother was exhausted, and knew that he didn't want any of them to have to go through this.

"Kilauea, don't be so harsh with them. They haven't done anything wrong," Officer Jenkins softly warned him, bringing Jace's attention momentarily back to them. Officer Jenkins looked at them gently. "First question: are you guys okay?" He focused his attention on Philips first.

Jace blinked in quiet surprise, though he figured he probably shouldn't be. He knew that police officers were human too, and they all looked thrashed.

Studying the rest of his friends again, he eyed all the bruises they all seemed to be hosting. Kory's neck was clearly getting worse, and he still hadn't let go of his inhaler, which said more about is mental state than anything.

Their eyes looked like his had looked in the mirror: dark and shadowed with recent scarring memories invading their thoughts. *Are we ever going to have light in our eyes again?*

No one answered at first, all seemed to be waiting for someone else to do so. Philips, who was still being watched by Jenkins, finally mumbled an "okay" that was almost too quiet to hear.

He turned his head toward Lisa. He couldn't see much of her injuries as she was actually lying on her side in a ball on one of the recliners with the blanket wrapped around everything but her head. She didn't look like she was going to be moving anytime soon, but she nodded her okay Jenkins went on to the others one by one.

"Alright..." Hazel said softly "Could be better."

Jenkins nodded and switched his piercing green eyes to Jace. The green of the man's eyes reminded Jace of Darrin and he had to look away.

"Relieved." Jace touched his neck again, and then quickly pulled his sleeve back down to his wrist as he saw the red line slip into view.

Officer Kilauea's eyes shot in the direction of his arm, but Jenkins was already onto Kory.

"Fine," he mumbled with a worried glance at Jace.

"What about you guys?" he asked Jason, Rob and Devin.

"We weren't in there," Devin said.

"Yes... but you're here and I'm sure it wasn't easy for you guys either."

"Tired," Jason admitted. His eyes looked almost as dark as theirs. "Happy that they are okay." His eyes flicked to Jace.

Devin nodded in agreement, but Rob didn't move. "I think I should leave," he stated, starting to stand.

"Why?" Devin asked in confusion.

"Because I just met you guys, I feel like I'm intruding."

Jason grabbed his arm before he could take a step and Devin spoke up before anyone could. "You only intruded when you slept in my truck and scared the shizzles out of me. I've grown to like you too much for you to leave now," Devin smirked, tone joking, but Jace didn't doubt the words.

"Wait... What?" Kilauea's eyebrows rose.

Rob's eyebrows rose as well. "Is that one of your questions?" he asked innocently. Officer Kilauea narrowed his eyes at him.

"Yes."

"He was there when we went to... um..." Jason hesitated. Jace knew that people didn't typically go to that abandoned town, and he didn't really want to get in trouble. It wasn't illegal but it was disapproved. "...went to the abandoned city. He slept in our truck, and he jumped out at Devin," Jason told him with a small smile.

"The abandoned city? Why did you go there?" Officer Jenkins asked in surprise. "Is that where they were?"

At Jason's nod he continued.

"How did you know to go there?"

Jason scratched his ear. "We went there when we were younger once, and I just had this strong feeling that we should try there."

"So how did you get away? And why did he take you?" This time Jenkins eyes flicked toward Jace and his friends. Hazel was staring at Jace. He looked at Philips who was watching Jace as if waiting for an answer. They all were. Jenkins and Kilauea's eyes went from Jace to the others, studying them, and Jace's eyes widened. So, they wanted him to tell the 'story.'

"Jace?" Kilauea looked at him with narrowed eyes, as if daring him to make a mistake. "You good to answer?"

Jenkins nudged his partner harshly—probably for the tone of his voice. Jace clenched his jaw, and with one last desperate look at Kory, turned back to Kilauea.

"We got away because someone helped us out. She couldn't lead us all the way out, so we were lucky that Jason and the others found us." Jace's voice was icy with frustration and nervousness he could barely control. "He wanted us for a reason unknown to me, except maybe he wanted more people to beat up to do what he wanted." He hadn't lied exactly. They had all gotten beaten, but Darrin had wanted information, not slaves.

"You don't look very beat up. Only they do," Kilauea observed.

"I think he's in worse shape than any of us are, even if you are unable to see it." Hazel snapped at him irritably.

"Are you blind?" Kory asked at the same time, tone condescending.

"How?" Kilauea asked testily. "Unless the bruising is hidden underneath the jacket and gloves. Is that why you are covered up and not them?"

Jace was sure that this officer was just trying to figure stuff out, but the way he was going at it made Jace feel cornered. His body shook with frustration, stress, and tiredness. He looked at his friends again. Some of them were covered with blankets anyway! How was wearing a jacket suspicious?

Jace suddenly became very aware of the scratch on his cheek and head, and the pain in his nose. How did he *not* look beat up too? Even though his most obvious sign of abuse was hidden along the right side of his body, it wasn't like he looked fine and dandy.

He could see that the others were also getting angry at the older cop's questions. Jason looked like he was about to punch the guy, hands clenched and eyes angry. Grandpa Henri was also glaring at him.

"Kilauea! Do you need to go out until you remember that you are not dealing with delinquent kids!?" Jenkins snapped, irritated.

Jace stood up, trying to blink away the tears that almost blinded him. "I don't think you want to know how I was beaten," he said calmly, a lot calmer than he felt. "And I also think I'm done answering questions. They can do the rest." He walked to the door a little unevenly with the pain down his leg, ignoring the looks that bored into his back, and slipped out. He moved up the stairs quietly, going into the room furthest from the top of them, which just happened to be a guest room, shutting and locking it behind himself. He sunk down onto the bed, head falling into his hands.

Weakling, just like the rest of them. He heard Darrin's voice enter his mind again.

No one would notice or even care if you weren't around. No one loves you; everyone is too harsh for that. The world is too harsh.

He pushed Darrin's voice away along with the tears. The constant bombardment from Darrin was getting harder to deal with and he wasn't sure how much more he could handle.

But he couldn't show weakness, he had to be strong—or at least hide the weakness that he actually felt.

His jaw clenched as someone knocked on the door. He wiped his eyes and stood to open it. He was extremely surprised to find that it was Officer Kilauea. He would have suspected anyone but him.

"What do you want?" Jace asked him sourly.

"I wanted to tell you something," the officer answered bluntly, pushing past Jace softly and shutting the door before leaning on it.

Jace couldn't help the fear that washed through him as he took a step back, then another, trying hard to control his breathing as he moved as far from the man as he could.

Kilauea spoke quickly, not moving any closer to him, possibly sensing his rising panic. "I'm a friend of your grandpa's. My name is Frank, don't know if you have heard of me. I know about Darrin, his magic and all, and I also know that what you have hidden under your sleeves is from Darrin's poisons. Sorry for being so harsh, but I needed to be sure you wouldn't say anything you shouldn't. I don't mean to scare or hurt you, but I want to talk to you alone."

"Are you going to tell that to my friends too?" Jace asked in surprise, fear overshadowed by curiosity. He also felt quite a bit of irritation at the revelation. He hadn't talked for Darrin, why would he have talked for some police officers?

"You can later, but no, I am not going to. Officer Jenkins doesn't know."

Jace nodded and Frank turned to leave but paused before opening the door.

"How far did the markings spread for you?"

Jace didn't need to ask what he meant, already knowing, but he just looked away quickly. He didn't like everyone questioning him about the marks and the torture he'd endured.

"It's okay. I thought I'd ask." He turned away but Jace stopped him, forcing himself to speak. If the man had any helpful information…

"It goes up my neck." He pulled the hood down as Frank turned around. He looked at the sight in horror.

"What?" Jace asked the officer worriedly.

"Did you know that it doesn't have to wrap all the way around to kill?" Frank asked him. "It can just wrap around the chest, neck or head… though it didn't wrap all the way around your neck, it should have killed you."

"Will it still kill me?" Jace asked warily, pulling his hood back up.

"I've only known one other person who survived it when it traveled to the neck… He has… problems." The officer shook his head. "Occasionally he'd have a coughing fit that, if he didn't control, could kill him. It didn't even go as high as yours."

"So, I might still die from it." Jace knew it was just false hope to believe that it was over. "That's great." His voice turned bitter.

Frank smiled sadly at him, then luckily changed the topic. "Are you going to come back down?"

Jace shrugged at his question. He was achy with fatigue and almost wanted to just lay down here now. "I guess so," he mumbled, and then gave a weak smile as he thought about his grandma's cookies. "I am rather hungry."

ꊶ   ꊶ   ꊶ

Jason shifted uncomfortably, wanting to get up and check on his brother. It bothered him that he couldn't because Officer Kilauea had gone up after him to supposedly apologize and wanted a minute with him. Having Jace so clearly hurt and exhausted alerted every single one of his brotherly protection genes, and he felt his insides were itching to get him to move.

It was quiet for a moment until Officer Jenkins cleared his throat.

"Can I learn all your names?" he asked softly, looking slightly embarrassed. Jason barely heard the question or any of the responses and when Jenkins turned to him, he had to remind himself what the officer had requested.

"Um… Jason. Sorry." He had missed the others giving their names, but he knew all his brother's friends decently well. He looked away from the officer as the door opened, and Glenda walked in with a plate of cookies in hand. She placed them on the coffee table between them all.

"Where'd Jace and your friend go?" she asked Officer Jenkins in confusion.

"Well… um. My partner was kind of harsh with Jace. He went to apologize," he said uncomfortably, looking at her with apology in his green eyes.

She nodded and left the room again. Hazel's hand reached out for the cookies as soon as the door had shut, grabbing three.

Philips stared at her in surprise while Kory just laughed and reached for his own.

"What?" she asked indignantly as she popped an entire cookie in her mouth. "I'm hungry."

Philips shook his head. "You just keep surprising me, that's all." He shrugged and grabbed a cookie of his own.

"You mean like how she beat Thomas to the ground?" Kory said with a laugh. Hazel flushed red, even though a slight smirk of pride flickered on her lips.

"You're still laughing about that? It wasn't that funny!" She insisted.

"Who's Thomas?" Jason looked up in surprise as Jace's voice joined the conversation again. He grabbed one of the cookies, walked around the couch that he'd been previously sitting on, pulled a chair beside Jason, and sat, straddling it backward. He still seemed guarded, but his gaze was calm now. Kilauea came in behind him.

"Thomas was one of the people in charge, and he also helped us get out," Lisa said, her eyebrows drawing together at her own sentence, probably still confused about the whole way they had been able to get free. Then flashed a small smile towards Hazel. "And it was pretty great."

"What?" Jenkins mouth was open in a way that made Jason think that he wanted to laugh but was unsure of why he should.

"Hazel beat the crap out of one of the men there and then took down two other men as well..." Philips shrugged. "She's a deceptively strong girl."

Hazel took another bite, her face still bright red. Jason saw Jace smile out of the corner of his mouth. He guessed that he already knew how well Hazel could fight since they had been friends for a while now.

"Why'd you beat him up?" Kilauea asked patiently. Jason was surprised by his mood change.

"Because he was hitting Philips," she said innocently, like he should have known that already.

"Why?"

She shrugged. "He wanted something."

"What did he do after you beat him?" Jenkins asked worriedly. Hazel flushed a deeper shade of red at that question and snuck a glance at Jace before turning back to her cookies. Jace looked like he was trying to read Hazel's mind, and it seemed like he succeeded as a second later his jaw clenched, and his eyes narrowed.

"He attempted to kiss me." She laughed nervously. "He gave up pretty fast, though."

Jenkins nodded, his face whiter than before. "What else can you tell me?"

She shrugged. "I don't know. Not much else to say."

"Were you all together?" he asked, looking between them.

"Mostly," Kory said, and then looked like he regretted his comment.

Jason understood. How would they explain that Jace was in another room the entire time?

"Mostly?" Kilauea asked, shooting a glance at Jace.

"Yeah," Jace spoke up. "Darrin wanted one of us as his… errand boy, I guess. I was with him most of the time when he wanted something." Jason was impressed by his quick thinking—but then, he was not speaking far from the truth.

"Who was that person?" Jenkins asked. The glint in his eyes told them that he already knew who it was.

"Jace." Philips looked at him. "We were together." He gestured to the others.

"Is there a reason he chose Jace?"

"I guess maybe because he kind of took charge, and Darrin knew we wouldn't leave him. Not that we'd leave anyone." Lisa looked at him. "Are we almost done? I'd like to sleep and wake up to see my family when they get here."

"Yes, I think that's about all we need to know, at least for now." Kilauea stood, and Jenkins followed him. "The reporters will most likely flock to this house as soon as they catch wind, and unfortunately I cannot help you there, but you'll see your parents as soon as they get here."

Jason suddenly wished his grandpa didn't live quite as far away from their families, though he had been glad that he was so close to the abandoned town last night so they could get Jace help quickly when he'd needed it.

Kilauea went towards the door. "If there is anything we can help with let us know." He opened it and waited for Jenkins to exit before nodding at Jace and mouthing something to him. Henri followed them to let them out of the house.

Jace nodded and looked away leaving Jason confused at their silent conversation.

"What was that about?" Hazel asked him as soon as the door shut.

"Kilauea's name is Frank, he's a friend of Henri's," Jace said easily as he stood up and went back around the couch for more cookies. "He already knew about Darrin, and I mean everything we know. He was only being harsh because he needed to make sure we wouldn't say anything." He paused, looking thoughtful.

"And?" Jason asked him worriedly.

"Nothing…" Jace's eyes narrowed. "I'm just trying to figure out if I want to eat or sleep first."

"It might be a debate for you, but I already know what I'm doing," Hazel said over her yawn as she stood up. Jason watched in amusement as she took a step to the kitchen. Jace shook his head with a small laugh before following.

"That girl has a bigger appetite than most guys," Kory said, starting to stand.

"Don't tell me you're eating too…" Lisa said from her curled position.

"Aren't you?" Kory asked teasingly, turning toward the kitchen.

"Are you too?" Lisa asked Philips.

He nodded sheepishly. "If I can get myself up."

"Well, I'm not going to be the only one sleeping!" Lisa tossed a hand up, knocking the blanket off her shoulder.

Jason put his head in his hands and rubbed slowly, trying to wake himself back up. His exhaustion suddenly hit him full force.

"You, my friend, should go sleep," Devin said with a yawn, "and so should I."

Jason nodded and looked up. He was surprised to see that Philips and Lisa had already left the room.

"Rob, you want to stay here? My grandpa has plenty of extra space."

Rob looked away and scratched his neck awkwardly. "Um… well… I haven't really… been in a… well… a house for like two years." He looked embarrassed. Jason looked at him questioningly, hiding the pity he felt for him.

"Do you want to?"

"I—I guess…"

"Great!" Devin said. "You're among friends now!" He stood up. "Let's go figure out where to sleep."

Henri came in at that moment and looked them over with a critical eye. "Are you guys hungry, or do you just want to sleep?"

"Sleep for now," Jason answered. "Where?"

"I'll have you three in here if you don't mind," Henri nodded towards the couches. "Get some food when you feel like it. I'll get some blankets." Jason stood up and looked at Devin and Rob.

"Which couch do you want?" he asked them. Devin shrugged while Rob sat on the couch closest to him and laid back.

Jason smiled and took the recliner to the side of him.

He was asleep before he knew where Devin had chosen to sleep.

Chapter Fifteen

JACE AWOKE AROUND one almost as tired as he'd been when he'd finally made it to bed. After his grandma had stitched up the gash on his head, Grandpa had led the boys to one guest room while the girls slept in the other. He wasn't even sure when exactly they got to bed, but it had to be around seven in the morning.

He wanted to go back to sleep, but he had tried for close to half an hour and it was no use; besides, the doorbell had gone off. He didn't want to meet with the reporters, or really even his parents, but laying there was merely postponing it. He would have to face them eventually.

He figured that everyone's parents had all gotten there some time in the last few hours, and he could've sworn he had a vague impression of his mother brushing back the hair on his forehead, but he'd been far too exhausted to wake up fully so he wasn't sure if it really happened.

He finally sighed and stood up, pulling on the jacket from the bedpost and pushing his arms through the sleeves.

"You're up now?" Jace jumped as he heard a quiet voice.

"Yeah, I'm up." Jace turned to Philips as casually as he could with the scare he'd just received. "How long have you been up?"

"Not too long this time," Philips shrugged. "I haven't been able to sleep very well though, kept waking up."

Jace pulled socks onto his feet, ignoring the pain and marks. "Well, that's understandable. I seem to hear voices when I try." Jace turned away speedily as that came out, but Philips didn't comment on it. Really, Jace had heard voices the whole night, except when he'd fallen asleep and darkness had inhabited his dreams.

Philips sighed heavily, shifting his slinged arm slightly with a wince and staring toward the door.

"Are you ready for this?" Philips asked.

Jace turned back in surprise. There was an obvious strain at the corner of Philips' eyes, the pain from the arm surely, but probably from memories and nightmares as well. "Which part? Being in the news, seeing my parents, trying to continue my life like nothing happened?"

Philips gaze lowered, and Jace felt bad for snapping at his friend.

"We don't have to act like nothing happened, because it did," Kory's sharp tone joined in, voice still a little harsh from the rough treatment at Darrin's hand.

Jace looked over at him. He was still lying on his side on the floor, but his eyes were open now.

"So, just continue living knowing that we failed and were tortured?" Jace said sourly. "Great. Sounds like a plan."

"Yes! We failed!" Kory snapped. "We didn't even believe it in the first place, and now all this happened, and we were hurt, but we know better now!" He sat up. "We are back now, safe. Isn't that a good thing? I personally would much rather be alive in my bed knowing that I tried my hardest and be able to try to find the Power again, than die in the hands of people trying their hardest to achieve the same thing for a horrible purpose! We can't give up now."

Jace and Philips stared at him in surprise.

"Wait..." Jace shook his head. "Try again? You're planning on trying again?" He felt worry slide in, his hands twitching anxiously.

"Aren't you?" Kory raised his eyebrows.

Jace couldn't respond.

"Well?"

Jace hesitated, then opened his mouth to object but Kory made a sharp gesture with his hand that cut Jace off. "There's no way you're going alone, so yes, I am planning on going!"

"But—"

"No buts, I'm going," Kory said. "For now, let's make this story as believable as we can, continue with our life the best we can, and leave when it's a good time." Kory stood up and put his hand on Jace's shoulder encouragingly.

"What about our families? We can't leave without telling them," Philips objected. "Everyone will think it strange that the same people who got kidnapped leave again soon after."

"True…" Kory tapped his lip thoughtfully. "One problem at a time though, let's go see our families." He shoved them toward the door, a glimmer of excitement in his eyes and voice at the thought of seeing his family again. Jace stumbled, trying to regain his balance, and threw a glare at his friend who just shot an innocent look in response.

Jace smirked and tossed the hood over his head. He grabbed the half gloves that he had placed on the dresser before falling asleep last night and wriggled his fingers into them as Philips opened the closet door, quickly finding himself a jacket, but he couldn't get it on by himself with the sling limiting his mobility, so Kory quickly undid it and helped guide his arm through carefully.

The navy-blue jacket fit him quite nicely, easily able to slip his injured arm in without it drowning him. Jace watched them redo the sling before he opened the bedroom door slowly.

"You guys are loud." Hazel pushed away from the wall she was leaning on outside their door. She, too, was wearing a jacket—or more of an open front sweater. It looked really good with her green shirt. Her eyes were hazel, but had a tint of green to them as well, which was more evident with the color she wore.

But she still had some dark bruises showing around her wrists, neck and face.

"I'm sorry, did we wake you?" Jace apologized. He hoped she hadn't heard the conversation.

"Nah, not me, I've been awake for a while." She shrugged and looked back toward her own room.

He followed her gaze and found Lisa shutting the door quietly behind her. "I was hoping to get some food before all the boys got there," she said with mock sourness in her voice. She had not grabbed a jacket and he wondered if it was because she didn't want one or they didn't have one in the room.

"Okay, you don't want to eat with us boys, but you're okay to have Hazel there? You do know how much she eats, right?" Philips said jokingly.

"Uh… Duh," Hazel laughed. "Girls are much more fun!"

"Ouch. I am doubly hurt right now!" Kory said dramatically, hand on his chest to make it look more ridiculous. Jace pushed softly past them, chuckling quietly, and started for the stairs.

"Do you know who's down there?" Lisa asked anxiously.

"No." He shrugged. "I guess we will find out." Jace paused. Sure enough, he heard people on the bottom floor, lots of voices that he didn't recognize. Reporters.

"Dang it," he muttered under his breath and took a step back, away from the stairs, and behind the wall.

"Who is it?" Hazel asked, trying to glance around him, her face downcast, the question redundant as she clearly knew the answer.

"Reporters," Jace said quietly, tugging the hood over his head a little better. "I was hoping to eat first."

"Maybe they'll let us," Hazel said, though her gaze didn't seem like she believed it. Why were the reporters inside anyway? Jace felt his hands tremble at the thought of all that attention on him.

"Maybe." Jace waited for someone else to move, but no one did. He sighed heavily. "I'm going to have to go first, aren't I?" he asked quietly, feeling a little frustrated. Was he frustrated at the reporters? His friends for making him the unspoken leader?

Yeah, maybe a bit of all.

"I'd say, yes." Kory tried to smile at him but stopped and rolled his eyes. "I'm not even going to pretend to be happy for you."

"I wouldn't want you to." Jace shook his head, took a breath, then took a step down the first stair. His leg was still painful, so even one step wasn't easy for him. He used the railing to keep himself up. He felt relieved when he caught sight of their families also in the room.

They turned immediately when Jace descended far enough on the stairs, the room falling silent. Kory's little sister was the first to move. She ran up with a shout and gave Kory as large of a hug as her small arms could handle. He lifted her into his arms and hugged her close. Silent tears came down his cheeks as he shut his eyes.

Jace turned his attention away from them and back toward the crowd. A few of the reporters lifted cameras in their direction, and Jace turned away just as quickly, heading toward his parents who had stood and were making their way toward him as well.

They embraced him with the warmest greeting he'd had in years.

His mom was crying. "I am so happy that you're okay!" She pulled him close, checking him over with a sharp eye before he was pulled back into her arms, even firmer. "I thought I'd never see you again!"

Jace was pretty sure the others were receiving the same greetings from their parents and couldn't help but feel relieved at the thought. It just showed that his parents did love him. Either that or they were acting like it the best they could, but he hoped it was the former.

"I thought I was going to die." His words were muffled by his mom's shoulder, his dad enfolding them both into the hug, one of his hands in his hair, holding his head steady. They both seemed to tighten slightly at Jace's words. His mom's tears were falling on his cheek, and his dad's hand was shaking slightly.

After a couple long moments, what felt like minutes, in which he sunk into their arms and refused to part, they eventually pulled back to look him over again.

"What is this?" Jace stiffened as his mom's fingers grazed his neck. He pulled his hood tighter and took a step back.

"It's nothing." His mother looked at him doubtfully and Jace saw his dad reach for him in concern. "I'll explain later. Can they leave?" He brushed his dad's hand away slightly, glancing at the reporters. Were the reporters going to hang onto every word meant only for their families?

"It looks like Grandpa is already on it." Jace looked at Laura who had come up behind him. She nodded to Henri who was holding the door open and telling the media to leave, at least for the moment. Laura finished the explanation: "Grandma let them into the house because she thought it was rude to leave them outside for so long, with the exception that they would leave when you guys came down here." She smiled in amusement as she came closer, but her expression changed as she stepped close.

He allowed Laura to pull him into a tight hug. He could feel stifled sobs coming from her. Jace hugged her just as tight, though he was honestly more surprised about Laura hugging him than his parents. Laura had been in her pre-teen and teenage rebel and independent stage for years; her friends seemed to be the only thing she cared about.

"Are you okay?" she asked as she finally let go.

"Yeah... I think so." He looked around in concern. "Where are Jason and Korren?" He asked his parents when he didn't spot either of them.

"Korren is using the restroom, Jason is still sleeping I think," his dad answered. His gaze flickered down to Jace's neck worriedly, though he said nothing. Jace wasn't sure why he was so fixated on them.

Well… besides the fact that he'd just gotten home after being kidnapped and the marks on his neck were the most evident abuse he'd received.

But why did he look at them like he'd seen them before?

"I'm so sorry mom, dad. I shouldn't—" Jace stopped talking as he realized his parents didn't know that they had left on their own. What would he have to apologize for in their eyes?

"Sweetie, don't apologize." His mom reached out and wiped his cheeks gently.

When they fell into a slightly awkward silent moment, he looked around. Hazel's mom and her brothers were with her. He was honestly surprised to see her older brother wrap his arms around her tightly, but maybe he really shouldn't be surprised. Clearly their families were more worried than Jace thought they would have been.

"Can I eat?" Jace asked desperately, more because he wanted an excuse to think. "Or will I have to talk to the reporters first?"

"No. I'll make sure you can eat first," his dad said firmly, turning slightly toward the door. He looked imposing, as if he was serious about not letting anyone bother his son while eating.

"Thanks." He was sure that he, along with his friends, looked thinner than before they'd left. Sure, none of his friends had ever been fat, but now they all looked slightly sick.

He didn't bother getting his friends to join him in the kitchen, leaving them to greet their families as he turned toward the door. But he paused suddenly as he remembered what Jason had said last night.

"I think they have something they should tell you…"

"Mom, Dad, Jason said you needed to tell me something?" Jace blinked slowly, not really up to discussing it right now, but not sure there would ever be a better time. Besides, he was curious about what they thought he should know.

His mom looked shocked, and maybe slightly worried, which in turn made Jace think it was something he wouldn't like.

"What?" Jace asked when the silence stretched for a few seconds. He stepped closer to them, anxious to hear whatever it was. But his dad only shook his head.

"I guess we have a lot to talk about in some of our next conversations," he muttered faintly. Jace understood what that meant, his gaze once more drawn to Jace's neck. Not now. They would *all* have stuff to talk about later.

He nodded slowly, his eyebrows furrowing slightly, before he relaxed and turned back to the kitchen. He wanted to stay and visit with his family and to head home, but the food he'd eaten last night seemed to disappear into the body where he needed it or something; and once again he felt like he was starving.

He met Hazel's gaze from across the room and held it until she turned back to her parents and said something quietly to them. A second later she walked towards him. She seemed perturbed, depressed almost.

"I'm going to eat, too," she told him, avoiding his eyes. There was a large bruise on her jaw that Jace hadn't noticed before. Maybe it was only just forming, or maybe it was a few days older so it was starting to fade.

"Are you okay, Hazel? I mean about… everything." The question seemed redundant, something you would say after something like this had happened only for a lack of anything else to say. The truth was, he didn't know how to speak to her about what he really wanted to say. He wanted to apologize to her for this entire mess. For telling them about the quest and inviting them to come with him, but he couldn't get the words past his mouth, even if she would let him.

"Jace, I don't even know." He nodded and she continued. "It's not something that I can even express how… It just… is what it is." He'd never heard her so lost for words. She shook her head, tears filling up her eyes. Turning her head slightly away, she opened up the door to the kitchen, effectively stopping the conversation before it even started. And maybe that was a good thing, because Jace had nothing else to say either.

"What are you doing?" Kory asked them. He stood a few feet away, his mom's hand grasping his right hand, and his dad's resting on his left shoulder. Zory was still wrapped around Kory's leg. Jace frowned in confusion until Kory's lips cracked into a small grin. "Hungry again?"

Jace nodded but realized that he was staring at Hazel, waiting for her answer.

Hazel snorted and waved dismissively at him, otherwise ignoring the comment, and stepping through the door.

"I'm going to eat too, okay?" Jace heard Kory say to his parents behind them.

He was met with the smell of pancakes, and how he hadn't

smelled them before he wasn't sure.

"I thought you'd be hungry." His grandma was standing over a griddle, flipper in hand, and she wore an apron around her waist. Jace never could have imagined his grandma in the kitchen cooking, let alone with an apron and a smile. Shows how little he knew his grandparents. She had a plate of pancakes to the side and was pouring more batter on the griddle now.

"We have a lot of extra people here, thought I should make a lot," she murmured as if as though she was just hosting a family reunion. Jace wished he could just brush it off like she did. It was almost as if she thought he'd merely been in school with his friends. And his parents? He just couldn't figure out his feelings toward them. A part of him wished he could go back in time to before the quest, even if he had been doubting that his parents loved him.

At least then he wouldn't have the regrets he had; wouldn't have gone through the torture, and wouldn't have to see the pain that he had caused his friends and family.

Unfortunately, he couldn't do anything but go on living knowing that his choices had almost killed him and his friends.

Do they believe that it's my fault, too? Do my friends blame me? Jace eyed Hazel from under his hood anxiously, barely registering the concern in her eyes when she met his distant gaze. *I couldn't be upset if they did.*

He could feel his insides shatter even more, contradicting his thoughts. No. He couldn't *blame them* if they did, but he still would be upset about it.

He gave Hazel a small smile when he realized that he was still staring at her and her expression had turned into concern rather than confusion. The smile felt completely fake, and he was sure that Hazel thought the same as she continued to watch him for a few seconds, her eyes scanning him in a way that only she and Kory seemed to do. It was only Kory's entrance into the kitchen behind them, followed by Lisa and Philips, that made her gaze break from his at last.

"Do any of your parents want to eat?" Glenda asked. Her blue-green eyes were bright this morning, and he wondered vaguely if she'd been crying. "Maybe Jason and his friends? Or your other siblings?"

"I'll go ask Jason," Jace mumbled, leaving quickly. He knew that his older brother and his friends had slept on the couch in the family room so he looked there first.

Rob was sitting on the edge of his couch putting on some

shoes. He moved quietly and Jace paused to watch him.

"Hungry?" Jace asked him after a moment, and the other man turned sharply, eyes wide at being caught.

"Um…"

Jace's eyebrows drew up questioningly, and he knew that he'd spoken a bit warily. He just hoped Rob hadn't noticed.

"My grandma made pancakes." Jace stepped closer to Jason who had still not awoken.

"He was pretty tired." Rob looked at him. "I need to thank him for letting me stick with him for a bit."

"You're staying, aren't you?" Jace still wasn't sure if he wanted this random man to hang around, but Jason and Devin seemed to like him, so he was determined to try and be friendly with the guy.

He shook his head. "I don't think I should."

Jace didn't try to contradict him. "Want to eat first?" he asked instead. He wasn't sure if he imagined Rob's shoulders sinking slightly and couldn't help but feel a bit guilty. He wished he wasn't so wary, he just found it disturbing that Rob hadn't known them for long and already he knew some of their deepest secrets. And Jace had lost any ability to trust new people after the kidnapping.

"Yeah… I guess I'll do that." Rob agreed quietly, turning to leave for the kitchen swiftly.

Jace sighed and turned to nudge Jason awake. However, his brother did not open his eyes, and his breathing stayed even, deep in sleep.

"Jason," he tried again.

Devin blinked awake on the other couch. "What is it?" he asked.

"Breakfast." He nudged Jason again, and his brother finally opened his eyes. He met Jace's gaze and tried to sit up, eyes blinking heavily.

"Are you okay?" Jason asked, words barely above a mumbled slur in his exhaustion, managing to look at him as he asked. His eyes looked tired and bloodshot, strangely reminding Jace of his own.

"Some food… pancakes. Want some?" Jace nodded in the direction of the kitchen.

"Yeah… I think so." Jason's dark eyes scanned the room slowly. Jace felt bad for waking him up since he knew that his brother hadn't had much sleep in the last few days—but still, it was breakfast.

184

He'd fallen asleep last night without food. He needed to eat.

"Where's Rob?" Jason inquired after he assessed his surroundings. His eyes closed and his body relaxed, and Jace couldn't help but wonder if he'd fallen back asleep.

"He's eating already."

"Okay." Jason stood up, teetering slightly as he did so. His hand massaged the back of his neck. "I don't think that recliner was the best place to sleep," he muttered, moving his fingers to his head and digging them into the spot between his eyes.

"It would also have helped if you'd slept the last few days," Devin said dryly.

"Yeah, I guess." He yawned and blinked tiredly. His hair was sticking up slightly at the back. He smiled at his friend, then slowly over to Jace.

"Are you okay?" Jason asked him. Jace frowned, unsure if his brother remembered asking that already, and Jace deflected the answer again.

"Yeah… Mom and Dad are here, and the other parents." He paused before adding, "And the reporters."

"Oh." Jason shook his head. "Not in the kitchen?"

"No, Grandpa sent them out." Then after a moment of silence he added, "Rob is leaving after breakfast," As he turned to the kitchen. He expected something from his brother, some words protesting and saying that Rob should stay, but he just nodded solemnly.

"Yeah."

Hazel was sitting with her back to the door when he entered so he couldn't see her face, but Philips had the kind of smile on his face that made Jace think he missed something funny.

"How are you going to hide that?" Philips asked Jace as he stepped into the room. He pointed to his neck.

Jace's shoulders sunk. "I don't know."

Lisa shrugged. "Just put a bandage on it," she said through a mouthful of pancakes. "They won't question that, since we have been gone for ages. Or wear a turtleneck if you can manage that. Plus… speaking of covering, I need to get a jacket as well. I don't want to go in front of the reporters looking like I was dragged through the mud."

Lisa was right, she did look like a disaster. Although in Jace's opinion she seemed to have gotten off better than anyone else. Hazel was probably bruised the worst, but Philips' stab wound was a deeper injury. Although, the bruise and swelling at Kory's neck looked painful and the fact that Jace caught Kory with his hand in the pocket, fingering the inhaler more often in obvious fear showed a huge change in his friend's demeanor.

"Yeah… A bandage may work, for a little bit at least." He wasn't a huge fan of turtlenecks, but it might have to be something to get used to.

Jace sat down in one of the empty chairs thinking about his own return to school. He didn't really want to go back, but now he couldn't stop thinking about it, which was ridiculous because it was surely not the most worrying thing in his life right now.

Jason sat in a chair across from him and laid his head on his arms. Jace looked around to see that Jason, Devin, and himself were the only ones who hadn't grabbed any food yet, the others already digging in.

"He looks exhausted," Kory said, glancing at Jason worriedly.

"I am." Jason lifted his head and rubbed it quickly before grabbing a pancake. There was enough for them to each have one.

"Also, not sleeping," Kory said, nodding in acknowledgment as he passed the syrup bottle to him.

"Not yet, at least," Jason agreed.

"Are any parents eating?" Jace asked, voice going slightly higher near the end when he poured a little too much syrup on his pancake and quickly tipped it up to a stop. He passed the bottle to Devin and used his fork to even it out.

"Nah, they all had breakfast." Philips shook his head. "They're all talking to the reporters?" He rolled his eyes slightly. It was strange how willing their parents were to talk to the media, when Jace and the others didn't want to.

The door opened again, and Korren came in. He looked dejected as he looked up at them. "I missed you," he said to Jace. "I was in the bathroom, and then you came in here," he added, walking around the table. Jace pulled him onto his lap, beaming at his brother, wincing slightly when he put his brother's weight on his hurt leg and quickly shifting him to the other side.

"Sorry, I was hungry, want some food?" He held his little brother tight, glad when Korren leaned back against his chest.

His brother looked over at what they were eating. Jace knew that pancakes were his brother's favorite, so he wasn't even a little surprised when he nodded his head enthusiastically.

186

"Do you have jam?" Korren asked their grandmother. Glenda opened the fridge and scanned it quickly before grabbing a glass jar full of purple—probably marionberry flavored—jelly, and another plate from the cupboard. She put the items and another stack of pancakes in front of Korren, and he quickly grabbed two. Jace grabbed another one as well and smothered it with syrup.

"Mm…" Korren smiled at Glenda. "You should make me pancakes more often." He shoved the rest of the pancake in his mouth, then had trouble chewing it.

"You'll have to come over more often if you want me to," she smiled back at him.

"Aren't you supposed to be in school?" Jace asked Korren.

He just shrugged. "Aren't you?"

Touché. Jace almost laughed, then Korren continued, "They let me skip to see you."

"Aren't you lucky?" Hazel smirked at him, and Korren stuck his tongue out at her. Hazel and Korren knew each other well enough to do that without hard feelings; the only disgusting thing was Korren hadn't finished swallowing before sticking out his tongue.

Jason once again had his head on his arms next to his plate, and after a few more seconds he lifted his head to grab another pancake, his other hand rubbing his head again.

"Thanks for letting me hang with you for a bit," Rob said after grabbing another one.

"You can stay for longer," Jason told him, lazily pouring more syrup and lathering it with a fork. *He is totally out of it.* "We often have people over."

Rob hesitated for a minute. "I… can the offer stay open for visits?"

Jace assumed that he didn't want to be a bother now, but didn't want to fully have the offer rescinded in case he needed the option later.

"Of course." Jace wondered if Rob was going to stay for the reporters or if he would just leave them to it. He wondered if his presence would help or hinder the story.

"Who are you?" Korren asked Rob. He had just swallowed down the next humongous bite and his words were a bit garbled.

"My name's Rob." He wore a grin that Jace realized he'd already become accustomed to. "You?"

"Korren. So how come you're here?" He gestured around him

as if to emphasize the situation. Jace tried not to laugh at the question and shifted Korren slightly.

"I was just with Jason when he found them." Rob colored slightly. Huh. Perhaps Rob didn't like the attention on him. He might have been a lot more like Jace than he had originally thought.

Korren narrowed his eyes at him and directed his fork to Rob as he spoke. "That's cool." He glanced at Jason. "You found them? Where?"

Jason blinked at him. "Remember the abandoned city that I took you guys to once?" he asked.

Korren nodded, his eyes wide. "Whoa… you were there?" He turned to Jace and then the others. "Someone take you?"

"Yeah, they took advantage of the place." Jace tried to smile at him but couldn't seem to. Memories of the dark buildings, pain, and syringes flashed into his mind again, and he took a bite in a hope to distract himself and act casual.

The door opened and Kory's mom and little sister came in.

"You about ready?" his mom asked. Jace wanted to tell her, *no*. Why was she so ready for them to go out there anyway?

Zory ran over to Kory and clambered onto his lap. She gasped as she saw his plate. "Can I have some pancakes?!" she asked excitedly, with a hopeful glance at Glenda.

"Of course," Glenda said as she put more on the main plate. She placed a pancake on an extra plate and handed it to Zory.

Zory thanked her and looked around the table. Her gaze landed on Jason, and she looked at him with fondness. "Thank you, I knew you would do it," she said.

Jace was confused at her remark but said nothing.

Jason paused with a pancake halfway to his mouth and set the fork back on the plate. "Of course, I wasn't going to give up until I found them," he said.

Ah… that made more sense now, but Jace wondered when she and Jason had the chance to talk.

Jace faltered as another sound filled his ears and something dark flashed across his vision, pulling him from the room that he was currently in.

Darrin ground his teeth as Michael came into the dark office, the dead plant sitting on the desk, unmoving. He stopped pacing and spun to face the man, the plant in his grasp.

"How could you let them escape?!" Darrin yelled, tossing the plant toward the other man.

Michael sidestepped it and took another step toward Darrin, his expression one of forced casualness. "There was nothing I could have done. It was just Thomas and myself. You and everyone else had been knocked out by the boy, and we couldn't take them ourselves, the one girl obviously knew martial arts, and Jace had his magic." The words came out in a rush.

Jace, through the thoughts of Darrin, could see that Michael looked a bit beat up, and Thomas, who had stepped in behind him, looked just as bad. He wondered what had really happened, because Hazel and the others had made it sound as though the others had helped them, not attacked.

Darrin grumbled for a few more minutes before pushing past Michael harshly. Thomas moved out of the way before he could touch him. In a flash, Darrin shut the door they'd just come through and turned back to face them.

Jace stared at his plate as the image played out in his mind. Was this his imagination? What was going on? He shook as the scene continued to play out. It was weird to not only see what might have been happening back at the town, but to also feel the frustration that Darrin was feeling.

"We need to leave now," Michael suggested. "They'll come by here to check out the town to try to bring us all to jail."

"There's no reason to stay here any longer now," Darrin snapped.

"I'll go get the car going and bring it out front." Michael insisted, not reacting to the snap.

The scene and Darrin's voice left his mind as swiftly as it came, and he found himself back at the table with the others.

Hazel was staring at him in apprehension. Jace's body was shaking and the fork had clattered to the plate.

"Jace? Jace? Are you okay? What happened?" she asked, one hand on his arm. Other than Hazel, the room was silent as death. Jace's brain was slow, and it took him many moments to register that everyone was staring at him, and Hazel had been talking to him, probably said his name many times before he'd focused on her.

"I d-don't know, I... one second buddy." He shifted his brother from his leg and onto the seat as he stood up. Pain flashed in his leg as he made his way to the door, but he didn't dare stop. He pushed through the pain and hurried through the room with the parents and reporters, ignoring the cameras and microphones that a few shoved into his face. He didn't even hear the questions that they asked as he made his way to the bathroom. Locking the door behind him, he slid, his back at the door, to the floor. What had just happened? Was it just his imagination?

No. *It couldn't be*. It had been too real... Hazel had told him that he had used magic at the abandoned town—was this just another form of it? Had he had some sort of vision?

He tried to still his trembling body but when he couldn't do so, he just laid his head back against the door, breathing deep. Fear wove its way through him as he wondered just what kind of monster he was.

I don't want this!!!

He finally calmed himself enough to stand back up, though he still felt shaky. He looked into the mirror and saw the red marks on his neck, just barely in view. He sifted through the cupboard—the gauze, where was the gauze? He didn't want to go back out without some. He looked in the rest of the cupboards and finally found some in a first aid kit under the sink.

A soft knock echoed on the door, causing Jace to clench his hands. "You alright?" It was Jason. Jace felt a flash of relief and gratitude for his brother as he relaxed and unlocked the door.

"Can you help me? I want something to cover this up." He gestured to his neck.

"Of course." Jason's eyes were still red, the skin around his eyes swollen and black from not having enough sleep, and his complexion rather wan, but he stepped in and let Jace shut the door behind him.

Jace took off his jacket, and then his shirt so Jason could get to the marks easier.

Jace felt his eyes widen as he looked into the mirror at the bruised veins, for the first time able to see the red lines covering most of his back, and the side of his chest. Besides the chest area the only place the red marks could be seen from the front was along his right side.

The thought that he was a kind of monster flashed into his mind again and he looked down at his feet, worried that the new fear was correct.

Maybe he was a monster.

"I don't think there'll be anymore swimming for me," he mumbled. At least he wasn't the biggest fan of the activity.

"Not unless we get you the full-on scuba outfit." Jason flashed Jace a smile and he was glad for his brother's attempt to make him laugh, but then Jason sobered. "What's wrong, Jace?"

Jace didn't know what had happened during the vision in the kitchen, but the noise from dropping the fork would have been enough to alert everyone.

When he didn't answer right away Jason continued, "Was it Darrin?"

Of course, Jason would think that Jace heard Darrin, which he had—but it was different this time. He had *seen* what Darrin was *doing*.

"No, it's okay. It's just memories," he lied. He didn't want someone to think he was insane—especially not his brother.

Jason nodded somberly, but Jace wasn't sure if he'd convinced him or not.

Jason cut the gauze with the little scissors from the bag and got the tape to keep it on Jace's neck. After he'd finished, Jace put his shirt and jacket on, pulling the hood back up as he looked into the mirror to make sure he could only see the bandage.

"Thank you."

Jason nodded tiredly and blinked before opening the door. "If you need anything, Jace, I'll be there for you this time. I promise." He watched Jace for a minute before closing the door and leaving him alone again.

Jace's sigh filled the room, and, after another moment of apprehension, he finally followed Jason back out. He slowly moved through the quiet hallway, not wanting to go back through the reporters to get into the kitchen.

After a long moment, he finally forced himself to take a deep breath and entered the room.

The closest reporters turned to him the second the door opened, gathering around the entrance too densely for Jace to slip past. He almost sighed in annoyance as the microphones were shoved into his face.

"What did they want?" one of them asked. He didn't catch what anyone else asked, as they were talking over each other. He shook his head at all the noise. There were more questions before he could even open his mouth to answer and when they finally calmed down Jace just shook his head again. "I'll answer when I'm ready, not before," he told them, afraid of what their reaction was going to be but starting to push his way through them.

A few tried to get him to talk but Jace just forced his way through them and quickly slid into the kitchen. "Jeez, they're desperate," he muttered as the door shut behind him.

"What did they do?" Kory asked. He picked up a glass and took a swig of water, leaning back in his chair with only a slight tightening around his eyes to show he was in pain by the swallow. Jace wondered how much he'd been able to eat.

Jace shrugged. "Nothing unusual I'd guess." He took his seat again, Korren sliding off to make room for him. He tried to avoid their gazes without making it look like he was doing so.

Korren slid back onto his lap, but Jace barely registered the pain that flashed up his leg as he did so. His mind was still going between the visions he kept seeing and focusing on the pain and terror of his time while kidnapped. He was struggling to pull himself out of it.

Jason, Rob and Devin were no longer in the kitchen. Rob had probably left by now, and he wondered if the other two went back to the living room to sleep some more. Jason needed it.

And even though there were extra seats, Korren still sat on his lap.

"I'm so happy you're back," Korren told him quietly, laying his head on Jace's chest.

"Me, too," he answered, *although somehow it didn't feel much different... I still can hear Darrin, and I'm still hurting,* And wasn't that just a painful realization? He thought he'd be free once he escaped, and instead he felt just as trapped. He forced another bite down his throat. He had lost his appetite, and he couldn't very well eat that much at one time anyway after nearly starving. He pushed the plate away a few inches and immediately Korren grabbed it with a short glance at Jace to make sure he was done.

"Are you alright, Jace?" Hazel asked after a long silence. Her eyes flashed sadly, and she looked down at her plate. He couldn't help but think that the sadness was somehow connected to something he'd done.

"Yeah, I'm okay." He figured the lie was obvious, because he didn't think that any of them were exactly *okay*. He ruffled his brother's hair and sat back in the seat.

Before they could continue more of a conversation, Jace's dad came into the kitchen, eyes immediately finding Jace and quickly going over everyone else as though to check that they were all okay.

"Everything okay?" he asked, grabbing a dry pancake in his hand as he came closer and taking a hefty bite out of it. He sat in the chair Jason had left and leaned back. "It's way too crazy in there." Clearly Jace had gotten the distaste of attention from his dad.

"That's kind of why we're hiding in here," Philips told him as he pushed his plate away as well.

"Don't blame you. I wish you guys didn't have to talk with them at all. We could ask them to leave if you want, but I think they'll follow you around and hound you until you tell them at least something." His dad winced at the thought, eyes seeking Jace out in concern, but he changed the topic. "Is Jason in the family room?"

"Yeah, I think so." His dad nodded at him and grabbed another pancake before standing to leave, one hand gently rubbing Jace's hair, settling momentarily on his face as he headed for the family room.

"I'm going to go check on him," he announced as he shut the door behind him. Jace stared at the door for another few moments before turning back to the others.

"We should probably get out there," Lisa said with a sigh, leaning her head on her hand.

Hazel exhaled long. "I guess." She pushed off the table to stand and grabbed the plate that she'd just finished using to take it to the sink.

Kory followed her and Korren quickly hopped off Jace's leg so they could both stand as well.

"Thanks for the food, Grandma," Jace said as he swept past her. He gave her a quick hug from behind as she smiled at him.

"Anytime." She glanced at the others, as if telling them that the offer was open to them as well.

Jace yawned. He was still tired. He hadn't been able to sleep very well since the quest started, and especially not since he'd been kidnapped. He didn't want to sleep either. The dark unsettled him because he could always hear voices that seemed too far away to ever understand.

Hazel led the way into the living room, pushing the door open, and they were all once again bombarded with reporters. Jace had been hoping that they would be able to stick together for the interview, but that didn't seem like it would happen now. Maybe they should have asked their grandpa to have them settle down and sit like some sort of press conference instead of them getting close and separating all of them.

He noticed his mom and sister making their way over to him as the reporters fired question after question at him.

"Where were you?"

"What did they want?"

"How did they treat you?"

"Were you really at the abandoned city this whole time?" Jace tried to concentrate on a few of the questions, but they all seemed to pass through his mind as they were asked. He curled his hands into fists and decided to answer the first question he remembered.

As he opened his mouth the reporters surprisingly shut up long enough that he could hear his own voice. "We were at abandoned city," He affirmed, chewing nervously on his cheek in between sentences as he thought about the next things to answer. "We were pretty much there the whole time." He purposely ignored a few of the questions. He felt Korren's hand grab his and he smiled down at him thankfully, pulling him against his leg. Korren hid part of his face in Jace's leg, and Jace wished he could do the same.

Another one shoved a microphone in his face. "Were there any other kids there?" she asked. She looked hopeful.

"Only a few other people that I saw," he told her, remembering the girl who had helped them out, "but I was kept apart from others most of the time." He forced his hand to release from their curled position, rubbing Korren's head to keep himself grounded. The lady's gaze looked defeated, but she continued holding the mic without moving.

"You were kept apart? What do you mean by that? Were all of you separated?" A few more questions were thrown at him, and he sighed as he looked down at his feet.

"Yes, I was kept by myself. I don't know if the others were separated or not as I was not with them." He didn't really know enough about what happened to the others to know.

"Did you guys all know each other before this happened?" someone asked.

194

"Yes, we have been friends in and out of school for years." he was feeling overwhelmed already, hands trembling almost enough to be twitching.

"What was your first thought as you were captured, and what do you think now?" *Well let's see...* he thought, a little surprised at the question. *What I think about it now? Probably would still be stuck on the fact that I wish to finish what I set out for and the fear of Darrin.*

"First thought? I was thinking of my friends and family, I guess." He stuck with something more believable. "They took us to an abandoned building and the whole time I just hoped that the others would be okay." That probably *was* his first thought anyway, he had been terrified for his friends the whole time.

"Now I'm happy to be back safe with all my friends, but—" He froze as he realized that he was about to tell them that he blamed himself for the others getting harmed. How would he explain why he thought that without giving everything else away? "I guess it's just trying to get back to normal."

I really hate this... And I will probably have to go through it for another few weeks. He took a deep breath.

"How did you get captured?" A lady shoved a microphone a little too close and he pulled back sharply from it as he racked his brain quickly for some sort of excuse. What would he say about that? He had no way of knowing if his friend's stories would match up. They really should have talked about it more—but they hadn't had a whole lot of time to do that.

"I was just hanging out with my friends. I guess they thought we would be easy enough targets." *It would be rather hard to get five kids without a lot of people noticing though,* he thought.

"Do you know why they wanted you?"

"Not entirely." He closed his eyes. "I still don't know, not really." He wasn't going to add any more than that.

"What did they do to you?" He looked at the man who'd asked the question, glancing away and finding his dad through the people.

"I–" His answer was cut short as Darrin's voice came into his mind again. Was he having another vision?

"...Yes and?" Darrin drove past a stop sign before looking up at Michael who sat in the passenger seat.

"The cops are there. You can't go back," Michael said calmly. Anger rose in Darrin. Michael was right, he knew. He pulled into an empty parking lot and found a spot before jumping out quickly.

As Michael stepped out, Darrin pulled out a gun, shoving him harshly with the barrel. Thomas got out of the back and stood out of the way.

"I need those things!!" Darrin shouted at Michael. Shifting the gun, Darrin pointed the barrel up into the air between them. The shot was loud in the air between them and Michael flinched.

"I'll go back and get them when it calms down," Michael said quickly, running a hand along his thigh in obvious nerves.

"You had better."

Jace could feel the energy within Darrin—so fierce, so strong. It made him feel something new. Something that could let him do anything he wanted.

Darrin pointed his gun at Thomas. There was another loud bang. Thomas fell to the ground screaming as blood came gushing from above his right knee. He tried to grasp it.

"If you don't, then that's what will happen to you. Right there." He pressed the gun into Michael's chest and held it there until he nodded.

"I will." Michael's gaze was filled with fear, but under that there was sadness.

For a split second Jace could feel the guilt gnaw at Darrin's heart, but his power pushed the feeling away quickly, leaving only success and disgust to replace it. *A smile grew on Darrin's face as Thomas's moaning sounds filled the air. Darrin liked that sound and the feeling that came with someone else's pain.*

When Thomas continued to sit there, Darrin snapped, "Get up!"

Thomas looked up at him and pushed himself up to his feet. He leaned on the car heavily and opened the car door to slide onto the seat.

"Now—"

Darrin's voice slipped back out of Jace's mind and was replaced by the reporter's faces. They were watching curiously, and it took Jace a while to remember where he was and what the question had been.

"I'd rather not talk about that," he mumbled as he tried to calm his beating heart. They looked displeased with the answer—some concerned—but they didn't press anymore on the subject.

The power... That's what was making him do these things?

But if he had the power then why were they searching for it?

He chewed on his lip. The 'Power' they were looking for must be something that Darrin wants. And this other energy that he kept feeling from Darrin must be the Shadow. It was dark enough to be so.

And that struck a chord in Jace, something in him telling him that he was right.

He forced himself not to think about that right then. He needed to finish with the media first.

You can't have it. I won't let you get it, he told the Shadow silently. Of course, there was no answer, but just how was *he* going to get it?

Chapter Sixteen

JACE WAS RELIEVED THAT his mom let him go to school the next week. He didn't want to stay home and answer any more questions or continue to live in assault of his mind replaying the time captive over and over. He wanted some semblance of normality.

His mom had protested at first. "You just got home. You shouldn't go back to school yet." But after telling her that he was okay she'd finally relented and told him to come back home if anything went wrong. He was terrified of going, but somehow more terrified of not.

And he still hadn't told his parents about the spider-veins. He wasn't sure if he was going to, but he'd done a lot of research since being home, and spider veins or varicose veins were the closest things he could find to explain what he now had, except his were bright red, and there was no explaining that.

He really wanted to talk to his friends, but he didn't have a phone anymore. They had gone home with their own families after they had finally finished with the reporters, and he hadn't seen any of them since. It had only been a few days, but still. He would have to memorize their numbers next time he got them.

Jace grabbed his school bag after making sure the hoodie was covering his neck, and that the bandage was still on. No one in his family was up this early, which was fairly normal as Korren and Laura both went to different schools that started a little later.

He grabbed a granola bar and ate it as he stepped out the front door. He usually walked since he hated the bus, and the school wasn't *too* far from his house. Even though he had a license to drive, he didn't have a car yet so he couldn't drive himself.

Jace saw a couple of other kids walking as well. They were in his grade at school, and they had a few classes together. He wrapped his hands around the straps of his backpack, hoping that they wouldn't notice him.

One of them gave him a wave and Jace quickly lifted his fingers in a small wave without pulling his thumb from under the strap. To his relief they turned to each other and continued their conversation instead of trying to bombard him. Maybe he'd given enough of a pathetic look to keep them from approaching.

He turned his gaze to the ground to avoid any other awkward interactions, wondering if any of his friends would be going to school today, or if he'd have to sit alone. He didn't think Kyler—one of the kids at school who was something of a bully—would mess with him when he'd just gotten back from being kidnapped. Or would he?

He could feel plenty of eyes on him as he entered the school, though he refused to meet their inquiring gazes. The place was loud, footsteps, chatter, and random yells making a cacophony, but he tried to keep focused getting to class.

The crowd made him more nervous than usual, after all the abuse of the past week. He worried someone would try to talk to him about what happened. But this was better than being alone with the noise in his head.

He startled when he heard a familiar voice behind him: "Jace, can I talk to you for a minute?" and looked up to see Principal Harold— a foot taller than himself, wearing round glasses and a suit— just a few feet away.

"Of course." Jace stared at the back of his principal's balding head as he walked through the halls. Principal Harold was a good man. He enforced the rules, but he wasn't mean about it.

Even so, when Jace entered his office and the door shut behind them, he couldn't help but feel worried. He didn't think that he was ever going to get over the fear of being alone in a room with someone else. His thoughts flew to Darrin and he had to force himself to keep breathing deeply.

"Are you doing okay?" His principal's concern was obvious.

Jace sat cautiously, folding his hands in his lap. His eyes flickered around the room. He had once been able to sit in the room comfortably—even when he'd gotten in trouble—but not now.

Now he sat stiffly not daring to relax.

"Yeah, I think so," Jace replied, meeting the man's gaze, but immediately looking away. Honestly, he *wasn't* okay. He was tired from lack of sleep, still sore, still terrified, and still feeling lost.

"You know you don't have to be back here so soon." The tone was gentle.

Of course, Principal Harold would think that. Maybe he thought Jace needed a week or a month, or at least *some* time off to get back on track with his life.

"I know," Jace shrugged, feeling jittery, leg bouncing, eyes not settling on anything for longer than a second. "I just didn't want to stay home. It's easier this way."

I need to get out of this room, he thought frantically.

The man nodded carefully, unsure. "If you need anything let me know, okay? And we have school counselors if you feel like you need to talk to them. I highly suggest you do."

Jace nodded, recognizing the tone as one that allowed Jace to leave now if he desired. He stood up, pausing a moment to ask a question:

"Do you know if any of my friends are here today?"

"Lisa's parents are keeping her home, but she's the only one I've heard from, and I haven't seen any of the others yet." Principal Harold studied him. "Sorry."

"It's okay. Thanks."

He fled the office quickly, catching sight of Vice Principal Dean as he left. Strange he hadn't noticed her—or much of anything else—on the way in.

Vice Principal Dean always had her hair pulled into a tight bun, standing about the same height as Jace. She cast him a sad look before turning back to her computer as he left without a word.

He was halfway down the hall to his room before he finally looked up at the other students, scanning the crowd for his friends and not registering any other faces as he did so.

"Hi Jace!" He looked behind him at Kory's voice, his friend coming to walk beside him; somehow chipper, even if it did sound a little forced.

"Hi." Kory wore a jacket as well, hands in his pockets, but without the hood up. His neck looked even worse than before, now with a motley-colored bruise encircling the entirety of the front, and Jace remembered Darrin using his power, much like the force was used in Star Wars.

Terrifying thought when it had been used in their real life.

"That looks painful," Jace said as he touched his own neck.

Kory followed his movement.

"It's still weird to breathe." Kory rubbed it absently but stopped with a wince. Jace was very aware of the people watching them, but Kory almost acted as if they were alone. "And to swallow," he added.

Jace looked at him worriedly. "Do you need to go to the hospital to see if something's wrong?" He had no idea what was normal, or what needed to be looked at.

"My parents took me on the way home the first day. I'll be fine." Jace didn't know if he'd just imagined it, but he felt like Kory's voice was off somewhat, hoarse maybe? What sort of damage had Darrin caused? Jace wanted to insist on him stopping at the hospital again.

"What about you, man?" Kory continued. "Are you alright?"

Jace nodded uncertainly, "Yeah. I still hurt, too." He tugged his sleeves down. "I think that the next little while is going to be crazy."

Kory nodded in agreement, once more grimacing at the movement. "Yeah, I think so, too. I can't say that it sounds fun."

"Not really." Jace looked Kory over with a sharp eye. His friend looked pale, and his face seemed to have shrunk slightly, clearly not getting enough nutrition. "Did they hurt you anywhere else?"

"Sure, they did, but I'll be fine." He insisted, pulling his hands out of his pockets with a sigh, his inhaler gripped in one hand. Jace wondered if he noticed that fact, especially when Kory had tried so hard to hide it from others previously. "I've been having random times when I get really, really hungry and only a few bites are needed to fill me up—super strange if you ask me—" he lowered his voice. "—and I keep replaying everything; the girl dying; me nearly dying, finding you like... well, like you were. Then it doesn't help when I wake up to a sore neck and realize that it had actually happened." Kory slipped around some people before continuing in a lower voice, coming even closer. "Jace, what did you mean; when you said that Darrin manipulated your mind?"

Jace forced himself not to cower from the question. He didn't know if there was anyone around them that could hear their conversation since they were talking really quietly but Jace didn't want to explain it, even to his friend.

"Honestly, I don't know what I meant." Jace barely spoke above a whisper and Kory stepped even closer to hear. "It was weird and 'manipulated my mind' was the only way I could think of explaining it. It was like an oncoming migraine that spread through my whole body, but then I heard his voice, and the pain wouldn't go away."

Kory tilted his head to the side but before he could say anything else on the subject, Jace changed it.

"Did the principal talk to you yet?"

Kory shook his head, but a voice interrupted his answer.

"Kory, can I talk to you?" And of course, it was the principal.

"Speak of the devil," Kory whispered in his ear with a short laugh. "Of course," Kory told him enthusiastically. Jace was pretty sure Kory was the only one who was able to go to the principal's office—whether it was for a good or a bad reason—with a smile on his face and his voice as happy as could be.

Jace shook his head and slipped into his first class. Lisa was the only friend who had this class with him, so with her being gone he would have to wait for next period to find out if any of his other friends had decided to attend school today.

He made his way to his usual seat; it was in the second to last row on the side, one of the furthest from the door. Their teacher hadn't come in yet, which was to be expected. The man usually stepped in right when the bell rang, literally.

It felt like a long couple minutes as he sat there, having pulled his journal out to draw to appear busy. He began to grow more agitated by the people giving him the side-eye and clearly talking about him in whispers, until his shoulders were tight, and he was about to jump up and leave the room.

Finally, the bell rang. Mr. Durnge had not entered yet.

He snapped his eyes shut as he heard Darrin's voice in his head. "*Jace. Oh, Jace. I know where you are. I will get you.*"

Michael passed through the dark building, Darrin right behind him, the darkness encroaching Jace's vision as he watched.

They were back in the building in the abandoned town, looking for something, but before Jace could figure out what, the click of the door shutting jerked him out of the vision.

"Jace. It's good to see you. I'm glad you're back safe." Mr. Durnge was looking straight at Jace. Uncomfortable, as they all stared at him, Jace didn't really know how to respond.

"Thanks. It's good to be back." His voice stuck in his throat a little. He wasn't sure if that was necessarily true. He didn't want to be here. Suddenly, he was wishing he'd stayed home. It felt like the underside of his skin was itching.

Mr. Durnge nodded before starting the lesson, and Jace squeezed his palm over his forearm, wishing the deep itch of anxiety would leave.

Mr. Durnge taught history, and he liked this class more than most—not because he really liked history but because Mr. Durnge could make it interesting.

However, Jace couldn't concentrate on anything today, and was relieved that his teacher didn't call on him. He could feel flickering glances the entire time.

He opened his notebook when his teacher asked but didn't write anything down. Instead, he drew, mind drifting.

"Jace." He looked up quickly from the page he was doodling on to see his teacher standing over him. All the other students had left. How had that happened?

"Sorry, sir." He stuffed his notebook in his bag, hands shaking with nerves, and started to stand, but the man put a calming hand on his shoulder.

"You're okay, Jace." He smiled at Jace and stepped away. "I saw you on the news. You didn't look like you liked the attention very much."

"I didn't." He was relieved to see that the classroom door stayed open but he couldn't help but edge closer to it.

"Even more so when they asked what they did to you," his teacher added, his eyes watchful.

Jace stiffened slightly, then hoped Mr. Durnge didn't notice.

"Anyway, I just wanted to make sure you're doing alright." He looked like he wanted to say something else but stopped himself.

You and everyone else... Jace thought bitterly. "Yeah, I'm okay."

Mr. Durnge opened his mouth, paused a moment, then went with; "Have a good day" before turning to leave.

Jace quickly followed him out, moving quickly through the hall to try and make it before he was late for the next class.

He entered right as the bell rang and sat in the chair closest to him—his regular seat. He was relieved to have an easy and fast exit.

Luckily Mrs. Noti didn't say anything about him being back, just went straight into the math lesson that went completely over his head. He would never understand how they got answers by doing the steps.

He started doodling again. He didn't know why he was, but he just couldn't concentrate.

And then *it* happened.

His next breath didn't come in correctly, as though something was holding him tight, wrapping slowly around his neck and chest. He sat there for a second, eyes widening as he tried to breathe.

It wasn't working.

He dropped the pencil, clenching his fists and squeezing his eyes shut for a moment. He needed to get out of there.

Jace raised his left hand—even that seemed impossible to do, as his whole body felt constrained by some invisible source, but it worked better than his right one, which felt entirely immobile.

"Yes, Jace?" his teacher asked softly.

"Can I go to the bathroom?" he gasped.

Her face creased with concern as she nodded.

He stood up hastily, trying his hardest to act natural. As he entered the hall, he quickly looked around to make sure no one was out there as he fled to the bathroom.

Was this what Frank was talking about? When he said that he would have problems?

He grabbed the lockers tightly, the air pushed from his lungs. He was suffocating! How did the man Frank told him about usually get this under control?

He forced his feet to stumble to the bathroom, nearly hunched over by the tightness over his entire body, right side seemingly in a spasm, but his mind singly focused on merely making it somewhere no one would see him.

Opening the bathroom door, he fell to the ground, relieved in the quick glance to find that there wasn't anyone in occupying the space.

His chest ached as gasped, desperate for air, hands curling into tight fists as brought them to his chest in panic.

The door hit his foot as someone tried to open it.

No. No, please.

"Jace?" He knew it was Philips, and a flood of relief that it was his friend washed through him.

Another pair of feet squeezed through the gap in the door, and he realized that Kory was in there too. His vision was starting to darken, and he didn't even try to answer Philips.

He was going to die! He was suffocating and he was going to die!

"Jace, calm down." Philips grabbed his hands to keep him from scrabbling at his neck. "Calm down, I need you to look at me and try to take a breath." But Jace couldn't.

He closed his eyes, about to give in to darkness, and it was in that moment that his airway suddenly opened, his chest relaxing, a gasp loud in the near quiet room.

But the darkness still heaved, finally taking him.

₪   ₪   ₪

Kory felt his shoulders release as he sat down next to his friends. Jace was breathing now, even if he wasn't awake. His face, moments ago an almost blue color, was slowly going back to pale. Kory would have suggested that they take him to the school nurse, but he knew that Jace would not like that at all, and they had no way to really explain what was going on.

So, Kory just leaned on the door to make sure that no one could enter.

"What was that?" Philips asked him.

"I have no idea." Kory shrugged. "I'm guessing his marks can still kill." That was the only thing Kory could think of.

When Jace finally opened his eyes a few minutes later, he pushed himself up against the wall and took a few trembling breaths. When he calmed and the confusion left his gaze, he muttered a quiet "thank you."

"What happened?" Kory asked him quickly, keeping his tone quiet and narrowing his eyes to study him. Jace's grandma had stitched up the wound on his head and given him painkillers, but it still looked painful. Kory was wishing he'd taken his own painkillers this morning because his neck and other muscles were screaming at him. Philips didn't look like he was in too much pain, so he must have taken his.

Jace hesitated, hand rubbing his chest. "I don't know. It felt like something was squeezing my chest." As he spoke Kory felt someone push against the door behind him.

"What the crap?" The words on the other side were muffled

by the door, but he still heard them. Kory stood up quickly, Philips and Jace following the movement, and stepped away from the door.

"Sorry," he told the boy that came in. It wasn't someone he recognized, but he obviously recognized them. His eyes flickered toward them, lingering on each of their various injuries, and back to the floor as he stepped the rest of the way in.

"Is everything okay?"

He must have thought it was pretty weird that the three boys who had been kidnapped were randomly in the middle of the bathroom during class, blocking the door.

"Yeah," Kory answered. He had spotted Jace through the glass in the classroom door walking—stumbling—to the bathroom minutes before. He'd gestured to Philips, who sat next to him, and gestured to the door before asking their teacher if he could go to the bathroom. Philips, despite his confusion, had followed his example.

Now they slipped past the boy who'd finally stopped staring at them and moved to enter a stall as the three of them left.

Kory and Philips had to stop back by their classroom to grab their bags before heading to their next one. Kory touched his throat softly. It really hurt to even move his neck to the side. Breathing was bothersome, and swallowing was worse. It wasn't normal, he knew that, but there was nothing he could do about it, so he wasn't going to make a big deal out of it.

"Jace!"

Jace jerked awake, disoriented for a long moment. It had been two days since he'd started going back to school, and he'd just gotten home and had gone straight to bed—his exhaustion making it so that for once he was able to sleep without Darrin's voice.

It had been his mom's voice that roused him.

Grumbling under his breath, he sat up. He'd barely gotten any restful sleep while he'd been kidnapped, and now—well, sleep wasn't much better. His clock showed him that he'd had about an hour of sleep.

"Coming!" He called groggily. He didn't need to worry about getting his jacket and gloves since he had slept in them. He'd basically stepped into his room, dropped his bag, and had fallen onto the bed.

He stepped out of his room and went down the steps as fast as he could. His mom was at the bottom. "Mayor Vercet is here to see you," she said.

He glanced over, surprised to see that the Mayor did, in fact, stand in front of him, his large body filling the doorway. He gave Jace a cursory glance, probably trying to figure out what had happened to him.

"Hi." Jace furrowed his eyebrows in confusion. Why was he here?

"How's it going?" Mason asked casually, as if they were just friends seeing each other again.

"Fine, how about you?"

"I'm good. I heard that you're back at school already. Is that correct?" *Did he come here just for small talk? To check up on me?*

"Yes, I thought that it might be easier to just get back on

track.”

Mason nodded as though in agreement. “Look, I can’t stay long,” he said quickly. He looked back at the door. “I’ve got a lot to do, including check on the others who got kidnapped. I just wanted to make sure you’re okay and see if there’s anything I can do to help.”

Jace was about to protest when he suddenly had an idea. “Um… thank you.” He chewed on his lip before pushing forward with the question. “Is there any way you can get the news reporters to back off?” They had even followed him to school, and that wasn’t cool at all. Luckily, they hadn’t asked him as many questions, but they had taken pictures of him from a distance.

Mason smiled. “Well, I could definitely try talking to them, but I’m sure many of them wouldn’t listen.”

Jace nodded. That may be better than nothing.

Mason started for the door again. “Have a good day.” The door closed before Jace could respond. He turned to his mom.

She smiled at him. “I'm so happy you’re back,” she said through the uncomfortable silence, and hugged him again. Closing his eyes, he let himself sink into the embrace.

“Me, too.”

“We were planning on going out to dinner tonight, you know, with the family.” She didn’t let go of him, just rubbed her hands up and down his back comfortingly. He wasn’t quite sure how to react. He wasn’t used to his parents giving this kind of attention to him, so he just stood there with his hands wrapped around her loosely.

“Yeah.” Jace felt tears start to come up, but he blinked them away. “Yeah, I’d love to do that.” As she pulled away, she wiped her own tears.

“We’ll leave in a half hour, okay?”

Jace nodded, then she left the room.

With the room empty, a random thought entered his mind. He remembered the foreign man that had shown them the cave, and then had been knocked unconscious, like he himself had been. What had happened to the man? Had he been killed?

Then he thought of the voice that he’d heard while in the cave. He couldn’t recall what it had said. He was pretty that was because he’d been hit in the head with a branch about five seconds after he’d heard it. He remembered something about not trusting anyone they didn’t know, and supposedly it had been Isaac who told Darrin about where they had gone. Jace didn't want to believe that.

He slowly wandered up the stairs, a hand on the wall in his tiredness as he tried to recall anything from the voice he'd heard before being taken. The injuries he'd received made him doubt he'd even heard it in the first place, but if he had… well, he would take any form of guidance at this point.

He sat on his bed, rubbing his forehead slowly, then looked up to see that Korren stood in the doorway. He held his hands behind him and stared at Jace with his head tilted to the side.

"Need something?" Jace asked him, and Korren came closer, his hands still behind his back.

"I made something for you," he said, pulling his hands from behind his back and revealing a piece of paper. "I made it while you were gone, to give to you when you got back, but I forgot about it." It was a picture of them all as stickmen. The thought warmed Jace's heart.

"Thank you," Jace breathed, taking the picture from his brother's hands carefully. He scanned his eyes over it. Korren had set the drawing in front of the ice-cream place that they would go to. In the background were trees—or in this case green blobs with lines— and Jace remembered the day, just a week before they had left for the quest and then gotten kidnapped, that they had been at this ice-cream shop. They would always go as a family, but it was Korren's favorite place.

Jace sat on the floor, still holding the drawing. He felt tears cloud his vision again, but he smiled up at Korren as he came closer. His younger brother sat on Jace's lap and Jace held him with the picture in one hand.

"You like it?" Korren looked up at him, then put his head against his chest.

"Yes, I do." He put the picture on the ground next to him and put his arms around Korren. "Where do you think I should hang it up?" He looked up at his walls. A few pictures from Korren were already pinned to his wall, the rest were photos of his friends and family and a poster of *Imagine Dragons*, his favorite band.

"There's a spot right over your bed that's free," Korren said softly. He grabbed Jace's hand and started messing with his gloved fingers. Then he put his hand against Jace's and looked back up at him. "My hands are almost as big as yours."

Jace smirked. He had about two inches to go but Jace didn't

tell him that. "I know, you're getting too big."

"Too big for what?" Korren looked curious, innocent eyes staring up at him. Jace felt winded as he realized that he would probably never look like that again.

"Too big for me to hold you... to play with you." Jace watched Korren's eyes widen in dismay.

"No!" He shook his head. "See look." He grabbed their hands and turned them as though to help Jace see them better. "See, I'm still teeny, not even that big yet!"

Jace tsked sadly. "It's going to be so sad when I won't be able to hold you anymore," Jace continued in mock seriousness as if he hadn't heard him.

Korren fell to his knees on Jace's lap, putting his hands on his cheeks. "No... no, I'm small, you can still hold me."

Jace forced himself not to wince from the painful pressure on his injured leg and couldn't help but feel a glimmer of amusement at how much that worried Korren.

"Do you want me to hang up the picture?" Jace asked instead, ruffling Korren's hair.

He nodded and got off his lap, grabbing the picture.

"Where are we putting it? Above the bed?"

Korren turned to him with his arms up and Jace knew that he wanted to be held. He picked him up, then grabbed a tack. "We'll just put it over the bed." He gave it to Korren. "You can do it."

Kory reached over to the wall and stuck the pin in, then turned back and wrapped his arms around Jace's neck. "We're going out to eat aren't we?" he asked.

"Yes."

"I'll go get ready then." Korren squirmed to get down and ran out the door. Jace took a deep breath then gave one last look at the picture before pulling his thoughts back to the cave, trying to recall anything he could.

The very little he remembered didn't help at all. It was all things that had already happened, or too vague to help him at this point.

Besides, as much as a part of him wanted to go back out and find this Power, the other part of him thought it would be better to leave well enough alone.

He sighed at his tumultuous thoughts and plopped back onto

the bed. As his eyes closed, memories reared their ugly heads up and he jolted back up with a gasp. His heartbeat had picked up to about twice the speed. He pulled his hand to his chest, trying to calm himself, and spotted Jason standing in the doorway.

"You okay?" Jason asked, coming closer. Jace nodded in response and let his hand fall, feeling it tremble.

"Yeah, fine." He stood up and met Jason by the door. Jason knew he had left home to find the Power originally before being kidnapped, but neither of them had spoken about it.

"How are you doing?" Jason asked, hugging him. His older brother seemed to always know what he needed.

"Fine, now." He ignored the contention in his thoughts and hugged him back, relaxing into his embrace. "Thanks."

₪ ₪ ₪

Licking his lips—dinner had been really good tonight, and mom had even let him get dessert this time!—Korren looked up at Jace from his seat in the car. Jace had leaned on the door almost as soon as they got in, eyes closed, and possibly asleep.

But when Korren wrapped his arms around him and leaned into his side carefully, he felt Jace's arm wrap around him. He couldn't help but feel relieved that Jace was still holding him even though earlier he had been saying that Korren was getting too big. Korren felt like he was getting bigger, but he was still way smaller than his siblings, and he was glad.

Jason was sitting on Korren's other side, watching them both warmly.

Korren was so glad that Jace was back safe. Not only was Jace here, but Jason was still here as well, staying with them to make sure they were all okay. He had gotten both of his brothers back.

It only took a few minutes for them to get home, and as soon as the car turned off Jace opened his eyes, got out, and headed into the house, messing with the half-gloves on his hands. Korren wondered why he wore such things—it wasn't like it was too cold out or anything and he didn't look like he liked them much—but he followed Jace into the house without saying anything.

Jace was heading to his bedroom, yawning as he did so, and so Korren moved to his own bedroom next to Jace's. It was still early in the night, only seven, so Korren had time to play before he had to go to bed, but Jace looked really tired and maybe he would be able to sleep so he didn't want to bother him.

He grabbed one of his toy cars, his favorite one because it was the first one Jace had given to him—a brown truck—and started adding other cars to the game, like a robber that got chased by the police car, but he had to stop when his parents came in, telling him it was time to get ready for bed.

He paused on the way to the bathroom and peeked into Jace's room. He could see the picture that they'd just hung up from the light in the hall, and he smiled. His brother would always hang up his pictures as if they were the best thing he had ever seen.

But Jace was whimpering.

Hesitantly, he walked into the room. Jace let out another whimper. Was his brother having a bad dream? Korren got them sometimes, and mom would help him. Maybe he should help?

Before he could move, Jace started thrashing around in the bed. *What do I do*? In a panic, Korren put out a hand on Jace's arm, gently alternating between patting and rubbing to calm his brother down. The motion seemed to work, Jace relaxed under his hand and his breathing softened so Korren kept it up for a minute.

Remembering that he was supposed to be brushing his teeth he carefully patted once more, then pulled his hand away and turned to leave.

He wasn't even at the door when a scream as loud as a firecracker came from Jace's mouth. He jumped high, spinning back around with wide eyes.

Jace sat up in bed, pulling his legs up to curl into a ball. His eyes were as wide as Korren's, scanning the room quickly. After a long moment, Jace met his gaze and the panic slowly faded as his eyebrow furrowed, something unidentifiable crossing his expression.

Korren was about to move closer when he heard someone rushing up the stairs. He turned to see their dad enter; going to Jace without hesitation and wrapping him in his arms.

Jace fell into his father's embrace, mumbling 'it's just a dream' over and over as his fingers dug into their father's shirt.

The hand in Korren's hair surprised him and he looked up to see his mom.

"Go get ready for bed," she said, turning him away from the

scene. She gently nudged him toward the door where Jason was watching worriedly.

He slipped out of the room, listening to his parents' voices in the other room as he brushed his teeth.

What had scared Jace so bad?

Chapter Eighteen

"DID YOU SEE THE LATEST news article?" Hazel asked Jace. She had come over after school and looked very apprehensive.

"No?" He framed it as a question and glanced at Kory.

"I can't believe that they would do this!" She started pacing.

Jace couldn't help it; her anxiety rubbed off on him. "What?"

She didn't answer but he saw her phone gripped in her hand, the light on, and grabbed for it; convinced that this was what she was riled up about.

"Don't. You don't want to read that," she said. He easily held the phone out of her reach as she tried to grab it back. Already scanning the page, he ignored her, and she plopped down beside him.

There was a picture of Jace on the front with Kory in the background. He was tugging at his sleeve absently with his gloved hand, while Kory was looking over his shoulder. In big words it said, "What are they hiding?"

Jace's shoulders sunk. They had gotten the perfect picture for a statement like that. "Why would they do that?"

Kory read the heading over Jace's shoulder. "Jeez, bad publicity. It's not like we're not dealing with enough as it is." He shook his head. "Why can't people mind their own business? We weren't doing anything to bother them."

Jace tossed the phone onto the bed with a sigh. He could feel tears start to threaten his gaze and stood quickly, exiting the room and hoping that his mom was still in the kitchen. She was.

She looked up as he entered, giving a warm smile. "Hi." Jace knew that his friends had followed him in. She looked at their distraught expressions and stopped cutting the vegetables. "What's wrong?"

"The news."

"Yeah? We knew they'd be posting stuff." Despite the words, her look was inviting. She sat in a kitchen chair and Jace plopped in a seat next to her, his friends following his example.

"They think we're hiding something."

Her eyebrows drew up. "Aren't you though?" She asked gently as she touched his neck. "You won't even tell me what this is." She was right, but he really didn't want to tell her about it yet.

"But they don't need to know! It's just going to make people hate us," Jace added in a lower voice.

She sighed. "I'm sorry, Jace. I know it's rough. I wish I could help more with that." Then she hesitated for some reason, looking at his friends before deciding to continue. "I think I need to tell you something now: Jason told us that you think we have been distant with you. Is that right?" He felt discomfort flood through him at the topic, not ever planning to confront his parents about that.

He bit his lip. He knew that if he objected, she wouldn't believe him, but he wasn't just going to go right out and say it.

She nodded sadly. "I had never meant to do that, but looking back, I realize it's true. I have been. It's just... I've been trying to prepare myself for you leaving." She wiped her hands on her pants, obviously nervous. "When you were born, your dad and I were told that you would leave on a quest in your teen years, something about the Power. The same thing your grandparents have been distracted searching for so long."

"Wait..." He tried interrupting but she continued on.

"Yes, I know you weren't kidnapped, initially anyway." She frowned, concern marring her features in the little lines around her eyes. "I didn't want you to think that I loved you any less, but I guess there was a part of me that protected myself in my fear of possibly losing you. I didn't want to lose you."

There was silence in the room. Jace knew his friends were waiting for his response, and he was still trying to process the information through his tired brain; a feeling of bitterness filling him, and yet a strange sense of hope.

"You know that's why I left?" He wondered what she thought of her distance being the main reason he'd gone on the quest anyway. He wondered if he would have even gone if he had felt the love from his parents.

He gave a quick glance at Hazel and Kory. They both looked

uncomfortable. Jace understood that feeling. It's why Jace hadn't wanted to ever bring this up. He was just kind of enjoying this new relationship with his parents without confronting their issues.

Mom looked sad, possibly surprised. "Not exactly."

The silence was back. This time it seemed to pressure him into talking. "This…" He pulled his hood down, "...was from Darrin." He put a hand on the bandage. He wasn't going to take the gauze off. It was too hard to get back on—he really ought to figure something else out. Hazel thought he would look good in a turtleneck, but Jace wasn't a huge fan of them, nor did he want to spend money on new clothes.

Instead, he pulled his jacket sleeve up. He knew for a fact that his parents hadn't seen this yet. Not even while he was sleeping because he hadn't really slept much, and every noise woke him back up. Yes, he heard voices, but even more than that were the visions that came occasionally, and the memories that plagued him anytime he closed his eyes. He'd been having both a bit less as time passed but he kept replaying the moment when Darrin had shot Thomas, the hunger for blood that he had felt from Darrin. He'd recognized that Darrin's personal feelings had been shoved down in place of the Shadow, but how could he beat something that evil and powerful to the Power; a power which the Shadow wanted?

He heard the door open behind him. He didn't need to look back to know it was his dad walking in with his heavy footsteps, and Laura's quick inhalation alerting him that she had joined them as well. Dad looked down at Jace's arm and he blinked a few times before turning to his wife, eyes slightly glassy. "You told him?"

Laura was still looking at Jace's arm. Even though all the attention on his marred skin was making him uncomfortable, he forced himself not to cover it back up.

His mom nodded shortly, still staring at the marks. "What did he do?" she gasped at last. He could hear tears blocking her words.

"He wanted me to tell him where the Power is. I didn't even know, and I tried saying that much but he kept trying." He looked down and bit his lip as his jaw trembled. "Is it bad that I really wanted to tell him?"

"No… it's understandable, sweetheart," she said, trying to soothe him, one hand automatically moving to cover his shaking one.

"It hurts a lot. I just want it to end." Saying the words, he realized his mistake. He had said 'want' instead of 'wanted'. He wanted

216

the visions, and the voices to stop, the pain and the choking, and the fear of something else happening to his friends and him.

"What? You want *what* to end?" Mom asked worriedly, her eyebrows furrowed. He heard the door open again and Jason stepped in with Philips and Lisa lingering behind. He didn't know why all his friends were here. They hadn't said they were coming over. Of course, they didn't have phones yet. Probably just came over to talk about the news article.

Even now he could hear a few voices whispering in his head. He had gotten used to them, and now they were like background voices.

But just because he was used to the noise it didn't mean he liked it.

He squeezed his eyes shut, instantly regretting it as he was dragged into another vision.

Darrin stood in the way, blocking the exit of the cave so that Jace couldn't get out. He felt the darkness pass through Darrin slowly, an energy that rivaled anything Darrin had ever known, until it was suddenly erupting from him, a dark void jumping clear from Darrin and charging toward Jace.

In the vision, he watched himself fall to the floor as he struggled with his breath. He'd felt this pain and desperation before in the school bathroom, like he was breathing in really thick air, and he couldn't get anything through.

The Shadow's void swirled around him before finally leaving him alone.

He found himself back in the kitchen, but he still couldn't breathe. His mom was watching him anxiously, but he didn't think he had turned the blue color yet that Kory said he had last time. Not yet anyway. He needed to know what Philips had done to help him.

Even though he knew panicking wouldn't help, he couldn't help it. "Philips," Jace gasped quietly, standing from his chair, and nearly wincing as it screeched back along the floor. "Philips, help." Philips looked confused for a second before his eyes widened in understanding. He quickly skirted around Jason, coming closer to Jace. Kory slipped to his side as well.

Jace still had no idea what had helped him last time, but he did know that it was right when Philips had tried to help him. Was it just Philips, or anyone? He didn't really want to find out.

He tried taking another step but fell instead. Pain flashed up his right side, along his veins. His entire body doubled over in pain, his mind screaming at him.

"It's okay Jace." Hands gripped his arms that he had subconsciously brought up to his ears. The voices swirled in his mind, louder, more persistent, yet slurred together so he couldn't understand them.

Again, as Philips grabbed him, he could breathe, but the voices didn't stop like he was hoping they would. He couldn't even concentrate on what they were saying.

He flinched when he felt a hand touch his back lightly. It didn't hurt; he was just tense. He almost expected Darrin to be behind him, hovering over him, tormenting him.

He kept his hands over his ears allowing Philips' tight hold on his arms to slowly ground him back to reality despite the swirling voices.

After another few minutes he brought his head up slowly, still plugging his ears even though it didn't do any good at all. In fact, he figured being able to hear the surrounding voices instead of everything in his head.

Hesitantly, Jace let go of his ears. He wished he wasn't in the kitchen right now. He didn't want to explain to everyone what had happened—has been happening.

"What's going on?" Dad asked quietly as he crouched in front of him. "What is it?"

"Darrin…" He looked into his eyes, scared that if he let them close he would be thrust into another vision. He did not want to tell them, but how could he not after that? "Darrin… he manipulated my mind somehow, made me sort of… connected to him."

He didn't know if that was what it was exactly but it was the only way he could think to explain it. "I don't know what he did, but I keep hearing people talking now, and no matter how hard I try they won't go away, and every once in a while I feel like I can't breathe, and… and…" They would think he was crazy if he told them, wouldn't they?

"And what, honey?" His mom was suddenly stroking his back, or had she been all along? He wished that he could close his eyes. He didn't want to see how they would react, but he definitely didn't want to see another vision.

"I don't know…" He leaned into the cupboards, trying to

218

think.

You've got to do better than that, idiot, he heard Darrin say in his mind, and Jace startled at the thought that the other man could see what was happening to Jace as much as Jace could to Darrin.

He wasn't sure how he knew, but Darrin's presence suddenly disappeared. It was almost like a dark block in the back of his mind was gone.

"Visions," he said at last, voice coming out as a mere mumble.

"Visions?" He didn't even try to figure out the few who had asked. He was so tired that all he wanted to do was sleep, but he doubted that would happen. Sleeping made it worse.

"Yeah. Like what Darrin could be doing..." Jace's eyes closed against his own will. He was relieved when the enshrouding darkness didn't come for him.

"The dark makes it worse; I can't even sleep and I'm really tired."

"What's going on?" Jace forced his eyes open when he heard Korren's voice. Laura went over to him and scooped him into a tight hug.

"They're just talking for a bit, are you ready to go play now?" He had his shoes on, so Jace had to assume that she had promised to take him out somewhere.

"Yes, I've been waiting for you, but when you took longer than you said I thought I'd come get you to see if you had forgotten." He looked at them, confused. "What are you guys talking under the counter for?"

Jace looked up to see that he was right. He was now under the overhang where stools would be if they had any.

"Much more fun than under the table, don't ya think?" Jace told him with a forced smile.

"I suppose." Korren looked thoughtfully at him. "You look tired," he said. Before Jace could answer Laura encouraged him out the door, following after one more lingering glance at him.

"He shot Thomas," Jace said after a few seconds. He looked at Lisa and Kory, shuddering as the horror from the bloodlust, ignited from the Shadow, washed over him.

"Why?" Hazel asked.

"He was trying to prove a point I think." He shook his head and continued in a mumble. "Michael was right, though. Darrin isn't the one that's bad." They had no idea what he was talking about. He knew that, but he needed to say it out loud because it was starting to make him really stressed.

His eyes were closed again.

"Korren is right. You look tired. I think it's time for you to get some sleep." He heard his dad come closer and nodded. He didn't care to open his eyes again because, for once, the darkness left him alone. Jace was pretty sure it was because he had talked to his parents, and it relieved the stress slightly.

He shifted his position as he felt arms slide under him. He wanted to protest, thinking that he was too big to be carried, but he just couldn't find it in him.

ᴎ   ᴎ   ᴎ

Jace was looking worse the last day and a half than he had when they'd first gotten out of the abandoned city, and that was saying something because, even then, he'd looked terrible.

He wasn't the only one; Philips was more exhausted nowadays as well. But Jace... well, Philips wondered if he'd had a single good night of sleep since they'd been back—heck, since they'd been captured.

"I'm fine," Jace had insisted after Philips had told him to get some sleep earlier this week. He had also put his guard up, even with Hazel. Now Philips understood why. Had Philips been in his position, he probably would have reacted much the same way, though Philips seriously doubted he could have ever handled voices, dreams, and visions. He was pretty sure he'd have gone insane and completely irritated at everyone. Jace was still gentle, even if distant.

One thing he hadn't told Jace—or anyone for that matter, was that when he helped Jace be able to breathe again, he'd felt his own energy leaving, his own breath stopping for a terrifyingly long moment.

It was weird and crazy alarming for a long moment, but then that feeling would pass and they'd both be okay. He figured that Jace was using his magic to take it in, even if he wasn't aware of it happening.

He wouldn't tell Jace in any case, his friend would only worry about it and refuse to let anyone help him next time.

"Did you know about that?" Lisa asked them suddenly. They

220

were still in the kitchen, having moved to the table with Jace's brother and parents—his dad sitting with them after he'd come back from carrying Jace to bed.

"I knew that he had times where he couldn't breathe, but nothing else," Kory confirmed with a nod as he looked away, his gaze thoughtful. "Did you see it move?" he asked after another second. Both of Jace's parents paused in their quiet talking as they all looked at Kory.

"What moved?" his dad asked.

Kory rested his hand on the table. Philips guessed that he was as uncomfortable with Jace's parents as he was himself. None of them have really spoken much, and now they were talking about something so… confidential. "The veins. They moved," Kory said. He touched his neck and drew his finger along his skin. "Here. In the front. I think that may be what's choking him."

His dad looked thoughtful. "I need to make a few calls." He stood to leave.

They all sat there in silence, Philips shoulders hunching more and more. Yes, he was tired. He'd probably got more sleep than Jace, but he could still feel the lack of a restful night wearing on him. No, he didn't hear voices or feel darkness, but his thoughts always went back to the time as a captive... the one girl who'd tried to help them and gotten killed for it, magic flying Kory across the room, and the knife that had been shoved in his arm.

The pain from the wound didn't help things either.

"How are you guys doing?" Riley, Jace's mom, asked them after a few more seconds. She looked close to crying herself, but her shoulders were pulled back in determination.

Philips didn't answer, his mind drifting to Jace who lay upstairs.

"You know he's going to try again, right?" Philips asked them quietly. He didn't even know if the others had answered Riley's question, wasn't sure how long he'd been thinking.

"He wouldn't, would he?" Jason asked.

Kory shook his head. "No, he's definitely going to. You can tell with Jace because he won't speak about it. He'll try to make us believe that he's just trying to forget but he's probably more or less planning a way to get back out there."

"His biggest thing—which is ours too—is our families," Hazel whispered. "We don't want our parents to freak out, especially with us just getting back." Hazel paused. "I'm going to go with him, but I'm not sure how we can get away without causing mass panic."

Philips shifted, gently touching his injured arm with his good hand. He'd taken pain medication to make the healing hurt less, but the effects were starting to wear off.

"He doesn't want us to go," Lisa said as she leaned back in a chair.

Kory looked at her. "Of course, he doesn't."

"So how will we know when he leaves? He won't tell us."

"I hadn't thought of that," Philips whispered.

You won't leave without us, will you, Jace? Philips frowned. He honestly would be surprised if Jace *did* tell them.

Chapter Ninete...

IT WAS A LOT WORSE AT school the next day. There wasn't just attention on them now, but many eyes actually held suspicion. People always seemed to believe what the news told them.

"Hey, Jace?" It was the end of his first class, and Mr. Durnge had settled onto the desk in front of him while he'd been packing up his bag, most kids already out of the room.

"Yeah?" He didn't stop putting his things in his bag. He was still tired. He'd gotten more sleep last night than recently, but he'd still awoken around three and couldn't get back to sleep. He'd looked at himself in the mirror earlier and knew that he had dark circles around his eyes, which in turn made him receive a lot of strange, worried looks.

"Can I talk with you for a minute?" Math was his next class, and he didn't really care if he missed part of it.

"Sure." He finally looked up when he heard the door shut. His eyes flickered from Mr. Durnge settled on the table to the now closed door then back again. Obviously, Mr. Durnge had asked the last person to leave to shut the door, but why?

His teacher's eyes narrowed as if he saw Jace's worry. "Sorry, but it would be better if no one else heard what I want to talk to you about."

"What is it?" Jace stood up, slinging his backpack across his shoulders. He curled his hands slightly, trying to breathe though panic was slowly unfurling inside his chest.

"Your dad called me—please don't panic on me right now, okay?" He took a step away and raised his hands slowly, eyeing Jace carefully. "He told me what happened with Darrin."

"What?" Why would his dad do that? Jace's panic was

replaced with disbelief.

"Frank—I think he told you about me, didn't he?" Mr. Durnge stuttered over the question a bit, as though not sure how to speak about it.

"What?" Jace racked his brain. Frank? How did Mr. Durnge know Frank? "Wait…" Jace began, as his eyes widened in disbelief. "Frank said that someone he knew had…" his voice trailed off as he gathered his thoughts, eyes flicking to Mr. Durnge's long sleeves. He didn't know how he was going to ask when he didn't even know what *it* was.

"Yeah, that's me." Mr. Durnge hesitated, throat bobbing nervously before he undid his tie, unbuttoning the first button and pulling his collar down. A red line went up the back of his neck a bit. "He asked me to help you with… trying to figure this out."

He pulled his tie tight again, fingers fidgeting after he finished. "Darrin took me when I was twenty-one… He wanted to know about this thing called the Power, which I assume is what you were kidnapped for."

At Jace's nod he continued: "Someone helped me escape back then. Darrin thought that I had died because he used one of the liquids on me that made it so I couldn't breathe. But I got help.

"Soon after that I had what some people call a coughing fit, honestly it's more like I was suffocating than coughing but it stuck." His smile looked more like a grimace. "My friends freaked out when it first happened, but we learned what would help soon after."

"What?" Jace asked quickly as the thought of suffocating again came into his mind.

"Magic." At Jace's startled look he smiled, still a little bitter. "Yeah, when I touched them, I actually took some of their breath."

"Wait…" Jace's eyebrows furrowed, trying to process that information, panic starting to unfurl as he realized what that meant. "Is that the same for me? I'm taking their air when I touch them?" He didn't want to take someone else's breath. He didn't want to hurt anyone!

"You've been having them already?" Mr. Durnge shook his head in surprise. "You have magic, too, then?"

"I've—I've been told that I do." Jace looked down. "How does it work?" He didn't know exactly what part he was clarifying.

"Um… Well, you should know that—like everything in life—

if you do something there is a consequence. If you use magic you have to expect that it will take energy, especially for more advanced things."

"What kind of things can I do?" He thought of his visions. He'd been taking Philips' breath without knowing it. Was it the same thing with visions?

"A lot of things. I'm sure. I don't know exactly what you can do, as I've never been around many other magic users long enough to learn too much."

"What about the visions? Are those my doing?"

The man looked startled. "Visions?"

"Uh... and voices."

He looked thoughtful. "When did they start?"

Jace scratched his head, "When Darrin manipulated my mind." He shrugged. "I don't know if that's what's it's called, but it's what it felt like."

"I don't know what that is." There was a knock on the door and they both turned toward it, Mr. Durnge sighing as he moved to open it. One of his next students came in. The student looked at Jace for a minute before returning his gaze to Mr. Durnge, and clearly that conversation was over.

As Jace was about to slip out, Kyler was moving in with his friends, and Jace moved out of his way, hoping to avoid any contact with him.

"Wait... Jace."

He turned back again, and Mr. Durnge handed him a piece of paper. "Here's your late slip."

"Thanks." He started for the bathroom. He didn't really need to go but he had a late slip now anyway, so he didn't need to hurry to class.

Kory was washing his hands as he entered, they were the only two in there. He smiled brightly at Jace as he entered.

"Did you know..." Kory looked up at him and touched his own neck "...that when you had the... attack thing, the vein things moved?"

"What?"

"I take that as a *no*." He pushed Jace's hood down. "It came around like this." He ran his finger from his right shoulder to his left. "I'd say that it's choking you."

"That's weird..." Jace said slowly. But as weird as Jace

thought it was, he couldn't say that anything really surprised him anymore. Jace shifted closer after a quick look around, leaning toward his friend. "Mr. Durnge has magic, too," Jace whispered—not sure he should have said anything, but pretty sure Kory would care that he had. Kory's eyes widened but before he could respond, another boy was coming in.

Kory gave him a grim smile. "It's really crazy here today," he said, then left Jace alone in the restroom.

Jace didn't need to go to the bathroom but he didn't want to go to class yet. Instead, he turned the water on and slipped his gloves off quickly when the other boy went into a stall.

After a few seconds he turned the water off and dried his hands. He heard someone else come in and pulled the gloves on before they could see. At the same time, he heard the toilet flush, signaling that the other boy was done.

"Hey, Jace." He looked up quickly to see Kyler in front of the exit to the bathroom. Jace felt his face blanch and suddenly wished he had pulled his hood back up.

"Hi." He felt small. Why hadn't he left right after Kory? After everything that had happened, he'd been hoping Kyler would leave him alone, he'd done so until now.

He didn't think that anything Kyler would want would be good.

"How's everything been going?"

"Fine." Jace looked around, but the only thing that might help was the other boy who had just finished using the bathroom. He stepped out and watched them warily, not even trying to make it to the sinks.

"I watched the news." *Of course you did...* Jace took a deep breath as two other people came in, jaw nervously twitching . He knew he wasn't going to get help from them since they were Kyler's two closest friends, and the other boy wouldn't be able to do much against the three of them. "They aren't the only ones who want to know what you're hiding."

"What are you talking about?" Jace's fingers twitched, then curled into fists. He wished that Kory or Philips was with him still.

"You've been hiding something since you got here. What is it?"

"I... ah, need to get to class."

"Kyler, leave him alone," the other boy snapped. He took a step closer, angling to be slightly in front of Jace.

"Stay out of this, Hector."

"No, you stay out of it. It's not our business if he *is* hiding something. He's already been through enough, and he just got back! For heaven's sake, leave him alone!" The gratitude Jace felt at having someone with him to defend him was strong, even though it probably wouldn't stop Kyler.

"We just want to know what happened. It's not a big deal." Kyler stepped closer, pushing Hector to the side.

Jace backed away. Unfortunately, he was just being forced into a corner. "I don't know what you're talking about," Jace tried again. He tried pushing past them but neither boy would budge. They grabbed for him, and he flinched, trying to pull himself away. Darkness swirled in his mind, memories assaulting, Darrin's voice wheedling—

He stumbled, almost falling to the floor.

"Stop it," Jace commanded as forcefully as he could, unsure of exactly where he was anymore. But the boys didn't listen. Jace pulled his arms closer to his body, but that only made them pull at them. Hector was somewhere, his hands trying to pull the others away, his voice warning them off, but Jace was currently drowning at the voices that were rushing in his head.

Kyler's friend, Zack, grabbed his jacket and pulled. His jacket slipped down his arms, bunching at his wrists.

The boys froze.

Jace closed his eyes tightly, not wanting to see their reactions, not wanting to believe that *that* had really just happened. His breaths were coming rapidly and he was trembling.

When he finally had the courage to open his eyes, they were staring at his arm in surprise. None of them moved as he came back to awareness. Jace swallowed hard, then tore his jacket from their loose fingers, pulling it back over his shoulder.

They just continued to stare, even as Jace left the bathroom.

No question about it; they were going to tell someone— everyone. He had to get out of here! What was he going to do? They would all know, all—

Someone came out of the bathroom behind him, calling out for him to wait, but he didn't look back as he practically ran to the school entrance. He didn't want to cry but he couldn't help it.

He had no idea where he was heading.

॥ ॥ ॥

"Sorry, sir, can I interrupt?"

Kory looked behind him from the desk to see a boy standing by the door. His teacher, Mr. Gentor, looked up in irritation.

"You already have. What is it?"

"I need to talk to Kory." Kory's eyes widened in surprise. It was the same boy that had stepped into the bathroom before he had left. He didn't know the kid, but figured he recognized them from the news.

He stood quickly, before Mr. Gentor could even answer, and grabbed his bag, slinging the strap over his shoulder.

As soon as they were out in the hall, and the door shut behind them, Kory rounded on him. "What's wrong?" he asked.

"Kyler and his friends came into the bathroom after you left, and they surrounded Jace," the boy said. Kory slipped his hands into his pockets and started to mess with his inhaler in his left one.

"Why?"

"I'm getting to that part," he snapped. "They wanted to know what he was hiding, because of the *stupid news*," he hissed the last part out bitterly. "They got his jacket off him."

Kory felt the color leave his face; he opened his mouth as he tried to find something to say.

"They were surprised and Jace slipped out."

"Where is he now?" Kory finally managed.

"He left." He pointed to the exit. "I don't know where, though." He hesitated. "Sorry, I was trying to get Kyler to stop but he had his friends with him."

"It's okay, thanks for coming to tell me." Kory looked down the hall, trying not to panic. As the boy walked away Kory opened the door to his class and immediately found their friend.

"Philips."

He looked up, his eyes narrowing in concern. Kory was sure his panic was showing through his eyes, so Philips was up and out the door swiftly, leaving the teacher dumbfounded.

Fortunately, Philips brought his bag out with him.

"What?" he asked when the door was shut.

Kory didn't answer. He turned and walked to the class he knew Lisa would be in.

"Go get Hazel, fast!" he breathed. Philips looked like he was about to object and ask more questions, but hurried down the hall instead, running in the direction of Hazel's class.

The door to Lisa's class was open. Kory knocked on the wall instead and peeked in. "Sorry, I need to borrow Lisa." Her teacher looked over her reading glasses and gave a quick nod before returning to reading out loud. Lisa closed her journal and shoved it into her backpack before coming out.

That probably wouldn't have worked before they'd been kidnapped. All the teachers seemed to give them some leniency out of concern for their mental health.

"What's wrong?" she asked. He didn't answer, instead, he headed back down the hall the way he had come.

Philips and Hazel met them.

"What's going on?" Hazel asked him sharply. Kory didn't slow down and quick footsteps stayed up with him.

"It's Jace. Kyler came into the bathroom and cornered him. He pulled Jace's jacket off," Kory said in one breath.

"What?" Lisa asked. At the same time Philips said, "Are you kidding?"

"How do you know?" Hazel looked horrified.

Their faces all probably matched his own expression.

Kory shook his head. "One of the boys came in when I left the bathroom and was there when Kyler came in. I guess some people took that 'what are they hiding?' thing just a little too seriously."

"Where is he?"

Kory shook his head at Lisa's question. "I have no idea."

"Where are we going?" Hazel asked.

Kory stopped right in front of the door. "The only places I can think that he would go are the tree house or his house. Do you guys have any ideas?"

"I have a phone now," Lisa said. "My parents bought me a new one, so let's call his mom. If he stops there, she'll know."

"Do that." Kory glanced around anxiously. The bell for the next class was bound to ring soon.

"Hey, is Jace there?" Lisa shifted the phone to her other ear. "No? Okay, yeah I know, he had a bit of trouble at school and left; we don't know where he went... I'll tell you later. No. Okay, will you let us know if he shows up? I know you're worried. We'll find him. Thanks."

After pushing the off button, Lisa slid the phone into her pocket. "Let's go."

Chapter Twenty

Hazel quickened her pace alongside Kory, confident that Jace would be at the tree house. She was also positive that it would be hard to convince him to leave.

After another few minutes she saw the forest come into view. When they reached the bottom of the tree house, Hazel called up, "Jace?"

She was the first one on the ladder. There was no response but she did hear sounds—someone was definitely moving up there. She sighed in relief and climbed faster. The rope ladder swayed as someone started up below her. She looked down to see Kory.

She reached the top step and entered the room. Jace was lying on the biggest beanbag, his arms slung over his face. Was he crying? She had always liked that Jace wasn't afraid to cry.

Jace had once spent two days in the tree house. It had been a time that Kyler had beaten him up. He hadn't wanted to go home to see his parents so instead he'd told them that he was having a sleepover and stayed here. None of them could convince him to come out, but at least the stay had been during the weekend, so he hadn't missed school.

"Jace?" She watched him closely, and heard the others arrive behind her.

His jaw trembled slightly. "What?"

"What happened?"

Jace didn't answer, just flipped over so his face was toward the beanbag, arms under forehead for breathing space.

She tried again. "Jace, come on."

"What are you doing here?" he asked.

"Seeing you," Lisa said softly. "What happened, Jace?"

"Nothing, I was just stupid."

Hazel closed her eyes tightly before stepping closer to him. She didn't know how to help him anymore, ever since Darrin had him. He didn't seem to trust them anymore—not half as much as he used to.

"Did I do something wrong, Jace?" she asked, sitting on the ground next to him.

He looked up. "No. Why do you say that?" His eyes were bloodshot, and his face was slightly blotchy.

"It seems like you don't like me anymore, ever since we got out." She knew that it was more from just being with Darrin than anything having to do with her, but she *needed* to get Jace talking… even if she used a little guilt-trip.

Fresh tears came down his face and Hazel could have sworn that she saw some fear in his gaze before he let his head fall back into the beanbag. "No, it's…" He stopped. She could see him shudder, and she forced herself to dive deeper, hating herself a little.

"It's just what?" she probed.

He sighed before looking back up at them. "I'm sorry. He is just making me feel… like I don't deserve anything."

"How so?" She saw Lisa give her a glance, probably confused as to what she was trying to get at.

"He keeps saying that he's going to kill you guys and that he'll get me." His shoulders sunk and he looked down. "And he keeps making me—saying things like I don't deserve to live, that I've already done enough damage." He let his face fall back into his arms.

Hazel couldn't respond. She didn't know what to say.

"I think he's right." Jace's words were muffled, but still easily deciphered. He pulled his head from the beanbag but turned away from them. "If it wasn't for me, you guys wouldn't have been hurt, and our parents wouldn't have to worry."

"Jace—"

"I don't think it's fair that you guys were hurt for something that I did."

"Jace."

"I just don't want to do this anymore."

"Jace!" She didn't want to yell at him, but at this point it was the only way to get his attention. He flinched slightly, his body tensing. "Jace, please stop it, you're my friend and I don't want you to talk like that." She felt a tear dampen her cheek.

232

He looked back at them again. "I don't want you guys hurt." He took a trembling breath. "The Shadow is strong—I can feel it, like, all the time now, and I don't want you guys to have to feel it too."

"Jace, I want to help you." Hazel watched his eyes intently. "I want to be your friend, please don't do that. Don't start to close up on me. On us."

After a few seconds he nodded slowly, hesitant and hopeful. "Do you—you don't blame me then?"

That's what this is about? She shook her head. "No, it's as much our fault as it is yours. Remember you tried to convince us not to go, but we insisted on doing it anyway."

Jace tilted his head. He looked relieved somehow. She just hoped that she was right in saying that they didn't blame him. She could only speak for herself after all.

Lisa smiled as she came closer. "Are you going to tell us what happened then or no?"

Jace returned a shaky smile. "Mr. Durnge wanted to speak to me, so I stayed in the room after class. Apparently, he was kidnapped by Darrin when he was twenty-one, and he has magic as well as the marks. He was trying to help me understand it a bit more."

Jace's eyes suddenly narrowed as he turned to Philips. "He said that when I have those 'coughing fits' whenever someone touches me, I take some of their breath."

Philips' jaw tightened.

"Why didn't you say that was happening?" Jace pressed. Kory looked at Jace in surprise.

Philips looked really uncomfortable. "I didn't want you to worry about it. It's not like it's a lot, just feels like I got the wind knocked out of me without any of the actual pain."

Jace shook his head. "I don't want to take air from you, Philips. That just feels wrong."

Before Philips could object—because clearly it was better for Philips to lose breath for a couple seconds than for Jace to die of suffocation—Jace continued: "After we were done talking, he gave me a late slip and I went to the bathroom where I saw Kory. He told me about my veins that seemed to move, and I told him about Mr. Durnge. Someone else came in and Kory left."

Jace ran his hands along his pants "I should have left right after, but I washed my hands first…" he stopped and pushed his palms into his eyes. "Kyler wanted to know what I—*we* were hiding. The other boy, Hector, tried to stop him, but… yeah. Well. Yeah." He shrugged. "It mostly sucked because it reminded me of how it was with Darrin, the fact that I couldn't actually do anything. But anyway, Zack took my jacket off and saw—well… this." He gestured to his arm.

"Do you think they'll say anything about it?" Kory asked him as he plopped onto a beanbag.

"I don't know, probably." Jace shrugged. "He doesn't have any reason not to." Hazel was pretty sure he was trying to act indifferent about it, but his eyes gave him away.

"Maybe he won't," Philips said hopefully.

"Yeah maybe." It didn't sound like he believed it though.

Philips blew out a slow breath. "I can't believe he would do that…" Jace shrugged again, looking helpless.

Ringing interrupted them, and Lisa jumped and quickly pulled her phone from her pocket. "It's so funny how I hate the freaking things and I'm the one who ends up with the new one first." The ringtone stopped as she pulled the phone to her ear. "Hello. Oh right yeah, sorry." She smirked and covered the receiver with her hand. "I forgot to call her back."

"*Who*?" Jace mouthed the question toward Hazel.

"Your mom."

"Why?" He looked upset, as if he already knew the answer.

"We called to see if you had gone home," she explained to him. Lisa had walked further from the group as she talked but came back a second later.

"She wants to talk to you." She tossed the phone to Jace before he could respond.

Jace sighed. "Hello?" he said, slinging an arm over his eyes. "No, I'm fine. Someone just pulled my jacket off, so I left… No." Frustration was vivid in his voice. "I've got to go Mom." He tossed the phone to the end of the beanbag and grabbed his backpack instead, going through the things in there.

"We should probably get back," Philips said quietly.

Jace nodded. "Go ahead." He grabbed a granola bar from his bag and started eating it.

"You too."

"No, I'm not going back."

"You're just going to let us take all the heat?" Kory asked

indignantly.

"You don't have to go." Jace looked guilty for a minute.

Kory smirked. "We'd take the heat either way bro, from our parents or from our classmates..."

"Fine, let's go back then." Jace stood up stiffly, and made his way back to the door, eating the bar as he walked.

"You don't need to," Lisa said, but Jace didn't stop walking to the ladder. Hazel flashed Kory a smile, thankful that he'd been able to get Jace out quickly. She'd expected a longer fight, but Kory also used the guilt route. Which she should probably feel worse about, and would, but Jace would self-destruct at times, and she didn't want that.

₪ ₪ ₪

He had to leave now. Well not *right* now. Jace couldn't risk any of his friends being around when he left. He couldn't wrap them up in this again. They might not blame him, but there was no way he was going to let them come with him now that he knew the danger.

He should have been embarrassed going back to school right after crying. He knew that his face was still blotchy, but he didn't really care about that right now. Actually, he didn't really *care* about anything. He just needed enough time to learn a little bit more about his magic from Mr. Durnge. Would he teach Jace though?

Why would he want to teach you?

Jace walked ahead of his friends as he entered the school. He didn't want them to guess that he was planning on leaving. He thought it would be best to finish up the day at school, talk to Mr. Durnge after classes, and then leave later tonight.

His previous class was out when they walked into school and he received a few stares as he made his way down the hallway. He was pretty sure they were just staring because of his puffy eyes and blotchy face—not because Kyler had told anyone yet. At least he hoped that was it.

Not that he wanted people staring because he'd been crying, but still; lesser of the two evils.

He hesitantly broke away from the rest of his friends, though he wasn't sure he really wanted to be alone in school again. His friends had their next classes in a different area of the school and unfortunately, his next class went by slowly, making the time drag on until he could again talk with Mr. Durnge before the final bell rang. He put his bag over his shoulder quickly and was the first one out of the classroom. He wanted to find his teacher before he had to leave.

Jace walked against the flow of people and found his teacher right before he was going to exit the classroom.

Mr. Durnge caught sight of Jace and flashed him a quick smile before pushing the door back open to allow them both back into the classroom, allowing the door to shut behind for privacy.

To his surprise, he saw the furtive glance his teacher shot to the door and realized that he was still freaked out about Darrin, and his time locked alone with him.

Mr. Durnge shook his head. "Sorry, Jace. Sorry that this happened to you."

Jace paused by the door, hands curled in his pockets. "I was the one who went looking for trouble. I got my friends dragged into it as well." He blinked past tears and stepped closer to his teacher earnestly. "How do you control the magic?" he asked.

Mr. Durnge's eyes looked thoughtful. "It usually happens when I think about it, focus on it. Like it's the thing I want most." He sat on his desk. "When you're having a coughing fit your mind is on getting air in, so you easily take it. And when you want to help someone, it's usually on your whole mind, so you are able to help them."

Jace thought back at how he had used magic when Kory was dying; he had wanted to help Kory more than anything, so he had. "That's it? You just concentrate on it?"

"Yes. But you have to be careful, because you can easily use too much magic at once and the outcome of that can be disastrous— or on the flip side, you might not use enough to accomplish your goal."

Jace nodded in understanding, chewing on his lips. Tentatively, he sat down on the table closest to his teacher. "Is that all I should know?"

The man squinted at the wall behind Jace. "I really don't know what else you need to know. But I think I should tell you a poem I heard about the Power."

"A poem about the Power? Why?"

"I think it might help you figure out where the Power is. I've tried to understand it, but maybe you'll have more luck." His voice changed slightly, falling into a semi-rhythm.

Darkness searches, cannot find, people wander, cannot hide.
Eyes seek, now blind, never noticing the light.

Jace immediately felt riveted by the poem.

Two places, back to back. Open skies here to there.
Looking for that open gate, nothing showing, it's all too late.

His voice became deeper, more urgent as if Jace had to make a choice right then and there.

Dark clouds come, fear sets in. You close up and fight again.
Hard to find, hard to see, is it there within thee?
See it here, so far away, losing something you thought so dear.
There it is so close now, but this is just where it gets hard.
Will you make it; will you fall, will it be time to draw?
He will come; he will see; he will take thee if not foreseen.
He could kill yet he could die.
What...

He paused and looked at Jace.

...will you decide?

Jace stayed quiet for a few minutes. He was sure that the part that said 'Darkness searches, cannot find,' was the Shadow trying to find the Power, but he wasn't sure what the rest meant.

"Do you know what any of it means?" Jace asked him, nose scrunched up as he tried to think it through.

Mr. Durnge cast a look toward the door before answering. "I'm sure that Darrin will find you, from what it says at the end, but it might be what already happened for all I know. And I think you will lose something, but who knows what..." He ran a hand through his hair. "I think you should keep a piece of paper with this poem on it and mark what you know, your thoughts on everything so you can continue and add to it when ideas come to you. It's a pretty scattered poem, don't you think?" Then he rolled his eyes. "And honestly, who even knows if it actually means anything?"

Jace nodded and pulled his backpack off his shoulders to find paper and a pen. He grabbed the first notebook he saw, opened it, and found an empty page free of doodles. He had his teacher repeat the poem, slower this time, so he could write it down, making sure to leave plenty of space to write down his ideas as they came to him.

Darkness, obviously Shadow… Maybe the two places back to back is the place where we can find it. Probably will be found by Darrin. Gets harder. Lose something.

He looked down at his hand, smudged black from his pencil, and looked back up to see his teacher looking over his shoulder. "Anything else you got from it?"

Jace watched his teacher shake his head, feeling disappointed. "No, nothing that you don't already have, and most everything else that I've thought of may be way off." His teacher looked at his hands. "Be careful, Jace. I don't know what will happen, I don't know how much of it, beyond magic and the Shadow, is even real, but I know it will be hard. I'd hate for you to get hurt again."

Jace closed his notebook, knowing that it was time to go if the man had nothing else for him. He'd have to work on this some more.

"Thank you, Mr. Durnge. Really." He gave him a small smile and started for the door. "And I'll try to be careful." He knew that his friends would most likely be waiting for him at the front of the school and he didn't want them to wait for much longer.

He pulled the door open, relieved to get out of the closed room, then headed toward the front of the school.

"Hey." Jace didn't need to turn his head to know that it was Lisa. Her class was down this way, and she was always slow to get out of the room since she always finished what she was working on before exiting.

"Hi." Jace looked at her and forced a small smile.

"What're you doing down this side of the school?"

"I was talking to Mr. Durnge."

"Oh." They walked twenty steps before saying anything else. "Anything new?"

"Not a whole lot, he just told me how the magic worked." He thought about telling her about the poem but was scared of what she might say. She might see more than just curiosity in the reason why he'd written it down.

"Oh," she said again.

But how could he not? He told his friends everything, and they all cared for him. He hesitated a long moment, fighting the indecision before finally pulling his backpack off his shoulders, stopping to lean against the wall. She stopped next to him, a question in her eyes.

"He also told me a poem, about the darkness and Power." He looked down at his notebook rather than at Lisa.

She looked at the page over his shoulder and read his scribbled handwriting. He wasn't sure if she could read his thoughts on it since they were even sloppier than the poem itself.

"That's interesting." Her eyes flashed slightly, but Jace was unsure what emotion was traveling across her face.

"That's what I thought too." Jace put the notebook back in his bag then started walking again, zipping it up as he went.

Lisa caught back up and slung her arm over his shoulder. She had to walk on her toes since she was shorter than him, but she did it good–naturedly and he couldn't help but smile. "You know… you should share that with Hazel. She's good with words."

"Yeah?" Lisa was probably right. But Hazel wasn't just good at words. She was good at figuring *him* out too.

They exited the building and Jace found his other friends. Philips was leaning against a wall looking up at a tree beside him; Kory, who loved climbing, was almost hidden from view in the branches above. Teachers had asked him to *get down* countless times and he'd do so, but then the next day he'd do the same thing again.

Hazel was lying on the ground, face toward the sky, hands behind her head.

"Hey, this bird's nest has eggs in it now!" Kory looked through the branches and smiled down at them.

Jace was surprised that no teachers had asked him to get down—or maybe they had. Recently, Kory had been given more than a few minutes in the tree before getting caught and that was probably because he'd just returned from being kidnapped, and the teachers were simply glad he was back, even if he was a nuisance.

Kory stood from where he was crouching on a branch and grabbed hold of another one above his head with his right hand. "What took you so long?" he asked as they drew closer. Philips pushed away from the wall as they walked closer, but Hazel didn't move. Jace was convinced that she'd fallen asleep.

Jace smirked and let his backpack fall beside her. "I was talking to Mr. Durnge," he told them with a small shrug. Hazel still didn't wake up. "I guess we're going to take a nap," he breathed down at her.

Philips looked at her and laughed. "I didn't even realize she fell asleep."

There was a crack from above and a branch suddenly hit the ground next to Hazel. She jerked up, eyes wide, looking at the branch next to her. Her eyes scanned the tree and up to Kory, who was holding onto another branch, eyes just as wide as Hazel's.

She swore as she pulled a hand to her chest. "You scared me to death."

Kory clambered down the tree closer to them, breathing heavily. "Sorry."

But Jace was sure Kory would do the same thing the next day, despite the fact that a branch he'd been holding had collapsed.

Hazel shook her head. "Are you okay?" She studied Kory closely and stood on her feet.

"I'm fine, just startled me."

A teacher drew closer and Jace knew Kory was in for a scolding.

"Let's go, before she gets here," Kory said under his breath, but he was too late.

"Kory, how many times do we have to tell you not to climb up there?" The teacher looked angry and worried.

"Sorry," Kory muttered and looked down at his hands as his face colored slightly.

"Sorry means you won't do it again." She folded her arms.

"I guess I'm not sorry then." He shrugged sheepishly, making her look at him in annoyance. She sighed as her arms fell to her side.

"I'd prefer if you'd stop climbing up there. You're going to get hurt one day." She scanned him worriedly, as if that day were today, then turned and walked away with the same purpose in her stride, obviously knowing that she wouldn't get any further agreement out of him.

Her heels clicked loudly on the cement.

Jace saw Kyler across the grass, who glanced up and happened to meet his gaze at the same time. "Can we go now?" Jace asked them quickly as he turned away, not wanting to be there any longer.

Hazel looked behind him, at where Kyler was. "Yeah, let's."

She grabbed her bag from the ground and Jace followed her in the direction of home. They lived in the same direction but had to break away to different roads when they got about five minutes from his house—other than Kory who lived next door to Jace.

Only when he was alone would he be able to think about his next step

Chapter Twenty-One

HE WAS IN THE MIDDLE of packing when Hazel came over. Jace had managed to shove the bag under his bed and grab out a book just as his door opened.

It had been a couple hours after that before she finally left, and Jace couldn't remember what they'd even talked about, he'd been so worried about leaving again.

He then had dinner with his family before getting back to packing, keeping his door shut, and knowing that they would all respect the shut door, knocking before they came bursting in. The exception to the rule was if he was having a nightmare.

He knew he couldn't carry that much stuff with him, but he made sure to grab the notebook so that he could have the poem.

He did make sure to grab the clothing too—four sets.

How was he going to get away? Kory lived next door to him and could easily see him leaving. He grabbed his toothbrush from the bathroom across the hall, adding it to his backpack, then quietly made his way downstairs. All the lights in his house were off and he didn't care to turn any on.

He made it to the front door and closed it softly behind him, taking off down the road.

He wasn't even half past Kory's house when his front door opened, and Kory came out. Jace didn't stop moving for Kory to catch up, instead quickening his pace.

As his friend came up beside him, he shook his head.

"Please go home, Kory." he begged him quietly, keeping his eyes on the road before him.

"Don't go Jace, please? At least let me come, too." Kory

didn't even pause.

"You can't, you gotta stay home. Stay safe." Jace stopped to face his friend.

Kory shook his head stubbornly—and seriously, what did he expect? Kory was the most stubborn of all of them. "I'm coming with you Jace—you can't do this on your own."

Jace felt his throat tighten, surveying Kory closely. "You can't... You might get hurt. You don't even have a bag. And... you can't make your parents worry again."

"Jace, I'm coming with you. Are you going to come back to my house with me to let me get my bag or will I have to go without anything?" There was really no chance of talking him out of following him.

He couldn't let Kory come.

He felt his magic push on the borders of his mind, his fingers twitching at the extra vibration on energy, straining to be released. The only way he could get Kory to stay here was to use magic. He studied Kory carefully. He could use magic, he could feel it and knew that it would work.

But what if he used too much and ended up hurting Kory?

He's gotta stay here, he can't come.

"Fine, let's go get your bag," Jace said quietly. As much as he hated the feeling—hated knowing what he was—he could feel the magic deep inside of him, waiting for him to use it and it suddenly seemed dominant. He was fearful of how strong it felt.

They moved back to his house quickly. Kory's parents and Zory were gone at the moment, so they didn't have to worry about being seen by them.

Jace felt tears crowd his eyes and felt ashamed that he was going to do this to his friend. Would he hurt his friend by using magic on him? Would using his magic be worse than having Kory come with him?

When they got into Kory's room, Jace left the door open. He questioned whether he should just let his friend come—but the magic in him was so forceful that Jace had no more time to think about it. He felt the magic burst out of the confines he had put it in, and he felt the energy surge straight toward Kory.

Jace couldn't stop it.

Kory's eyes widened as his feet suddenly sunk into the floor about two inches. He tried taking a step but couldn't move. He looked up at Jace, his eyes shocked, but Jace was already backing away, tears slipping out of his eyes.

"I'm sorry, Kory. I'm so sorry." He pulled his hand to his mouth to keep from totally breaking down, before wiping his cheeks. "I can't let you come and be hurt because of me again."

He spun away, striding to the exit of the house and trying his hardest to ignore Kory calling for him.

Jace was mortified at what the magic—what *he*— had done, knowing that there was no room for forgiveness after purposely using magic in such a way.

It would be better this way. Jace was a monster, and this quest was dangerous. His friends would be safer away from him.

ℼ ℼ ℼ

Kory stopped calling for Jace when he heard the front door close. He tried moving his feet again. They still didn't budge. He felt sorrow choke him and wanted to fall to his knees but couldn't do that either.

He couldn't even tell if he was in pain, there was a sort of numbness that had settled in his feet.

"Jace." He let out a short sob, panic about being unable to move setting his breathing off. He couldn't believe that Jace would stop him like that, even if he was afraid of them coming with him, and trying to protect him in some weird backward way.

Minutes passed, and Kory felt his already wrung-out nervousness turn into a deep-rooted fear. Was he going to be stuck like this forever? How would he explain what happened to his parents? To anyone?

He looked around his room for the home phone. He wanted to call his friends. Maybe they could help. And they had to go after Jace before he got too far to find.

He caught sight of the phone lying on his desk, but that was a good five feet away. He tried reaching for it, but it hurt his legs to do so. He used a chair to lower himself closer but, still felt a sharp pain in the back of his legs.

The pain added to his panic, his mind swirling in complete desperation as he tried harder to reach for the phone.

He was just about to crouch down when he was suddenly

released. His feet came out from where they had sunk in, and he fell to his knees. Scrambling up quickly he grabbed the home phone, calling Lisa first thing.

"Hello?" A sleepy voice came from the other side. Kory felt relief flood through him, the panic of being stuck slowly leaving as he heard Lisa's voice. He was free. Maybe the magic had worn off. He looked back at the ground where he'd been standing.

"Lisa, you were right. Jace left." The spot he had sunk into looked normal now, no holes or divots.

As if nothing had happened.

The pounding in his chest and the numbness in his feet were the only evidence that he'd been trapped in the floor.

He never wanted that to happen again.

"Left?" Her voice was sharp. Kory sat on his bed, though his floor looked normal again, his shoes did not. They looked a little misshapen at the bottom.

"I tried—I swear I tried to stop him, or at least go with him, but he stopped me."

"How?"

"He used magic on me." He pulled his shoes and socks off to look at his feet, wincing as he did so. They felt sensitive.

"Are you okay?" He could hear her moving around, the concern in her voice palpable.

"Yeah." His feet were red and blistering. He winced at the sight. That wasn't good, and he probably should go to the doctor, but if he wasted time doing that, Jace would be long gone. "Can you get the others? We can meet at the tree house." He put his hands to his feet carefully, feeling relieved that it helped the pain lessen.

"I'll get Philips, do you want to get Hazel?"

Kory nodded even though she couldn't see him. "Yeah, I will." He hung up the phone before she could ask any other questions and pulled on some other socks and shoes, face stuck in a grimace as he forced them on.

Ignoring his feet, that ached somewhere between throbbing and numb, he moved to grab his backpack and stuff it full of clothes and some food from the pantry before exiting the front door again. He went in the same direction that Jace had been headed, toward Hazel's house.

She was on the way to the tree house.

The lights were off at her house, but he knew which window

was hers. He walked around the house until he came to it and threw some small rocks at the glass until she turned her light on and came to open it.

"What is it, Kory?" She kept her voice low. She looked confused and sleepy.

"Can you get out of the house?" His voice was trembling, he knew it. He also knew that she could hear the tremor. Her eyes narrowed slightly as she caught sight of his bag.

"Yes, why?"

He closed his eyes and tried to keep his voice steady. "Jace left." He fingered his strap and took a step back so he could see her without having to kink his neck as much. Her jaw clenched and she disappeared from view, closing the window behind her. He waited for her to come out, but after a few minutes, when she didn't appear, he started to worry. He saw a few house lights turn on and knew that something wasn't right. Hazel wouldn't turn on lights to sneak out.

He went around to the front of the house right when the door opened. Hazel was talking to her mom quietly.

"Mom, we have to go. Jace needs us. He hasn't been doing well since we got kidnapped; he took it harder than the rest of us."

Her mom shook her head. "Let me take you."

"You can't, he won't come back with you. I don't even know if he'll come back with us, and I think he'll be staying away from the roads anyway. I'll stay safe, please, Mom."

Suddenly, her mom caught sight of him standing behind Hazel.

"Could you tell my parents not to worry?" he asked. "Tell them that we're together and we went after Jace? They're not home right now, but I don't want them to freak out." Luckily Kory's sister was with them—he wouldn't have dared leave his sister home alone.

Hazel's mom sighed and turned back to Hazel. "I don't want you to go, it's not safe. But you're almost eighteen and I know I can't lock you up." She ran a hand down her face, the stress-lines obvious, then pulled Hazel into a tight hug. "I just want you safe sweetheart. We thought we lost you once already. Everyone else kidnapped by Darrin had been killed, so we all thought we were going to lose our kids… So I need you to promise me you'll be careful, and make sure to call me, okay? I bought you that phone today, so make sure you use it." Then she looked at Kory, her expression resigned and pained. "I'll

246

tell them."

"Thank you." Hazel hugged her mom tightly. "Thank you so much. I'm sorry, I just need to find him. He's our best friend, and he needs us."

Hazel let go of her mom and joined Kory, waving as they started walking down the sidewalk. He could feel her mom's gaze on them until they'd turned the corner.

"What happened?" Hazel asked immediately.

"I saw him leaving so I ran out to intercept. He was determined to go, so I told him I was going with him." Kory could feel his hands shaking. "I didn't have my bag, but he agreed to let me go get it, and he came with me." He bit his lip and took a few more steps before continuing. "He used magic to keep me from following him though." As he spoke, he could feel the pain increase in his feet. He slowed down slightly.

"He used magic *on* you?" Her eyes scrunched up, almost disbelieving.

His mind flashed back to Jace's tears, of how scared he looked when he'd used his magic on him, how worried he'd been. Kory was almost positive that Jace hadn't wanted to do it, maybe he hadn't even meant to.

He stopped fully now looking at the ground. Most people would think having magic was cool, but Jace seemed to think of himself as someone capable of hurting someone no matter what he did. As though he were a monster.

"What is it?" Hazel stopped in front of him.

"He doesn't want us hurt." He shook his head and leaned on the fence, reaching into his pocket and fingering his inhaler when his breath caught. He didn't pull it out, just held onto it as he focused on keeping his breathing even.

"We already know that Kory—"

He cut her off with another shake of his head. "No, I mean he doesn't want us to get hurt *by him*." He clenched his jaw "That's why he wouldn't let me go, he's scared of hurting us."

She was silent for a few minutes. "He doesn't know how to control it," she finally muttered.

Kory didn't respond. They needed to get moving again, but he couldn't pull away from the fence. He was convinced that his feet were getting worse.

Hazel gave him a hug. "It's gonna be okay, we'll find him."

Her tone was hopeful.

He nodded into her shoulder. They were almost the same height so he didn't have to bend over much. Kory had never been a very big kid, and was close to the same size as half of the girls, even after hitting his supposed growth spurt.

"How did he stop you?" Hazel asked him after another few minutes.

"He made my feet sink into the floor and get stuck." He grabbed hold of the fence to keep some of the weight off his feet, starting to walk to the treehouse again.

"What?" Hazel still seemed disbelieving.

His feet were really starting to pound, the numbness retreating and the throbbing doubling. Maybe he was running out of adrenaline. Still, he had to move, he couldn't stay here. With more endurance than he felt he had, he followed Hazel the rest of the way in silence. Kory searched the darkness, hoping to see Jace even though he knew he wouldn't.

When they got to the tree house Lisa and Philips were already there. He could hear them talking. He climbed up the ladder carefully and walked into the room where they were.

"Do you know where he went?" Philips asked Kory as they entered.

"He was heading west, probably to Jurade or somewhere," Kory said, plopping into a beanbag, but his feet didn't feel any better sitting. His shoes and socks were only agitating the burn. But he didn't want them to worry about him, so he tried to ignore it. He repeated what he'd already told Hazel, including the part that Jace didn't want to hurt them, but he couldn't stand it anymore. He slipped his shoes off, aware that Hazel was watching him curiously and slid his socks off before putting his hands on the bottom of both feet, the coolness of his hands helping calm the heat.

"What happened?" Hazel asked worriedly, coming closer to him and looking at his feet. Kory followed her gaze to see that it was blistering even worse now.

"I think it burned me, when I stuck to the floor," he said, his gaze still on his feet. Lisa suddenly stood up next to him and walked to the other side of the tree house. He didn't want to say that Jace had burned him because he still wanted to believe Jace wouldn't willingly do that to him.

Lisa came back over with a cold pack in her hands. She was always the most prepared for an emergency since she studied a lot about medicine, so she moved the pad gently onto his feet with confidence. The cold stung a bit at first and then it started numbing it.

"Tell me how it feels," she asked.

He wasn't sure what to say. It didn't hurt, but it wasn't helping yet. It just felt cold.

"It feels fine," he said at last, staring down at his feet. "We should go after Jace."

"Let's wait for twenty minutes and see if your feet get any better, and we'll get some stuff gathered for us." She stood and grabbed her backpack as she went through some snacks. Philips and Hazel moved to help.

"I can help," Kory said, starting to get up again.

"We got it, Kory," Hazel said, looking up. "Just wait there."

He complied and took his bag off his shoulders to lay down on the beanbag, his eyes growing tired. For a split second, he saw Jace. His face was sad and scared.

"I can't stop it," he was saying. "I don't know what to do."

When the image disappeared, Philips was shaking him awake. "Do you still want to go tonight?" he asked.

Kory nodded and sat up, feeling even more tired after the short nap. His feet were almost numb now.

"How are your feet doing?" Lisa asked as Philips helped him up. She grabbed the cold pad and put it back in the small fridge, which was powered by three extension cords leading to the treehouse.

"Better, I think." He slipped his socks and shoes back on and grabbed his pack. He was anxious to go find Jace. He stood, relieved to find that his feet felt much better. He was actually surprised at how much better they felt.

Thinking again of Jace, they began heading once again to Jurade.

"Wait…" Lisa pulled out her journal and opened it to the last page. "Hazel, this might help us."

"What is it?" he asked, coming closer.

"A poem. Mr. Durnge gave it to Jace, and he showed it to me." She shrugged. "I memorized it and wrote it on my phone on the walk home."

"You saw it and memorized it?" Philips asked incredulously. "Just like that?"

She nodded. "Yeah, it's like a story, easy to remember."

He smirked at that. Her memory was impressive like that.

Lisa handed the notebook to Hazel. "Think you can find any hidden meanings?"

Hazel sat back on a beanbag, staring at the notepad and tapping her lip in thought. "I think the most obvious parts are about the Shadow trying to find the Power, and that something will happen, but the 'you close up and fight again' could either be how Jace is closing up to us and fighting letting us come, or something even deeper. But because it says 'dark clouds come now, fear sets in' I think that it's something we haven't seen yet, or that he is already struggling with. I also think where it says, 'eyes seek now blind, never noticing the light' and the 'what will you decide?' are the most vital clues as to how we will find it, and the 'two places back to back, open skies here to there' is where we will be."

She paused and studied the page for another few seconds before standing up again. "It's going to drive me insane. I feel like I'm missing something obvious." She shifted forward on the beanbag to hand the journal back to Lisa. "I'll keep working on it."

Lisa nodded in response and shoved it back into her pack before zipping it up. "Are you okay, Kory?"

He nodded even though he wasn't sure if he really was.

"Can I try something, to try and help it?" Kory raised his eyebrow at her.

"What?" he asked tentatively.

"I read that honey helps burns; I think we need to wrap it in something better than a sock." Then she shook her head. "Honestly, I think you shouldn't even walk on your feet."

Kory shrugged. "You can try it." He gave them a small smile that felt forced. "Honey will be weird to walk on."

They started in the direction of the 24-hour Wal-Mart, Lisa in the lead. The moon grew higher in the sky and more stars appeared.

Not long later, Kory was surprised as a car slowed next to them. Jason's head leaned out the window, eyes scanning them all. "What are you doing? Jace isn't with you?" He looked disappointed as Kory shook his head. "Do you know where he is?"

What's Jason doing out here? Maybe he'd also noticed that Jace was missing.

"No." Hazel looked at her feet and shifted them, "but we're

going to go find him."

"I think he's going to Jurade," Jason said after a few seconds. "I saw him looking up caves on Google."

Kory's shoulders relaxed slightly, now that he had more of an idea of where he could be going. "That's where we thought he'd go."

"Is that where you're heading?" He looked confused as he glanced behind him. "That's the other way."

"We have to stop by Wal-Mart first," Philips said, giving a glance at Kory.

"Do you want to ride? Then we can go to Jurade after." Jason unlocked the car, and Kory noticed Devin for the first time.

The ride would be tight—it was an Impala after all, with only six seats.

"Sure." Lisa nodded and opened the back door on the driver's side. She slid to the opposite side and Philips and Hazel followed her in, leaving the front seat for Kory. Devin slid into the middle seat so Kory could climb in next to him.

He opened the door. "I can sit in the center," he told Devin softly, shuffling his feet and waiting to see what Devin wanted to do before getting in.

He just shook his head. "It's okay, I'll just stay here." Kory climbed in, wincing as pain flashed back into his feet. He was hoping that it would just stop hurting. A fool's hope.

With the door shut, Jason started back toward Wal-Mart.

"So how do you know Jace left?" Jason asked them after a few seconds in which the song, "Over and Over" played softly in the background.

When Kory didn't answer right away Hazel responded for him. "Kory saw him leaving, and tried to stop him so he could go too, but Jace used magic to keep Kory from coming." She said it all in one breath and Kory stared down at his feet, trying not to look at anyone.

"Jace used magic *on* you to stop you?" Jason sounded disbelieving as well.

"He didn't want to," Kory muttered, feeling everyone's gazes on him. "He doesn't want to hurt us, so he has been keeping us at a distance. I think he just doesn't know how to control it and is panicking."

They entered the Wal-Mart parking lot, so he didn't have to say anything else. He grabbed his wallet out of his backpack and checked to see how much money he had.

"Do you want to get some snacks while we're here?" Jason asked them, digging through his wallet as well. He shut off the car and looked at them.

"Sure." Kory could see Hazel shrug out of the corner of his eyes. He closed his wallet after he'd confirmed he still had forty-seven dollars.

"Stay here, Kory," Lisa said firmly, making him pause with his hand on the door. Her door opened and she slid out.

"But—" Kory tried to protest but was interrupted.

"Get in the back but stay here." Kory's shoulders sank, and he looked down. As much as he wanted to protest, he didn't, knowing that they were just trying to help him with his feet. It wouldn't be long, and then they'd be back. He told himself that, nervously fingering his inhaler in his pocket.

"Here, I have money." He tried to hand it to Lisa, but she ignored it.

He watched the others leave the car and sighed. Jason and Devin cast him confused looks as Jason passed him the keys, but they said nothing as they all went in together.

Kory waited in the quiet car for a few minutes, watching a teenage couple sitting in the grass at the Wendy's in the next parking lot over, before finally opening the door to move to the backseat so he could stretch out, figuring the easier access to work on his feet was why Lisa wanted him in the back.

He felt his feet give a throb as he stood. As much as he hated being left behind, his feet were grateful for the reprieve. Slowly he lowered himself into the back seat, sliding in against the other door.

Yep, that sucked. His feet were not happy with him. It still felt better than it had before the ice, but not great.

Ten minutes later, while his feet continued to throb and he'd resorted to careful breathing to try to keep himself calm, his friends exited the building. He watched them come closer. Kory popped the trunk and while most of his friends emptied the cart, Lisa moved to the side and opened the door at his feet. He started to sit up, but Lisa's calming hand was immediately on his leg to keep him still.

Jason returned to the front seat and watched, confused, as Lisa carefully took off his shoes.

Why didn't Jason just ask him what was wrong? Kory knew he wanted to.

Devin and Philips slid into the front seat and watched her as well.

"What happened?" Jason asked Philips quietly.

Kory bit his cheek as Lisa started taking his socks off. He could feel the fabric sticking to the wound.

"We think Jace accidentally burned him."

Devin narrowed his eyes. "You're using honey?"

Lisa nodded, looking sure of herself. "Yes, I read that it helps, so we're going to try it out." Kory caught sight of the honey on the ground next to her. She was still working on getting his sock off, obviously aware that the fabric was sticking slightly.

"How do you know what you're doing?" Jason asked, eyes concerned. Lisa finally got his sock off. Kory couldn't see the bottom of his feet, but he could see Lisa's reaction. She looked worried, her eyebrows drawing up in concern.

"I take a lot of time to look these things up," she said distractedly in answer, mostly focused on Kory.

"Has it gotten worse?" Kory asked after she'd gotten the other sock off.

"Um…" She hesitated. "I think you broke a blister."

"So?"

"You're more likely to get an infection if it breaks. Does it hurt more now?"

Kory winced before sitting up slightly. "It does."

Lisa opened the honey and grabbed a spoon. She scooped some out and smeared the yellow goop on his left foot; it was feeling a bit more painful than the other.

His jaw tightened but he didn't give any real reaction to the sticky substance or the pain. After a few more seconds he closed his eyes and leaned his head on the window, ignoring the throb.

Lisa moved the spoon away from his foot for a few seconds before returning. "Is it okay?" she asked.

He swallowed heavily and shrugged a response. He wasn't sure how it was supposed to feel.

But when Lisa got to the ball of his foot, pain shot up his leg like a zap, and he hissed, jerking his leg toward himself, which only made the honey get on the seat.

"Sorry," he told Lisa. He let his leg relax again and looked at Jason apologetically. "Sorry." He tried wiping the honey off the seat with his fingers, but it just smeared. "I didn't mean to pull away."

"It's okay, Kory," Jason said, though he leaned over and shuffled through stuff in the glove box before pulling some paper napkins out.

"Do you want me to continue?" Lisa asked him quietly.

Kory nodded. "Yeah, sorry, it's just sensitive right there."

"That's where your blister broke," Lisa started again, and Kory held his breath as she finished and wrapped his foot up with the gauze.

Jason handed him the napkins, slightly damp. "See if this cleans it up better."

Kory nodded and shifted his body slightly, placing his wrapped foot on the car floor so he could reach the spot easier. The stickiness came off—mostly—but the color was still there. He cleaned off his fingers before scrunching the napkin up into a ball and squeezing it in his hand. He didn't really think that honey would help with the pain.

Hazel paced while looking around. Kory knew that she was feeling anxious to get going, like Kory himself. He clenched his jaw determinedly as Lisa worked, refusing to keep jerking away. They needed to get going as soon as possible, so he let himself drift as Lisa worked, his mind slipping into a vast void that seemed to separate him from the pain. The trick to handle pain from a young age, for himself at least, was to slip fully into his mind like this, even if he didn't love the apathy that seemed to follow.

₪   ₪   ₪

Jace walked through the forest, eyes straining to see anything in the darkening forest. The sun had almost gone down by now, and he felt like an idiot leaving so close to night, especially without bringing any camping gear other than a flashlight. Clearly, he hadn't thought this through—he was even less prepared than the first time around. And it was far freakier to be out in the forest alone. He wished he had his friends with him for company to distract from what might be hiding in the trees.

His friends. His mind flashed back to Kory, and a pang of sorrow made his eyes water. What had he been thinking? Kory could have been with him, he had wanted to come, but Jace had been so panicked about his magic hurting them—and for good reason because his magic had stopped Kory; he just hoped it hadn't actually hurt his friend.

The magic was so strong though, like it had a mind of its own, almost. Or at least, acted on his fears. As of yet, he had no idea how to control it.

As much as he wanted them with him, Kory and the others would be safer if he stayed away from them.

Taking a deep breath, Jace turned his focus on what he had to do from here, and the poem he still had to figure out. It had potential to be one of the most vital things in his search for this Power, and he wished that he had talked to Hazel about it when he'd had the chance. He still hadn't come up with anything else to help decipher it.

When he heard twigs snapping and the crunch of footsteps behind him, he was finally pulled from his thoughts. He froze and listened, turning until he faced the sound with his flashlight. His heart was beating frantically as he realized it was a person, but who would be out here?

Jace was surprised to see the person who stood in front of him.

"Rob?"

Rob's eyebrows rose. "Jace?" He came closer, squinting at the light in his eyes. Jace lowered it. Rob's own flashlight was already directed below Jace's chest. "What are you doing here?"

"What are *you* doing here?"

"Going to Jurade, it's the fastest way there when you don't have a ride." He shrugged and gave a huge smile.

"Yeah... same."

"Sweet! Could I walk with you?"

Jace bit his lip. He didn't want anyone with him, but if they were already heading the same way it might be safer to go together—at least for a little while until Rob went his separate way. As uncomfortable as Jace had originally felt around the man, it had never been because he felt dangerous, but because he hadn't known him yet.

"Sure." They fell into step at an easy pace.

"Where are your friends?" Rob asked after another few seconds.

Jace felt the tears fill his eyes. "At their houses I think." He gave his new friend another quick glance. "I need to do this on my own."

"Ah... gotcha." Rob side-eyed him with a shrug, and Jace was relieved that their conversation came easy with no judgement. "I'll leave you alone if you'd like."

"No, you're good for now."

It was quiet again as they walked for another five to ten minutes. Neither one felt they needed to entertain the other, but Jace finally spoke up again as the sun fully dipped below the mountains.

"Why are you heading to Jurade?"

Rob's head tilted in seeming thought. "More places I can stay for free." He slipped his hand in his pocket and pulled a bar out. "Want some?"

"I have my own, thanks."

"Okay." He took a bite with a shrug. "How are the others doing?" His eyes flashed sadly, reminding Jace of the last time he had seen him. He had been pretty open about not trusting Rob. Perhaps he should have given him a chance.

"They all seem to be doing pretty good, healing and such."

Rob nodded in relief, again flashing that smile of his that seemed to somehow never leave his face.

"Good."

"I feel like I owe you an apology," After another long moment Jace spoke again, a little uncomfortable, shifting his backpack with one hand, the other gripping the flashlight tighter.

"What for?" Rob's eyebrows furrowed at the comment.

"I was pretty rude to you, open about how I felt." He looked down. "I thought, not knowing you well, you'd judge us, or make a big deal out of something we were trying to keep private, and I definitely didn't trust you, but I shouldn't have been so... unkind to you."

Rob looked like he didn't know how to respond, and once again, they found themselves in silence.

"Well... thanks, Jace. I appreciate it." Rob finally said, looking uncomfortable, yet sincere. "You know, most people don't seem to care how I feel, being homeless. And, I mean, I know I can't compete with them, but everyone seems to judge me as worthless and won't even give me a chance." Shocked at the sudden vulnerability from the man, Jace watched him more than his feet as they walked.

But then Rob stopped and Jace turned to face him, meeting his eyes.

"But, you know, I'm not homeless because I can't get a job. I just… I find that the people who have so much—a good house, cars, phones—most seem to miss the bigger picture. They miss out on life and family, you know? They just… float. They could be happy and out doing all these amazing things, but instead they spend their days stressing about things that don't matter." Rob shrugged as though what he was talking about wasn't important.

As they started moving again, Jace listened without interruption.

"I just don't want to be lost in those types of things." Before Jace could agree he continued: "I don't want to push anyone away, you know, tell them that they can't do something, or can't go somewhere, and I don't want to miss gaining new relationships or opportunities."

Jace wasn't sure if Rob knew how what he was saying affected him. He thought back to Kory again, stopping and leaning against a tree as tears came down his face. *Why didn't I just let him come? He just wanted to do the same thing I did, and I stopped him.*

And Jace *knew* how being left behind or excluded hurt Kory. He'd always been worried about being left out of anything they did, FOMO to the extreme. Because once Kory made friends, he clung to them harder than even Jace did.

He figured that it had to be because of Kory being in foster care for years, but Jace had never asked.

"Did I say something?" Rob's voice was nervous, his feet shuffling in place.

"No. Well, kind of." Jace shook his head but didn't worry about the tears. "What if… what if you let them do something and they get hurt?"

Rob studied his eyes for many seconds before releasing a slow breath and leaning back on his own tree. "Jace, people can get hurt wherever they are and whatever they are doing. That won't change. I wish I could say that there was a way you could keep them from harm but there isn't. And it's a good thing, too."

"What if *I* don't want to hurt them?" Jace looked away and curled his fists. "If they are with me, I can hurt them."

Once again it took Rob a few seconds to respond, and when he did his voice was quieter. "Switch the roles, Jace. How would you feel if your friend wouldn't let you come on something that you knew could very well end up bad for both of you? Would you rather—even with the risk of that friend hurting you—he make you stay home, away from him? Would you rather have the relationship with this person and have something turn out wrong, or pretend like nothing is going on and simply go your separate ways?"

Jace didn't have to think about it for long to know that he would hate it if the roles were reversed.

"I need to tell him I'm sorry," Jace said softly, looking back the way he'd come, though Jace couldn't convince himself to walk another few hours back to see them.

"You're nervous about your magic, aren't you? That you'll somehow hurt them with it?" Rob asked suddenly.

Jace eyed Rob carefully, noticing how perceptive he was and how little he seemed to show that fact. He seemed to take a lot of info and keep the majority inside.

"Yes. I don't know how to control it, and I don't want to be the cause of them getting hurt."

Rob's eyes narrowed. A low humming sound came from his lips. "There is danger everywhere, Jace. And I'd say it would feel much worse to have your friends die from something else and not being there for them because you're out there on your own journey."

Jace rubbed a hand down his face before meeting Rob's eyes again. "Thanks," he told the man, suddenly very grateful for having Rob with him. "And I'm sorry for judging you harshly."

Rob gave him another large, earnest smile. "I think you are the first to have said *sorry* to me about anything."

Jace returned the smile, and his heart felt warm. He hadn't expected that. All the tension of the past few days suddenly released itself, and all he could think about were his friends who still liked him for who he was and wanted to stand at his side.

As he and Rob continued their conversation and their walk toward Jurade—the light from two flashlights was brighter than one— they chatted more about what they had been doing since they'd gotten back, and how it had affected them, Jace continued to feel grateful that someone was with him, though there was no question that he would miss his friends from home.

Chapter Twenty-Two

KORY WOKE UP TO the sound of a car door being shut—the slam quieter than usual, but the click still enough to rouse him—and found his head resting against the window, and ache in his forehead letting him know it had been there for a bit. He saw Philips, Lisa, and Hazel getting out of the car. He looked around, but didn't see any reason why they were doing so. There were no buildings around them, only trees. And it was dark.

"What's going on?" Kory asked Philips, whose passenger door was still open. Kory opened the back door as Philips let the front one shut.

"We're going to see if we can find Jace in the forest." Philips put his hand on his door and looked like he was going to close it, but Kory swung his feet out and put his palm against it to stop him.

"Okay, cool, let's go." He could feel Jason's and Devin's gaze on him. Lisa and Hazel walked around the car to his side.

"Stay here, Kory," Lisa said sternly, but Kory wouldn't be swayed. He'd come out here to find Jace and that's what he was going to do.

"No, I'm coming," he said firmly, unbuckling his seatbelt and standing up, but Philips put an arm on the car and blocked him from moving. He grabbed his bag in his left hand, frowning at them all.

"Kory, stay here. We'll try to find him, and you can wait for him with Jason. He's going ahead to Jurade to see if he can catch him coming in." Philips voice was also firm, matching Kory's own tone.

"I'm not going to wait for him. I'm going to come find him with you guys. I came out here to find him and that's what I'm going to do." Jason and Devin looked on with amusement and worry but didn't give their input. The others looked exasperated, but, really, they should know him better by now.

"You'll just slow us down. Stay please." Hazel looked embarrassed, perhaps she regretted telling him that he'd be slow. "I don't want you to hurt more than you already do."

He clenched his jaw, his frustration making him feel suddenly vulnerable. He tried to ignore the screaming in his mind that was telling him he couldn't do anything and pushed his hands into his pockets as he swallowed heavily.

"So?" he sighed. "Jace doesn't want us hurt, yet we're going to follow him anyway. Me coming with you guys is just like how we are all following him. Should we just stop looking and go back because we don't want anyone to get hurt?"

He heard a snort from either Jason or Devin and knew he had made a good argument.

"You'll still be helping, though," Philips argued, "But you won't have to walk." He tried pushing him back into the car, but Kory wasn't going to budge.

"We're not leaving until you get back into the car," Lisa said.

He shrugged—then quickly went under Philips' arm and moved past them before they could grab at him.

"Well." He turned to face them. Walking backwards on his still tender feet, he pointed toward them with a slightly smug smile. "While you guys are waiting for me to get back into the car, *I'm* going to go find Jace." He pointed behind him then spun around and entered the forest without another word. He didn't need to look behind him to know that they were all frustrated with him.

He didn't even look back to see if they were following. Instead, he slung his backpack onto his shoulders and headed northwest, deeper into the forest. He didn't want to pass Jace, so he hoped going northwest, rather than straight west, would make him run into Jace sooner rather than later. It was a long shot for them to find him, but he was hoping.

Footsteps came up to the side of him, and even before turning his head he knew the light footsteps were Lisa's, her flashlight bouncing as she caught up. "You're a stubborn bull," she huffed. "I don't know what to do if it gets worse, and you're not supposed to get the bandage dirty, 'cause I'll have to change it a lot more. Honestly, we should have taken you to a doctor."

He shrugged again, aware that everyone was walking alongside him. "Sorry."

"Sorry means you won't do it again, Kory." Lisa had a teasing smile on her face, and Kory couldn't help but return it.

"I guess I'm not sorry then."

"How are your feet?"

He wiggled his toes in his shoes. "They aren't hurting too bad right now."

"When they do, is the pain more of a throb, a sharpness, or a tingle?"

Kory thought about Lisa's question for a minute before choosing his answer. "Probably more like a throb, or a shooting pain, like something's squeezing, kinda…"

"And it doesn't hurt right now?"

He shook his head. "No, it's been off and on."

She nodded, her eyes narrowing thoughtfully. "And, on a scale of one to ten, one being it doesn't hurt, ten unbearable, how would you rate it?"

"When it hurts, probably a seven or eight, but right now I'd say two," he answered, wondering what all the questions were for.

He looked back at Philips and Hazel, not surprised by their expressions. They were all clearly bothered by his coming with them while injured.

"It sounds like you have a mixture of breakthrough, acute, and resting pain."

He had no idea what any of those were. "Okay?" his eyebrows rose in question.

"*Breakthrough* is pain that is off and on." She smiled, as if she was enjoying the chance to explain this to him, "And *acute* is close to the same, but will hurt when you change the bandage or something like that, while *resting* is background pain, always hurts, but not intensely."

"Oh." He still wasn't exactly sure, but he figured it was probably a second-degree burn.

"If it gets painful, let me know and we'll stop until it's better." Kory nodded and looked up into the night sky.

"Will the honey really help it?" Kory knew that doubt showed through his voice.

Lisa tilted her head. "Hopefully."

He continued to doubt anyway but turned his attention to the dark trees, hoping to catch sight or sound of any movement.

₪ ₪ ₪

Jace was tired, but somehow Rob seemed to have endless energy. He had agreed to stop and sleep as soon as a sufficient place to lie down was found. A little before dawn, a good place to sleep was discovered, and Jace didn't have to try hard to convince himself to eat and drink first. He hadn't eaten anything since the journey had begun, and he was hungry.

Jace had been surprised to find how much he had actually enjoyed Rob's presence the last few hours; having someone for company was much better than being alone, but Rob himself was great.

"I'll keep watch the first few hours if you'd like," Rob said as he ate his own bar.

"That'd be nice. Wake me up if we have any problems, or you want a break." Jace pulled his jacket close to his body and leaned against the tree, hoping that not too many bugs would find their way into his clothes.

He dozed off surprisingly quickly but didn't dream. However, it didn't feel like much later before he was being shaken awake by Rob. There was light brightening the trees and the chirping of birds, so at least it was dawn now. He slept maybe an hour?

He heard the rustle of leaves and Rob's face looked slightly worried. "Something is moving around out here…"

Rob was looking around, not quite sure which direction the sound was coming from yet. His apprehension continued to grow as the noise continued, fluttering the leaves, and stirring up the dirt, but something in his mind settled when he heard what sounded like whispers.

"Jace?"

Jace gasped in surprised relief as Hazel stepped out of the trees.

"Hazel? what are you doing here?" She looked tired. Her hair unkempt, and a second later their other friends stepped out of the trees as well, including Kory. Jace was amazed that his friend would still come looking for him, even after what he'd done.

"We came to find you," Hazel said, biting her lip. "We don't care that you have magic, Jace. We know the risks. We want to be with you."

Go home! his mind screamed. Except he wanted them with him more than he wanted them gone. He rushed closer, immediately moving to give Kory a hug. "I'm so sorry, Kory. I didn't want to stop you."

"I know," Kory mumbled next to his ear. "I know you didn't mean to, it's okay." Jace pulled away slightly.

"Are you okay? I didn't hurt you, right?"

He shook his head. "Don't worry about it Jace, I'm fine." He saw the look that Lisa gave Kory but didn't question it since Jace was now giving Hazel a hug.

"I can't believe you guys came after me after what I did."

"I don't plan on losing our friendship over something I know you didn't mean to do." Hazel smiled, relief in her eyes.

Jace shifted his hug to Philips, then Lisa, noticing that Rob was still off to the side looking uncomfortable. Jace gave him a smile, hoping that he'd realize it was okay to come closer. He took the hint with his own smile.

"Hey, Rob, long time no see." Philips shook his hand but then must've thought better of it and pulled him into a hug as well. Lisa and Hazel reached out for a hug.

"Group hug!" Rob sang with a laugh, and Kory immediately complied, even though, by Rob's wide eyes, he could tell he had intended it as a joke. Jace laughed and joined his friends.

After they pulled away, Rob tugged at his shirt, looking embarrassed. "That was intense. I wasn't actually expecting... you know."

But Jace was already feeling something else. An unbreathable darkness suddenly enveloped him. The shroud was extreme and could only have been only one thing: the Shadow. He looked around anxiously for Darrin, taking a step backward, toward his friends.

Everything had changed; the sky, the trees, but mostly the air in which he breathed. It was all made to suffocate him, spiraling him into panic.

"What's wrong, Jace?" Rob asked.

"The Shadow. Can't you feel it?" He turned toward them, eyes wide. "We need to run!" None of them moved. Even Jace's feet felt glued to the floor in his panic. Where was the fight or flight instinct now? The darkness thickened.

It was too late.

Darrin came out of the trees in front of them, and Jace wondered if he was imagining the dark shadow that seemed to silhouette the man.

"Jace." Darrin smiled. "You really have made it easy to find you again. Haven't you figured it out yet? I'm going to find the Power before you." Jace felt a sudden burst of dizziness. He was going to fall over! Opening his eyes—when had they closed?—he watched in vague alarm as the Shadow erupted from Darrin and toward him, the fuzziness in his head making it hard to move or care.

When he fell to his hands and knees, he realized only vaguely that it wasn't because of the Shadow or the sudden dizziness that he had fallen, but because of something else.

Someone else. The lasting impression of hands that had shoved him lingered on his back and he looked up.

It was Rob who had stepped in just seconds before the Shadow had got to Jace and had pushed him out of the way.

Jace tried to scramble to his feet, but before he could, the Shadow reached Rob, the darkness surrounding him, making him disappear from view. Rob let out a scream and Jace could sense the fight, sense the Shadow digging it's grasp into Rob, as though clawing its way straight into Rob's soul and—

Jace felt the tremble in the air as the Shadow rushed back toward Darrin, coalescing back into the man.

And Rob was gone. Vanished. Only a hollow sound of the scream echoing in Jace ears evidence of him having been there a moment before.

"Rob!" Jace scrambled for the spot Rob had been, hoping to be wrong, but no, Rob was gone.

Darrin walked closer, the glint in his eyes and clenched fists showing his anger. And that was his cue to get out of there.

As much as Jace didn't want to leave before he'd discovered what had happened to Rob, he knew that they had no choice. His friends being there with him jerked him out of the funk that made him want to curl into a ball and give up.

"Run!" Jace yelled again. This time his friends ran the way they were heading, hopefully toward Jurade.

Jace was following behind them, alarmed to watch as Kory started to fall behind the others. He played soccer, so he was always quick on his feet. Maybe his bruised neck was affecting his breathing more.

Suddenly, Kory dropped to the ground with a cry, making Jace tremble with terror. Was Darrin doing something to him?

No! That can't happen, not again! He felt a rush of magic leave him, but was focused on helping Kory back to his feet, aware that Philips had also come back to slip under Kory's other side.

Kory's pale face wasn't Jace's only concern, he was biting his lip as if in extreme pain, and that made Jace worried.

"Ten," Kory gasped as Lisa and Hazel found their way back to them. "It's a ten."

"What?" Jace was confused, but he didn't have time to think about it. He noticed Lisa's face form a frown as they continued to run. Jace didn't really believe that they could outrun Darrin, but it was another few minutes before he realized that he no longer felt the presence of the Shadow.

Gradually, cautiously, he started to slow, his friends moving with him, not questioning him, even as they glanced concernedly around.

Once he was sure that Darrin and the Shadow were gone— and maybe that had been Jace's doing; he wasn't sure what he'd done, but he'd clearly used some sort of magic— Jace finally stopped, and his friends came to a standstill next to him.

Jace glanced around to make sure they really were alone before turning his attention back to Kory. Kory groaned. His lips were slowly paling. His feet didn't touch the ground with Jace and Philips carrying him, and Kory wasn't even trying to get free, his face scrunched in pain.

Lisa was already moving, coming close to Kory. "Sit him down," she ordered. "Hazel, open my bag."

Jace did as she said and then looked up at them.

"What's wrong?" Jace knew the sudden pain wasn't from Darrin. Lisa wouldn't know exactly what was going on and what to do if it had been.

"His feet were burned," Lisa said.

Jace drew back, shocked, and knew immediately that it was his fault. His hands clenched in his lap, but he didn't move away since Kory was leaning on him.

Kory's hand searched Jace's leg until he found his hand, then he squeezed it and seemed to relax slightly, breathing shallowly.

As Lisa started to take Kory's shoes off, Hazel opened the bag beside them before crouching close to Kory and Jace.

"Get me the bandages, and the Aloe Vera." She took off the socks now to reveal bandages, then grabbed the green goo from Hazel, muttering something before saying louder; "Kory, we've got to get you to a doctor, I really shouldn't be doing this."

But Kory's eyes were glazed over. He seemed to be looking at nothing and had probably not even heard her.

"Why are his fingers and lips almost... blue?" Jace asked. Kory tried to sit up, and Jace held him, trying to calm him.

"Water, please?" Kory coughed then sobbed. "I want water." Jace moved to give him some, but Lisa shook her head.

"Don't give him any yet." Lisa focused on Kory's feet but gave a short answer to Jace's question. "He's in shock, can't have water, he might choke on it. Can you lay him on his back gently?"

Jace and Philips both nodded and shifted before lowering him. Kory wouldn't let go of his tight grip on Jace's hand, so it made it slightly harder to move. Lisa and Hazel propped Kory's legs on a root before continuing.

"It's okay Kory," Jace said, pressing a hand on his head carefully. It felt slightly cold.

"I can't..." he coughed, trying to speak. "I can't breathe."

He was trying to get his hand into his pocket and Jace realized that his friend was trying to reach his inhaler. Jace plunged his free hand into Kory's pocket and held the inhaler to Kory's mouth. Kory grasped Jace's hand over the inhaler and took a trembling breath before letting his hand fall away, though he didn't let go of either of Jace's hands when he relaxed.

"Hazel, get my phone out and call Jason, we've got to get Kory somewhere better. I'm sure they're still out driving to find Jace."

Lisa continued to switch bandages as Philips spoke up. "Tell him to meet us about three miles North of where he dropped us off, and we'll call him and tell him where we are when we get close to the road." Lisa looked stressed, and Jace knew why. He assumed they were at least two hours from the road.

Jace looked down at his hands and took a shaky breath. Should he help with his magic?

Last time you tried to use magic you ended up hurting him.
Still, it might be better than any other hope.

"Can I… I can try to help." Jace looked at Lisa, whose own eyes showed understanding.

"If you think you can do it, then try," she whispered.

Jace looked down at Kory's pale face. Tears streamed from his closed eyes, obviously biting back a sob.

Jace felt the magic rise at the opportunity, somehow knowing that he was planning on using it. This time he wasn't going to let the magic control him, he was going to control the magic. He exchanged one glance with Philips before hesitantly closing his eyes and reaching for where his magic felt like it came from. Once he was in there—at the heart of this newfound power—his mind felt at ease as it seemed to know his intent.

Help him, please.

Rather than letting all of the magic go to Kory immediately, he sifted through the rays slowly and opened his eyes to see how Kory responded.

At first, the redistribution of magical energy didn't seem to do anything, but after a few minutes Kory's fast breathing slowed down and he relaxed a bit more. Jace looked back at Kory's hand to see that the blue from his fingertips had faded mostly as well. After another moment, he rolled onto his side, further onto Jace's side, drifting to sleep.

His shaking softened quite a bit, and the tension in his face smoothed out.

Hazel's hand found his shoulder. The movement distracted him and he panicked a moment. Would his magic race to Kory before he was able to rein it back in?

No… somehow he was doing it. It was working.

His own head pounded, but Kory looked like he was sleeping. He wasn't as pale anymore, redness returning to his cheeks.

Jace looked over at Lisa, who had stopped wrapping his feet, just staring at the bottom. From the one foot he could see, it was still a little red and swollen, but his friend no longer seemed to be in shock, and the blisters started to clear up before his eyes.

Lisa slumped, shoulders drooping and hand covering her eyes as though suddenly exhausted, but then she looked up at Jace with a wide smile as Hazel spoke.

"Good job." Hazel smiled and gave him a soft kiss before turning back to the bag. She grabbed a blanket and covered Kory with the thin fabric.

Jace blinked and smiled at her softly before turning his attention back to Kory and Lisa. Kory's hand had finally loosened its grip, confirming his earlier thoughts of him falling asleep.

Lisa nodded at him. "It really looks like it helped. It might be almost back to fully healed." She didn't move from her slumped position. He wondered how long they'd all been out looking for him for her to look so tired.

He looked at the trees surrounding him—the atmosphere was back to normal, birds gradually chirping again, light filtering through the trees instead of darkness—and he could feel peace within his heart. Still, if Rob hadn't been there with all of them, he wouldn't have been taken by the Shadow. He felt a sudden sorrow for his new friend. He was dead, had to be.

He remembered what Rob had said about knowing a person and missing them after they were gone, rather than never having the relationship at all, and he wondered about that. Did Rob regret it in his pain before the Shadow killed him? Jace hated to be the reason for his death, but he couldn't argue with Rob's logic. Jace wouldn't want to be left behind if it was any of his friends.

But how could he just let them come when he knew of the danger?

Hazel stood up, grabbing Lisa's phone, and Jace knew that she was going to call Jason. Hazel's phone conversation was a complete blur to Jace with his fatigue of using his magic.

As soon as Hazel finished, they all got up to make their way to the road to meet Jason; Jace and Philips carrying Kory between them. It was a long walk, and even though Kory was smaller than them, carrying him the whole way strained both of their shoulders.

But they wanted to get out of the forest, and Jace needed Kory to be okay.

He wanted to take his friend to the hospital, but he also knew that if he did, his plan of sneaking away wouldn't work as all their parents would be called.

Besides, it appeared his healing job had worked, and if so, maybe they wouldn't have to swing by the hospital.

They got to the edge of the road, after taking many breaks along the way, and sat to watch for cars to pass while staying hidden in the trees, hoping that one might be Jason. He was tired, but he wanted to get somewhere safe before he went to sleep.

It was only as they sat there for about ten minutes—Philips on the phone with Jason to describe where they were, before remembering he could just use phone location to send to Jason instead—that Kory woke up. His friend groaned and shifted in his place with his head in Jace's lap, slowly looking up at his face with confused eyes.

"What happened?" Kory asked, weary. "I just remember darkness, and… my feet don't hurt so badly anymore."

Jace hesitated. "We're waiting for Jason to come pick us up."

"From… you mean…" Kory sat up. "How'd we get by the road?" He looked so lost. "I seriously… I don't remember."

"You passed out," Lisa told him.

Kory shook his head softly. "But it didn't feel like I did," he whispered, barely audible. Jace furrowed his eyebrows, wondering what he meant about that, but then a honk from a car jerked his gaze up, and Jace saw a minivan waiting on the side of the road.

His eyes narrowed in confusion, wondering who in the world could be waiting for them. Jason had an Impala—which Jace just realized they would not all be able to fit in. Did some random person want to give them a ride? They must have seen Philips, who was still pacing just outside of the tree line.

The lights in the car turned on as the door opened, and Jason stepped out. Jace blinked in surprise, unbelieving that his brother was driving a minivan. He hated minivans.

"Jason?" Jace asked in shock.

"Jace?" Jason mimicked. "I know, I know, the car sucks, but unfortunately I had to have a brother who left the house without a word to anyone, and I took on more people than my car can chew, so for now you get this rental car, all right?" Despite the sour words, Jason was heading quickly to Jace and pulled him into a hug. "Get your butt in the car, Jace, and don't you ever dream about leaving alone again."

Jace smiled in his brother's shoulder, holding him tight. The relief that he didn't have to go through this alone brought tears to his eyes and he sniffed without pulling away from his brother.

It had been a terrible two days, and the hug was exactly what he needed.

He hadn't realized how hard it was going to be coming alone, and all he'd done was walk through a forest. It had been scary enough facing Darrin and the Shadow with his friends again, he didn't even want to imagine doing it alone.

"I won't leave." Jace assured Jason once he finally pulled away. "We need to get Kory to the hospital."

"What?" Kory jerked away from them and stared at Jace worriedly. "No way! You'll just leave me again, besides, I think your healing fixed my feet, because I don't feel any more pain."

"Kory…" Jace frowned at him.

Kory folded his arms. "Don't '*Kory*' me! If you're going to be using your magic on me, I'm not going to be going to any hospital, got that? Now let's get this show on the road." Jace wanted to argue, but he knew Kory wouldn't relent, and he also knew that he was extremely exhausted, so he and his friends filed into the back of the minivan as Jason hopped back into the driver's seat without any more argument. Maybe after they got some sleep and checked his feet once more in the morning, they could revisit the debate.

Jason turned to face them once they were all in and comfortable. "So," he said. "Now what?"

Jace took a deep breath. It seemed that his magic *had* worked on Kory's feet, which meant that they didn't necessarily have to take him to the hospital. So where did they go next?

"Now," he answered slowly, "We find the Power before Darrin does."

The Power of Silence

Finding the Power has not been easy for Jace and his loyal friends, and they want to go home. But there can be no rest now, as the task is getting more dangerous, the challenges more extreme, and their enemies more threatening each time they meet. The friends struggle making any headway in their search as the Shadow becomes almost overpowering, finding new ways to get what it wants.

And what happens when a long-kept secret from one of Jace's friends is unknowingly weighing them all down?

Will they finally discover the truth about the Power?

In *The Power of Silence*, expect to find true friendship amidst challenges, and the strength that can only be had when many come together to carry each other's burdens.

To be released: Winter 2025

M. C. Topham was raised in various places inside the state of Utah and California. She'd gone on a church mission to Japan for a year and a half, enjoying getting to know a new culture and plenty of people while she taught about Jesus Christ and the English language. She now lives in Utah with her husband of two years, a dog, and a cat.

She graduated from a Massage School and Footzone School, and has been house-cleaning since fifteen. She now enjoys all of those as self-employed, part-time jobs, making all her days diverse so she never feels bored.

However, writing is her real passion and becoming a published author has been her goal since she started weaving stories around age thirteen. She published her first book at sixteen and looks forward to continuing her dream.

Follow on Instagram: **m.c.topham**
Follow on Facebook: M. C. Topham

www.ingramcontent.com/pod-product-compliance
Lightning Source LLC
Chambersburg PA
CBHW071411300726
48976CB00006B/2061